Annie's Christmas by the Sea

ALSO BY LIZ EELES

Annie's Holiday by the Sea

Annie's Christmas by the Sea

LIZ EELES

Bookouture

Published by Bookouture
An imprint of StoryFire Ltd.
23 Sussex Road, Ickenham, UB10 8PN
United Kingdom
www.bookouture.com

ISBN: 978-1-78681-294-0
eBook ISBN: 978-1-78681-293-3

For Sam and Ellie, with love

Chapter One

My dad is the rugged hero of Scandi-Noir dramas on TV. A Viking-tall actor with cheekbones to die for who cycles across Copenhagen when not kicking arse on screen. So it's hard to fathom why this odd little man in front of me is claiming to be my father.

'I met your mother at a music festival in the late eighties and we kinda hooked up,' says the man who's apparently called Barry. Not Sven or Ulrik or Axel, but *Barry*, which is possibly the least Scandinavian-sounding name ever.

He adjusts the mirrored sunglasses he's worn since turning up on my doorstep and glances through the window at the waves smashing into the harbour wall.

'Spandau were headlining the festival. Nice lads. And I was in an up-and-coming band that was about to sign with a record label.' His voice has a strange Essex-meets-mid-Atlantic twang. 'Did your mother tell you about me?' When I shake my head, he shrugs, before tugging at his leather trousers which are bunching up in the crotch area. 'That's weird.'

'What's weird is you arriving out of the blue,' I say, sharply. I'm not trying to be a bitch but Barry's abrupt arrival feels like an ambush and my heart is hammering. 'Maybe you could have written first, before just turning up.'

'Could have, probably should have, but that's not my style, babe. I'm more a spontaneous doer than a writer,' he drawls. 'I suppose this has come as a surprise then.'

Uh, yeah, Barry. I'd say some random bloke invading my home and claiming paternity is a surprise. I'd go so far as to call it a humungous shock, even worse than waking up to discover that Trump is leader of the free world. My hands are shaking and I clamp my arms to my sides so Barry won't see.

It's not that I'm unused to long-lost family suddenly appearing out of the blue. I only met my great-aunt Alice for the first time earlier this year, and I've met my slimeball, distant cousin Toby Trebarwith since. But that was almost a year ago, and none of us were expecting my absent father to crawl out of the woodwork.

When I stay quiet, Barry pushes his bottom lip forward and frowns. 'Didn't your mother tell you anything about me at all?'

'Not really. Just a few bits and pieces.'

Like letting slip when I was a child that my dad was a Viking. Just one tiny fact, but it sparked my imagination and my father became a Scandinavian superhero living in a perfect IKEA world. My unusual bright blue eyes only gave credence to the story which began to feel real over the years. It's daft, I know, but I thought 'the Viking' might have become an actor, which is why I'm obsessed with Scandi dramas like *The Bridge* and *Borgen*.

I never once imagined that my dad was a short man called Barry with a paunch hanging over the top of his trousers and greasy hair down to his shoulders.

'If you really are my father,' I say slowly, my voice wobbling as he sinks with a loud *oof* onto Alice's sofa, 'how long have you known about me?'

'For sure? Only since I Googled "Trebarwith family in Salt Bay" a couple of weeks ago and your photo came up. It was some news story about you being caught in a flood. Did this place get swamped then?' He takes in the bare plaster walls of Alice's sitting room and the new jute carpet. 'I'm surprised that your mum kept quiet about me. I never forgot her. She was the first woman I ever sha—' he presses his lips together tightly '—made love to and you always remember your first time, don't you, even though it's all fumbled and frantic. Anyway—' he glances at my aghast face and ploughs on '—I heard on the grapevine that she was pregnant with my baby.'

'Did you take the trouble to check if the baby she was carrying was yours?'

Now, that really does sound sharp but I don't care. He's talking about Mum's pregnancy like it was a piece of juicy gossip; something to be bandied about on the tour bus. If his daft band had a tour bus – they probably all crammed into a clapped-out Ford Cortina between gigs.

'Nah, afraid not,' says Barry, his trousers creaking as he shifts in his seat. 'I'm not proud of that but I was young and not ready to be tied down. You've got to understand that my band was on the brink of being discovered. We were going to be stars. I tried to get in touch later but—'

'So, realistically, anyone could be my father rather than you,' I butt in. My desire not to share DNA with this strange man is overcoming any misgivings I might have about painting my poor mother as a slapper.

Barry shakes his head. 'The newspaper piece said you're twenty-nine so the timing's right, and then there's this.'

With a flourish he whips off his sunglasses and stares straight at me. Oh. My. God. His eyes are the same piercing periwinkle-blue as mine.

'Heavens!' Alice has slipped into the room unnoticed and is standing right behind me. She leans forward with her hand on my shoulder and gazes into Barry's face. 'And who might you be?'

Barry scrambles to his feet and wipes a hand down his AC/DC T-shirt before stretching it out towards my elderly great-aunt. 'I'm Barry Stubbs, Annie's dad.'

Stubbs! I'm seriously going to have to rethink the whole Scandinavian heritage thing.

Alice falters for a moment before grasping Barry's hand and shaking it vigorously. 'How marvellous to meet you. Did Annabella know that you were coming to visit us?' When I shake my head, on the verge of tears, she gives me a sympathetic smile. 'I see, and do you intend to stay in Salt Bay for long, Mr Stubbs?'

Barry sniffs and shifts from foot to foot. 'For a while probably 'cos I'd like to get to know Annie, um, I mean Annabella, now we've finally caught up. I mean, how often do you get to meet up with long-lost family?'

'More often than you'd imagine,' I murmur, thinking back to the unexpected letter I received from Alice in January, back when I was a free spirit living in London. I was a real city girl then and didn't realise that sleepy Salt Bay on the wild Cornish coast would steal my heart, along with Alice, and the amazing choir I've set up here – and Josh. Lovely, handsome Josh. When I think of the kind, gorgeous man who's taking me out this evening, my stomach flutters.

'Where are you staying, Mr Stubbs, or do you live in Cornwall?' asks Alice, pulling her shawl tightly around her frail body. There's a nip in the air now November's almost here. And the house, though dried out after the flood, still has a lingering air of damp on days like today, when sea and sky are the same steely grey.

'We've come down from London but we'll find a B&B round here somewhere.'

'We?' A horrible sense of unease whacks me in the pit of my stomach.

'Yeah, we.' When Barry swings round, I notice a bald patch on the top of his head that he's tried to hide with a comb-over. 'I was going to mention Storm at the right moment – which might as well be now. She's outside in the car.'

'Who's Storm?' I ask, sending up a silent prayer that Storm is Barry's loveable, uncomplicated, not-related-to-me dog.

'She's my daughter, which makes her your half-sister, though she's considerably younger than you. Sixteen, going on twenty-five,' he laughs, while my mouth falls open but no sound comes out because I can't quite believe this is happening.

All my life it was just me and Mum until she died of breast cancer. For twenty-nine years I had no other relatives and now, within the space of a few months, I've got more feckin family than I can shake a stick at. And I think Barry might just be a relative too far.

'Fetch her in,' orders Alice, with a glance at me. 'You can't leave the poor girl in the car.'

Barry moves to the stone-framed window and raps sharply on the glass. 'Storm,' he hollers, above the dull boom of a high tide ebbing and flowing against granite. 'Come in here now.' He beckons towards his grubby white Fiesta that's parked outside with two wheels on the grass verge.

While Alice goes to open the front door, Barry sits back on the sofa and stretches out his chunky legs. He's a total stranger. Someone I'd pass in the street without a backward glance. How can he possibly be my dad, even with the eyes? My legs are feeling wobbly now so I take a seat opposite him and fold my arms tightly across my chest.

'So where exactly was this festival where you met my mum?'

Barry breathes out slowly as though he realises he's being tested.

'In a field near Melton Mowbray.'

Hhmm, that tallies with another piece of information I managed to drag out of Mum. She told me she met my father at a festival in Leicestershire.

'The ironic thing was,' adds Barry, leaning forward with his elbows on his knees, 'it was called the Sunshine Festival but it rained for two days solid and the mud was up to our knees. Some people came in Jesus sandals and got trench foot.'

Oh crap. I rarely tell people my full name because they invariably take the mick. I mean, why would any woman call her child Annabella Sunshine Trebarwith? You just wouldn't, would you, unless you were drunk or stoned, which is what I've always assumed Mum was when she named me. But what if she chose 'Sunshine' for the bona fide reason that it was a link to her child's father?

'I can't believe your mum didn't tell you anything about Va-Voom and the Vikings,' says Barry testily. 'We were brilliant.'

'The Va— whats?' I stutter.

'That was the name of my band that almost got signed by a top record label. We would have done if our lead singer hadn't got rat-arsed and vommed all over their A&R man, silly sod. I was a Viking.'

And with those final four words the last piece of the paternity puzzle slots into place. Barry Stubbs is my father.

Before I can fully digest the arse-clenching magnitude of this, there's a flurry at the door and in walks a tall girl with a messy bun so tight it's pulling the skin at the corners of her eyes. Thick bleached-blonde streaks litter her brown hair.

'Hey Storm, babe, meet Annie, your half-sister.' Barry grins, looking very pleased with himself.

'It's good to meet you,' I squeak, good manners trumping the wave of nausea that's tightening my throat.

'Yeah.' Storm dabs at the blue eyeliner beneath her lower lashes as though she meets half-sisters every day of the week. She's wearing a shedload of make-up though I'm sure Barry said she was only sixteen. My mum wasn't the most hands-on of parents, but even she would have baulked if I'd cleaned out the Rimmel counter in my mid-teens.

There's an awkward silence broken only by a tinny *chugga-chugga-chugga* coming from the earphones slung around Storm's neck. When Barry nods towards them, she pulls her phone from her pocket, with an exaggerated sigh, and turns off the music.

'Can I get you both a drink?' asks Alice, who's leaning for support against the door frame. 'Storm, would you like some orange squash?'

Storm snorts and picks at her purple painted nails. 'Nah, have you got any Red Bull?'

'I— I don't think we've got any red drinks, have we, Annabella?'

'I'm afraid not but we might have some lemonade.' Storm wrinkles her nose and gazes around Alice's sitting room which is sparsely furnished and cold. 'Things are a little unfinished in here because we had a flood.'

'Rad!' Interest flits across Storm's face. 'Did anyone die?'

'Thankfully no, but all the furniture was ruined so we're replacing it bit by bit.'

I could say more about the pretty river that flows through the village turning into a torrent and sweeping through the centuries-old house. Or Josh fighting his way through the swirling water to rescue me. But Storm has already lost interest now she knows the fatality count was zero. Folding her arms, she perches on the back of the sofa and pouts. Her jeans have trendy rips across the knees and I catch a glimpse of fake-tanned skin.

'I'll have a cup of tea, please, if there's one going,' says Barry, giving Alice a wink. 'Lots of milk and two sugars. Three if it's in a mug. I've got a sweet tooth.'

Alice never uses mugs for tea. She gets sniffy at the very idea but she smiles serenely and heads for the kitchen, with me scurrying after her. Five minutes with my father and half-sister is quite enough and I can't wait to escape.

*

'Well, this is all rather unexpected,' says Alice, the Queen of Understatement, as she spoons Earl Grey leaves into a china teapot. 'They're an odd couple, though anyone could tell that Mr Stubbs is related to you. I've never seen eyes like yours before – the same brilliant blue. And you and Storm look very similar.'

'Really? I can't see it myself.'

Sitting down heavily at the kitchen table, I scratch my fingers across the pale oak to check that it's solid and real. Which probably sounds weird but my head is spinning and everything feels like a dream – one of those surreal nightmares that wake you with a start and keep you huddled under the covers even when you're desperate for the loo.

'Oh yes,' says Alice, flicking the switch on the kettle. 'Her eyes are different but she has the same shaped jawline and pretty face. You could be sisters. Indeed, it seems that you are sisters!'

Pulling an oak splinter from beneath my fingernail, I suck at the bubble of blood that follows it, only vaguely registering a tang of salt and metal.

'Half-sisters. We're not fully related. And it's all very well, Alice, that I've met Barry and Storm and know they exist. I guess it ties up a few loose ends. But the really important thing is, how do we get rid of them?'

Alice has just taken the biscuit tin from the cupboard and hesitates slightly before tipping Hobnobs onto a plate. 'Are you quite sure that's what you want, Annabella, when you've only just met them both? You didn't get rid of me and that wasn't so bad, was it?'

When her face creases into a smile, I can't help but smile back at the feisty eighty-three-year-old who's become so dear to me over the last few months. London seems ages ago now – it was a different life and I was someone else. Someone without family. Without roots. Without Josh; lovely Josh whose smile still makes me catch my breath.

'I know this must be hard, Annabella,' says Alice, leaning across me to place the plate on the table. 'And I can only imagine what a shock it must be. But I think you need to welcome your father and sister – half-sister – and see where it leads. After all, I won't be here forever and then you'll have no family left, apart from Toby.'

Jeez, that's a terrible thought! Grabbing Alice's hand, I stroke my thumb across her soft, papery skin. 'Please don't say that. I don't want you to go anywhere.'

'I'm certainly not planning on popping off any time soon but we have to be realistic,' says ever-practical Alice, letting her hand rest in mine for a moment. 'I'm getting older, my health isn't getting any better and Stephen says I'm deteriorating, though it's an ugly word and I wish he wouldn't keep using it, even if he is a doctor.'

'But I don't understand why Barry's tracked me down now,' I say quickly, keen to move on from any suggestion of Alice's death – though I'm obviously not going to let her die, not ever. That's why I've been shovelling multi vits and echinacea into her like Smarties. 'He could have looked for me ages ago while Mum was alive, and he hasn't even asked about her.'

'Which are all valid questions that need answering but you won't get those answers by sending him and his daughter away. You need to spend some time together.'

'Maybe it's nothing but a scam and Barry's only taking an interest in me now 'cos they plan to ransack the place.'

'There's nothing much left to take,' murmurs Alice, still keenly feeling the loss of so many of her possessions. Photos and ornaments were swept away in the rising waters; precious items that the insurance pay-out can never replace. 'Find out more about Mr Stubbs and Storm, by all means. That's only sensible. But give them a chance, like you did me. You were lonely for far too long, Annabella.'

She's right about the loneliness thing, though I didn't always realise it when living the high life in London. Having no roots or responsibilities was brilliant during my twenties but then my friends started settling down, the big three-o beckoned, and what I wanted from life began to change.

I'll be thirty a few days before Christmas and will celebrate my special birthday here with family, new friends and a man who might just be the love of my life – *and*, says the niggly bitch-voice in my brain, *none of that would be happening if you hadn't given Alice a chance. So maybe she's right about Barry and Storm after all.* Ugh, this is all far too weird and confusing.

'Trust me on this, Annabella,' says Alice, switching off the kettle, which is billowing clouds of steam. It doesn't turn itself off these days and, as a result, steam-blistered paint is flaking from the ceiling. 'Learn from my hard-earned wisdom so at least there are some benefits gained from me being this ancient.'

'I know you're wise, Alice, but maybe you're wrong this time?' I venture, but Alice is having none of it.

She snorts and pulls her mouth into a thin line. 'The Trebarwiths are very rarely wrong.'

I think about my mum, but it seems unnecessarily cruel to add, *Except when it comes to dealing with knocked-up teenagers.*

So, instead, I jump up to help as Alice pours boiling water into the teapot with an unsteady hand but she bats me away. 'I suppose you'd better carry the tea or I'll slosh it everywhere but I'm perfectly capable of managing the biscuits, thank you very much.'

*

When we take the tea and biscuits into the sitting room, neither Barry nor Storm has moved but there's an atmosphere as though they've just had words.

'Thanks very much.' Barry takes the cup I'm offering and has a sip. 'Ooh, fancy tea. Cheers.'

'So tell me about yourself, Mr Stubbs. What do you do?'

Alice switches on a lamp to chase away the early-evening gloom and closes the curtains she's borrowed until the room is decorated. They're covered in orange swirls and utterly hideous but I feel cross when Storm looks at them and sniggers. Alice chooses not to notice and settles herself into an armchair.

Hugging his tea to his chest, Barry grins. 'I'm still playing guitar in a rock band which is why my hearing's so rubbish but it's worth it 'cos we're about to hit the big time.' Storm groans and rolls her eyes. 'We just played support for The Bank Trains.'

When I look at him blankly, he says, 'They're big in Blackpool.'

'I hate stupid Blackpool,' mutters Storm, fiddling with the tarnished stud in the side of her nose that looks like a blackhead. 'Are those chocolate Hobnobs?' She grabs two biscuits from the plate on the telephone table and takes a huge bite, scattering crumbs across the carpet.

'So tell me, Mr Stubbs, exactly why you've come to Cornwall to see my great-niece.'

I'm used to Alice's directness but Barry looks ill at ease for the first time since his arrival.

'Having found out where Annie was hiding…'

Hiding? Indignation flashes through me but Barry carries on, oblivious.

'… I thought it was time to meet her and get my two girls together. It's not right that they're apart. Though I didn't realise Salt Bay was so—'

'Backward,' scowls Storm, rubbing a hand across her neck, which is a different colour from her made-up face. She puffs out her cheeks and more crumbs scatter everywhere.

'I was going to say far away,' says Barry, nudging Storm off the back of the sofa with his shoulder. 'Sorry, Storm's in a bit of a grump but it took us ages to get here and we still need to find a local B&B before it gets properly dark. Then if Annie's up for it, maybe we can all get together tomorrow and talk about things properly. I'd really like that.'

He turns towards me and stares with his piercing blue eyes until I feel obliged to give him a curt nod. It's either that or punch him and, even in the most trying of circumstances, I'm not a punchy person.

'That's settled then,' says Alice, her lined face pale in the lamplight, 'but I'm afraid you won't find a bed and breakfast establishment in Salt Bay. It's not that kind of village. You could stay here overnight if you'd like.' What the hell? She ignores my panicked expression and pushes a hand through her straight, white hair. 'Storm would have to sleep on a put-you-up in the box room but it's comfortable enough for a youngster.'

Storm looks as though she'd rather sleep on wet harbour sand than in Alice's spare room but Barry leaps at the chance of a free bed for the night.

'That would be awesome, if you don't mind, and we won't be any trouble. We'll grab our stuff from the car and get settled in. Come on Storm, give your dad a hand.' He grabs Storm's arm and drags her into the hall.

Once I hear the front door slam, I swing round to face Alice, who's sitting serenely in her chair, next to the stone fireplace with its gleaming brass fender. 'What did you say that for? You can't let them stay here at Tregavara House.'

Alice shrugs. 'They are a little eccentric, I'll give you that, but they seem harmless enough and you need to get to know them. I'm sorry if you think I'm meddling, I truly am. But they're your family.'

'At the moment they're nothing but strangers.'

'As were you the first time you spent the night under this roof, Annabella.'

'That was different,' I protest.

'Was it?' Alice smooths down the soft fabric of her olive-green dress. 'Your attitude at the time was rather like Storm's, albeit without the teenage rudeness, but I'm so glad that we took a chance on one another. I must admit that I'd be lost without you.'

It's a touching admission from my great-aunt which rather takes the wind out of my sails. As she knew it would, because she's a canny old bird. Stephen, her doctor, once said he'd learned never to underestimate the Trebarwiths, and I've done the same. Once Alice has her mind set on a course of action there's no budging her.

So, though I sigh as Barry bowls back into the sitting room with a bulging holdall, I keep my mouth firmly shut. Storm trails in after him with a bright pink wheelie case, her full mouth turned down at the corners and a crease between her eyebrows. The wheels of the case leave a dark smudge of mud across the new carpet.

'Annabella will show you to your rooms and perhaps, Storm, you could help her to set up the spare bed.'

Storm grunts and her shoulders drop as she, like me, accepts the inevitability of the situation. It seems that she and I will be getting to know one another whether we like it or not.

'This is good of you, Mrs Trebarwith,' says Barry, slinging the holdall over his shoulder and narrowly missing a large china cat on the mantelpiece. It's Alice's ugliest ornament and, sadly, the only one that survived the deluge.

Alice smiles but doesn't correct him that she's now Mrs Gowan and has been for years since marrying a local fisherman. Though she's been a widow for well over a decade now and was alone in this big house – the Trebarwith family home – for ages. 'I'm sure Annabella will tell you where everything is but let me know if you need anything.'

Barry and Storm follow me into the hall and I let them go ahead of me up the elegant staircase which bends at its middle into a perfect L-shape. They certainly are an odd couple; Barry in his too-tight trousers and Storm, whose baggy jumper rides up to reveal her belly-button ring as she hauls her case up stair by stair. Her dad doesn't offer to give her a hand and neither do I, though I probably should.

Are these two strangers really related to me? I thought I finally had this family thing sorted out, but you can always count on life to throw you a curveball when you're least expecting it.

Chapter Two

Storm is more impressed with the first floor landing of Tregavara House which, untouched by flood waters, has a thick, pale carpet, embossed cream wallpaper and a large stained glass window. It's gloomy outside but the rich reds and blues of the Victorian glass are vibrant and the intricate pattern traced by the leaded edges of the panes looks like lace.

'Posh,' mutters Storm under her breath, pulling at her case, whose wheels are stuck in the shagpile. In the end, she swings the case into her arms and carries it past the closed door of Alice's bedroom.

At the doorway to the spare bedroom, the one that Toby uses when he's visiting, I pause and gesture for Barry to go inside. 'You can have this one and I'll set Storm up in the box room, which is at the end of the landing.'

'Why can't I go in here?'

Storm peers into the pretty bedroom opposite, whose stone-framed windows face the dark sea that's flecked with white. There's a yellow lamp fringed with glass beads on a bedside table and a tall, thin wardrobe with enamel door knobs.

'This one's already taken. It belongs to Emily.'

Storm swings around so fast that the chunky gold necklace she's wearing bashes against her collarbone. 'Who the hell's Emily? Not another sister!'

'No, don't panic. Emily's not related to either of us, but she lives here and provides help for Alice.'

'The old lady? Why, what's wrong with her?'

'Alice isn't terribly well and needs some support.'

There's no way I'm telling this surly teenager about the neurological condition that's making Alice increasingly slow and unsteady on her feet.

'I s'pose she is getting on a bit,' mutters Storm, her lip curling in disdain at the huddle of soft toys on Emily's bed.

There are quite a few toys – some of them battered and moth-eaten from Emily's childhood – but they're soft and warm and hint at Emily's kind, loving personality. Storm, on the other hand, is unlikely to ever have a cuddly giraffe nestling on her pillow. A shark, maybe – a tiger with its teeth bared, or a velociraptor.

Firmly closing the door to Emily's room, I lead Storm away and start sorting out clean bedding from the airing cupboard.

'Here you go.' The pile of sheets I hand to Storm are old but have the fresh smell of washed linen. 'We'll get you settled into the box room and your dad sorted, though he already seems to be making himself at home.'

Barry, just visible through his open bedroom door, has abandoned his holdall in the middle of the floor and is stretched out on the bed with his boots still on. 'This'll do nicely for the night,' he calls out, his stacked heels rucking up the worn candlewick cover. 'I like a nice hard mattress and it's good for my back after all that lugging heavy speakers about. Our band can't afford roadies. Thanks, Annie.'

'Don't thank me, thank Alice,' I say with a tight smile, pulling more blankets from the airing cupboard.

'Maybe we can have a chat about family stuff tonight if we're staying here,' shouts Barry from his bed. He raises himself on his elbow as I come into the room laden down with thick, prickly blankets and stares at me with his unnerving bright blue eyes.

'I'm out tonight and it can't be changed,' I say briskly, dumping the bedding on top of his legs.

'Ah, I get your drift,' Barry winks and kicks off his boots, which skid across the carpet. 'Hot date, is it?'

'Hardly. I run a choir – the Salt Bay Choral Society – and we have a rehearsal tonight.'

I don't mention the steaming hot date with Josh afterwards because it's none of his damn business.

'A choir? That sounds lame.' Storm has crept up silently behind me, like an assassin.

'Actually, the choir's amazing. It's good fun and it's helped bring some joy into the village following the tragedy.'

'Ooh, what tragedy? Did something terrible happen here?' There's that unattractive spark of ghoulish interest again.

'Yes, something terrible did happen here but it was a long time ago.'

Storm folds her arms across her black jumper and glares at me when she realises I'm not going to elaborate. She pulls out her phone, presumably to Google 'Salt Bay tragedy', though she'll be disappointed. Salt Bay is the village where the Internet comes to die.

'A choir, fancy that. You really are a chip off the old block,' laughs Barry, plumping up the pillow behind his head. 'Music's always been a huge part of my life though being an artist has its challenges, don't you find? People don't always fully appreciate my creativity.'

'Yeah, right,' grumbles Storm, shaking her mobile as though that will magically produce a signal. It won't. I've tried. With a sigh, she shoves the phone into her jeans pocket and puts her hands on her hips. 'Can we stop chatting and get this all sorted out because I'm starving to death. All I've had all day is a bowl of Cheerios and some Hobnobs and I bet there isn't a McDonald's for miles.'

'Where can we eat around here; is there a caff or something?' asks Barry, lacing his fingers across his chest. 'I noticed a tea shop when we came through the village but it was shut.'

'Maureen closes at four o'clock once the summer season's over.' My voice sounds clipped and cold. 'Your best bet is the Whistling Wave, which is the pub on the outskirts of the village. If you head away from the sea and go past the green, you can't miss it. The cod and chips there are always good.'

Storm opens her mouth but, before she can complain about fish being too fishy or something, Emily pokes her head around the bedroom door. Thank God; I've never been more pleased to see Alice's familiar, uncomplicated carer who's part of my life in Salt Bay – the life that these two weirdos are making more complicated by the minute.

'Um, hello,' says Emily shyly, peering at me from under her fringe. 'I just got back and Alice said you were up here. Can I help you set up the beds?'

She glances at Storm and begins to wind a tendril of long brown hair around her middle finger. She does that when she's nervous and it always makes me feel maternal, although there's only a decade or so between us.

'Thanks, that would be really helpful.' I turn towards Barry and Storm, who are staring at Alice's live-in carer. 'This is Emily and, Emily, this is Barry and Storm, my um…' Nope, I just can't say it so I leave the sentence hanging.

Storm looks Emily up and down, taking in her frilled floral skirt, plain beige jumper and the thick, untidy plait snaking down her back. Though Emily's a teenager, she dresses like a frumpy sixty-year-old, which doesn't matter here in Salt Bay where the height of fashion is wearing your jeans low-slung. But Storm looks like she's about to laugh. Emily flushes bright pink and stares at the floor until I come to her rescue.

'Maybe you can help Barry make his bed and I can sort out Storm in the box room?'

Emily gives me a grateful smile as I usher Storm onto the landing, wishing I could *really* sort her out in the box room, with some ground rules on being nice to people. It's not worth the hassle when she's leaving tomorrow but so far she's been nothing but sullen and rude.

Proving my point, we're hardly out of earshot when she suddenly demands, 'How old is that Emily girl?'

'She's eighteen,' I say, shepherding her past the bathroom and towards her tiny bedroom at the back of the house.

Storm's snort of disbelief echoes along the landing and down the stairs. 'No way! Do all teenagers dress like that round here, like something out of an old film? This place is unbelievable. It's Hammer Horrorville by the sea!'

'Keep your voice down,' I hiss through gritted teeth, picking up the case she's dragging behind her and dropping it none too gently onto the box room floor. Storm watches from the doorway while I unfold the put-you-up bed and does nothing to help, even though the bed is ancient and keeps trapping my fingers. She could learn a thing or two from eager-to-please Emily, if she wasn't so busy mocking her.

After a while, as I'm shoving a pillow into a faded pillowcase, Storm saunters over to the window and perches on the cold stone sill.

'So have you lived here, like, forever then?' She peers out at the dark cliffs towering over the house and shudders.

'No, only about nine months, on and off.'

'Where were you in Cornwall before then?'

'I wasn't in Cornwall at all. I'm a Londoner, like you, and lived there my whole life until I came here. The last place I lived was Stratford, close to Westfield shopping centre,' I add because the centre's large Topshop is probably on Storm's radar.

'Huh!' She huffs and wrinkles her nose. 'You're telling me you gave up London and all those shops to come and live here! Are you, like, mental or something?'

'I can assure you I'm perfectly sane,' I say in the same strangled tones Mum would use, right before she launched into a rant about nosy neighbours, or intrusive teachers, or whoever was bothering her at the time. The pillow won't go into the case so I start punching it to make it fit. 'Alice needed me so I said I'd stay for a while and I'm glad I did because Salt Bay is starting to feel like home.'

At the mention of 'home', Storm's lower lip begins to wobble until she pulls her mouth tight. Damn! There I was, disliking her intensely and then she reveals a glimpse of upset teenager to confuse me.

Abandoning the half-in half-out pillow on the bed, I join her at the window. 'Look, I know this place seems a bit out of the way and odd at first but it grows on you and you'll get to like it.'

Remembering how much I hated Salt Bay at first, I'm tempted to put my hand on her shoulder in solidarity. But Storm pushes past me and heaves her case onto the bed with a grunt. 'We won't be staying here long enough for me to get to like it,' she snarls, snapping open the locks. She lifts the lid and starts rooting through the jumble of clothes inside, before muttering, 'You can go now. I'll sort out the pillow.'

Feeling thoroughly dismissed, I scoot past Barry's door and into my room where I throw myself onto the bed and stare at the ceiling. My heart is still hammering because I am, as Alice would put it, completely discombobulated.

My body has turned into an emotional pinball machine, with chaotic feelings pinging through me, and it's impossible to think clearly. All I know for sure is that everything was fine an hour or so ago. There I was, settling into a new way of life in Salt Bay with Alice and Josh and the choir. And then Barry knocked on the door and my inner peace was well and truly shafted.

So what do I do now? Concentrating on hairline cracks in the wall to calm my racing thoughts, I make a mental list of my options. It doesn't take long:

1. Throw a mega hissy fit and insist that Barry and Storm leave Tregavara House immediately.
2. Put up with my father and half-sister for one night and then get rid of them as quickly as possible tomorrow.

Option one is tempting but risks upsetting Alice, as well as confirming Storm's suspicion that I'm mentally unstable. Plus, that option became unworkable, really, from the moment Barry put his dirty boots on Alice's candlewick and claimed his bed for the night.

So, option two it is then. Sighing, I roll over, snuggle my cheek into the soft pillow and vow to make the best of it. Maybe Alice is right and spending more time with Barry and Storm will do me good. Heaven knows how but first impressions aren't always right – I know that more than most – so I'll grit my teeth and give them a chance. Until tomorrow, and then they're out. And though I don't have high hopes of our family reunion, maybe Barry can tell me more about Mum when she was young – preferably minus details of his first proper leg-over.

Stretching out my hand, I pick up the framed photo of Mum on my bedside table and gently trace her outline with my finger. It's my favourite picture of her, looking windswept and happy in Hyde Park before she got ill and lost her lovely dark hair.

'Barry – really? What the actual fuck were you thinking?' I whisper to the faded picture.

For so long it was just the two of us against the world and I thought I knew her so well. But it turns out I was wrong. She kept information from me; really important information like the truth about her parents throwing her out and about Barry being my father. And now there's no chance of ever asking her why.

I place her photo carefully back on the bedside table and Mum smiles back at me across the years, blissfully unaware that the secrets she took to her grave are coming back to bite me on the backside, big-time.

Chapter Three

Light is spilling from stained glass windows and throwing shadows across tumbled stones as I hurry through Salt Bay's tiny graveyard. The temperature has dipped in the last couple of days and the jacket I threw on is too thin, but the church will be warmer. Just so long as Hilary remembered to leave the heating on after her Bible Studies class.

If she forgets, we end up singing with our coats on for the first hour, and Roger has started bringing a hat and scarf too, just in case.

'Hilary is hideously forgetful because the menopause is messing with her mind,' he complains regularly, pulling the woolly hat over his sparse strands of hair. 'That's the trouble with women vicars of a certain age, and she's the most hormonally challenged in all of south-west Cornwall.'

Roger, landlord of the Whistling Wave, is the most misogynistic dinosaur in the *whole* of Cornwall but I've grown fond of him over the last few months, in spite of his views. In fact, I've grown fond of all the singers in Salt Bay Choral Society and look forward to our weekly rehearsals, although – I snatch a quick glance at my watch – I'm late for this one.

Sorting out the beds and then my head took ages and I only had time to wolf down a quick sandwich before heading out. I probably should have offered to make one for Barry and Storm, but it's better if they go to the pub. I don't want them imposing any further on Alice's hospitality and a sandwich made with the remains of last night's roast chicken would be unlikely to meet with Storm's approval anyway. She's probably vegan, just to be awkward.

A thick wave of heat hits me when I push open the heavy church door – hallelujah! – and the stresses of the day start to fade as I slip inside. I love this granite church, which has become so familiar. Its cool, bumpy walls and worn flagstones are steeped in history that intertwines with mine: history I didn't even know existed a year ago. Tregavara House had the same safe, familiar vibe until a bunch of new relatives rocked up this afternoon and turned my world upside down. But at least in here I can catch my breath for an hour or two.

Most choir members are already in their seats in front of the simple stone altar. Jennifer, who runs the village newsagent store, is talking loudly at poor Arthur, who's glancing around desperately for an escape route. She can be horribly overbearing but she means well. Elderly Cyril is shuffling into his chair and, ah, that's sweet, Pippa and Charlie are holding hands in the corner, with their heads bent together. Young love! When they got married several weeks ago, Salt Bay Choral Society sang at their reception and mostly hit the right notes, which was a wedding gift in itself.

I cried as they said their vows, which was embarrassing, but seeing their hopeful, loved-up faces caught me off guard. Salt Bay has unleashed my inner waterworks and I cry far more easily now than when I was haring around London with no ties.

My friend Kayla laughs at me for being a cry baby but her eyes looked suspiciously shiny as Pippa and Charlie promised to love one another for all eternity. Which is a *very* long time. Where is Kayla tonight? While I'm peering around the church for my Aussie mate, barrel-shaped Roger spots me and wanders over.

'No Kayla tonight,' he says brusquely, adjusting the collar of his faded grey polo shirt. 'She had to stay behind the bar because Daniel didn't turn up for his shift. Reckons he's got the flu.'

'Poor Dan, the flu makes you feel terrible. I had it last winter and thought I was going to die.'

A memory of my ex, Stuart, dabbing ineffectually at my forehead with a wet flannel springs to mind. That's funny, I haven't thought about him in ages. Probably because he was such a useless boyfriend.

'Huh, flu my arse!' grumbles Roger. 'He's got a hangover more like, after going out on the town to celebrate his birthday. He thinks I was born yesterday, the useless lump of lard!' He wanders off, still muttering under his breath.

'Come on everyone, take your seats and we can get started.'

I know that deep voice with its soft Cornish burr. Josh is standing almost out of sight at the piano, looking at sheet music over Michaela's shoulder and pointing something out to her. He must have come straight from school, where he's a teacher, because he's in navy cords, rather than jeans, and a crisp, white shirt that's open at the neck. His raven-black hair is curling slightly where it touches his collar and there's a five o'clock shadow across his strong jawline. Jeez, he's absolutely gorgeous! Glancing up, he catches my eye and his handsome face breaks into a smile. Just for me. Phwoar! Oops, I think I might have said that out loud.

Josh and I had a rocky start and every now and then I have a wobble about 'us'. Which is not surprising, seeing as I've never felt this strongly about any man before. There have been other boyfriends, like Stuart, of course – I'm not a nun. But that was back in my London days when commitment frightened the pants off me and moving on was my greatest skill. This time I don't want to move on, and that's what really scares me.

Before I start over-thinking things and getting anxious – one of my particular talents – Josh strides up and kisses me briefly on the mouth, with lips that taste of mint toothpaste. I lean in for a longer kiss and lose my balance slightly when he pulls back, but I cheer up when he whispers, 'Good grief, I've missed you.'

'You saw rather a lot of me yesterday evening.'

'That was ages ago.' His dark eyes twinkle as he snakes his arm around me and gives my waist a quick squeeze. 'The hours since then have seemed endless.'

I giggle and snuggle up against his chest. 'I missed you too and a lot has happened since yesterday. I've got something to tell you about my family.'

'What?' Josh drops his arms and steps back. He eyes me warily. 'Toby hasn't turned up to wreak more havoc, has he?'

'Toby hasn't turned up but my father and half-sister have. They arrived at Tregavara House a couple of hours ago and are making themselves at home.'

'Bloody hell!' Josh glances at the huge silver cross on the altar and bites his lip. 'Did you know anything about them?' When I shake my head, he frowns. 'That must have been quite a surprise – a good one though, I suppose?'

'Not really. It was more of a shock… they're not what you'd expect.'

'In what way?'

I shrug, not sure how to answer Josh's question. I thought my father would be more, well, dad-like, plus more Viking than failed rock star wide boy. And as for Storm, she and I have nothing in common apart from some dodgy DNA. Just thinking about them makes me feel agitated and I can't wait to talk things over with Josh. But now isn't the right time.

'I'd better tell you later when she's not on the warpath,' I say, nodding towards Jennifer, who's tapping her watch impatiently, backcombed blonde hair bobbing up and down with every tap. 'I love you.'

Josh smiles but doesn't say it back. He never does when we're in public but I don't let it bother me; not really. Josh Pasco is deep and dark and buttoned up, and that's just his way.

'We can talk after the rehearsal, when we're not being watched by lots of people,' he says quietly, brushing his lips across my hair. He's trying to be discreet but his show of affection is spotted by Jennifer, who tuts, and Cyril, who beams. Overall, the choir are delighted by our budding romance. Florence reckons we're like Romeo and Juliet – though hopefully without the double suicide ending.

The choir has grown since our first concert in the spring. I wasn't sure about starting up the choral society again, not after the tragedy. But Kayla persuaded me that it wouldn't be disrespectful and she was right. The choir has breathed new life into the village, and into me too. And now I wouldn't be without the ragbag of amateur singers who meet every week to make music.

'Come along, you two. Chop chop! We need to practise.' Jennifer's loud voice bounces off the stone walls. 'It's not long until the next heat of the competition and we want to win.'

'I don't know about win,' grumbles Roger, who's slumped in his seat with his arms folded across his large belly. 'I'd settle for not being totally shite.'

Jennifer shoots him a filthy look but Roger's got a point. It wasn't my idea to enter the Kernow Choral Crown, a prestigious competition for amateur choirs in Cornwall. In fact, I'd have said we were nowhere near ready to take part, but Jennifer suggested it and I got swept along by everyone's enthusiasm for the idea.

The problem is they're thinking back sixteen years to past glories, when Salt Bay Choral Society beat off all competition to lift the Crown – but a lot has happened since then. Just a few months afterwards, the choir was destroyed by a fierce storm which swamped fishing boats and drowned seven of its singers, including Samuel Trebarwith, the grandfather I never met.

Alice says I worry too much but I can't help thinking that our newly resurrected choir is expecting to emulate the old choir's success. And my anxiety is only ramped up by Jennifer's comments and the feeling that I'll be letting everyone down if we don't do well. Samuel will probably come back to haunt me and make my life a living hell. Though he'll have to stand in line behind Barry and Storm.

'Don't worry about it, Roger. We'll do just fine in the competition,' calls Ollie, oblivious to the fact that his inability to sing in tune might be a problem. Though, as Kayla keeps telling me, his Greek-god good looks might work in our favour if the judges are female. She's biased because she and Ollie are an item but I'll put him in the front row anyway, just in case.

We've decided to sing a Gilbert and Sullivan piece in the semi-final, plus a sea shanty which is meant to sound slightly rough around the edges. We can always claim we're aiming for authenticity if our tuning's a bit pitchy, though tonight everyone is singing really well. They must have been practising at home.

I conduct the first songs and then Josh takes over to lead the traditional Cornish song 'Lamorna' that we've lined up for the final – well, we might as well act as if we're confident.

Watching Josh conduct is one of my favourite things in the whole world so I sit on a bum-numbingly hard pew and enjoy the moment. His thick black hair flops across his forehead and his shoulder muscles strain under his shirt as he marks out the beat and gets caught up in the music. It's very sexy, especially when he turns mid-song and gives me a slow wink.

Emily notices and smiles at me before casting longing glances at Jason in the tenor section. Poor Emily. Jason – who prefers to be called Jay – is eighteen years old with gelled, light-brown hair and the sort of clean-cut features that belong in a boy band. He's popular and good-looking – and he knows it. There's no way he'll give a gentle mouse like Emily a second glance and, even though she's been mooning over him for weeks, I don't think they've ever spoken.

My heart breaks for her because I still remember the exquisite pain of the unrequited crush: that heady mix of excitement and hope which slowly leaches into bitter disappointment. Mum's penchant for moving flats meant I spent my adolescence hopping from school to school so any teenage crushes rarely had a chance to go anywhere. Apart from Simon Shalpiton in Battersea, who turned out to be a dork in the end, as I fear Jay would too if Emily ever got her hands on him.

Emily scuttles off home with her head down at the end of the rehearsal but Josh and I head for the pub. This is the date part of the evening and we hold hands as we saunter past the village green. It's too dark to see the crystal-clear river which cuts through the open ground but we can hear it tumbling over stones on its way to the sea.

'So tell me about these mysterious long-lost relatives,' says Josh, giving my hand a squeeze.

'Well, my father's called Barry and—'

'Barry!' Josh stops in his tracks and swings round to face me. 'I thought you said your father was Scandinavian? That's why your eyes are so amazing.'

'It seems I was wrong and my father is actually from Essex, originally, or so he tells me. And he's in some rock band I've never heard of, though he's getting on a bit, and Storm, his daughter, is sixteen.'

'Storm?' When Josh laughs in disbelief, his teeth shine white in the beam from the green's single lamp post. 'Good grief!'

'I know, it's an unusual name, but it suits her. Storm is quite a grown-up sixteen, with lots of make-up and attitude.'

'Yeah, I know someone else with attitude.' When I give his arm a gentle punch, he pretends to rub it and grins. 'But how do you feel about them turning up unannounced on your doorstep?'

'Shocked and confused and not great, to be honest. I've got no idea why they're here and they're not at all what I would have expected, but maybe I'm being a snob. Am I a snob?' I ask, anxiously. Snobbery was a cardinal sin in my mum's eyes and I can imagine her shaking her head at me.

'I don't think so. I've haven't noticed any snobbish tendencies, not since you got over the whole Salt Bay not being cosmopolitan London thing.'

'And maybe I wasn't what Alice was expecting when I arrived on her doorstep and that's turned out OK.'

'More than just OK.' Josh puts his fingers under my chin, tilts my face towards him and, now no one is watching, kisses me extra slowly for ages. I love being kissed by Josh. It makes my toes tingle.

'Anyway,' I continue, coming up for air and rubbing my chin where it's been grazed by his stubble. 'Throwing them out straight away would probably have been a bit harsh so they're staying until tomorrow because Barry wants to have a chat with me.' My stomach churns at the thought and I grab hold of Josh's arm. 'Do you think I'm doing the right thing? First impressions can be wrong, can't they?'

'Of course they can – as you found out with me.' Josh gives a short laugh. 'Your first impressions of me were *way* off.'

'I don't know about that. I thought you were grumpy, arrogant and a pain in the backside so I was pretty much spot on.' Josh snorts and shakes his head. 'But I haven't got much family so I'm going along with Alice's advice that it's best to give them a chance.'

'That sounds like a good plan, especially if they're only here until tomorrow.' Josh laces his long fingers through mine and pulls me on towards the pub. 'We all need family, even when they turn out to be a bit of a pain.'

'Talking of which, how's your mum doing? Though she's definitely not a pain.'

Josh sighs and loosens his grip on my hand. 'Not great. She's still quite breathless and tired and she's got a hospital appointment coming up to see if they're going to operate.'

'Really? I didn't realise an operation might be necessary.' I link my arm through Josh's and snuggle up close. 'No wonder you're worried. But if the doctors think an operation might help her, it must be for the best. Try not to dwell on it too much. That won't help her, or you.'

'Yeah, I'll try.' Josh shrugs off my arm and marches ahead as I hurry to keep up, feeling I've said something wrong. I sometimes misjudge family situations because they're still new to me. But I'm upset about Marion being unwell and meant to be reassuring, not bossy.

Marion is really lovely. I got to know her pretty well when I stayed with the Pasco family after the flood, while Tregavara House was still uninhabitable. There were six of us squeezed into their cottage in the old part of Trecaldwith – Marion, me and Josh, his sisters, Lucy and Serena, and Lucy's five-year-old daughter, Freya.

It could have been a nightmare and I came close to throttling sixteen-year-old Serena for hogging the bathroom and playing ear-splitting music. The secret services could use top-volume rap as a torture device. But overall it was brilliant to live with a proper family because I never had that growing up, seeing as Barry scuttled off.

And now Barry's back, with a stroppy sibling of mine in tow – as if he'd only nipped out for a pint of milk, rather than being absent from my life for three decades – but it feels far too late to play happy families.

Chapter Four

People are piling out of the Whistling Wave when we get closer and music is wafting into the cool evening air. The pub was deathly silent when I first came to Salt Bay – no juke box, no live bands, no singing, nothing. Mind you, the whole village was like that, as though the Great Storm had washed away any joy. But things have improved since the choir got going again and the whole place seems brighter. Or maybe I've changed and my brighter outlook on life is casting a rosy glow across the village.

Either way, the Whistling Wave now has a folk band who visit once a month to play live. They're pretty dire but that's not the point – it's music! And Roger sometimes plays low-level background music in the bar which drives poor Kayla mad because she doesn't share his musical tastes. She can just about stomach Val Doonican but she threatened to smash up the place when he played his pan pipes CD on repeat.

Tonight, Kayla must be in charge of the CD player because Ed Sheeran's voice is lilting around the pub. There's a fire burning in the huge blackened stone fireplace and lamps in the deep window nooks are casting yellow pools of light. But Kayla doesn't look happy. In fact, she's looking flustered behind the bar, fairy lights glinting on the rust-red strands of hair which have escaped her ponytail.

'Mate, how's it going?' she calls, putting down the wine glass she's wiping. 'It's a right pain I couldn't come to the rehearsal, thanks to Dipshit Dan. How did it go?'

'Pretty well, and it's not a problem that you missed it. You can come to the next one.'

'I know, but the next heat of the competition is coming up fast. Time is ticking on, Annabella.'

Don't remind me! A shiver goes down my spine and I mentally kick myself for getting in a tizz about nothing. The Kernow Choral Crown is completely unimportant compared to Marion's health.

'Have you been busy in here?' I ask, changing the subject.

'It's not been too bad, though it's filling up now the choir's chucked out. But that couple over there have been running me off my feet.' Kayla tips her head towards a table at the back of the bar. 'Most emmets are OK but they've been a nightmare. That woman was so rude, I came close to punching her lights out.'

My stomach does a weird lurch when I realise that the couple she's dissing are Barry and Storm. Barry is sipping at a pint and Storm is slumped across their table, picking at her nail varnish and looking bored.

'How long have they been in?' I demand, stomach churning.

'I dunno, ages. They've been keeping me busy ordering food and drinks.'

'Is that them?' asks Josh, glancing at my ashen face. 'Are you going to tell her?'

Kayla has started pulling a pint of St Austell's Tribute for Josh but stops mid-way. 'Tell me what?'

I take a deep breath and go for it.

'That man over there is called Barry and he's my father, apparently.' Kayla's jaw drops open but I carry on. 'And the girl with him is my half-sister, Storm. They turned up out of the blue this afternoon.'

'No freakin' way!' Kayla leans towards me with her elbows on the bar. I can see straight down her top and a couple of men nearby nudge one another. 'You're kidding me, right? Crikey, *EastEnders* eat your heart out! Did you know about them?'

'Nope. The whole thing has been a huge shock. I knew I had a dad, obviously, but not who or where he was.'

'I thought you said he was Scandinavian? He doesn't look Scandinavian.' She stares hard at Barry. 'And I don't mean to be rude but your sister is a right piece of work.'

'Half-sister. She is quite challenging but perhaps we were the same at sixteen.'

I don't think so for a moment but maybe I should stand up for her, what with her being family and all.

'You what? I don't believe it!' Kayla slams down Josh's half-empty pint so hard, beer slops over her hand and slicks across the bar. Then, she marches across the pub, with me scuttling after her, and gives Barry and Storm her best death-stare. 'What the hell do you think you're doing?'

Barry pauses with a pork scratching halfway to his mouth. 'You what, love?'

'You!' Kayla glares at Storm, who straightens in her chair, looking slightly less bored. 'What's your game? Are you trying to get me sacked?'

'Kayla, what on earth is going on?' I put my hand on her arm but she shakes it off.

'Is this woman a friend of yours, Annie?' asks Barry, carefully putting the scratching back into its packet.

'She is and you seem to have upset her. What's the problem, Kayla?'

'The problem is—' noticing that people in the pub are watching us, she lowers her voice from foghorn to merely mega-loud '—the problem is that she didn't tell me she was only sixteen when she was ordering Bacardi for herself at the bar.' She swings back round to Storm. 'Do you know that's illegal and you could get the pub and me into all sorts of trouble?'

Good grief! Roger will go nuts if he finds out. He's so obsessive about checking people's ages before selling them alcohol, we reckon he's been hauled over the coals before for underage sales.

'Whatever.' Storm rolls her eyes and sighs.

Kayla's face is almost the same colour as her hair. Ooh, this is not good. I've only seen Kayla explode once, when a drunken punter insisted that Australia was an insignificant island off the coast of New Zealand. It was not a pretty sight and I don't want to see it again.

'I think what Storm really means is that she's very sorry and she shouldn't have been ordering spirits at the bar,' I gabble, eyeing up Storm's glass of what looks like Bacardi and lime.

'No, what I *really* mean is you all wanna stop getting so stressy. You're gonna be dead soon.' Storm takes a slow sip of her drink and watches Kayla through narrowed eyes. She might as well be lighting a touchpaper because Kayla is about to go *Full Metal Jacket* any minute.

'Let me introduce myself,' says Josh, stepping between Kayla and Storm and stretching out his hand towards Barry. 'I'm Josh, Annie's boyfriend.'

I've never loved him more, especially as it's the first time he's introduced himself to anyone as my boyfriend. At least this evening hasn't been a total bust, even if World War Three does erupt.

'Ah, so you're the hot date.' Barry shakes his hand and nods at Josh, who's still acting as a buffer between Storm and Kayla. 'What exactly are your intentions towards my daughter then?'

'Um.' Josh glances at me nervously.

'Only joking! You should have seen your face!' Barry leans back in his chair and slaps Josh soundly on the back. 'Storm, apologise to the angry lady, and Josh, it's very nice to meet you.'

'So-rry,' says Storm with a scowl, somehow managing to make the situation even more fraught with her apology. 'The pubs I go to in London don't care what I order at the bar and I didn't realise you were so anal about it in Cornwall. It figures, though.'

'And just what is that supposed to mean?' Kayla is trying to peer around Josh's back but he's swaying gently to block her view.

This is so not how I wanted my friends to meet my family. In fact, I wasn't planning on introducing them at all. What's the point if Barry and Storm are leaving tomorrow and won't ever return to Salt Bay? Naively, I thought they'd have a quick meal in the Whistling Wave and keep their heads down. But I see now that I seriously underestimated Storm's pain-in-the-arseness, and it's up to me to ease the tension. Somehow.

'Look who's come in!' I yell with relief as Ollie bounds through the pub door like an enthusiastic puppy. He catches sight of us in the corner, waves and rushes over, golden hair bouncing up and down.

'Sorry I'm late. I gave Tom a quick lift home from choir because he's not feeling well. There you are!'

Sweeping Kayla into his rugby-player arms, he plants a smacking kiss on her cheek, totally oblivious to the strained atmosphere. He's much more relaxed about public displays of affection than Josh, not that it matters.

'I missed you at choir,' he booms, hugging Kayla close. 'I sang extra loud to make up for you not being there.' That's true. It was awful. 'Who's this, then?'

Here we go again. Screwing my hands tight, I nod towards the odd couple still slouched at the table.

'This is my father, Barry, and my sister, Storm. Half-sister,' I add as Storm opens her mouth to correct me. 'They arrived earlier today. Unexpectedly. Out of the blue. It's all been a bit of a shock...' I trail off, not sure what else there is to say.

'Wow, that's amazing! Are you staying for long?'

'Long enough to get to know my daughter,' says Barry as I wonder just how long that might be. A few hours, a week, a month? He does know that they're leaving tomorrow, right?

'How was the journey over from Denmark?' asks Ollie, shaking Barry's hand vigorously. Good grief, I appear to have told the whole wazzocking world that my father is Scandinavian.

'Sorry, what? Denmark?' Barry looks flummoxed.

'He's from Essex,' I hiss at Ollie, who frowns briefly before his wide signature smile lights up his face. 'OK, that's cool. Essex is nice too. Not so much snow. Fewer mountains. But nice.'

Storm slowly shakes her head at Ollie, which only infuriates Kayla more. She starts hopping from foot to foot, like a boxer building up to a knock-out punch.

'If you two have finished your food, I'll walk you back to Tregavara House. You must be knackered after all that driving.' I'm gabbling in my desperation to get them out of the pub, pronto.

Storm pulls her phone from her jeans pocket and gasps in horror, 'But it's only quarter past nine.'

'Alice goes to bed early and we don't want to wake her up when we come in,' I say decisively, dragging Storm's chair across the flagstones so she has to stand up or end up on her backside. Grumbling, she grabs her jacket from the back of the chair, gives me a scowl, and stomps off.

'Teenagers!' chuckles Barry. 'Mind you, she's always been a bit of a handful. I expect you were the same at her age, weren't you, Annie?'

I smile weakly, not up to talking about the years he missed, not here in the pub in front of my friends who obviously think my family are a complete nightmare.

'Hadn't you better go and catch up with Storm? I'll be out in a minute.'

Barry hoicks up his creaky leather trousers and grins. 'I suppose I'd better check she isn't having a hissy fit and throwing herself into the harbour. Daughters, who'd have 'em? Not me.'

That's a Freudian slip and a half. But Barry ignores my ice-cold stare and gives a cheery 'Bye all,' before sauntering through the bar and out of the pub.

'Unbelievable!' mutters Kayla, breathing deeply to calm down as Ollie strokes her back. She's grimacing so much, her eyebrows are meeting in the middle.

'I'm so sorry, Kayla, about the ordering drinks and the rudeness,' I blab, feeling dreadful. 'I'd never have suggested they eat in here if I'd thought for one minute that Storm would be buying alcohol. It didn't even cross my mind.'

'That's all right, it's not your fault.'

But she doesn't catch my eye or react when I pat her arm in an apologetic way. Great; I'm obviously tainted by association.

'They're not staying in Salt Bay for long, are they?' Kayla demands, collecting up the discarded pint and the Bacardi glass. It's empty because Storm knocked back the dregs while her father and Ollie were talking. What kind of father lets his young daughter drink spirits? And on a Wednesday, for goodness' sake. For some reason, the fact that Storm is boozing mid-week seems even worse.

'Well, are they?' she asks, sharply.

'No, of course they're not staying for long. I hope not. Probably not.'

'I know you're related, and all that, but I'd get shot of them as soon as possible if I were you. I've got a bad feeling about them.'

'Don't be so dramatic, Kayla. They seem all right,' says Ollie, giving my shoulder a sympathetic squeeze.

'Really? You always think the best of people, you drongo.' Kayla sounds cross but she leans against Ollie and nestles her head under his chin. 'All in all, you're far too smiley and trusting. You want to be more cynical and reserved, like Annie's boyfriend. No offence, Josh.'

'None taken,' murmurs Josh, his mouth twitching in the corner. 'Annie, shall I come with you?'

When he touches my arm, a tingle shoots down to my toes. There's nothing I'd like more than my gorgeous boyfriend coming back with me to Tregavara House. After such a confusing and difficult day, I'm in desperate need of a ginormous out-of-the-public-eye Josh Hug.

But I shake my head. 'Best not. I'll get them home and into bed and hopefully they'll head off tomorrow. Sorry.'

Truth be told, I want to keep Josh as far apart from Storm and Barry as possible. He's already putting up with my awful cousin, Toby, and I don't want him having to cope with even more. The Trebarwiths turning into the Addams Family might put him right off me.

Icy cold fear suddenly grips my stomach and digs its nails in. I can't imagine what I'll do if Josh goes off me, because moving on from this man isn't an option right now. I glance at him anxiously but, although he's frowning – Kayla describes it as 'glowering' – he seems more disappointed than annoyed.

'I was really looking forward to seeing you, Annie,' he whispers, bending his head to kiss me on the cheek.

Ooh, me too. As I breathe in the familiar citrus tang of his aftershave, I'm tempted to throw myself into Josh Pasco's arms and beg him to come home with me. But keeping my life in Salt Bay separate from Barry and Storm seems important right now. And Josh would be embarrassed if I suddenly went all emotional on him in the pub. I'm not sure I'm a begging kind of person, anyway.

So I just murmur, 'Me too,' and leave it at that.

Josh is standing so close I can see tiny streaks of gold in his dark brown eyes. 'Just make sure that when they leave you don't go back to London with them.'

'Of course not,' I laugh, though I'm not one hundred per cent sure he's joking. 'I just need to get this sorted out first. Is that OK?'

'Of course. Do what you have to do and we can get together later in the week.' He shrugs his broad shoulders and gives a lopsided smile. 'Family comes first, I guess.'

Yeah, I guess.

Chapter Five

I'm woken early next morning by the sound of hammering. Sharp bangs are reverberating around the house and ignoring the din proves impossible. I do try for a while but it's hard slipping back into sleep when it sounds like an episode of *DIY SOS* is being filmed directly beneath your bedroom. Nick Knowles could barge in at any moment and I wouldn't be surprised.

Yawning, I roll over onto my back and open my eyes wide. Jeez, I'm knackered. Storm stomped off to her bedroom as soon as we got back last night and Barry soon followed, saying he was tired, so I got an early night. But it was weird having them in the house and I tossed and turned for hours, going over the day's events in my head. And every time my feet strayed across the cold bed, I was aware of the space where Josh should be.

Thinking of Josh wakes me up even more, and eventually, when the hammering starts to crescendo, I give in and crawl out from under my snug blankets. Brrrr. It's freezing in here, although the enormous radiator under my window should be on – I brush my fingers across the hot metal to check. Yep, it's definitely working but Tregavara House is big and old and draughty, and has seemed even more so since the flood.

Which reminds me: pulling back the curtains, I carry out a swift recce of the narrow river that meanders along the fold of the valley, where Salt Bay nestles on the edge of the sea. Recent dry weather means the river is low but glancing at it every morning has become a habit since water breached the bank and swamped us. Checking has become a nervous tic to keep me safe: the river isn't flooding, so today is not the day I drown. Woohoo!

Bang. Bang. The noise is getting louder and, when I go onto the landing and peer over the banisters, Barry is on his knees in the hallway bashing hell out of the skirting board. He's leaning forward and exposing a wide expanse of builder's bum, which is inappropriate because he's my father and – well, it's just generally inappropriate.

'Barry!' I yell, but he only stops hammering when I clump down the stairs and tap him on the shoulder. He drops the hammer with a clatter and swings around.

'Annie! Hell's teeth! I thought you were a ghost – this creepy old place is really messing with my mind. Didn't I hear you say that you worked for a charity somewhere? Why aren't you getting ready for work?'

'One, because I texted my boss yesterday and arranged to take today off, and two—' I glance through the open sitting room door at the clock on the mantelpiece '—because it's only seven-fifteen.'

'Really? Is it that early? My watch is rubbish at keeping time 'cos I bought it down the market and was fleeced. Armani, my arse.' Barry sits back on his heels. 'Oh well, it's good to grasp the day and push ahead with what you're doing.'

'And what the hell are you doing?'

'Yes, indeed,' calls Alice from the top of the stairs. Now, she *does* look like a ghost in her grey dressing gown with white hair fluffed out around her pale face.

'Morning, Mrs Trebarwith. I didn't wake you, did I?' says Barry, turning to give her a little wave. His long hair is caught into a ponytail with a glittery pink scrunchie which sparkles under the hallway light. I so hope it belongs to Storm.

'I was already awake but the hammering was rather loud,' says Alice, holding on to the banister with both hands as she carefully negotiates the stairs. 'What are you doing, Mr Stubbs?'

'I noticed when I came in yesterday that your skirting board hasn't been fixed on properly. Shoddy workmanship. So I thought I'd sort it out for you, to thank you for letting us stay for a while. And please call me Barry.'

For a *while*? Does an overnight stay count as 'for a while'? Oh God, it probably doesn't. 'For a while' sounds like three days at least. Or even longer. Maybe four, or five, before I can get Barry and his rude daughter out of my life for good. But I can't take another day off work to be around and make sure they leave. I close my eyes for a few seconds and breathe deeply.

'Don't worry,' Barry adds cheerfully. 'I know what I'm doing because I work as an odd job man between rock gigs, when money's tight.' He dabs at his forehead with a greying hankie from his trouser pocket – he's swapped his leather trousers for faded jeans with rips at thigh level that would look better on a teenager.

'Where did you find the hammer?' asks Alice.

'In my car. I carry a minimum of hammer, screwdriver and chisel so I'm always prepared to do odd jobs for people.'

Or to break into their houses, flits across my mind and, in spite of my reservations about Barry, I immediately feel ashamed. Just because my father comes across as a bit of a wide boy, he's not a criminal. Not necessarily. Maybe I am a snob, after all.

'Is Storm awake?' I ask, deliberately nicely to make up for being such a horribly suspicious person.

'God, no! She slept through my gigs as a toddler so she's used to noise. She won't be up until midday at the earliest.'

'I thought you'd be the same, what with being a rock god used to late nights.'

That's not meant to be particularly sarcastic but Alice gives me a straight look.

'Tinnitus,' chirps Barry cheerfully. 'All that loud music has totally knackered my ears and, as soon as I wake up, the infernal noise stops me going back to sleep. It's like hand-bell ringers on crack having a party in my head.'

Alice flinches at the earthy language but pats Barry on the shoulder. 'It's a little early for DIY but it was a kind thought all the same. Thank you.'

What exactly is Alice up to? She's being far too nice to Barry and we don't want to encourage him to stay, do we. When I try to catch her eye, she keeps her head down. If I didn't know better, I'd think she was avoiding me.

While Barry is gathering up scattered nails, I examine the mended skirting board and have to admit that it looks more secure. His frenetic hammering has left a few dents but Alice seems pleased with what he's done. She even tells him that it's nice having a man around the house again, as though I'm not capable of banging a few nails into a bit of wood. I think feminism may have passed her by. But doing a bit of bodged DIY is hardly going to make up for being a rubbish father, is it.

*

An hour later, I'm dressed and morosely eating a slice of toast slathered in marmalade when Barry slopes into the kitchen. He's pulled a Rolling Stones sweatshirt over his vest top and, though his hair is still in a ponytail, he's swapped the pink scrunchie for a plain black band.

'I was hoping to catch you, Annie. Maybe you and I can have that little chat now?' He sits at the table and grabs the piece of toast I was planning to eat next. Then, cutting slices of butter as thick as cheese, he watches them pool into the golden bread before taking a bite.

Alice is busying herself at the sink and has her back to me but I can tell she's earwigging. Of course she is; I would too. But I don't want to be judged by Alice for making a balls-up of this 'little chat'. And I might have things to say to Barry that Alice wouldn't want to hear.

'Why don't we go for a walk by the harbour?' I suggest.

Barry stares out of the window at plants bending in a brisk breeze coming off the sea. 'What, outside?'

When I nod, he shrugs and mumbles with his mouth full, 'All right. Outside seems a bit unnecessary but I'll get my jacket and see you at the front door in a couple of mins.'

He takes the toast with him, dripping greasy butter over the kitchen tiles as he heads for the hall.

When he's gone, Alice turns slowly from the sink and smiles at me. 'Good luck, Annabella. Just remember to give him a proper chance.' Like she's the voice of my conscience, or something, even though the one with the guilty conscience should be Barry.

*

Seagulls dip and dive above us as Barry and I head for the harbour, which is one of my favourite places. I love its strong granite arms which stretch into the sea and shelter Salt Bay, as if they're giving the village a hug. It can be a wild place on windy days with white waves crashing up and over the stones but today's breeze shouldn't be a problem.

'Are we walking or sitting?' asks Barry when we reach the harbour wall. The tide is going out and there's a patch of washed sand below us. Brightly coloured fishing boats are resting on the shore, tethered by rusty chains and thick rope to metal rings driven into the stone.

'Let's sit.'

Folding my scarf underneath me like a cushion, I sit down and dangle my legs over the edge of the smooth wall. And, after a moment's hesitation, Barry joins me, his knees cracking when he stoops down.

'God, these stones are freezing. I'll end up with a numb bum.'

His jeans have a trendy rip over his left buttock so he's probably right. Maybe he'll get piles and spend the rest of his life buying haemorrhoid cream, which is no more than he deserves.

I blink rapidly to shift a vision of Barry's backside from my brain and then we both sit looking out across the churning sea to the grey horizon. Now we're alone together, it's really awkward and I have no idea what to say to this strange little man. There are loads of questions I could ask – about my mum and why he and Storm are here – but I'm not sure where to start. The seconds tick by as we listen to the suck of the waves and a car revving its engine in the distance.

Barry is the first to break the silence. 'It was a shame about your mum dying,' he blurts out, eyes towards the horizon.

'How do you know about that?'

'It said in the newspaper piece about the flood that your late mother lived here. But it didn't say what happened to her.'

Banging my heels against the harbour wall, I take a deep breath of salty breeze before answering. I thought I wanted Barry to talk about Mum but, now that he is, I just want him to stop.

'Breast cancer,' I say curtly. 'She died four years ago.'

'That's a bummer,' murmurs Barry, which is accurate but probably not the best response to such sad news. 'Still,' he adds, sounding more upbeat, 'it must have been great growing up here by the sea. Sandcastles on the beach, ice creams, surfing, big house and all that.'

Jeez, he really doesn't have a clue about the grenade that his quick shag lobbed into the lives of my mother and her family. A fumbled five minutes for him led to decades of estrangement for the Trebarwiths – and I was the grenade that blew everything apart. A heavy feeling of guilt washes over me; a guilt he should share.

'I didn't grow up here. In fact, I didn't know anything about this place until last January.'

'How come?' Barry winces as he shifts about on the hard stone.

'When my grandparents found out that my mum was pregnant with me, they threw her out. She was eighteen and on her own. She must have been scared to death.'

'That was harsh.' Barry swallows so hard his Adam's apple bobs up and down. 'I didn't realise they'd done that.'

'You wouldn't have, what with you abandoning her too.'

Barry zips up his jacket against the chilly breeze and stares at the dishwater-grey sea for a few seconds. Then he sighs. 'So what happened to the two of you then?'

'Mum gave birth to me in London and we stayed there, moving from flat to flat because we didn't have much money and mum was often ill.'

'What, ill with cancer?'

'No, mentally ill.'

Usually I sugar-coat the story of my upbringing because no one really needs to know the truth. But feckless Barry doesn't deserve the sweetened version.

Puffing out his cheeks, Barry pulls mirrored sunglasses from his jeans pocket and slides them onto his face. 'Joanna seemed a bit wild when I knew her but I didn't realise she was, you know—' he lowers his voice even though there's no one around '—doolally.'

Good grief, this is just the kind of crap I had to put up with in the playground, when Mum didn't behave like the other mothers. When she'd turn up early and insist on taking me out of school to go on some wild goose-chase, or she'd forget to turn up at all and I'd be left waiting with some teacher desperate to ditch me and get home.

'My mother wasn't doolally, Barry,' I say through gritted teeth. 'She was mentally unwell but in spite of that, and also in spite of having *no support whatsoever*—' I emphasise those last few words '—she loved me and looked after me.'

'Yeah, she did a good job with you. I'll give her that,' says Barry, which is big of him. He waves his arm at Salt Bay behind us. 'So how did you find out about this place in the end?'

'Alice tracked me down in London and sent a letter asking me to visit her. I didn't even know she existed until then.'

Barry nods. 'She seems like a sound woman. I'm surprised she went along with throwing Jo out all those years ago.'

Now is the time to tell him more about the circumstances of Mum's estrangement from her family. I could tell him the whole sorry story, about how Mum rebuffed my grandmother's attempts to get in touch over the years and lied to me about it. But that might make Barry feel less guilty and I'd quite like him to suffer for abandoning us.

Does that make me an awful person? Probably; and my life wouldn't necessarily have been better with Barry in it – I mean, look at how Storm's turned out. But it can't be right that he side-stepped his responsibilities and had fun gigging round London while we were scraping by.

'It was really sad, what happened to your mother,' says Barry, smoothing down strands of long hair caught by the wind, 'but I guess everything's ended up all right in the end. You seem to be well in with the Trebarwith family now.'

'With Alice, yes.'

I deliberately don't mention Toby, who views me as an inconvenience at best.

There's another strained silence, punctuated by the screeches of seagulls high above us and the mewling of a stray black cat that wanders over and butts its head against Barry's thigh. It stretches out on the cold stones when Barry runs his hand along its back and, even though its ribs are showing through matted fur, I can't help envying its freedom and total lack of angst. That's the effect my long-lost father is having on me – I have a lovely home and a fabulous boyfriend but I'd quite happily swap places right now with a flea-bitten moggy.

'Look, Barry,' I shuffle round to face him, fed up with tiptoeing around the subject. 'What exactly do you want from me?'

'Nothing!' Barry holds his hands palm up towards the scudding clouds. 'Honest, babe, I want nothing.'

'Then why are you here?' My exasperation is reflected back at me in Barry's shades.

'I don't know. I was curious, I suppose, and wanted to get to know you. It's like being a new father all over again.'

I'm tempted to make a cutting comment about it being a bit late to come over all paternal but Alice's words are ringing in my head: *give him a proper chance.* And the quicker we get this over with, the quicker he'll leave. So, I grit my teeth.

'OK, I understand that you were curious and I don't mean to be unwelcoming but a lot has happened to me this year, and you and Storm turning up is hard for me to get my head around.'

'That's fine. We can take it slowly. Actually, me and Storm are heading back to Brixton later 'cos I've got a pub gig tomorrow but we can email and Facebook and stuff.'

'Of course we can.'

Hooray! I feel faint with relief that 'for a while' really does mean one night only.

'And maybe you can come to a gig soon and see me rocking out.'

'Definitely,' I lie, already sure that I will never ever watch Barry bump and grind onstage.

'And you and Storm will end up being great friends.'

That's about as likely as me copping off with Ryan Gosling, but I nod and smile. Alice would be proud of me.

Chapter Six

Back at the house, Barry goes straight upstairs while I head for the kitchen, desperate for a celebratory cup of tea. Thanks to the sea air, I'm always gasping for a cuppa these days, and getting shot of Barry and Storm is worthy of celebration – though I'd still like to know why they really came here in the first place. No one travels for hours with a surly teenager to the back of beyond because they're suddenly curious.

I'm at the sink filling the kettle and deep in thought when two strong arms snake around my waist and the kettle clangs into the tap.

'Jeez!' I yell, as metal hits metal and cold water sprays all down my T-shirt.

'Oops, sorry,' Josh murmurs into the back of my neck. 'I didn't mean to make you jump.' He tightens his hold on my waist and kisses the top of my damp shoulder, where my skin is exposed.

'What are you doing here?' I relax my muscles and lean back against him. He feels so solid. Putting the kettle down in the sink, I twist around in his arms and clasp my hands behind his neck. He grins down at me, dark hair flopping into his eyes.

'My first class are away on a trip and I'm helping with a school event this evening so I'm going in a bit later. And I thought I'd nip in to see you, if that's all right, seeing as you're playing truant today.'

'It's more than all right.'

'And is it all right if I kiss you?' asks Josh with a mischievous glint in his deep-brown eyes that remind me of molten dark chocolate. 'If you wouldn't mind.'

'Ah, just go for it!'

He laughs before kissing me hard on the mouth and pulling me tight against his lean body. Ooh, this feels lovely.

We're really getting into it – nothing too pornographic obviously because we're in Alice's kitchen – when the door from the hall bursts open and Storm bundles through it. She stops dead when she sees us and rolls her eyes with a loud sigh. Josh gives a small groan as he breaks off the kiss and lets me go.

'Storm! Is everything OK?'

My breath is coming in short gasps and I can still taste Josh on my lips.

'Where exactly is the shower in this place?'

'There's one over the bath.'

'That thing is the shower? It's ancient and the water that came out was brown which is disgusting.'

'It'll clear if you run the water for a few seconds or you can have a bath if you'd rather.'

'I want a shower. Only old people have baths in the morning.' Storm rakes her fingers through her shoulder-length hair. Without make-up on she looks much nicer – younger, prettier, less hard. 'Oy, watch out!' She rubs at the arm that Barry's just bashed into with the door.

'You're up then. It's a miracle!' says Barry with a grin. 'It's well early for you.'

A glance at my watch shows it's almost ten o'clock.

'I couldn't sleep,' grumbles Storm. 'It's too noisy around here.'

Josh glances up from the magnets and postcards he's studying on the fridge door. 'Don't you live in the middle of London? It must be far more noisy there.'

'Yeah, but that's traffic and sirens and drunk people shouting. I'm used to that but I can't be doing with seagulls that screech all the time like they're being murdered. Plus, I kept being woken up by a weird booming noise.'

'That'll be the sea,' I murmur.

'Huh!' Storm looks unimpressed. 'I don't know how you stand all these country sounds all the time. It'd do my head in. When are we leaving, Barry?'

It's strange that she doesn't call him 'dad'. Perhaps it's not allowed because 'dad' doesn't fit his rock 'n' roll image.

'Don't get stressy, babe, we'll be heading off this afternoon.' Storm and I share a look of relief. 'But I thought before then Annie could show us around the village so we can see where she's living before we go.'

'Actually, Josh has just called in—'

'No, it's fine, Annie. We can catch up later.' Josh picks up the mini magnet of the Acropolis that's just fallen onto the floor. 'You take your family on a tour of Salt Bay and I'll see you another time.'

'Why don't you come too?' asks Barry. 'I'd like to get to know Annie's young man.'

Storm lets out another long, deep sigh. 'No one says "young man" any more, Barry. You think you're so cool and you're really not. And Annie and, um…?' She raises her eyebrows at me.

'Josh.'

'Yeah, Annie and Josh aren't that young anyway so it sounds even more stupid.'

'Charming,' I murmur to Josh but he's already at the back door with his fingers curled round the handle, desperate to escape.

'Thanks, Barry, but I need to get to work so I'll give the tour a miss.'

'Are you sure?'

I raise my eyebrows and open my eyes wide, which in universal code means: *For the love of all that's holy, stay with me!* I'm so looking forward to spending some time with Josh. We've been so busy recently, what with his teaching job and looking after his poorly mum, and me working in Penzance and helping Alice get Tregavara House back to normal.

'I'm absolutely sure,' he says, decisively, walking over and giving me a frankly perfunctory kiss on the cheek.

I'm all for the tall, dark and introverted vibe Josh has got going on. It's sexy as hell, especially since he's far more unbuttoned when we're alone. But he really is hopeless with anything that smacks of affection when other people are around. And it's only got worse since his mum's health has deteriorated and his emotions have been firmly focused on his family.

'Come with us,' I urge him softly. 'It won't take long.'

'You need to spend time with your family and I need to get to work,' he whispers, his breath hot on my ear.

'Don't let us chase you away, Josh, mate.' Opening the bread bin, Barry pulls out a slice of bread which he folds in half.

'You're not. It was good to meet you and Storm.'

Josh winks at me but I ignore him for abandoning me so swiftly with these two. He frowns slightly and a glimmer of disappointment flashes across his face which makes me feel mean. And though I give him a big smile to make up for it, it's too late because he's already gone.

'Where's that other girl?' asks Storm as the back door closes. 'The weird one.'

'Emily? She's nipped out to see her family who live in Penzance, just along the coast.'

'Why doesn't she live with them? Are they weird like her?'

I can't let it go a second time. 'Emily isn't weird. She's a lovely girl, as you'd realise if you knew anything about her.'

'There's no need to be stressy about it,' bristles Storm, folding her arms across the long Drake T-shirt she must have slept in. 'She doesn't look that normal.'

'Really? And I thought you teenagers were all about inclusivity and acceptance these days.'

Storm wrinkles her nose and we eye each other warily across the kitchen, while Barry stuffs bread into his mouth and beams as though seeing his girls bickering gives him a rosy glow. He seems to be away with the fairies half the time and I'm starting to think he's taken a few too many drugs over the years.

By the time Storm has showered and plastered on make-up, Barry has eaten two more slices of bread and loaded his belongings into the car. He's also put together a small, flat-pack bookcase that I've been tripping over at the back of the sitting room. The bookcase looks good, and it was kind of him to make it, but he's acting like he deserves a medal. He's already called in Alice to inspect his handiwork and taken a photo to put on Facebook later. Rock 'n' roll!

I could really do without showing Barry and Storm around Salt Bay – what's the point if they're about to leave? But I get wrapped up against the cold when Storm reappears and give myself a pep talk while waiting for them by the front door. Just a couple more hours and then they'll be gone and my new life in Salt Bay can get back on track.

Chapter Seven

When Storm appears, she complains about having to walk into the village and wants us to drive, even though it would take longer to pile into the car than amble the distance. But Barry puts his foot down for once and insists she walks with us along the narrow road towards the village green.

Storm stages a passive-aggressive protest which consists of walking so slowly it would make Alice look nifty. But she soon tires of it and catches me up.

'How many people live in Salty Cove?' she asks.

'Salt Bay. I'm not sure; not that many. Two hundred maybe?'

'Is that all? There's more people than that in the block of flats where we're staying.'

She scuffs at a stone with her black ankle boots which are similar to ones I wore on my first ever visit to the village. Though I soon learned that high heels and Cornish potholes aren't a great combination unless you fancy a few weeks in traction.

Barry has wandered off to look at the river and is out of earshot, throwing stones into the rushing water.

'Is it just you and your dad in your flat?'

'More or less; just us and some friends.'

'He hasn't got a girlfriend or a wife then?' I say it as nonchalantly as possible, but inside I'm bricking it in case there's a stepmum out there that no one's bothered to mention.

Storm snorts and points at her father. 'What, Barry? Who'd have him?'

She's got a point. Barry is currently standing with his hands on his hips, quacking at a duck on the opposite bank. His T-shirt has ridden up, revealing a red, blue and yellow tattoo that snakes down his back and under his trousers. His buttocks must be multicoloured. Yuk!

'What about your mum? Is she still about?'

'Yep. She lives in Richmond which she reckons is in London, even though I reckon it's Surrey.'

'Do you see her much?'

'Nope, she's got another family now.'

I steal a glance at Storm, who's watching Barry with a pained expression. He's taken off his shoes to paddle and is swearing loudly about how cold the water is. In late October.

'Do you have any more half-sisters or brothers?'

'What are you, the family police?' Storm ducks as a screeching seagull flies low over her head. 'I don't have time to see my mum or her new kids because I'm so busy with all my friends. OK?'

OK. I let the subject drop because I know more than most about dodging family questions. My school friends used to quiz me all the time: 'Why haven't you got a dad?', 'Why do you move house so much?', 'Why does your mum dress funny and sing at the school gates?' It wasn't easy growing up with my mum. But it must be harder having no mum around at all.

Storm starts playing with her phone while Barry climbs out of the river and wipes his feet on his socks. After balling the damp socks into his pocket, he pushes bare feet into his trainers and wanders over.

'What's Salt Bay got to offer then, Annie? Give us the Grand Tour and hit us with the sights. I've already seen your ducks.'

The Grand Tour doesn't take long. First I show them Jennifer's newsagent shop and the grocery store which Storm declares 'tiny', then the church ('spooky'), the ancient Celtic stone cross on the edge of the village ('boring') and the historic whitewashed pub in daylight ('full of freaks'). I don't suggest going into the pub just in case Kayla is working behind the bar and might be on for a Bacardigate rematch.

The village is surrounded by awesome countryside. Steep hills rise away from the brown stone cottages and are dotted with patches of sunlight streaming between clouds. It's very pretty but neither Barry nor Storm seem impressed and I'm put out at first, until I remember my initial bad-tempered impressions of Salt Bay. Let's just say that I wouldn't have got a job with the Cornish tourist board.

As a last ditch effort, I take them up onto the cliffs above Tregavara House so they can marvel at the jagged coastline stretching into the distance. Storm huffs, puffs and grumbles all the way up.

'So what do you think?' I ask Barry, who's shielding his eyes against the midday glare as he stares towards Land's End.

'Nice. What do you reckon, Storm?'

'Is that seagull shit?' Storm points at a huge grey splat in the grass. 'There's loads of it.'

'That's because there are loads of seagulls,' I say calmly.

Storm stifles a yawn. 'Tell me about it.'

'But what do you think of the view?'

I'm not sure why I care but it's suddenly important that Storm appreciates how magnificent this place is. London might have culture and shops and fabulous buildings, and I still miss it. Some days I *really* miss it, especially the buzz of Covent Garden and Camden Market and Portobello. But tiny, peaceful Salt Bay has its own unique charm.

Storm gazes out across the roiling sea which is a different colour every day. Right now, the waters are deep turquoise with thick bands of white-flecked green stretching to the horizon.

She sniffs. 'It's all right, I s'pose.'

'There's a beach if you look over the cliff edge. Carefully,' I add as she stomps towards the end of the land and peers over.

The tide is out and far below us lies a perfect curve of golden sand. There are two huge rock stacks, standing guard a few metres out to sea, and the waves are sparkling with diamonds as they crest onto the shore.

'Yeah, not bad.' Which is the closest to enthusiasm I've had all day.

A couple of people I don't recognise are sitting on the sand, wrapped up in jumpers and enjoying winter sun on their faces. And a large white dog is careering along the bay with what looks like a sandwich in its mouth. The whole beach will disappear in a few hours' time when the tide turns.

Barry peers over my shoulder. 'How exactly do you get down there then?'

'Do you see that path that runs down the cliff over there, that narrow track? That's the way down.'

Barry nods while I cross my fingers behind my back. *Please, for the love of God, don't ask me to take you down there.* It's pathetic but I've only been to the beach three times and two of those were via water, thanks to Peter Seegrass, who took me there and back in his rowing boat. The truth is I'm too chicken to use the cliff path because it's absolutely terrifying. The first and only time I tried it, I ended up sliding down the track on my backside until I whoomphed into Josh at high speed. My death-slide was only halted by me ramming into

Josh's goolies – thinking about it, our relationship didn't have the most conventional of beginnings.

Fortunately, Storm has the attention span of a toddler high on orangeade. 'What's that over there, with the fence?' She backs away from the cliff edge and nods towards a low white fence that's only just visible in a deep hollow.

'That's a cemetery.'

'Another one? Sick! There's already one at that toy church. How many do you need around here?' Her muddy brown eyes light up. 'Do you have lots of murders?'

'Only a couple last year.' For a moment, excitement flashes across Storm's face until she realises I'm kidding, and her perpetual scowl locks back into place. 'My grandfather Samuel is buried over there. He's the one who threw out my mum when she was eighteen and got pregnant with me,' I say loudly. I haven't let Barry off the hook yet.

'That was well over the top,' sniffs Storm. 'Everyone gets pregnant these days at, like, fifteen and there's counselling and stuff. No one chucks people out. What a bastard.'

'They were different times,' I say quietly, hardly believing that I'm standing up for Samuel but not wanting Storm to criticise him.

Mind you, Samuel is probably spinning in his grave right now because Barry, the man who got his precious daughter pregnant, is so close. It'll be like matter and anti-matter colliding if Barry's fingers brush Samuel's marble gravestone. Maybe a quantum singularity will open up and swallow Salt Bay whole – or maybe I grew up watching too much *Star Trek*. Either way, it seems right that the tiny cemetery, which perches above the village, is off-limits to Barry and Storm.

Mum's name is also engraved on Samuel's stone and I start wondering how she would feel about my dealings with Barry. Would she be angry that we're talking or sad that I can't wait for him to leave? I sigh and turn my face into the wind, realising it's impossible to second-guess a woman whose legacy is throwing curveballs at me from the grave.

Suddenly, Barry's mobile pings and he ferrets about for it in his jacket pocket. It's a small phone with a black Iron Maiden cover.

'What the—?' He frowns at the screen. 'Bloody hell.'

'Have you got a signal?' Storm scrabbles for her mobile and starts waving it frantically above her head. It's the most animated I've seen her since she arrived in Cornwall.

'Is there a problem, Barry?'

'More a misunderstanding but—' he stares at the screen as though he can't quite believe what he's reading '—I've been thrown out of the band.'

'What, again?' Storm stops windmilling her arms, phone still high above her head, and gives a loud sigh. 'All right, what did you do this time?'

'Nothing!'

'It's obviously not nothing or they wouldn't have thrown you out.'

'Like I say, it's just a misunderstanding. Pug reckons I've been flirting with his wife.'

'You have. Big-time.'

'Don't be ridiculous! I haven't been flirting with Shaz. I only chatted to her a bit. That's not a crime.'

'What about when you took her out for a drink to that bar in Tooting?' accuses Storm, switching off her phone and ramming it into her jeans pocket.

'I thought Pug was going to meet us there,' blusters Barry.

'Tricky, seeing as he was in Ipswich at the time. You're such an idiot, Barry. Are they still going to pay you?'

'Doubtful. Pug says he'll punch my lights out if he ever sees me again, so that's a couple of hundred quid up the swannee.'

Storm flushes and bites down hard on her bottom lip.

'It's OK, babe. Don't worry.' Barry snakes his arm around her thin shoulders. 'Just trust your old dad because something will turn up. It always does.'

Storm shakes her head, looking close to tears, turns on her heel and marches back towards the village with us scurrying behind. I can't help but feel sorry for her – her tight, worried face sparked memories of when Mum would buy ridiculous things we didn't need and our finances would get into a mess. Once she came home with a yellow cockatoo in a cage. But it's not my responsibility to sort out Barry's cock-ups. Although – a terrible thought strikes me – they might stay longer if Barry doesn't have a gig to get back to.

Fortunately, Barry has a plan in mind by the time we get back to Tregavara House and it involves him being three hundred miles away from Salt Bay.

'Right,' he calls out to Storm, who's stomped into the house ahead of him, 'get your things together because we need to head back to town, like now, to sort things out.'

I've never known anyone pack as quickly as Storm, who's back downstairs, hauling her case behind her, in five minutes flat. Barry follows a couple of minutes later and drops his holdall onto the hall tiles.

'Well, it looks as if this is it for a while, Annie,' he says, opening his arms wide. Stepping forward reluctantly, I stand stiff as a statue as his arms go around me. Almost thirty years old and this is the first time I've ever had a cuddle from my father – that's what goes through my mind as Barry's musky smell goes up my nose. It's awkward being hugged by him, but not as awful as I expected. In fact, it makes me feel a little bit sad until I quash that feeling down, hard.

When it all starts getting a bit too weird, I wriggle out of his clutches and hand him his jacket, which is hanging on the coat stand.

'Have you two exchanged contact details?' asks Alice, shuffling into the hall from the sitting room.

'Yes, we have.' I point towards a Post-it stuck to the radiator that has Barry's mobile number and email address scrawled on it.

'We're going to stay in touch,' beams Barry while I smile weakly. An email here and text there – that'll be fine. I don't have to ever see them again if I don't want to. And there's no need for Alice to look at me like that.

Stepping forward, she holds out her hand towards Barry. 'It's been good to meet the two of you and thank you for fixing the skirting board and making the bookcase. We could do with someone like you around permanently.'

'I'm always open to new job offers, especially now the band has gone tits up. Excuse my language.' Barry takes Alice's hand but then leans forward and kisses her on the cheek. 'Cheers for having us. Storm, say goodbye to your sister and Mrs Trebarwith.'

'Laterz.' Storm already has her hand on the front door latch. 'Get a move on, Barry, or we'll never get out of here and back to London.'

Yanking the door wide, she stalks out as Barry grins, picks up his holdall and follows her.

'Is there anything else you want to say to them before they go?' asks Alice as we stand shoulder to shoulder on the path outside.

'I don't think so. There's nothing more to be said.'

I deliberately don't catch her eye because I'm feeling sad again, which is ridiculous. I've coped perfectly well without Barry and Storm in my life for twenty-nine years and they've done nothing but cause chaos since they arrived. So why do I feel as though I might be missing out?

Dark grey clouds have blocked out the sun and a light drizzle is falling on Barry's car, whose wheels have sunk into the soft verge. He waves through the mud-streaked window and turns over the engine while I hold my breath. Just a few more seconds and they'll be gone, back to vibrant London. Then I can get back to adjusting to life in Salt Bay, with them and the pull of the city behind me.

The engine gives a low throaty growl and clunks to a halt. Barry tries again. And again, as my chest starts to feel tight. But the stupid car won't start. After a while, Barry slides out, lifts up the bonnet and fiddles underneath while Storm sinks lower in the passenger seat.

'Is there a problem?' calls Alice, who sways slightly until I put my arm under hers for support. She's not so good at standing still these days.

'Damn thing won't start.' Barry's voice is muffled under the bonnet. 'This car is more temperamental than my ex-wife but it'll be fine in a minute.'

He gets back into the driver's seat and turns the engine over again. This time it gives a nails-down-a-blackboard screech before spluttering to a halt. The cold rain is getting harder and starting to bounce off Barry's windscreen.

'You'd better come back into the house while we decide what to do,' calls Alice as I help her inside.

Barry bounds back into the hallway with Storm trudging after him, head down. Raindrops caught in her fringe shine like glass when I flick on the light to chase away the gloom.

'Is there a garage around here?' asks Barry, pushing damp hair across his bald patch. 'A cheap one 'cos I'm a bit strapped for cash at the moment.'

'Of course not, there's nothing round here,' splutters Storm. 'Nothing but sea and cliffs and stupid seagulls.'

Alice shoots Storm a straight look before saying calmly, 'I'm afraid not and we're unlikely to find anyone who can help you today. We might have to sort something out tomorrow instead. What time do you have to be back for your concert?'

'I don't. There's no rush. That work venture has fallen through but I need to get back to town asap to search for work and, of course, somewhere for us to live.'

'To live, you say?'

'Yeah, we were living at Pug's house. He was putting us up for a bit but I expect that offer's been withdrawn what with the, um, misunderstanding. Though his sofa was doing my back in anyway.'

'Where were you sleeping, Storm?' asks Alice.

'I was sharing a room with Pug's mum, who's barmy.'

'Sweet old lady but a few sandwiches short of a picnic,' agrees Barry.

Alice frowns and sinks down slowly onto the bottom stair. 'That doesn't sound ideal for a young girl.'

'Nah, it's not bad and Storm's used to it. Sofa surfing never hurt anyone and I can probably find somewhere for us to stay for a couple of days.'

A strange look has come over Alice's face and the back of my neck starts prickling. She wouldn't! I widen my eyes at her and gently shake my head, but Alice sits up straight and nods as though she's come to a decision.

'Perhaps we can come to an arrangement that's mutually beneficial, Mr Stubbs. If you're without a job and accommodation, you and Storm could stay here for a while longer. You could do the odd jobs that are piling up around the house and it would give you both a chance to spend more time with Annabella.'

Good grief! But at least Barry won't go for Alice's proposition. He's a tragic wannabe rock star, not an odd job man. It would be like Bruce Springsteen giving up his musical career to work part-time in B&Q. But Barry, as ever, continues to disappoint.

'Really?' He's almost hopping with excitement. 'I knew as soon as we met that you were a sweetheart. It would certainly tide us over and it would be brill to spend as much time as I can with my new daughter – well, not so much new, seeing as she's almost thirty.' He gives me a wink and laughs. 'Thank you so much, Mrs Trebarwith.'

'You'd better call me Alice.'

'Do I get any kind of say in this?' wails Storm, still poised by the front door.

'Afraid not, babe.'

Barry bundles her out of the house to get their bags from the car before Alice can change her mind.

'Why on earth did you do that, Alice?' I stoop down beside her.

'To be honest, I'm not sure.' Alice winces as the sound of Storm and Barry bickering drifts in through the open front door. 'It seemed like a good idea at the time and I can't bear to think of that girl with no home to go to.'

'That girl is tougher than you think.'

'Possibly, but probably not as tough as *you* think, Annabella. Do you know who she reminds me of? You, and how you looked when you first arrived – defensive, angry and vulnerable.'

'That's ridiculous. Storm and I have nothing in common.'

'Absolutely nothing, apart from the same father, a missing parent when you were growing up and an air of loneliness.'

'I'm not lonely.'

'Not now. Not since you came to us and met the lovely Josh Pasco.' She pats my knee and smiles. 'I'm sorry to spring it on you, Annabella, but sometimes I know what's best. As you said in the kitchen yesterday, I'm very wise.'

Huh. I'm beginning to rethink my opinion.

Chapter Eight

Barry and Storm have only been in Cornwall a few days but it seems so much longer. Josh and I have only managed to snatch a few precious moments together since they arrived and Tregavara House is no longer an oasis of peace.

Emily is always quiet and she, Alice and I muddle along well together. Often in the evenings, when I'm back from work in Penzance, we all sit and watch TV: me with an open book on my lap, Emily with her knitting and Alice with a blanket over her knees. She enjoys our company after spending so many evenings here on her own.

But now the house is filled with Barry banging away with his hammer until all hours. God only knows what he's doing exactly. And he insists on playing terrible music on tiny, tinny speakers that he hooks up to his phone. Music has saved me over the years by taking the sting out of disappointments and sorrows. I love everything from old music hall songs to hip-hop and Radiohead. But the songs that Barry favours can only be described as grown men with sore throats screaming their heads off into a microphone. They're ear-bleedingly awful and make me long for the good old days of living with Serena.

Barry also insists on watching TV with us and keeps commenting on the people on screen. Or he flicks between channels constantly until my head is reeling – what is it with men and remote controls?

Thankfully, Storm stays upstairs in her bedroom, much to Emily's relief because, if the situation is hard on me, it's equally disturbing for Emily, who's looked like a rabbit caught in headlights since our guests arrived.

She corners me in the kitchen on Wednesday evening, just before we're due to leave for our next choir rehearsal. Her hair is pulled back into the usual thick plait that falls down her back to her waist. But there's a slick of bright blue eyeshadow behind her glasses, which I presume is for Jay's benefit.

'Annie, can I have a quick word?' She flushes and starts twisting her hands together. 'I know Storm and Barry are your family and everything and this is your house – Alice's house.' She corrects herself before I can. 'And it's lovely that Alice has taken them in when they've got nowhere else to go. She kind of did the same thing for me.' She stops and bites her lip.

'But...'

'But when are they leaving?' she says in a rush. 'It's not that I don't like them. Not really. It's just that Storm—' She exhales loudly and shrugs. 'It's not that she's said anything horrible...'

'I know,' I say, giving her arm a reassuring rub.

Storm certainly hasn't said anything horrible to Emily, as far as I'm aware. The problem is she hasn't said anything to her at all, as though lovely Emily isn't worthy of her attention.

'I'm not sure when they're leaving but I wouldn't have thought it would be too long. Barry will want to get back to gigging and Storm will have to get back to school – and shopping.' Emily giggles. 'Actually, it's good that we're having a chat because I've been wanting to ask what you think of Jay.'

Ooh, I'm not sure I should be doing this but the thought of Emily's heart being broken is more than I can bear. Her self-esteem was battered at school by watching from the sidelines as the cool girls got off with the fit boys... she's never said as much but it's obvious. And, seeing as I remember exactly what that feels like, I don't want a player like Jay inflicting more pain.

Heat radiates from Emily's cheeks as she blushes fuchsia-pink. 'He's OK, I suppose. Why?'

'I just don't want you to be hurt, Emily. I get the feeling that Jay is a bit... flighty.'

'I don't know what you mean.' Her cheeks go from pink to puce.

'I'm not trying to poke my nose in and I know you enjoy choir.'

'I do, I love it.'

'Which is great and I don't want that to be spoiled by—'

Before I can say anything else, Barry crashes into the room with Storm close behind him like a truculent shadow. 'Sorry, are we interrupting?' he bellows.

Emily spots Storm do a double take at her glowing face and steps behind me to hide.

'Not really, but Emily and I were just going to choir so we can't stop.'

I shove an arm into my jacket to make the point that we're leaving right now. Perhaps Emily and I can continue our conversation on the way.

But Barry grins. 'It's good we caught you then because we've decided to come too.'

'No, you can't,' squeaks Emily from behind me. 'Not to choir.'

'What d'you mean, love? The choir's for the whole community, isn't it?'

'What Emily means is we're just rehearsing for a choral competition so there's nothing for you to listen to yet.'

What Emily *really* means is, for goodness' sake, man, please don't let your mute, uber-cool daughter spoil every single aspect of my life. But I doubt she'd thank me for saying so.

Barry grins and puts his arm around Emily's shoulders. 'Ah, bless! We don't want to listen, silly; we want to join in. I'm willing to give your amateur choir the benefit of my professional musical skills, which are extensive. Lemmy once told me my guitar playing was unreal. Do you want to hear—'

'That's great, Barry,' I interrupt, 'but we don't sing rock stuff. It's more traditional Cornish songs and choral works so not your type of thing at all.'

'No problem', says Barry breezily. 'My motto is I'll try anything once, though that's got me into a lot of trouble in the past, if you know what I mean.' He gives Emily a nudge and winks at me.

'You could come to choir but you're not going to be here much longer, so is it worth it?'

My voice has gone up an octave because I'm getting desperate. But Barry, oblivious as ever, doesn't take the hint.

'We'll be here a while because there's still a lot of work to be done. I had a look at the roof space today and your insulation is shocking.'

'I'm not sure Storm would enjoy the choir.'

To be honest, I'm not sure Storm would enjoy anything other than a Big Mac, a mahoosive shopping centre and a subscription to MTV.

'Of course she will and she's bored so it'll get her out of the house. Don't you reckon, Storm?' He takes her shrug as a 'yes' and smiles at Alice, who's just walked into the kitchen with one of the many used mugs he scatters around the house. 'Guess what? We're going along to shake up the choir.'

'That sounds like a fantastic idea, especially with your musical background, Barry. I'm sure the choir will be very grateful.'

Steady on! I could do with some backup here. 'Don't you think that it might not really be Barry's thing?' I raise my eyebrows almost to my hair-line, body language for: *This is the most appalling idea I've ever heard.*

But Alice wilfully chooses not to understand. 'I'm sure a man of Barry's calibre can cope and will be an enormous asset to the Salt Bay Choral Society.' She hasn't been so effusive since Andy Murray won Wimbledon.

Ah, I get it. Her murky motives become clear as I realise that it's Wednesday; *Coronation Street* is on in fifteen minutes and Alice wants some peace from Barry's running commentary on her favourite soap. He watches it with us and seems remarkably au fait with the plot for someone who reckons he's a rock god kicking against the establishment.

Alice suddenly gives a feeble cough and, when she looks at me with her tired, brown eyes, I know I've lost the argument. What a bummer. But I suppose getting Barry and Storm out of her hair for a while is only fair, even if she was the one who invited them to stay. Twice.

Chapter Nine

It isn't easy being the newcomer in a small village. As a Trebarwith, I had a head start because my family has lived here for generations. Tregavara House was built by one of my ancestors, who made a fortune from tin mining, and it's one of the oldest buildings in Salt Bay. But I've still had to work hard at being accepted and I'm bricking it that Barry and Storm, so obviously out of place here, will draw attention to my incomer status.

My worries are confirmed when we walk into the church and everyone in the choir stops talking and stares at us. Like we've got two heads or something.

'Hello everyone,' I call out. 'Um, this is Barry and Storm, who will be joining us this evening.' There's a murmur of surprise from the choir and Jennifer leans forward in her seat to give them a once-over.

'Are you the new people who've moved into Perrigan Bay?' she shouts down the aisle. 'The people from Carlisle?'

'Never been to Carlisle in my life, love. Too far north for me,' Barry shouts back, his voice echoing around the ancient building. 'We're from London – I'm Annie's dad and Storm, here, is her sister.'

'Half-sister,' grumbles Storm, banging her backside down onto a pew. Her short skirt rides up so high I can see the tops of her thighs.

'And why didn't I know about this?' demands Jennifer, Salt Bay's biggest gossip, who prides herself on knowing everything about everyone. She glares at Kayla, who's pouting a few seats along. 'I'd have thought you'd have mentioned it.'

'They were supposed to be leaving,' grumps Kayla, 'and it's Annie's business anyway. I thought she might not like the whole village knowing.'

She got that right. I'm about to give her a grateful smile when Barry suddenly steps in front of me and stretches out his arms, like he's about to confer a blessing on everyone.

'Hi all. You'll be pleased to hear that I'm a professional musician – a guitarist. I've never performed with an amateur community choir before, but hey, how rubbish can you be?' He starts chuckling as I cringe inside. 'This dinky little church is so cute and the smallest venue I've ever played, but that's cool.'

'The back room of the Dog and Biscuit was smaller than this,' murmurs Storm, 'and no one your age should say "cool", Barry.'

She rests her feet on an embroidered kneeler and folds her arms, while Barry does what he does best and completely ignores her.

'I've been a musician for thirty years,' he continues, as I pull music from Samuel's old briefcase with shaky hands. My two worlds are colliding while I'm a useless bystander who's too chicken to leap in and be assertive.

'A classical guitarist?' enquires Arthur, hopefully, obviously not taking into account Barry's ripped jeans and un-classically greasy hairstyle.

'Hell, no. I don't do any of that "Cavatina" crap. I'm more an Iron Maiden and Black Sabbath kind of guy. Back in the eighties, before I got into heavy rock, I used to play with a band called Va-Voom and the Vikings. We almost hit the big time – have any of you heard of us? No?' Barry shakes his head at the blank looks coming his way. 'No worries. I'm still happy to provide you with the benefit of my expertise, and I promise not to make you all look bad.'

His laugh echoes along the aisle towards my stony-faced singers. Well, this is all going swimmingly so far.

Summoning up the smidgen of assertiveness I do possess, I address my glum choir. 'Barry and Storm are just visiting and have come along to sing with us tonight, if that's all right with you?'

Jeez, I can't even get that right. That should have been a statement of fact, rather than a question, so the choir would have no choice. Barry and Storm *will* be singing with us tonight and there's nothing you can do about it – the Salt Bay Choral Society isn't a flaming democracy. But Mary rescues me from my faux pas.

'Of course,' she says brightly, 'the more the merrier. Come along, you two, and take a seat.'

Lovely gentle Mary, whose wavy white hair is caught behind her ears by two clips that are sparkling under the lights.

'Barry, are you a bass or a tenor?' calls Ollie.

'Dunno, mate.' Barry sniffs. 'A tenor, I suppose. I've always been good at singing the high notes.'

'You can sit by me then,' says ever affable Ollie, who grins at Kayla though she doesn't smile back. She's too busy giving Storm the evil eye. Storm hasn't noticed her yet but it's only a matter of time.

More than anything right now I need Josh by my side. Just seeing him would make all the difference but he doesn't appear to be here, even though he's always on time. Perhaps he had to work late at school or maybe his mum has taken a turn for the worse. A good girlfriend would know these things but Barry and Storm seem to be taking up all my brain space.

'Do you want to join the sopranos or altos?' I ask Storm, who's drumming acrylic fingernails on polished wood.

'Nah, I'm good.' She slides further down and rests her head against the back of the pew. Secretly I'm relieved she doesn't want to sing because it will make my job of keeping her and Kayla apart that little bit easier.

'Sorry I'm late! Did you miss me?'

Jay is standing framed in the church doorway; clean-cut and handsome in a tight black V-neck jumper with no shirt, and black jeans with the waistband resting on sharp hip bones. His boy band style doesn't do anything for me but it has an oestrogenic effect on the young women in the choir, particularly Emily, who's perked up no end. She sits up straighter in her seat and flicks her long, thick plait off her shoulder and down her back.

'That's not a problem, Jay,' I tell him. 'We haven't started yet. Why don't you take a seat and we'll get going.'

Jay gives us his dazzling snow-white smile and starts sauntering towards the front of the church.

'Hello, who's this?' He comes to a halt near Storm and tilts his head to one side. 'I don't believe we've been introduced. I'm extremely pleased to meet you.'

'Yeah, whatever.' Storm shifts uncomfortably on the hard pew.

Jay treats her to his megawatt grin and rakes fingers through his over-gelled fringe. 'I'm Jay, by the way. What's your name?'

'Storm.'

'What an unusual name. I love it,' gushes Jay, layering on the charm. 'Are you a new member of the choir? I really hope so.'

Out of the corner of my eye, I notice Emily's shoulders slump and feel an overwhelming rush of affection for her. Young love can be brutal.

'I haven't joined the choir,' mutters Storm, with a sigh.

'That's a shame. Why don't you have a go at singing? I can hold your hand if you're nervous.'

Jay runs his tongue along his top lip while I try to decide whether to congratulate him on his chutzpah – chatting someone up in front of an audience takes some balls – or vomit at his general cheesiness.

Storm stares at him, looking bored, but there's a flicker of something else. It's well hidden behind her perpetual mask of indifference but Storm is ill at ease.

'She's with me and isn't singing tonight,' I pipe up. 'Storm's just here to listen so why don't you go and take a seat.'

'Aw, that's a shame,' pouts Jay, giving Storm his best sexy wink before wandering off with his hips swaying.

'Cheers,' mutters Storm to me, though it's so indistinct I could be mistaken. Maybe she said 'Cheek!', directed at Jay. Either way, I'm too nervous to ask her to repeat it in case she rolls her eyes and makes some comment about old people being deaf.

Leaving Storm to stew at the back of the church, I start the rehearsal with vocal warm-ups I've picked up from singing with various amateur choirs. And we're just about to start practising proper for the Kernow Choral Crown when the heavy church door bangs open and Josh rushes in. He frowns at Storm and Barry before rushing down the aisle and giving me a quick kiss on the cheek. There's a faint 'yuk' from Storm behind us.

'Sorry I'm late,' he murmurs close to my ear. 'Mum's not feeling too good today.'

'Should you be here at all then?'

'I offered to cancel but she said she'd be OK for a couple of hours and I should go. You know what Mum's like.'

I do. Marion, widowed when Josh's stepdad drowned in the Great Storm, is a strong woman who hates making a fuss. She's the heart and soul of her family and has been incredibly kind to me over the last few months. They'll be devastated if her heart condition can't be fixed – and so will I.

I'm not a religious person, never have been. But I'm in a church so I send up a prayer, good vibes, positive karma – whatever you want to call it – for Marion and her poor ailing heart.

∗

We press on with the rehearsal and it goes pretty well, with Josh and I taking it in turns to lead the choir, who are in good voice tonight. Apart from Ollie, obviously, who never hits a note if he can just miss it. But we're an inclusive choir, open to all, and that's how I like it. The beauty and power of music should be available to everyone, regardless of singing ability. And I guess that should include Barry and Storm too. For one rehearsal, at least.

All credit to Barry, he makes a good job of sight-reading the music, and Storm slouches at the back without a peep. Everything's going well and I'm just starting to relax when Barry puts his hand up and waves it at Josh.

'Barry, did you want to say something?' Josh's soft Cornish accent sounds sexy, even when he's not talking dirty.

'I do.' Barry gets to his feet and glances around at his audience. 'So, is this the stuff that you're going to be singing in that Crown competition thingy? Only it's all a bit boring. Don't you want to sing something a bit less old? What about mixing it up with a bit of Bowie or Genesis?'

'Not again,' moans Arthur, who went off the deep end when Florence suggested singing Take That tunes at our first concert back in the spring.

'The competition is traditional and all choirs sing old Cornish songs. Those are the rules,' booms Roger from the bass section. His beer-stained sweatshirt indicates he rushed straight from the pub to be here.

'Yeah, but rules are made to be broken, babe.'

'Only if you want to be disqualified. And don't call me babe,' grumbles Roger, who's still wearing his woolly hat.

Barry holds out his hands and shrugs. 'You wanna be a little more courageous and less conformist, man.'

'Are you calling me a coward?'

Roger puffs out his cheeks and stands up so quickly his chair falls onto its side with a clatter. He's a big bloke, Roger. Far bigger than Barry, who holds up two fingers and, morphing from rock god to hippy, croons soothingly, 'Love and peace, man. Love and peace.'

'Are you giving me the V-sign?' yells Roger, pushing Arthur to one side and almost climbing over Tom in his rush to get to Barry. Jeez, there's going to be a punch-up in the church. We'll all go to hell.

I leap forward to keep the two apart but Josh is there before me, standing between them. 'Come on now, Roger. Calm down. Barry gave you the peace sign – his fingers were the other way around. Look.' Josh gives a demonstration. 'Isn't that right, Barry?'

'Absolutely. That sign means "peace". If I was trying to insult you, Roger, I'd have told you to eff off to your face, not flicked you the Vs.'

Josh blinks rapidly. 'Thanks so much for the explanation, Barry. Now why don't we just agree that it's a misunderstanding and we can all get off home. We'd just about finished the rehearsal anyway.'

Roger breathes out slowly, almost quivering with suppressed emotion. 'I suppose so.'

Placing her hand on his arm, Jennifer says soothingly, 'We don't want any trouble in here, Roger, however much you've been provoked.' She shoots Barry a daggers look but he's out of sight behind Josh so it goes to waste.

'No, you're right. This isn't the time or the place so I'll let it go. This time,' adds Roger ominously, rolling his shoulders and huffing.

He's led away by Jennifer while the rest of the choir gather up their belongings in stunned silence and start leaving. Barry strides to the back of the church and sits by Storm, who begins to berate him loudly for 'pissing people off'.

'Josh, thank you.' I'm almost crying with relief. 'You were brilliant and I'm so sorry.'

'That's OK, I'm getting used to being a buffer between your family and everyone else in Salt Bay.' He says it with a smile that doesn't quite reach his eyes but, when a tear slides down my face, he wipes it away with his finger and, pulling me out of sight behind the piano, gives me a crushing hug. 'When your dad and sister have gone back to London and Mum is better, we can get on with our lives. I know it's complicated at the moment, but things will get better. How is it going with Barry and Storm anyway?'

'OK, I guess,' I mumble into his shoulder, trying not to get make-up on his clothes. 'Though I've no idea when they will be leaving. It's all a bit open-ended, thanks to Alice and her penchant for asking people to stay.'

Oops. The round neck of Josh's long-sleeved, pale blue T-shirt looks suspiciously streaky. I lovingly stroke my fingers across his neck while surreptitiously trying to wipe off Yves Saint Laurent foundation.

'Are you sure you want them to leave?' asks Josh, moving his strong hands to my waist. 'They are your family, after all, and I guess *I* should get to know them if they're going to be around for a while.'

I pull back in his arms. 'Why? Why would you want to do that? You can see what they're like already – flaming awful.'

'First impressions can be wrong. You said so yourself, Miss Trebarwith. And anyway, they're a part of you and I like everything about you.'

Which is lovely and sweet, and all that. But obviously balls when it comes to my dysfunctional family.

By the time Josh and I emerge from behind the piano, Barry and Storm have scuttled off and the only other person left in the church is Roger, who's loitering near the vestry.

He sidles up, still very red in the face, while I'm shoving music into my bag and Josh is making sure the heating's off.

'I don't mean to be insulting, Annie, but your father is a total pillock.'

'I wouldn't want to be on the receiving end if you did mean to be insulting, Roger, but I take your point and can only apologise.'

'Huh,' huffs Roger. 'That's the trouble with people who aren't locals.'

'Don't forget that I'm not local.'

Josh wanders over and puts his hand on my shoulder. 'You're more local than most of us with your Trebarwith heritage stretching back over generations. And don't worry, Roger, they'll be heading back to London soon, won't they?'

He glances at me for backup but I shrug because who knows? Storm is desperate to get back to the big city but Barry seems to be getting his feet well under the table. Literally. I found him and Alice chatting at the kitchen table this morning about his career as a rock god. He was explaining to her what a groupie is.

'When exactly are they going?' demands Roger.

'I'm not sure but I know they'll be keen to leave boring Salt Bay soon and get back to far more exciting London. Not that I think Salt Bay is boring. That's what Barry and Storm think,' I bluster as Josh drops his arm.

'Well, as long as they behave themselves until then.' Roger huffs a little more for effect before wishing us both a pleasant evening – not much chance of that – and heading for the pub.

The bang of the closing door echoes around the church, which is suddenly cold and full of shadows.

Josh has pulled car keys from his pocket and is turning them over and over in his hand. 'I've got to get back to Mum, but why don't you come with me and stay over?' He leans forward, kisses my ear and murmurs, 'I've missed you so much.'

There's nothing I'd like more than lying in Josh's arms all night but I don't have my work clothes with me. And though the charity where I work as a PA aren't too hot on the dress code, I think they might object if I turn up in my scruffy jeans.

'Can you wait while I grab a few things from the house?'

Josh shakes his head and pushes his arms into his battered leather jacket. 'I'm really sorry but I can't. Serena is staying with a friend and Lucy's late shift starts in half an hour so I need to get back.' Seeing my face fall, he pulls me towards him for another quick hug. 'It doesn't matter. Lucy's in on Saturday night so why don't I come round to yours and we can all have tea together and I can get to know Barry and Storm. I'll bring fresh fish from Trecaldwith Market. Isn't that a good idea?'

It's an absolutely terrible idea but at least it's a way of spending time with my boyfriend, who's just glanced at his watch and is now literally running away from me, down the aisle.

'Got to go or I'll be late,' he calls back, over his shoulder. 'See you on Saturday. It'll be fun.'

Huh. His idea of fun and mine are rather different but we have to make it work. Because, right now, our families are pulling us in different directions – and we're getting lost in the middle.

Chapter Ten

'Is everything all right, Annie? You seem rather distracted.'

I slowly bring my focus back to Celia, who's tapping her fingernails on the desk in front of me. She tilts her head and regards me coolly.

'I'm so sorry, I zoned out for a moment. What were you saying?'

A glance at my scribbled notes leaves me none the wiser. I'm supposed to be taking down details to update her busy diary but my shorthand looks awful and I can't remember what she told me. Oops, Celia won't be happy if I send her to Truro at ten o'clock on Tuesday when she should be there at eleven o'clock on Wednesday. That kind of thing can get a girl fired.

'I really am very sorry but would you mind repeating that last little bit?'

Celia leans back in her office chair, takes off her blue-rimmed glasses and pushes them through salt-and-pepper hair onto the top of her head. Behind her, through the tall sash window, shoppers are wandering through the centre of Penzance with shopping bags full of Christmas presents.

'Is everything all right at work, Annie?'

'Absolutely. I love it here and I think – well, I hope – I'm doing a good job.'

Celia nods and starts tapping her pen on the desktop. 'You've fitted in very well and you seem to keep me under control. Not many people can manage that.'

Her lip twitches slightly and I grin. Some people find Celia brusque and intimidating but we've got on well since I joined the charity a few months ago. She's taken a liking to me and I admire her passion that's putting Notes Music Trust on the charitable map.

Notes Music Trust provides musical therapy sessions for vulnerable youngsters and also runs a couple of residential homes for older people with disabilities, some of them retired musicians. It does amazing work and cements my view that music is magical and can help to soothe even the most troubled of minds and bodies. My official title here is Office Manager/PA which sounds very grand but, in reality, I'm a jack of all trades because it's often all hands to the pumps.

There are other charities in Cornwall and further afield doing similar work but we're very localised with a relatively small budget. That means I earn peanuts compared to my London salaries, but job satisfaction makes up for it.

'So tell me, Annie, if it's not work, is everything all right at home?'

This is the first time Celia has properly asked about my home life because, though we get on, she's my boss so a girls' night out is unlikely. In fact, it would be weird.

'You know that I moved here from London a while ago to live with my great-aunt.' Celia nods. 'That's all fine and Alice is lovely but at home right now it's rather… um, challenging because my father and half-sister have turned up.'

'Is that so awful?' Celia looks confused.

'Not awful, exactly, but unsettling because I'd never met them before they arrived on my doorstep. I didn't even know that my half-sister existed.'

'Golly!' Celia's fountain pen clatters onto her desk while I wonder whether being open with my boss is such a good idea. I don't want her thinking that I come from some deadbeat family with undiscovered half-siblings all over the place. 'That does sound rather unsettling. Do you like them?'

'I'm not sure yet. We're getting to know each other.'

'Which can take some time.' Celia swings round in her office chair and watches a harassed young mum scoot past with a wailing child in a pushchair. 'It took me ages to get used to my stepmother and we never got along, though I don't suppose that's terribly reassuring for you.'

'Not really.' I laugh, touched that Celia would share personal information.

She's so different from me. Whereas I was brought up by a single mother in a succession of dingy inner-city flats, Celia is the daughter of a Home Counties landowner, and she went to private school, married well and had three children in her late thirties and early forties. Though her youngest child is now ten, her solicitor husband works long hours so her world is a collision of work meetings, childcare crises and school events. Something simple, like an over-running meeting or a childminder with a tummy bug, can throw everything into chaos.

'What about that young man you're seeing?' asks Celia, using a clean tissue to scrub blue ink from her hand. 'The one who called into the office for you a couple of weeks ago.'

'I didn't know you'd noticed Josh.'

Keen not to mix my work and personal life, I made sure he was only in the office for a few moments.

Celia sighs as she drops the stained tissue into the bin. 'I know I'm a lot older than you, Annie, and happily married for donkeys' years, but that doesn't mean I can't appreciate a handsome man. I'm not dead. Are the two of you still seeing one another?'

Crikey, this is beginning to feel like a well-intentioned interrogation.

'Not very much at the moment because of family pressures on us both.'

'Well, that's not very satisfactory.' Celia steeples her fingers under her chin and looks at me with her cool grey eyes. Her fingernails are long and painted red, her emerald earrings match her green jumper, and her make-up looks fresh and newly applied, though it's past lunchtime. How on earth does she manage it? I have far more time to tart myself up and co-ordinate my outfits, but Kayla still describes my look as 'shabby chic'. Today I'm wearing an ancient Hobbs dress that's gone slightly bobbly, and my black tights have developed a large ladder over the left knee, so she might have a point.

'When are you next seeing him?' barks Celia, making me jump.

'This evening, I hope. I thought I might call round to his house on the off chance.'

'Then we'd better get on with sorting out next month's diary and you can head off early. I don't want to stand in the way of young love.'

*

Celia is as good as her word and shoos me out of the office at half past four. I've already deciphered my scrawled notes and made a good job of updating her diary (fingers crossed) and I leave my desk tidy so it'll be good to come back to on Monday, but if I don't see Josh soon I think I might burst. I was so disappointed when he had to leave straight away after choir, and he was too busy doing private tutoring for us to meet up last night.

It's dark already and chilly but Christmas lights strung up between the shops lift my mood as the bus to Trecaldwith heads out of bustling Penzance and into the countryside. The minibus is warm and cosy and packed with workers going home after a long week. Carrier bags full of parcels fill the aisle and people have to pick their way over them as they get out at their stop.

When we reach the outskirts of Trecaldwith, lights are shining from the glass cube building where Josh teaches English and Music. Trecaldwith School has a great reputation in the area and, though I'm biased, I bet Josh is a brilliant teacher. Firm, and a tad grumpy at times, but always fair.

He talks about his students as though he really cares about them, and I bet that's reciprocated by plenty of the adolescent girls there – though perhaps not in the same neutral way. Teenage girls are obviously going to lust after a teacher who's tall, dark and fabulously handsome, aren't they. But Josh seems oblivious. When we're walking together through Trecaldwith, I've got used to teenage girls pointing at us and giggling. That's because we're a couple, right? And not because they can't believe that Sir would go out with a minger like me.

Trecaldwith harbour, where I get off the bus, is much bigger and busier than Salt Bay. There's a large stone quay where fishing boats land their catch and a low warehouse-style building where the fish are stored until being moved on. A few fish shops are dotted around the streets leading up from the harbour and crushed ice is piled up in the gutter outside as I walk past. It's so cold, the ice is hardly melting and glistens under the streetlamps. Inside the shops, hake, cod and sardines are laid out on the counter, though most of the displays are almost empty and staff, wearing wellies, are cleaning up.

Josh's cottage is close to the oldest church in Trecaldwith and part of a small terrace with terracotta plant pots outside. There's a front door key in my bag but, now I've moved out, it doesn't feel right letting myself in, so I knock.

Almost immediately, the door is pulled open by Marion, who gives me a beaming smile. 'Annie, sweetheart, how lovely to see you.'

It's lovely to see her too and I give her a huge hug. Mostly because I've missed her, but also to disguise the shock which I'm worried will show on my face. Marion looks awful – pale and stressed – and I'm taken aback by how much she's changed in the three weeks since I last saw her.

'Come on in,' she urges, pulling me inside. 'It's so cold out, I think it might snow.'

Inside her small sitting room, Marion beckons for me to sit down.

'I'm fine,' she says, noticing my concerned face. 'I just get breathless and feel a bit faint sometimes. Why didn't you use your key? You don't have to knock, you know. You're like part of the family.'

It's lovely when Marion refers to me as family – it gives me a rosy glow. But it makes me a tad nervous too, just in case it jinxes things with Josh. She probably told his ex, Felicity, that she was part of the family too, and that didn't end too well. Oh no, don't think about Felicity and her tiny, perfect body and beautiful long blonde hair. God knows what Josh sees in me, with my size twelve thighs and unremarkable light brown hair that goes frizzy when it rains.

'Josh isn't back yet,' puffs Marion, easing herself down onto the sofa. 'He's on detention duty this week, poor soul. He hates it. How are your father and sister getting on in Salt Bay? I'd like to meet them sometime; maybe when I'm feeling better.'

'They're fine, thank you.' I push down my guilt at not going straight home to give Alice and Emily a break from my relatives.

'Are you sure they're fine?' Marion stares straight at me. She's a canny one and has an instinct for when people aren't telling the truth. 'It must have been strange with them turning up out of the blue. I'm sure it can't be easy on you, Annie. Not when you've had such a year of change.'

Oops, don't be nice to me, Marion, or I'll start blubbing, which would be unforgiveable in the circumstances. There's you, on the one hand, putting a brave face on illness, while I'm finding it hard to cope with the appearance of an ageing rock star and a stroppy teenager. Jeez, I'm seriously pathetic.

'It's all absolutely fine,' I say, plastering a big, fake smile on my face. 'More to the point, what about the scan you're due to have at the hospital?'

'That's happening next week and I can't wait, to be honest. Once they find out exactly what's wrong with me, they can do something to fix it, so it's all good and there's nothing to worry about. Isn't that right, Lucy?'

Marion smiles at her elder daughter, who's just come downstairs.

'I'm sure you're right, Mum.' Lucy glances at me. 'I didn't realise you had company.'

'I've only just got here. How are you, Lucy?'

'Yeah, I'm fine.'

Lucy takes a seat next to her mum and smooths down her skirt. She looks like a teenager, though she's only six years younger than me, and it's hard to believe she has a daughter. Gorgeous Freya with her ebony plaits and dark, soulful eyes.

'Freya's at a friend's house for tea,' says Lucy, as though she can read my mind. 'How are you doing, Mum?'

'Not too bad but I'm feeling a bit tired so I might go and lie down for a while if that's all right with you, Annie. Josh will be home soon and I might see you later?'

'Of course. Go and get some rest.'

Marion smooths down her dark hair, which is streaked with grey, and gets to her feet slowly as though it's an effort. It's like watching Alice, who's thirty years older.

'Do you want me to help you upstairs, Mum?'

Lucy and I both jump to our feet to give her a hand but Marion gives a dismissive wave.

'No, of course not. You keep Annie company. It'll be nice for you girls to have a chat.'

It's very quiet without Marion, and the ticking of the clock on the mantelpiece sounds extra loud as Lucy and I sit in silence for a while. Lucy has always been ill at ease with me, which is not surprising bearing in mind my surname. And I've always had a faint feeling of guilt since I discovered her secret. Guilt and unease – it's not a great combination.

'What's it like, your dad and sister suddenly turning up like that?' asks Lucy suddenly. She looks so like Josh when she's being intense, it makes me catch my breath.

'It's a bit weird really.'

'Are you pleased though that they've turned up?'

'I suppose so, though it's hard in some ways.'

'What ways?'

I shrug. 'They're strangers really.'

'So why is that a problem? You'll get to know them.'

'I'm not sure I want to.' I laugh, trying to ease the tension that's flooding the room. But Lucy, deadly serious, leans forward with her elbows on her knees.

'Why don't you want to?' she demands.

Blimey, first there's Celia's interrogation about my love life and now it's a third degree about my family.

'I don't know. Because they might mess things up; they might ruin my life here.'

'How?' Lucy's stare is intense as her dark bob swings around her elfin face.

This is all getting a bit heavy and I have no idea what Lucy wants me to say. She obviously has some sort of hidden agenda. Thinking about it, I'm also not sure how Barry and Storm *could* ruin my new life in Salt Bay. They could never come between me and Alice.

But, with a blinding flash of clarity – one of those insights that come out of nowhere and punch you in the face – I suddenly know how. My life here is new and fragile. And, however much I tell myself I love it, I'm also finding it hard.

There's so much that roots me in Salt Bay – Josh, Alice, the choir – but I *do* miss London. This new life doesn't feel solid yet and the pull of London is still there. I've managed to bury it deep but, every time Storm criticises the village or slags off its inhabitants, I see Salt Bay through her jaded eyes.

Her corrosive comments burn away some of the sheen. They remind me that the village is quiet and remote and the weather's a bit shit. They take the shine off the magnificent views, salt spray in the air, Cornish folk I've grown to care about. And when I don't see Josh, when he's busy and distracted and our families are keeping us apart, my new life begins to feel like a house of cards that could come tumbling down.

I don't say any of that to Lucy, of course, because I don't want her reporting back to Josh that I'm having second thoughts about staying in Salt Bay. Because I'm not, not really; I'm just tired and confused and missing wall-to-wall Wi-Fi.

When I don't answer, Lucy scans round the room as though checking that no one can hear. Then she whispers, 'You know who Freya's dad is, right?'

I have no idea how to answer this. Yes, I do know, but I'm not supposed to because it's a secret. A huge secret. An 'I'll have to kill you if I tell you this' type of secret.

Lucy clocks my anguished look and sighs impatiently. 'I know Josh must have told you. Of course he's told you because of who your family are.'

'Don't be angry with him. I haven't told anyone else, not even Alice.'

Lucy looks surprised at that but I didn't think it was my place to tell Alice that Toby Trebarwith, the cousin she's so fond of, got Lucy pregnant when she was only seventeen and then did a runner to London as fast as his treacherous little legs would carry him.

'Good. I wasn't sure.' Lucy sucks in her lower lip. 'So presumably you know that—' she hesitates over his name '—that Toby has never wanted to see Freya or have anything to do with us. And I've been happy for things to be that way.'

I nod, wondering whether I should apologise to Lucy on behalf of the less louse-like members of the Trebarwith family.

'But things are different now and I've changed my mind.' Lucy takes a deep breath and her next words strike fear into my chicken heart. 'It's time for Freya to meet her father, Annie, and I need your help.'

'Are you sure you want Toby to be a part of Freya's life after so many years?' I don't mention the needing my help part in the hope that it might just go away.

'I've been thinking about it for a while and two things have happened to make me sure that now is the right time.' There's a creak from the stairs and Lucy waits for a moment and then lowers her voice. 'I don't want Toby turning up out of the blue when Freya is grown up, and causing chaos. Wouldn't it have been better if you'd known the truth about your father earlier?'

'To be honest, I'm not sure that knowing about Barry at any time would have been better.'

'But surely it would have been easier than him turning up unannounced when you're an adult? And you must have asked questions about him when you were little. Have you watched *Long Lost Family* on telly?' When I nod, Lucy ploughs on. 'But mostly I'm worried about Josh.'

'Why? What's the matter with him?' I sit up straight on the collapsed springs in the armchair, holding my breath.

'He's being run ragged with mum being ill. She doesn't admit it but she's anxious about being in the house on her own, and my hours at the shop have been cut so he's having to provide even more financial support for all of us. And it's just not fair. He's carrying the whole burden while Toby swans around London and comes down here in his fancy car – he drove past me a few weeks ago though I don't think he saw me. And he's never paid a penny in maintenance.'

'I agree, it's not fair but Josh said you wanted it kept quiet because you didn't want everyone knowing your business.'

'I didn't, but I've grown up since then and now there's more to consider than just my feelings. What really matters is what's best for Freya. Do you think Toby would want to see her?'

It's hard to imagine selfish, self-centred Toby being the slightest bit interested in parenthood, although… he did mention Freya to me once.

It was just a passing comment but, for a second, he looked vulnerable and a little less like a heartless swine.

'I don't know. He might.' I shrug and rub my tired eyes. 'What does Josh think about all of this?'

'Oh no,' says Lucy, getting to her feet and starting to pace up and down. 'You absolutely can't tell him. You know what Josh is like, he hates Toby and he'll just shut the idea right down. He'll say he can cope without his maintenance money but I can see it's really starting to affect Josh's health. He looks exhausted all the time and he's really irritable because he's so stressed.'

Josh did look pale and drawn the last time I saw him. And when we do spend time together these days, it sometimes seems that he's somewhere else in his head. But Lucy is asking for too much.

'You're putting me in a really difficult position,' I tell her. 'I don't want to keep secrets from Josh.'

'It's not a secret,' she insists. 'Not really, because all I'm asking you to do is raise the subject of Freya with Toby and let me know his reaction. It might go nowhere so there's no need to upset Josh for nothing. Please, Annie—' she grabs my hands and holds on tight '—you're the only person I can talk to about this who won't go ballistic and say no for all the wrong reasons. Please. I'm trusting you and it's best for Josh in the long run.'

I'm about to refuse because keeping secrets from the man you love can't be a good idea. All the agony aunts in the women's mags would say it's a complete no-no. Little white lies are probably fine, such as telling your boyfriend that his bald patch isn't visible or his *Monty Python* take-offs are funny. But not big humungous lies involving the man that your boyfriend has referred to as one of the biggest bastards of all time. Even if the lie is for his own good.

But I'm sideswiped when the front door opens and Josh comes in. His shoulders are hunched and he looks pale as he wipes a hand across his face and drops his bag, with a deep sigh, onto the carpet. The Josh Pasco I met on my first day in Salt Bay was, if I'm honest, a complete pain in the backside. But he was sparky and vibrant. Today, Josh – my Josh – looks done in and defeated.

When he catches sight of me, his face lights up. 'Annie, what a lovely surprise!'

He comes over, kisses me on the lips and squeezes into the chair beside me. It's funny but he doesn't mind being affectionate in front of his family – as though he has permission to be himself around the people he most trusts in the world. It's a squash in the armchair but I love the feeling of his thighs hard against mine. He puts his arm around me and cuddles me in tight.

'Are you all right, Lucy?'

'I'm fine but, more to the point, how are you?' says Lucy archly, glancing at me from under her dark eyelashes. 'You look done in.'

'I'm all right. Just feeling a bit under the weather, and detention duty didn't help. Why can't the kids just behave, or at least play up when people aren't watching. Jenson in 8A lit a cigarette in front of the deputy head and then complained when he was kept in after school. What an idiot.'

He gently rubs my arm and closes his eyes. He looks exhausted and vulnerable, like a child.

'I thought maybe we could go out this evening, Josh. You know, on a date, because we haven't seen much of each other lately. What about an early film in Penzance, or we could go to the Whistling Wave for a couple of hours?'

Josh opens one eye and peers at me. 'That would be lovely but could we stay in instead? It's been a hell of a week and I could do with saving money at the moment.'

'No worries. I can pay.'

'No, you're all right. Why don't we stay here instead and you can stay overnight?'

'I need to be at Tregavara House, really. It doesn't seem fair leaving Alice and Emily on their own for too long with Barry and Storm.'

'Oh yeah, I forgot about those two.'

There's a hint of annoyance in Josh's voice, which grates because I'm only following his lead and looking out for my family.

He rests his head against mine and exhales slowly. 'Look, I don't feel up to coping with Barry and Storm this evening and I need to be here overnight for Mum. Can you at least stay for tea and then I can run you home later? I'm really sorry. My life doesn't seem to be my own at the moment.'

'That would be lovely,' I say, but I'm worried. Josh seems different, as though the life-force has been sucked out of him. Lucy is right, family responsibilities are sucking him dry while Toby is getting away scot-free and living it large in London. It really isn't right.

Josh moves away from me and slowly levers himself out of the chair. 'Come on, Annie, let's go and raid the fridge. I'll cook you something magnificent.'

Lucy touches my arm, as I'm following Josh towards the kitchen, and opens her big brown eyes wide. 'OK,' I mouth at her. 'OK.'

Chapter Eleven

You know when you think things can't possibly get any worse… I'm staring out of my bedroom window the next morning, ostensibly admiring the view but surreptitiously checking the river level (obviously), when a shiny silver BMW zooms into view.

It can't be – not today! The car screeches along the road, revs past the green and approaches the harbour at speed.

Balls! The car screams to a halt outside Alice's front gate, sending a cloud of dirt and dust into the air. I stand back and peer around the curtains as Toby shoves open the driver's door with his foot and steps out.

He inhales deeply and sniffs as though the damp sea air doesn't measure up to his expectations. Then, after hauling a smart leather bag from the boot, he double-checks that he's locked his car before walking briskly up the garden path and ringing the bell.

Jeez, Barry's been downstairs for a while, hammering something to death, and might get to the door before me. Rushing down the stairs, I almost lose my footing on the bottom step and an icy rush of adrenaline whooshes through me. But there's no time to waste. Barry is already ambling out of the sitting room as I hurtle past him and wrench open the front door.

'Toby! How unexpected to see you here!' I burble, sounding like I'm high on coke or ketamine, or whatever illicit substance kids are using these days.

'Is it?' Toby's hooded grey eyes narrow. 'This is the Trebarwith family home and, the last time I checked, I'm a Trebarwith. Can I come in?' He pushes past me and drops his bag in the middle of the narrow hallway. 'I set off at stupid o'clock this morning to beat the traffic. Where's Alice?'

'Penelope picked her up half an hour ago. She'll be back later. She didn't realise you were coming,' I say distractedly, looking round for Barry, who's disappeared.

'No, well it's hard to plan ahead when I'm such a vital part of the team at work so I have to take time off when I can. I was going to St Tropez this weekend but my lady friend couldn't make it at the last minute so my plans changed. I didn't fancy going on my own.'

His eyes flit through the open sitting room door to the bare wall near the fireplace where the painting of my ancestor, a young woman in Victorian clothes, used to hang.

'Are you still looking after the painting, Toby?'

'Of course,' he huffs.

'The room should be finished soon and then Alice says she wants the painting back.'

'That's ridiculous. She should keep it in London for safe-keeping. It's worth a fortune. But—' he sighs '—it is her painting, I suppose.'

'Yes, it is and she'd never see it if it was in some vault in London.'

Or, more likely, on the wall of Toby's expensive Chelsea flat so he can show it off to his snobby art friends.

'She'll need to have the painting properly insured and get locks on the windows, and an alarm fitted.'

'Don't worry, we'll sort everything out before we have the painting back. Alice is very grateful that you saved it.'

That does the trick. Toby huffs but snaps his mouth shut, as he always does when the rescue of the painting is raised. Mostly because he chose to save the valuable oil painting, rather than me and Alice, when the flood hit Tregavara House. Fortunately, Josh and Charlie from the choir arrived like the cavalry in the nick of time to help save me and Alice from a watery grave. But the whole soggy event laid bare Toby's avarice and he knows it.

'Painting, what painting?' Barry has wandered out of the kitchen clutching two slices of butter-drenched toast.

'Who is this?' asks Toby primly, taking in Barry's too-tight jeans and straggly hair that today is falling free to his shoulders.

'This is Barry,' I say slowly, wondering if there's any way I can avoid saying the next bit of the sentence. Nope, there isn't. 'He's my father.'

As Toby's mouth falls open, there's a bloodcurdling screech from upstairs followed by a yell. 'Annie, this fucking useless shower is spewing brown water at me again. It's probably full of shit. Come and sort it out.'

'And that,' I add, holding Toby's horrified gaze, 'is my half-sister Storm.'

'You mean to say there's more than one of you?' mutters Toby, taking Barry's outstretched hand and giving it the limpest of shakes.

'Annie's family is growing by the minute,' says Barry cheerfully. 'And who are you?'

'I'm Toby Trebarwith, Alice's cousin. I didn't realise that Alice was running a B&B.' He sneers at the half-eaten toast which is cooling in Barry's paw-like hand.

'We're earning our keep,' bristles Barry. 'I'm doing all the odd jobs that need doing around the house. And I can hang the painting you were talking about if you'd like.'

'Good God no, don't ever touch the painting! It's very val—' He hesitates. 'It means a lot to my family.' He emphasises the word 'my' and gives me a filthy look.

There's another screech from upstairs and repeated banging as though someone is kicking the bath with boots on.

'I'd better go and sort out the shower for Storm. Why don't you unpack, Toby, and get settled in? Ah, give us a minute to rearrange the sleeping arrangements. Barry's in the middle bedroom at the moment.'

'He's in *my* bedroom,' bellows Toby, which is a bit rich seeing as this is the first time he's visited in weeks.

'I've been keeping the bed warm for you,' says Barry with a wink. 'I can sleep on the sofa for a couple of nights – I'm used to that.'

'I'm sure you are,' says Toby, like he's got a stick up his arse, and I get an urge to punch him. Yes, Barry is a bit rough and ready but there's no need to speak to him like he's the hired help. Toby has resented me since I arrived out of the blue almost a year ago so he's obviously going to resent my new relatives. But it still rankles. I can slag them off but I won't take it from Toby.

Balls, I forgot about Storm! Loud stomps echo through the hallway as Storm bangs her way down the stairs. She's naked apart from a large green bath towel wrapped around her, and her hair is standing on end. The remains of yesterday's mascara are trickling a dark trail down her left cheek and, I might be mistaken, but she looks far more orange than yesterday.

'Come on, Annie. I need to get in the shower to wash off my fake tan so can you sort it out right now.'

When she notices Toby, she pulls the towel up higher over her boobs.

'I presume this is Storm,' says Toby, sarcasm dripping from every word. 'You and Annie look very alike.'

Seeing as she's looking a total fright at the moment, I'll take that as an insult.

'Storm, this is Toby, Alice's cousin,' I sigh.

'So you're not related to me, then?'

'Heavens, no.' When Toby gives a little laugh at the very thought, Storm's orange face clouds over. Which is a Teenage Strop warning signal that I've come to recognise over the last few days.

'Come with me and I'll get the shower working.'

I grab Storm's cold, bare arm but before we can move, Toby looks over my shoulder and his eyes widen. 'Oh, for goodness' sake, this just gets better and better.'

When I turn around, Josh is standing in the kitchen doorway with a face like thunder. For a few seconds, no one moves. It's like that Edvard Munch painting *The Scream*, with me as the silent screamer.

Then Josh speaks in a low and measured voice. 'I didn't realise you'd be here this weekend, Toby. Annie didn't tell me.' Like it's all my fault.

'Annie didn't know,' I squeak.

Toby and Josh continue their glare-off while Barry shovels in half a slice of toast and Storm perks up no end. The last time Toby and Josh met there was almost a fight and Storm can feel the tension between them. This girl has a nose for trouble and thrives on conflict.

Toby finally breaks the silence. 'I can understand why Annie's father and half-sister are here. But what exactly are you doing in Tregavara House?'

'I'm here to see Annie,' growls Josh, 'not that it's any of your business.'

'Everything that happens here is my business,' says Toby pompously, as though he's the Sultan of Salt Bay. 'But I forgot the two of you were courting.'

Courting! Toby is thirty-three years old but sometimes speaks as though he's in the 1950s.

'How do you two know each other then?' asks Storm sweetly, looking between Toby and Josh. She is such a stirrer! 'Did you used to work together?'

'Christ, no! Josh is a teacher in Trecaldwith whereas I'm a senior partner of a prestigious arts and antiques business in London.' Toby says 'London' like it's a different world – which it kind of is.

'We're from good old London Town,' mumbles Barry, through a mouthful of toast. 'We might live near you.'

Toby wrinkles his nose. 'I doubt it. I live in an apartment near Chelsea Harbour whereas I expect you live farther out. Somewhere with an oh-two-oh-eight number, like Beckton.'

Storm scowls and actually bares her teeth at Toby while I put my arm around her waist and start frogmarching her to the stairs. 'Let's go and get that shower working before you freeze to death.'

I mouth 'sorry' at Josh as we go past and he shakes his head. 'Don't worry. I'll catch up with you later because you seem to have your hands full.'

'No, I won't be too long. Why don't you wait for me in the kitchen?'

'You can chat to me,' says Barry with a wink in my direction, 'about wedding dates.' I could cheerfully throttle him.

'That's kind of you, Barry, but I've got a few other things to do. I've put the fish for tonight in the fridge but we might need to rearrange this evening. I'll call you later, Annie.'

With a final death-stare at Toby, he turns and disappears into the kitchen and I hear the back door bang shut.

Fantastic! My hideously dysfunctional family has managed to put the kibosh on my lovely morning with Josh. We were planning to walk over the hills, high above the village, until we could see the houses huddled together in the fold of the valley and the indigo sea stretching out before us. Far away from everyone, there would have been lots of hand-holding. And hugging to keep warm. And kissing. Sometimes I really hate my family.

Storm hesitates at the bottom of the stairs and I tighten my grip on her arm. 'Come on!'

'Ow, you're hurting me,' she grumbles, climbing the steps. 'Don't get stressy with me just 'cos your boyfriend's ditched you and your cousin's a total tosser.'

I'm worried that Toby's overheard but, when I look back, he's disappearing into the sitting room, leaving his bag in the middle of the hallway floor. Barry kicks it to one side and watches Toby thoughtfully, munching on his toast.

After I've got the shower going – which is easy-peasy if you have even a modicum of patience – I give Barry a hand moving out of Toby's room. This consists mainly of picking his clothes up from the floor.

'I'm sorry you have to move, Barry.'

Wincing, I pick up a pair of discarded underpants with my finger and thumb and drop them into the carrier bag he's using as a laundry basket.

'No problem. It was his room before it was mine, and Toby seems the kind of spoilt, over-indulged man who's used to getting his own way.' That's surprising. Barry spends his life in an oblivious haze so I didn't expect him to get Toby worked out quite so quickly. 'Plus, he's a total dickhead who's probably never listened to Black Sabbath in his life.'

Yep, he's got Toby summed up all right, although—

'He is a bit of an idiot but he's had a few problems in his life.'

I'm not quite sure why I'm sticking up for Toby. But this 'blood is thicker than water' malarkey is turning out to be a real thing, which is a right pain. Because Toby is a distant relative, and Alice is very fond of him, I feel the need to fight his corner. Though Alice doesn't know the real Toby. He keeps his obnoxious side well hidden from his elderly relative who just happens to own a kick-arse painting and a rather nice house. Cynical, moi?

Barry chucks another T-shirt into his holdall, willy-nilly, and zips it up. 'We've all had problems, babe, but we don't all act like right ponces. Right, lead me to the sofa.'

When I go to move past him, Barry steps in front of me. 'There is one thing, Annie.' He swallows hard, looking shifty. 'It's only a little thing but do you think you could call me "Dad"? I know Storm doesn't 'cos she thinks it's cool to call me by my name – and, to be fair, I told her off for calling me "Dad" when she was little. It buggered up my street cred with the fans. But time's moved on and it would be good if at least one of my daughters called me "Dad". Because that's what I am.'

He bites his lip and looks so vulnerable all of a sudden, my stomach does a weird flip. This is so unfair. I won't be able to dislike him so much if he starts acting all human.

'I don't know, Barry,' I say slowly. 'I mean I'm still getting used to the idea of you being my father at all and turning up out of the blue with Storm. It's a lot for me to get my head around.'

'Yeah, whatever. Just thought I'd mention it,' says Barry, breezily, slinging his holdall over his shoulder. 'I don't want to rush you. Spending quality time with you is enough for now.' He wanders off along the landing towards the stairs, tight jeans straining across his ample buttocks.

I'm freaked out that Barry wants me to call him 'Dad' – that's a step way too far. But what's really worrying is him saying that spending time together is 'enough for now'. What exactly is he expecting later?

As I change the sheets on what will be Toby's bed, I wonder about Barry's real reason for coming to Salt Bay. If he's so desperate for a touchy-feely family reunion, why didn't he look me up ages ago, when Mum was still around to answer my questions? None of it makes any sense, I realise, screwing Barry's sheets into a tight ball and bundling them into the laundry basket. All I know for sure is that he and Storm, with help from Toby, are rocking my new foundations in Salt Bay and royally cocking up my love life.

Chapter Twelve

Josh doesn't come back. He texts to say it's probably better if he stays away from Tregavara House while Toby's around. And he's probably right, I conclude miserably, while hanging out of my bedroom window. Waving my arm in the air, several metres above the garden, is the only way to get a halfway reliable phone signal around here – and the locals have got used to me leaning precariously across the windowsill. I've only dropped the phone once and it landed in Alice's soft flower bed so no harm was done.

Sitting on my splintery floorboards, I forensically examine Josh's brief text for hidden meaning. Because over-thinking is what I do. At least the text ends with a kiss, which gives me some comfort. I put kisses on everything, even an email to work's Board of Trustees – though, to be fair, that was an absent-minded mistake. But Josh's kiss indicates that he's not too put out by encountering all my dysfunctional family in the same place, at the same time. Of course it does. Unless the kiss is merely to avoid hurting my feelings, until he ends our relationship for being far too complicated, and smashes my feelings to smithereens.

Ugh, my thoughts are sliding downwards in a ridiculous anxiety spiral so I go in search of Alice, who's arrived home from her outing. She's my shining pillar of stability amidst all the chaos that's surrounding me.

I eventually find her in the garden, sitting on the wooden bench that was delivered last week, with her face bathed in cool winter sun and her eyes closed.

'Is that you, Annabella?' she asks, eyes still firmly shut. 'Sit down with me for a few minutes, dear.'

When she pats the seat next to her, I settle down on the pristine bench. It looks out of place in the bedraggled garden, which hasn't fully recovered from being submerged. When Josh carried me out of Tregavara House, through the swirling flood waters, it was like wading through a lake. But I don't want to think about Josh right now.

'What are you doing out here, Alice? It's not that warm; you should have a thicker jacket on.'

'Oh, don't fuss.' She opens one eye and looks at me. 'I'm not your mother, Annabella. You don't need to look after me all the time.'

Alice is wrong because she needs a lot of looking after these days, but I settle back on the bench and let her remark slide over me. I've become far more mellow since moving to Cornwall, in a way that's impossible when living in the middle of a huge city. Try being laid-back in the rush hour crush for the Tube and you'll end up standing on a crowded platform for ages while hardier souls elbow you in the face to get a place inside the carriage.

'Are you escaping?' I ask Alice. She opens both eyes wide and smiles at me. Deep wrinkles furrow her pale cheeks.

'Is it that obvious? It's lovely to see Toby and such a nice surprise, but he's quite full-on and rather exhausting. He keeps badgering me about what security arrangements are in place for when the painting of *The Lady* comes home. I'm not entirely sure he wants the painting to come back to Tregavara House at all. And Barry and Storm are being particularly noisy today.' She stops and focuses on two small boats that are motoring into harbour, seagulls wheeling and dipping behind them. 'Emily's still in Penzance, shopping. I expect she'll be back soon.'

I'm not so sure about that. Emily has been spending as little time at home as possible since Jay hit on Storm at the choir rehearsal. And when she is here, I'm being as nice to her as I can because I feel responsible for bringing Storm into the house.

Alice steals a quick glance at me. 'Barry said that Josh called in earlier to see you. It's a shame he couldn't stay longer.'

'I think Barry, Storm and Toby en masse were too much for him.'

'I can see they might be rather overwhelming.'

Alice doesn't mention the bad blood between Toby and Josh and I keep my mouth shut. She doesn't seem to realise how much they hate one another, or why, and it's not my place to spill so many secrets. I'd just end up the bad guy in the middle of it all and everyone's whipping boy.

Peter Seegrass has just climbed off his boat and is wandering along the harbour wall. He's easy to spot in his bright yellow oilskin trousers, and Alice gives him a wave.

'Are you meeting up with Josh later? I think it will do you good. He's a decent young man and just right for you to settle down with.'

It's touching how keen Alice is to marry me off to a local boy who will stop me from ever running off back to London. I pat the back of her blue-veined hand, which feels chilly. 'I don't think so. I'll stick around while Toby's here.'

Truth be told, I'm too scared to leave Toby, Storm and Barry in the house on their own. I've been doing my best to keep them apart and am only taking a break in the garden because Storm is in her bedroom with the door closed and Barry is in the attic hitting something with a hammer.

Basically, I'm a prisoner at Tregavara House with the shittiest group of inmates ever, excluding Alice and Emily. While the man I love is miles away, looking after his own family. It's not right and I wallow for a few moments in self-pity as Adele's 'Someone Like You' – the soundtrack to this poignant moment – plays in my head.

When I sigh, Alice sits up straighter and pulls her thin, beige jacket tight around her frail body. 'I need to speak to you seriously for a moment, Annabella.'

I thought we were already, but I twist around so we're face to face. 'OK,' I say, with a sense of foreboding. I know she's getting on a bit and isn't terribly well but maybe she's had bad news.

Alice takes a deep breath. 'Make sure you and Josh spend lots of time together and don't take one another or your relationship for granted.'

Phew! 'OK, Alice, will do.'

'No, I'm being serious.' She grasps my hands, brown eyes squinting in the pale sun. 'You must try hard to make your relationship work, Annabella. I lost the love of my life because I took him for granted. I thought he'd always be around, and then he went off with someone else.'

'But David came back and married you in the end.'

'No, David was the second love of my life.' She laughs at my look of surprise. 'There's a lot you don't know about me, Annabella. I haven't always been this old and frail.' I desperately want to ask about the first suitor who broke Alice's heart but she blocks any questions with a slight shake of the head. 'However, now I am, so learn from a wise old woman and forge strong relationships with those closest to you, whenever you can. Otherwise you run the risk of losing them.'

She doesn't elaborate any further so I'm not sure whether she's just talking about me and Josh or if she also means Barry and Storm. The thought of losing Josh makes me feel light-headed and panicky whereas the thought of losing Barry and Storm… not so much.

'Brrr.' Alice suddenly shivers and points at a thick ridge of black clouds building up over the cold sea. 'We'd better go in because there's a storm coming. But think about what I've said, Annabella, and make sure you hold on tight to what's precious.'

Chapter Thirteen

Toby suddenly appearing out of the blue, apart from being a right pain, has presented me with a dilemma – a dilemma steeped in old secrets, which means I can't ask anyone for advice.

When I told Lucy that I'd raise the issue of Freya with Toby, I was banking on not seeing him for ages and there was always the chance she might change her mind.

But her mind remains unchanged and here he is, sitting on Alice's sofa, drinking tea, with his feet up on the coffee table. His purple socks look brand new and are probably made of cashmere gathered from the necks of Mongolian goats during a full moon. There's no nipping to the sock counter at M&S for a man of Toby's self-perceived calibre.

Peeking through the half-open door, I wonder again whether what I'm about to do is the right thing. Josh has made it crystal clear that he wants nothing to do with Toby, but whether Freya meets her father should be Lucy's decision, surely – and Josh needs some financial support or he'll crumble under the strain. He's starting to look positively unwell.

Those are both good reasons for Toby taking on the responsibility of fatherhood, but the clincher for me is what's best for Freya. She's going to find out who her dad is one day and it'll come as less of a shock when she's young. Plus, every time I think of fatherless Freya

I picture myself as a child, asking questions about my dad and Mum ignoring them until I just gave up. Freya has a right to know.

OK, I'm going in. After a couple of deep breaths, I push the sitting room door open as wide as it will go and march up to where Toby's sitting. He lowers his copy of the *Telegraph* that he brought with him and peers over the top of it.

'Oh, it's you. I thought it might be your family.'

'Storm's upstairs in her room and Barry's working on the house.'

'I heard him banging and crashing about.' Toby carefully folds his paper and places it on the cushions beside him. 'Are you sure you don't need to get a proper workman in? Someone who knows what he's doing.'

'Barry's quite skilled actually. He made that bookcase and he's fixing a hole in the roof at the moment. He does a lot of odd jobs in London when he's not—'

Aargh, I stop abruptly.

'When he's not what?' asks Toby, eyes narrowing as he senses my discomfort and moves in for the kill. Oh, what the hell; Barry will tell him anyway.

'When he's not playing in his band. Barry is a musician.'

Toby snorts and slides his feet off the coffee table. 'That's priceless! What sort of band? Let me guess. Judging by his long, greasy hair and unkempt appearance, I'd say death metal or heavy rock. I'm right, aren't I?'

He snorts again while I fight the urge to smash his face in. Barry's passion might be Def Leppard rather than Monet or Modigliani, but that doesn't mean Toby can take the piss.

There's no way I'm going to help bring him and Freya together. And yet – I take in his expensive chinos and cashmere jumper, and the flashy gold watch on his arm which would feed Josh's family for a year. He's living the high life while they're drowning in financial troubles, and it's about time Toby faced up to the consequences of his casual fling.

I perch on the edge of the chair opposite him. 'There's something I need to speak to you about.'

'I hope it's nothing to do with those two moving in permanently and taking advantage of Alice's hospitality. She's a fool to herself.'

'It's nothing to do with Barry and Storm. It's about Freya – your daughter,' I add pointedly.

Toby looks as if I've punched him in the face. His cheeks glow bright red and he sinks into the sofa like a deflated balloon. 'What about her?' he gulps.

'I wondered if you'd ever thought about being a part of her life.'

'Shut the door!' hisses Toby, scanning round for eavesdroppers.

Once I've closed it, he leans forward with his elbows on his knees. 'Have you been put up to this by Josh? He's jealous of how much money I'm making while he's grubbing around on a teacher's salary.'

'Josh knows nothing about this. But, talking about money, if you're so well off isn't it a bit rotten not paying any maintenance for your own child?'

Toby recoils as though no one has ever questioned him like this before. Then his features settle into a sulk. 'I didn't want Lucy to keep the baby anyway. It was her choice. I said I'd pay for her to get rid of it.'

Wow, what a gentleman! This isn't going to work, and I don't want it to. Getting to my feet, I shoot him a filthy look and am almost at the door when he says, 'You think I'm a heartless bastard, don't you.'

'Yes, that's exactly what I think.' I'm way past the point of lying for the sake of family harmony.

Toby loosens the collar of the mauve shirt that's peeping above the neckline of his jumper. 'Not that it's any of your business but I do think about her sometimes. I'm not a complete monster.'

'Just completely selfish, then.'

Toby thinks for a moment and shrugs. 'Maybe, but it's been just me for such a long time I've grown used to it. I saw it in you too, when we first met, but you've changed since you moved here. It's funny really. Salt Bay seems to have done you good whereas I couldn't wait to escape, and a child would tie me to this damn place.' He sighs and his chin drops to his chest. 'Show me, then.'

'Show you what?'

'Show me a picture of my daughter.'

Still not sure I'm doing the right thing, I scroll through the photos on my phone until I find one of Freya. She's smiling mischievously at the camera with her ebony hair in dark bunches. She's beautiful and more than this man deserves.

When I hand Toby the phone, he stares at the picture for a moment. The tiny muscles around his deep-set grey eyes tighten but the rest of his face remains expressionless.

'She looks like my mother,' he says finally, handing the phone back to me.

'Your mother who was horrified that you'd got a member of the lowly Pasco-Pawley family pregnant.'

Toby nods. 'Yes, she was upset but she's not here any longer to give her opinion.' He sits back, resting his head against the sofa. 'I don't suppose Lucy would let me anywhere near the girl anyway.'

'She might do if she thinks Freya should get to know her father.'

Toby stares past my shoulder into the distance. 'I'll think about it.'

Then he picks up his paper, shakes it open and holds it in front of his face to signal that our conversation is over.

I slip out of the sitting room with a sick feeling in the pit of my stomach. What have I done? It's hard to shake the notion that I've betrayed Josh, even though it was Lucy's idea and I'm trying to do what's best for Josh and, most of all, for Freya. But that just sounds like excuses now, and don't they say that the road to hell is paved with good intentions?

Chapter Fourteen

Tregavara House feels claustrophobic so, grabbing my jacket, I close
the front door quietly behind me and walk into the village. It's risky
leaving my family alone in the house – I have visions of Storm yelling
'dickhead' at Toby while Barry plays air-guitar behind him in an ironic
way – but I need half an hour's peace to think.

The storm clouds have dumped their rain on Salt Bay and moved on,
leaving pale blue patches scattered across the sky. But it's still cold and
the village is starting to look Christmassy. Jennifer – Salt Bay's version
of the Grinch – has already put up brightly coloured decorations in her
shop because she reckons that people feeling festive tend to spend more.

'Common sense flies out of the window when they see a bit of gold
foil and they'll buy any old tat,' she told me, Blu-Tacking a glitter-strewn
star to her window.

A huge fir tree has also been erected in a wooden tub on the village
green and some of the villagers are stringing lights on it. They wave
at me and I wave back but don't stop to help because I'm heading to
the pub. My go-to place in London when life was a bit rubbish was
Waterloo Bridge at dusk. There, I'd watch old and new London light
up as darkness fell and contemplate life while the Thames glittered
below me. Here, my go-to place is centuries-old pub the Whistling
Wave, where generations of people have gathered for friendship, fun

and solace. And, boy, could I do with some solace right now. Plugging in my earphones, I play Elbow's 'My Sad Captains' which matches my mood.

When I reach the Whistling Wave, I scan the bar looking for Josh but he's nowhere to be seen. It's Saturday afternoon and he'll be at home, keeping his poorly mum company rather than drinking in here. But I can't help feeling disappointed.

Sliding my bum into a seat near the roaring fire, I log on to the pub's Wi-Fi and send Josh a WhatsApp message. *I can't wait to see you once Toby has gone. Hope your mum's OK xx*

Are two kisses too much? Does it make me look clingy and desperate? Ugh, I didn't worry about things like that before. The relationship between me and Josh was easy and exciting and fresh but now, since family matters have been keeping us apart, it's become screwed up and weird between us. I delete one of the kisses and press 'send'.

'Hello, stranger. Don't you want a drink? It's not like you to be without one,' says Kayla, making me sound like an alcoholic as she slides into the seat next to me.

'I do, but if I start I might not stop.'

Which does rather make me sound like someone with an alcohol problem.

'Jeez, are you having one of those days? They're little buggers, aren't they?'

She waves at Tom from the choir, who's just come in with his parents.

'Do you need to go and serve them?'

'Nah, I'm on a break so Roger's going to have to get his arse into gear for once. It's big enough.'

We both watch as Roger lumbers to the bar and starts pulling a pint for Tom's dad. He rolls his eyes at Kayla as though she's bunking off.

'Give it a rest, Roger, and do some work for once,' mutters Kayla under her breath before putting her elbows on the table and her chin in her hands. 'Go on then, hit your Auntie Kayla with what's happening in your mad, crazy life.'

'Where to begin? Barry and Storm are still driving me nuts.'

'Understandable. They're awful, especially Storm. I can't stand her.'

Eek. Kayla tends to say exactly what she's thinking, which can be endearing. Though not so much when she's slagging off someone related to me. And she's made no effort to get to know my new relatives so isn't really qualified to pass comment. But that's not going to stop her.

'I mean,' she says, folding her arms and huffing, 'the way she acted in here was—'

'And now Toby's turned up out of the blue which is causing all kinds of tensions,' I butt in quickly before she can go off on one.

Kayla's mouth drops open. 'What the hell? I'm not surprised you're fed up. I bet they all want to kill each other.'

'They do, so I'm spending all my time keeping them apart, especially Toby and Storm. She's already said he's a total tosser.'

'Hhhmm.' Kayla shrugs, looking impressed. 'That's one thing on which I do see eye to eye with your sister.'

'Half-sister,' I protest, though I've lost the battle of trying to distance myself from her.

'Half-sister, schmister. So, what does Josh say about all of this?'

'I don't know because I haven't seen him properly for a while. He called in this morning, saw who was there and beat a hasty retreat.'

'Ha, can't say I blame him. He hates Toby for being such an arse in the flood.'

I'd love to tell Kayla that the bad feeling between them goes back so much further than that, but I can't. God, I *hate* keeping secrets so it's ironic that I'm rather good at it. I had a lot of practice with keeping Mum's strange moods and behaviour under the radar because I was terrified of being taken into care. But secrets mess up your life.

'Don't worry.' Kayla turns her back on the raging flames in the blackened fireplace and gives me a sympathetic smile. 'It'll all sort out. Toby will scuttle off back to his posh life in London, Barry and Storm will leave too – one day – and you and Josh can get back to getting it on unhindered. The two of you are great together.'

'Do you think so? I was kind of hoping he might be in here.'

'We haven't seen so much of him, not since his mum's been crocked again. Ollie reckons it could be pretty serious this time.'

'It's not great.'

More secrets, but I'm not sure how much I'm allowed to say about Marion's health. Josh is such a closed person in many ways and might not like family details being bandied about. Even to Kayla who, thinking about it, would be a terrible choice of confidante because she blabs about almost everything.

'That's a shame.' Kayla sighs and I look at her properly for the first time since I came in. I've been so caught up in my own problems, it hasn't registered that she seems pale and tired today and not her usual vibrant self. Even her clothes are dowdy and the black sweatshirt she's wearing makes her red hair look dull and lifeless.

'What about you? Are you OK?' I ask, mentally kicking myself for being so self-centred.

'Not really.' The corners of Kayla's full mouth drop. 'It's stupid but I had an email from a friend yesterday who's travelling around Asia and it made me feel a bit—' she waves her hand round the pub with its dark-wood beams and gleaming horse brasses on the walls '—tied down.'

'But you like it here, don't you, and what about Ollie?'

'Of course I like it here or I wouldn't have stayed so long. And Ollie's great.' She smiles broadly and stares dreamily into the distance. 'But this was only ever supposed to be a stopping-off location on my way to other adventures. I don't want to stay here my whole life. Salt Bay wasn't meant to be my forever place.' She bites her lip.

'You had a lovely trip back to Australia recently. That's further than I've been for ages, and you got to show off Ollie to the smug-marrieds.'

That's what Kayla calls her two older sisters who, she's informed me more than once, are 'boring as hell'.

Kayla giggles. 'Yeah, it's hard for them to heap their usual patronising crap on me when they're sitting there with their tedious husbands and two-point-four children while I'm snogging my gorgeous, thighs-to-die-for Cornish boyfriend on the sofa.'

'You didn't!'

'I did! Ollie was a bit surprised when I launched myself at him but he went along with it. Don't look so disapproving, Annie! They're always saying they feel sorry for me because I haven't settled down yet, so I wanted to show them what they're missing. I bet they haven't had mind-blowing sex for months. Probably years. Whereas me and Ollie are at it like rabbits every day.'

'Too much information.' I laugh, but I'm feeling panicky right now. Josh and I haven't had the energy or opportunity to make love for a while. It's hard to get in the mood when Storm could burst into my bedroom at any moment or his mum is coughing next door in Trecaldwith. And it's impossible for a tall man and a size twelve woman to get jiggy in the back of a Mini without risking serious injury. I had the backache to prove it for several days.

Or maybe, says the niggly bitch-voice in my brain, *Josh is using all this as an excuse and he doesn't want to make love to you any more.*

Aargh, I've never felt this strongly about a man before and it's making me feel insecure. Having more to lose is a seriously overrated state of affairs.

I cup my chin in my hands, mirroring Kayla, and we both give a deep, heartfelt sigh.

'Cheer up, girls,' demands Mr Paul, who's passing our table on his way to order another pint. 'It might never happen.' Which just makes me want to kill him.

Kayla and I sit in silence for a while, staring into the crackling fire. Then she shudders and pulls herself up straight.

'OK, we need a plan. I'll start broadening Ollie's outlook on life so he realises that Cornwall isn't the be-all and end-all.'

'How are you going to do that?'

She shrugs. 'I dunno. Maybe show him my travel photos and tell him about all the fabulous places I've visited. A slow drip-feed of information into his brain. I'll be very discreet and use my feminine wiles.'

Discretion is a foreign word to Kayla, but she's inordinately proud of her 'wiles' so I nod in agreement. It's easier. 'That sounds like a good plan.'

'It is. And what about your plan to get rid of your sis— um, half-sister – and "father"?'

She puts 'father' in air quotes though I'm not sure why. Sadly, it doesn't make Barry any less related to me.

'I don't know. I'm not sure but I reckon they'll soon get fed up with Salt Bay and with me and will move back to London.'

'Oh, Annie, have you learned nothing from me? You need to be proactive and make things happen.' She bangs her fist on the table, making me jump.

'What would you suggest?'

'You could murder them in their beds or, at the very least, pack their bags and tell them to sling their hook. But you won't do that because you're far too… nice.' She says 'nice' as if it's a bad thing. 'But you need to do something soon or it'll be just you, Alice, Barry and Storm around the Christmas dinner table. And you don't want that.'

I *really* don't want that. I can already imagine Storm sulking over the stuffing, and Barry drunk in a paper hat, while Josh is miles away looking after his own family. 'Getting rid' of family seems a little harsh but there's no getting away from the fact that my life would be far easier without them around.

'So,' I ask, 'what can I do that falls short of homicide?'

'I know.' Kayla's eyes light up. 'Send Storm to school.'

'How the hell is that going to work? I want them to go back to London, not get more settled in the local community.'

'Reverse psychology,' says Kayla loftily, tapping her forehead with her finger. 'She should be at school and no doubt thinks she's going to enjoy an extended holiday down here. So, tell her she has to go to school locally and she'll be mega keen to get back to London where she can probably bunk off for days on end with no one noticing. I don't suppose Barry keeps an eye on her.'

'I'm not sure that would work.'

'I know these things, Annie. I did an online course a while back about the workings of the mind, and reverse psychology is a proper thing. I mean, what else are you going to do?'

I'm not convinced but at least it's something to try and, at the worst, it'll get Storm out of the house for several hours a day. 'OK, I'll give it a go.'

Kayla claps her hands together. 'Great! Get your sexy, brooding boyfriend to find her a place at his school. Give him a ring now and sort it out.' She glances at Roger, who's coping with a sudden influx of customers and is puffing and panting. 'I'd better give Roger a hand before he carks it at the bar.' She grabs my hands and squeezes hard. 'Ring Josh. Now.'

*

Leaving the pub, I walk to the end of the village and up across the fields until I reach a weathered wooden bench. Then I stand on the bench and dial Josh's landline. It's the only private place you're guaranteed a phone signal round here if the phone box is busy or, like today, surrounded by people putting up a Christmas tree. There's often a queue for the bench when the phone box is out of action. But today I'm the only person here.

Spread out before me is the village, with smoke curling from cottage chimneys and colourful boats bobbing about in the harbour. It's like a postcard of cosy England. I blow on my hands, which are going blue in the cold wind, and enjoy the peaceful setting. The village has been like this for generations which means my ancestors must have seen what I'm seeing now. My mum too. That makes me feel drawn to this place but also slightly jumpy. Because sometimes the cord that binds me to this village feels more like a chain and that's when I get an overwhelming urge to escape back to London.

The landline at Josh's is ringing and ringing and I'm about to end the call when the phone is picked up, though no one speaks.

'Hello? Is that you, Marion?'

'No, Marion can't get to the phone right now,' says a high-pitched, slightly breathy female voice. 'Can I tell her who's ringing?' The voice sounds familiar but I can't place it.

'It's Annie calling.'

'Oh.' The woman on the other end sounds put out. 'Did you want to speak to Josh?'

'Please, if he's there. Um, who is this?'

There's a slight pause and the answer clicks into my brain a split second before she answers. 'It's Felicity. We've met once before, on the beach at Salt Bay.'

Flaming hell! We've met all right and she was trying to make things up with Josh at the time. Josh and I weren't an item then – in fact I still thought he was a git – but that's not the point. She's the woman who lived with Josh in Penzance and then broke up with him because he had to move back in to look after his family. And she's in Josh's house right now.

Closing my eyes, I picture Felicity, who's fluffy-blonde pretty with teeny tiny thighs and a gleaming white Hollywood smile. She's practically perfect, and I bet she has a fully functional family too, who are nothing like the shitstorm of dodgy genes I've inherited.

'Annie, are you still there?' she asks, breathily.

'Yes, I'm here.' I pull myself together. 'Of course I remember you from the beach. We had a lovely time.'

'Until you slid down the cliff on your backside.'

'Yeah, well, that's probably best forgotten,' I reply, through gritted teeth.

'Probably.' She gives a tinkly laugh and calls out to someone in the room. 'Thank you, just put the tea down there. It's for you, Josh. It's Annie. I answered the phone while your mum was in the loo.'

Josh is there and he's making her tea!

'Hi Annie.' Josh sounds distracted. 'Is everything all right?'

'Yes, fine. I'm sorry, I didn't realise you were busy.'

'Felicity called round to see Mum because she heard she was unwell.'

Of course she did, and I'm being uncharitable to think otherwise. I bet she and Marion got close because Marion thought Felicity would be her daughter-in-law one day. *And now she's stuck with you,* says my niggly inner voice which is starting to become rather tiresome.

'That was nice of her,' I manage.

'It was.'

There's a silence until I say, 'Actually, I was ringing to ask you a favour.'

'Anything,' says Josh, though he sounds wary.

'Can you check if you can get Storm a temporary place at your school?'

'Oh, for goodness' sake,' he splutters. 'They're not moving in long-term, are they? Isn't it a bit strange them turning up out of the blue? I know they're related to you but are you sure you know enough about them?'

'I know enough,' I say, trying to keep my voice measured though his reaction has taken me aback. 'Actually, I'm trying to encourage them to leave Salt Bay so we'll have more time together, and I have a cunning plan.' Great! Now I sound like Baldrick. 'If Storm thinks she has to go to school here, she'll nag Barry mercilessly to go back to London. It's reverse psychology.'

Josh's sigh reverberates down the line. 'You've been talking to Kayla, haven't you? Do you really think this is going to help?'

'Probably not,' I say miserably, horribly aware that Felicity must be listening in. 'I just thought it might be worth a try. I'd just like things to get back to normal…'

'Me too,' says Josh, sounding gloomy. 'All right. I suppose I can check it out. She should be in school anyway.'

'Exactly. Thank you, Josh, and I'm sorry.'

I don't specify what I'm sorry about because it's a blanket apology covering everything – Toby, Barry and Storm being around all the time, me enticing him away from Felicity (though heaven knows how that happened), and my occasional longing for London which I keep well-hidden but Josh seems to sense is still there.

'You don't need to apologise, Annie.' Josh's voice goes muffled as though he's covering his mouth. 'Let's not argue when we're both just trying to do what's right for everyone. I miss you, Annie, and can't wait to see you really soon.'

'I miss you too,' I gulp, the words catching in my throat.

After Josh ends the call, I sit heavily on the muddy bench and have a little cry. I can just picture the three of them – Josh, Marion and Felicity – sitting around, drinking tea and chatting about the good old days. Felicity will be flaunting her impressive cleavage at Josh and maybe he'll start thinking fondly about how much easier life was with her.

Chapter Fifteen

An uneasy truce has settled on the house when I get home. Barry is slouched in front of the TV watching an old war film, Storm is playing music in her room, and Toby is sitting at the kitchen table reading through what looks like work documents. He lifts his head to acknowledge my presence but doesn't say a word when I grab a glass of water.

I hover by the sink for a few moments in case he wants to chat, but soon give up – what could we talk about anyway? My family is out of bounds, Freya is too hot a topic, and I don't want to discuss Alice's health behind her back. Work is usually a safe area but he still hasn't forgiven me for ditching the job he got me in his London office.

Instead, I go in search of Alice. Her bedroom door is closed and, when I open it a crack, I spot her lying on the bed. She looks like a drowsy Queen Mother in her pretty four-poster bed with its rose-pink counterpane. She's sleeping a lot more these days and I can't help but be concerned about her. Particularly as she's getting more stiff and shaky and seems to slur her words occasionally. It's such a worry. A year ago, I'd never heard of Alice Gowan but now she's one of the most important people in my life and the very thought of losing her makes my throat feel tight.

I'll leave her to snooze in peace – well, kind of peace because Storm's music is thumping along the landing.

'Hey, Storm, can you turn that down please.'

Storm is also lying in bed, with her eyes screwed tight, and she jumps when I tap her on the shoulder. Frowning, she sits up and leans back against her pillows.

'What do you want?' she grumbles, rolling her eyes when I gesture that she should turn her music off. There's blessed peace as she clicks her phone and the music being pumped through the attached tinny speakers stops.

'Alice is asleep so can you keep the music down, please.'

'All right, no need to get stressy. I didn't know.'

Storm starts rolling across the bed to click her music back on but stops mid-roll when I sit down next to her. She shuffles across the bedspread, so there's more room for my backside, and regards me warily. 'Is your knobhead of a cousin still here?'

'Do you know, Storm, I don't think you realise quite how rude you are sometimes. You shouldn't be so insulting about people, especially when you know very little about them.'

'OK,' she concedes grudgingly. 'Toby is just a bit posh and sneery.'

'I know he can be rather full-on and snobby. You can imagine what he thinks of me, being brought up by a single mother in a succession of grotty flats.'

'No, you weren't,' scoffs Storm, picking at a clump of black mascara on her lower lashes. 'There's no point trying to get round me by making stuff up.'

'I'm not making anything up. I lost count of the number of flats we'd lived in by the time I was your age.'

'I bet they weren't proper grotty though. One flat we stayed in had so many mice, I couldn't sleep because I could hear them scrabbling about.'

'Our flat in Bethnal Green had cockroaches almost as big as mice. That's why we moved out after a week.'

'Hhmm.' Storm narrows her eyes and breathes out slowly. 'When we stayed with Barry's friends last year, their neighbour got arrested for drug dealing from his flat. The police raided it.' She pulls herself up against her pillows, looking smug.

'Really? One of my mum's boyfriends turned out to be wanted by Interpol for doing something dodgy in Spain. We never found out what but it might have been murder.'

Storm sniffs. 'When Barry's gigging, I'm left on my own with his weirdo friends who smoke dope all the time. And it was so fumy one evening, I got second-hand high. When I was twelve.'

'And my mum was often so mentally unwell she'd take to her bed for days and I had to fend for myself. When I was six.'

'Well,' declares Storm, pulling back her shoulders as she prepares to massively up the my-childhood-was-worse-than-yours ante. 'My mum ran off to go and live with a man who can't stand me.'

She nods in triumph and grins, though her lower lip wobbles until she sucks it between her teeth.

'That sounds painful,' I say, quietly.

'Not really.' Storm's face is tight with suppressed feelings. 'She had her reasons and at least my mum wasn't mental.'

Ah, a good old counter-attack, which was my only weapon in the playground when kids hurled insults at me about my family set-up. But it's a rubbish way of keeping out hurt and pain. All it does is build up a great big wall that no one, even kind and caring people, can get through.

'Do you know what, Storm?' When I pat her hand, she doesn't pull it away. 'I think that both of our mums probably did their best.'

'Yeah, probably,' she mumbles. And, for the first time since we've met, she gives me a proper smile which reaches her heavily made-up eyes.

'And Barry's doing his best too, I guess.'

'Yeah, though we often have to move 'cos he's pissed someone off or owes them money. He's a right div.'

'He doesn't seem to be the easiest of dads.'

'He's not.' She gives me another fleeting smile, looking much younger than sixteen. 'He's a total car crash of a dad – though, to be fair, he took it hard when Mum left.' She glances up at me from under her long, black lashes. 'What happened to your mum then?'

'She died, about four years ago now.'

Storms studies her fingers and starts picking at a ragged cuticle. 'That's a shame. Was she nice?'

When I nod, she starts biting the skin at the corner of her mouth.

'How long ago did your mum leave?' I ask her gently.

Storm carries on gnawing at her lip while I hold my breath, not sure she'll answer a personal question but hoping that she will.

'Seven years ago, after she met a posh idiot like your cousin, only he's called Simon. Simple Simon.' She leans past me and flicks on her music but turns the volume down low. 'Why does Alice sleep such a lot?'

'She's an old lady and she's not very well.'

'In what way not very well?'

'She has a neurological condition that means she's shaky and unsteady on her feet. And she gets very tired and it's affecting her speech a little, I think.'

'Oops.' Bright spots of colour flare in Storm's cheeks.

'What?'

'When she slurred the other day, I thought she'd been hitting the vodka shots. I didn't judge her though 'cos there's nothing else to do around here except drink.'

'There's lots to do if you look for it.' I start desperately racking my brain for things that might interest a streetwise teenager. 'There are amazing walks over the cliffs.' Nope, that one goes down like a lead balloon. 'And there's free Wi-Fi at the Whistling Wave, just so long as you don't order alcohol at the bar again. Or you can get to Penzance and its shops on the bus. There's a New Look.' Storm nods approvingly. 'Or you can join the Salt Bay Choral Society and make music with us. Singing is a brilliant way of expressing yourself and having fun, don't you think so?'

Storm patently does not think so if her bored expression is anything to go by. She slides back down onto the bed, closes her eyes and folds her arms across her chest.

'I'll keep the music down 'cos I don't want to wake the old lady. But I'm not talking to that Toby. Even his name is stupid.'

'It's a deal,' I say, getting to my feet and pulling the bedspread straight. Dizzee Rascal no longer being played at ear-bleeding level plus the added bonus of no conversation between Toby and Storm sounds like a very good deal to me.

*

Toby avoids me for the rest of the afternoon and I keep busy, trying not to think about Felicity visiting Marion. But I'm tortured by images of Josh and Felicity chatting, Josh and Felicity laughing, Josh and Felicity kissing, and Josh and Felicity falling into bed, a tangle of arms and legs.

I anaesthetise myself with *Midsomer Murders* on TV; bloodless murders in quaint villages can be soothingly soporific. But, by the time I head for bed, I'm exhausted, having been tortured by my thoughts for hours. Logically, I know nothing has happened between Josh and Felicity – Josh is loyal and lovely and, unlike my ex-boyfriend Stuart, not a cheater – but, in my head, they're already buying a Labrador and sending out wedding invitations.

Maybe my head will be less jangly in the morning. Kicking off my slippers, I pull back the bed covers and slip under the chilly sheets. My bedroom is an oasis of peace when Barry's not drilling unnecessarily on the landing, and tonight all is blessedly calm. I'm just getting all lovely and drowsy when there's a light tapping on the door.

My eyes fly open. 'Who is it?'

'It's me, Toby. Can I come in?'

What the hell does he want? After switching on my bedside lamp, I grab my dressing gown from the bottom of the bed and cover the nightshirt I'm wearing. Toby's opinion of me will sink even lower if he sees *Princess* emblazoned across my chest in thick gold thread. The shirt was a present from Josh; an in-joke because Freya thought I was a princess when we first met, because of my bright blue eyes. The criteria for qualifying as royal are rather lacking when it comes to a five-year-old.

When I'm fully covered, I call, 'Come in.' The door edges open and Toby's head appears around it.

'Sorry to bother you, Annie. Have you got a minute?' he asks, with a creepy smile.

Why is he being so polite and subservient? When I nod, Toby steps into the room and quietly closes the door behind him. He's changed his outfit from this morning – I have no idea why – and is now dressed in immaculate indigo jeans and a pale linen shirt. He must be freezing in this cold, old house.

Without another word, he walks over and plonks his backside down on the counterpane. Toby Trebarwith is sitting on my bed. This is a perfectly weird ending to a perfectly weird day.

Toby clears his throat and stares at the photo of my windswept mum in Hyde Park. 'I wanted a word about what we were talking about earlier. About—' He glances up from my mum's smiling face and meets my eye, willing me to finish his sentence.

'About Freya.'

'Yes, that's right. I've been thinking about what you said, and maybe it wouldn't do any harm to meet the child. Just once.' When he swallows, his Adam's apple bobs up and down. 'So, I was thinking maybe you could speak to her mother about it.'

'To Lucy.'

'Yes, speak to Lucy, If that's all right with you.'

I nod resignedly. Toby meeting Freya is like a huge juggernaut that I've helped put into gear and, now it's started moving forward, I'm too involved to jump off.

'That's great, then. Thank you. Right, I'd better leave you to get some beauty sleep.' Toby stands and wipes a hand across his bum as though sitting on my bed might have contaminated him. He walks briskly to the door but, before his fingers close around the handle, he looks back. 'You said that Josh doesn't know anything about this.'

'Nope, he knows absolutely nothing.'

'I thought as much or there'd be no chance of a meeting. And can I presume that you intend to keep him in the dark about all of this?'

I nod my head while crossing my fingers beneath the covers, which means that I'm not really betraying my boyfriend. However – surprise, surprise – I still feel rubbish after Toby has slipped out and the door has clicked shut behind him. Fingers crossed or uncrossed, I'm now in league with Toby and keeping a secret from the man I love, who trusts me. Felicity's shiny, pretty face drifts into my mind as I wrap my arms tight around my pillow, knowing that I'm in for a sleepless night.

Jeez, my life is getting horribly complicated. Pulling the heavy pillow on top of my head, I take a shallow breath and ignore the feeling of being suffocated.

*

Toby hangs around for much of the next day, which is unlike him. Usually he graces us with brief 'make sure Alice is still alive and Annie hasn't stolen the silver' visits. But this time I can't shift him. He has a stroll around the village, spends the next hour moaning about how 'provincial' Salt Bay is and then parks himself at the kitchen table with the Sunday papers from Jennifer's shop spread out across the scratched oak.

I spend much of my Sunday keeping the two factions of my family apart, which is exhausting. Barry slips my net a couple of times but beats a hasty retreat from the kitchen after asking to look at the paper and only being offered the *Sunday Telegraph*.

Toby sneers when Barry turns down the proffered paper, and I get an urge to kick my insensitive cousin. Yes, Barry is unsophisticated in Toby's eyes, but preferring the *Sunday People* to the *Sunday Telegraph* isn't a crime and Barry, for all his swagger, is a human being who can be hurt.

Finally, at close to five o'clock, Toby throws his leather holdall into the back of his BMW and bids me and Alice goodbye. Barry and Storm have made themselves scarce and Emily isn't back yet from visiting her family.

Lights from Tregavara House illuminate Toby's silver car and reach towards the harbour as Toby slides behind the wheel. It's a still evening and the thick silence is broken only by a faint whoosh of black waves pulling on wet sand. In the distance, towards the centre of the village,

Salt Bay's Christmas tree is just a dark smudge. Its festive lights won't be switched on until next month, during a special ceremony.

Toby's window suddenly slides down and he beckons me over. When I dutifully trot down the garden path, he leans out and says quietly, 'Are you planning on coming back to London any time soon?'

His question takes me by surprise and I shake my head. 'No, why?'

'I just wondered. I thought you might want to escape your dreadful family and things don't seem as lovey-dovey right now with Josh Pasco.'

'We're fine. Just too busy with families to spend much time together,' I splutter, wondering what subtle cues he might have picked up on. It's worrying if Toby Trebarwith, the most insensitive man on the planet, thinks our relationship has cooled.

'If you say so. I just want to make sure you realise there's no point in asking me to help you get another job in London. Not after the last fiasco. I was in Rafe's bad books for ages after you did that runner and we had to pay megabucks for an agency temp.'

'Sorry,' I mumble, feeling guilty even though Toby had a selfish, ulterior motive for fixing me up with employment in the first place.

Toby checks that Alice is still out of earshot on the garden path. 'And make sure you have a word with Lucy about that thing we spoke about, before you leave Salt Bay.'

'I'm not leaving Salt Bay.'

'Are you sure? I still can't believe a city girl like you is happy in this dead-end hole.'

Toby slides up his window, slams his foot down on the accelerator and screeches off towards the bright lights of London. Storm is so right – he is a total tosser.

Chapter Sixteen

One good reason for getting shot of Toby, apart from desperately *wanting* to get shot of Toby, is that Josh is coming for tea this evening. And I don't fancy another hostile stare-a-thon in Alice's hallway.

Secretly, I hoped Josh had gone off the idea of having a meal with Barry and Storm, but he called on Alice's landline mid-afternoon and she invited him round. Which was lovely of her, and we need to eat the cod he brought yesterday that's stinking out our fridge, but I'm nervous. Partly because Josh, Barry and Storm together in a small room is an unknown quantity. But mostly because I'm convinced Josh will sense I'm lying to him. Well, not lying exactly. Merely omitting to tell him that I might be helping Toby to meet up with Freya, his beloved niece. Behind his back.

Good grief; every time I go over it in my head – and I'm going over it a lot – I get all hot and clammy. Flinging open the kitchen door, I gulp cold, salty air into my lungs and try to calm down. Chances are that Lucy will change her mind and Toby will go off the idea of fatherhood anyway. Which will be great for me – but maybe not so good in the long term for Freya.

'Oh, puhleez! Shut the door before I freeze to death,' moans Storm, barging into the kitchen and throwing herself onto a chair. She glances at my burning face. 'Are you having a hot flush or something? Shaz, who we were staying with, has loads and spends most of her life shoving her face into the freezer.'

Exactly how old does Storm think I am?

I close the door and take slimy cod from the fridge while Storm wrinkles her nose and makes a right old fuss about the smell. But it feels good to concentrate on preparing food and the panicky fluttering in my chest starts to ease. There are potatoes to peel and beans to cut and, by the time I hear Josh's car pull up outside, I've convinced myself that the meeting will probably never go ahead. I'm just making a humungous mountain out of a piddly molehill. And right now I need to focus on getting through this meal.

'Hey, Annie. Hi, Storm,' says Josh, coming into the kitchen via the back door and giving the table an admiring nod.

Storm, with encouragement from me, has laid places for five and lit candles that she found in a drawer. They're dripping wax all over the tablecloth but they make the kitchen look warm and cosy.

'Have you gone to all this effort for me?' Josh whispers in my ear, before kissing me briefly on the lips. He smells gorgeous. 'Is there anything I can do to help?'

'No, it's all under control and I'll put the veg on now you're here. Perhaps, Storm, you could tell Barry and Alice that tea will be ready in a few minutes.'

Storm sighs and puts down Alice's magazine that she's only reading, she told me, because Salt Bay is so boring on a Sunday she might lose her mind. As she disappears through the kitchen door, Josh leans in for a lovely, longer kiss before doing a swift count of cutlery on the table.

'So Toby's definitely gone back to London, then.'

'Definitely. I saw him off the premises myself. And Emily called to say she's staying in Penzance until tomorrow morning. I don't think she can face an evening with Storm.'

Josh grins and brushes a strand of hair from my hot cheek. 'So it's just you, me and your family.'

'Afraid so. Can you bear it?'

'Of course. As your boyfriend, it is my solemn duty to get to know your family.' He clicks his heels and grins. 'And I want to support you. Having them turn up hasn't been easy and I feel guilty for not being around to help 'cos of Mum.' Hooking his arm around my waist, he pulls me so close his thick fisherman's jumper tickles my nose. 'Can you forgive me?'

I'm kissing him passionately – purely to show that all is forgiven, obviously – when Storm rushes back in, bashing the door against the wall.

'Can't you get a room?' she grumps, dropping into a chair. 'You two are a bit old for playing tonsil tennis in public.'

Which is exactly the wrong thing to say to my buttoned-up boy-friend, who thinks holding hands in front of people is pushing it. I could cheerfully crown Storm as Josh moves away from me and wipes a hand across his lips. But she's busy staring at Barry, who's appeared in the doorway, looking almost unrecognisable.

His hair is freshly washed and falling in waves to his shoulders, his clean jeans are un-ripped and he's wearing a paisley shirt I haven't seen before. He's making an effort which makes me feel – oh, I don't know, just a bit weird. It's quite touching, I suppose.

'Have you put your best clothes on?' scoffs Storm, picking up her knife and fork and tapping them rhythmically on her Birds of Cornwall tablemat.

'It's my Sunday best, in honour of Annie's young man. Things must be getting serious between you two if you're having tea with the in-laws, eh mate?'

And that's the father I recognise: an expert exponent of the inappropriate comment! Any warm feelings that were stirred up by Barry's clean-up swiftly disappear.

Josh, ignoring his remark, shakes his hand before fetching plates that are warming in the Aga. He lays them out in a line on the worktop while I start unwrapping parcels of fish. Ouch! The foil is piping hot but, hey, searing off my fingerprints is a small price to pay for perfectly cooked food – and this cod would put Delia to shame. Glistening with melted butter, the milk-white flesh falls apart at the touch of a fork and smells delicious. It's such a shame that my stomach is in knots and I've lost my appetite.

As it turns out, tea *en famille* goes far more smoothly than I'd anticipated. No one swears or farts and Barry keeps his inappropriate comments to himself. Even Storm, after having a tentative taste, declares that the cod is 'better than the Filet-O-Fish at McDonald's'. High praise, indeed.

But tensions in the room are hard to ignore. Josh does his best to make small talk with Barry and Storm but he's not properly himself around them. I want them to see the man I fell in love with – the kind, gentle, funny man who sings in the shower and does a brilliant impression of Roger. But he's on his best behaviour and comes across as a bit stiff and stilted.

For some unfathomable reason, I'd also like Josh to think well of Barry and Storm. So Barry making daft comments or Storm rolling her eyes puts my teeth on edge, though I do my best to hide it.

Alice doesn't get involved much at all, once initial small talk is over. Instead, she sits, picking at her fish and saying so little it's hard to know what she's thinking. Life's changed so much for her recently. Just a year ago, she was rattling round in Tregavara House on her own and now she's sharing it with four others, including my odd relatives. Perhaps she misses the peace and regrets ever getting in touch with me.

Suddenly, Alice reaches across the table to pat my hand and, not for the first time, I wonder if she's psychic. I've always thought it's mumbo-jumbo but my great-aunt does have an uncanny ability to judge my mood and offer comfort when it's needed. What will I do when she's no longer around?

Ooh, don't think that. Not now.

'What's wrong with your eyes?' demands Storm as I blink rapidly to ward off tears. 'It's the cod, isn't it? Fish fumes can be toxic. Honest,' she adds, clocking my look of disbelief. 'I learned that at school. Or maybe it wasn't fish… I wasn't really listening, to be honest…' Her voice trails off.

'Did you know that Josh is a teacher?' I ask her, keen to move on from 'killer cod'.

'Nope, though it figures.' She ignores my raised eyebrows and scans Josh up and down. 'So what do you teach, then – maths, physics or some other nerdy subject?'

'I'm terrible at maths and physics and all nerdy subjects. I teach mostly English and a bit of music.'

'Right,' says Storm, looking vaguely impressed, while Barry grins and points at Josh's long fingers.

'I thought as much. Your hands are like mine – the hands of a musician. Annie's got them too.' He waggles his fingers in my face to make his point.

'Actually, Storm, while we're talking about schools—' Josh glances at me and nods '—I'm finding out if you can come to my school for a while, so you don't miss too much while you're in Cornwall.'

Josh's words have an electrifying effect on Storm.

'School? I don't need to go to stupid school!' she splutters, sitting bolt upright and sending a glass flying when she flings out her arm.

'You really do.' Spilled orange juice is snaking across the table and I mop it up with my crumpled serviette. 'You need to go to school to learn and get qualifications or you'll end up in a dead-end job.'

'Like you,' she fires back.

'No, not like me! I went to a lot of different schools and didn't get the qualifications I needed to be a music therapist. But I did well enough and now I'm working at the charity.'

'Which sounds lame.'

'It really isn't. I enjoy my job. And I guess I've ended up doing a bit of music therapy anyway, through running the Choral Society.'

'Now that is la—'

I hold up my hand and cut her off before she can use the 'L' word again. 'You need to go to school, Storm, whether that's back in London or here.'

'I hate school,' she moans, sticking out her bottom lip like a sulky toddler.

'You and lots of people.'

'No, I mean I really, *really* hate it.'

She sniffs and rubs the back of her hand across her nose, leaving a streak of foundation on her skin.

'You must miss your friends at school.'

'Not really. I don't have that many.'

She's trying to sound off-hand, as though she doesn't care, but she can't kid me. Making friends is hard and keeping them even harder when your home life is in disarray. It makes you lonely.

'What do you think, Barry?' asks Josh.

Barry shrugs. 'I think if you can get Storm to go to school, you're a better man than me. Maybe she could be educated at home. I bet we could teach her everything she needs to know between us. Me for music, Josh here for English, Emily for cooking, Alice for manners, Annie for… charity stuff.'

His suggestion – the worst suggestion in the history of mankind – hangs in the air.

'Of course Storm must go to school if she's going to be in Salt Bay for a while.' It's the first time Alice has spoken for ages and takes us by surprise. She frowns, caught in the glow from a candle that's almost spent. 'There should be no debate about it. Storm must go to school and thank you, Josh, for organising it.'

Storm sinks lower in her seat and looks so upset I feel guilty for suggesting school in the first place. Flaming Kayla and her woo-woo reverse psychology! I know Storm can't bunk off forever if she and Barry insist on sticking around. But I suddenly remember what it's like to be the new girl in a new school: bitchy girls huddling together in cliques, in-jokes that make no sense, maze-like buildings. A shiver goes down my spine and I send up silent thanks that my schooldays are long gone.

Discussing school has put a real damper on the evening and Alice soon excuses herself and heads for the sitting room. Storm slopes off to listen to music in her bedroom and Barry follows Alice to watch TV. He's delighted when I turn down his offer of helping with the washing up; far more delighted than Alice will be when he starts commenting on her recorded episode of *Corrie*.

'Looks like it's just you and me, Pasco, doing the washing up.'

I grin at Josh and squirt Fairy Liquid into the deep enamel sink that's filling with hot water. Tiny translucent bubbles start clinging together in wispy clumps.

'It's fortunate, then, that one of my many talents is cleaning crud from crockery,' says Josh, scraping leftovers into the bin, his sense of humour staging a comeback now my family's left the room. Typical.

Josh piles plates, glasses and cutlery onto the worktop while I scrub them clean and refill the sink when the water gets too greasy. Phew, it's hot work! When I win the lottery, my first purchase will be a spanking new dishwasher for Alice's kitchen.

After a while, when Josh doesn't offer his opinion, I ask, 'What do you think of my new family then? Can you see why they freak me out?'

'A new family turning up would freak anyone out,' he concedes, tea towel in hand. 'But they're not too bad.'

'Really?' When I swing round, greasy water arcs off my rubber gloves and spatters across the floor tiles. 'Barry is weird and Storm is awful.'

'But apart from that…' Josh gives his sexy grin that turns my legs to jelly. 'Honestly, Annie, Storm's no worse than other kids at my school who've had a chaotic upbringing. And Barry's just one of a kind. A bit like you.' He ducks when I flick water at him. 'But I can see that it'll be better for you – for us, really – when they go back to London.'

'But we're OK, aren't we?'

'Um, yeah. Why?' Josh pauses half-way through drying one of Alice's serving dishes, which is a gorgeous pale green colour and ages old.

'Nothing. It's just something that Toby said.'

Josh's face clouds over and I immediately regret letting Toby's parting comment get under my skin.

'What did he say?'

'Nothing. Not really. He just mentioned that you and I didn't seem to be getting on quite as well. But what does he know?' I give a forced laugh, plunging my hands so far into the sink, greasy water floods the inside of my gloves. Ugh, that feels slimy and disgusting!

'As usual, Toby is talking out of his arse,' says Josh with a scowl. 'I can't believe you're taking any notice of a man whose idea of a relationship is seducing a teenager and abandoning her when she gets pregnant.'

'I'm not,' I protest, stripping off my clammy gloves. 'But it's just…'

Shut up, Annie! screams my inner voice. *Put a great big sock in it, right now.* Which, with hindsight, is fabulous advice but I'm so used to my inner voice being a right bitch, I ignore it.

'… it's just that we're spending so little time together and, when we do get to meet up, you seem distracted and not very affectionate. Not when we're around people anyway.'

Josh carefully places Alice's serving dish on the table and sighs. 'I'm tired, what with everything that's going on in my life, and it's just the way I am. Just because I'm not snogging you senseless in public, doesn't mean I don't feel things. I can't be like Ollie, Annie.'

'I know, and I don't want you to be like Ollie. But I just wonder why it's so hard for you sometimes to show how you feel.'

'Why on earth do you women need a reason for everything?'

Which is a *leetle* bit general and sexist but I let it go, seeing as I'm the eejit who kick-started this conversation.

Josh rubs a hand across his tired eyes. 'Look, my dad died of a heart attack when I was a child and then my stepdad drowned when I was a teenager and I had to keep things together while people around me were falling apart. Maybe that made me – I don't know – shut down a bit. Or maybe that's just psycho-babble balls.' He sighs. 'It's just the way I am, Annie. I've always been reserved around people. I've never worn my heart on my sleeve and I never will, even though it seems the whole world wants to emote these days. The important thing is that we want to be together and we trust each other. Isn't that enough?'

'Of course it is,' I cry, flinging myself into his arms and hugging him tight. Mostly because there's nothing else I'd rather do, but partly because scorching hot guilt zapped through me when he mentioned trust, and I don't want him to see it in my face.

I could tell him now about the meeting with Freya. But he'd only try to stop it and I still think, on balance, that it's best for her to meet Toby soon – while she's young enough to get her head round it. She doesn't want to end up like me in twenty-five years' time, with some random bloke invading her life.

Plus, I've already inflicted a double whammy on Josh this evening by bringing up Toby, and then accusing him of being cold. *And he's so fraught and tired at the moment, it might be three strikes and you're out,* chips in my inner voice. Oh, great, the bitch is back.

I snuggle into Josh's itchy sweater and clamp my lips tightly shut.

Chapter Seventeen

Josh doesn't stay over on Sunday and, though we text several times over the next couple of days, we don't manage to meet up. Emily returned from Penzance, looking like death with a filthy cold, so I've been rushing back from work to care for her and Alice. And Josh has been busy at school, keeping an eye on Marion and private tutoring in the evenings.

Life in Salt Bay is more hectic than when I was hurtling across London between jobs and social events. Though that's not surprising. Back then, it was just me and now my days are jam-packed with people. So many people. Too many fricking people. Even when I do manage to snatch some time to myself, my head is full of Barry and Storm – why they're here and when they're going to leave. There's no escape.

By Wednesday I'm desperate to see Josh so I get to the church stupidly early for the next rehearsal of the choral society. And my punctuality is rewarded when Josh rushes in just after seven o'clock, work bag slung over his shoulder. No one else has arrived yet so Josh makes a beeline for me and pulls me into his arms. Ooh, that feels lovely. He's almost crushing me and I can hear the *thump-thump* of his heart through his soft grey sweatshirt.

'I've missed you,' I mumble into his chest.

'Me too.' Josh puts his fingers under my chin, tilts up my face and kisses me. The kiss goes on for ages. I have so missed this. We should be getting the church ready for the rehearsal but he pulls me onto a pew and we sit side by side with fingers entwined and hips touching.

'How's your mum?' I ask, nudging my arm against his.

'Not feeling too good. We're making sure one of us is with her almost all the time because she gets anxious on her own. And I'm still on detention duty so I'm getting home late, and I've had loads of marking to do. And the kids at school are horrendously hyped up with Christmas just around the corner. Roll on the holiday – I'm knackered.'

He yawns deeply and I yawn in sympathy.

'Poor old you. Things will improve and we'll have more time together when your mum's better and Barry and Storm are back in London.'

'No date set for their departure yet then?'

When I shake my head, Josh's lovely mouth sets into a tight line. 'They're not coming tonight, are they?'

'They reckoned they might. Storm said that listening to us lot caterwauling was better than listening to Barry farting in front of the telly, which is what counts as a compliment from a teenager.'

Although I laugh, Josh doesn't and my stomach lurches. I really don't want him to get grumpy about my family during the little time we have together. I don't want them leaching into every precious area of my life.

Josh sees my face fall and puts his arm around my shoulder. 'Sorry, Annie. I'm just tired. Of course it's fine if they do come along but we'll just need to make sure Barry and Roger are as far away from each other as possible. We don't want any punch-ups with the semi-finals coming up.'

'Don't remind me,' I complain, snuggling into his sweatshirt. 'I feel nervous enough already.'

I've been anxious since an email arrived, a few days ago, informing me that competition judge Mr Simeon Kerroway would be arriving at ten o'clock a week on Saturday to hear us sing 'in situ'. The competition organisers are trialling a new way of choosing choirs to take part in the Grand Final in Truro, on the second Saturday before Christmas. We're in the 'New Choirs' category because there wasn't one for 'Resurrected Choral Societies'.

'It'll be fine,' murmurs Josh, leaning in for another kiss. But he pulls back and jumps up when the church door creaks open and Arthur and Fiona march in. They're closely followed by Pippa and Charlie, hand in hand, and Kayla, who's arguing loudly with Roger.

Other singers shuffle in soon afterwards – Cyril, Gerald, Emily with a bright red nose, who's refused to give the rehearsal a miss – and I've just started thinking maybe Barry isn't coming when in he walks, with Storm trailing behind him. Roger's face crumples into a scowl and even gentle Mary looks fed up. I know how they feel.

'Oh, brother!' Josh is carrying a chair past me and plonks it at the edge of the tenors, six people away from Roger. 'Barry, come and sit here,' he calls, motioning to the empty seat and ignoring an icy stare from Jennifer, whose chair is next to it.

Oh dear, a Barry-Jennifer combo could cause fireworks but, quite frankly, being the buffer between my family and the rest of the freaking world is wearing me out.

'Do you think he'll be OK next to Jennifer?' mutters Josh out of the corner of his mouth as he walks past me with the music stand.

'How should I know? She'll just have to suck it up.'

Josh frowns and shrugs. 'All right. I was only asking.'

'Sorry, I didn't mean to snap. Do you forgive me?'

But Josh doesn't reply and I'm not sure if it's because he didn't hear or if he's ignoring me.

Storm has taken her usual seat at the back of the church and gives me a wan smile as I approach her.

'No, I do not want to sing in your stupid choir.'

'Then why the hell are you here?'

Oops, my irritation is not under control this evening.

Storm yanks her black scarf tighter around her neck. 'What was I going to do instead? Sit and watch Alice staring at old-lady TV soaps? I'm missing all of my favourite programmes while I'm stuck here. You haven't even got MTV.' She pouts and gives an exaggerated shiver. 'Mind you, it's warmer back at Tregie-whatsitsname House.'

'If you are here, then at least make yourself useful by helping Michaela with her music. You can be her page-turner.'

'Wow, that sounds absolutely fascinating,' murmurs Storm in a monotone, but at least she stands up as though she might help. Then she glances at my face and smirks. 'I wondered why you rushed off early without us.'

'What do you mean?'

Nodding towards Josh, she wipes her fingers gently along her lips and chin. 'Stubble rash.'

Balls! That's the problem with designer stubble. It's sexy as hell on good-looking men but, when you snog them, it's a tell-tale sign. A beacon of shame. Like walking round with your jumper on back to front after you've been upstairs at a party. No wonder Jennifer gave me a straight look when I handed over her music. I'm now acutely aware of my chin, though my whole face is currently flaming bright red so any stubble rash should just blend in.

I'll have to brazen it out. With my hand over my chin, like I'm thinking deep thoughts, I stride to the podium (really a wooden crate donated by Maureen from her tea shop), pick up the baton that once belonged to Josh's stepdad, and the rehearsal gets underway.

It goes pretty well, considering. Barry can read music so he manages quite well, singing-wise, and he only sniggers once when Jennifer hits a high note and gives it extra vibrato. Just 'cos she can.

Everyone else is in pretty good voice, too. Even Ollie, who's standing next to Kayla and holding her hand in front of the whole choir. Which is really sweet, though Kayla seems distracted and out of sorts.

Josh and I take turns to conduct and we all go over and over the two pieces we'll be singing until we're more or less note-perfect. And, as an old sea shanty echoes round the church in four-part harmony, I start believing that perhaps we won't fall flat on our faces a week on Saturday. And maybe, just maybe, we could make it all the way to the Kernow Choral Crown finals. What a fabulous Christmas present that would be for the village.

The only fly in the ointment is Emily, who's very noble and all that for dragging herself out of her sick bed to rehearse, but she's coughing and spluttering all over the sopranos and if she gives them her germs before the competition, I'll kill her. People gradually move away from her until she's standing on her own – a little island of contagion.

She keeps gazing at Jay, who's the real reason for her being here, but his eyes are firmly fixed on Storm at the piano. Storm is supposed to be turning over the music whenever Michaela nods, but she keeps losing concentration and Michaela has taken to gently kicking her in the shins at the appropriate moment.

Every now and then, when she thinks no one is looking, Storm joins in with the choir. Her face softens as she sings along, hardly moving her lips, and I catch a glimpse of a vulnerable teenager lurking beneath layers of mistrust and stroppiness. Which is freaking awesome – I know music is powerful but it must be turbo-charged to break through Storm's brittle shell. Cyril catches my eye and winks while Josh is conducting and I grin back at him. He's noticed too.

*

At the end of the rehearsal, people break into two groups and either head for the comfort of home or a pint at the pub. Barry's gagging for a drink but his plans are scuppered by Storm complaining that being so close to the piano has given her a headache. Fabulous! Not that my half-sister is in pain, obviously. But Barry bends under the weight of her nagging and agrees to give the pub a miss and take her home. Which means that Josh and I can spend a blessed hour together – minus my family and his. It feels like Christmas has come early.

Josh holds my hand on the way to the Whistling Wave. It's dark and chilly, with a stiff breeze coming off the sea, but I leave my gloves in my pocket because I'd rather feel his skin against mine.

'Lucy's home 'cos she's working days at the moment so I can stay over tonight, if you like,' he whispers in my ear as we're walking past the green. Enid hasn't pulled her curtains and lamplight from her window is glinting and scattering across the dark river.

'I would like that very much,' I murmur back, feeling a shudder of excitement. 'We'll have to be quiet. I don't want Storm taking the mickey because my boyfriend is staying over, or Barry making lewd comments.'

'Yes, ma'am.' Josh lets go of my hand and does a mock salute. 'I'll creep home with you and creep out again before anyone gets up. It can be a secret assignation, which sounds very sexy. Like you.'

He bends his head and kisses me but, as we're still walking, his lips miss my mouth and brush against my cold nose.

At the pub, Josh holds the door open for me before ducking to avoid the low beam across the doorway. It's toasty warm inside, and festive, thanks to reams of colourful paper chains looping across the ceiling – the lick-and-stick kind of chains that decorated our flats when I was growing up. Mum didn't really do Christmas. It was a 'bourgeois bonanza of consumer consumption', according to her. But she'd nip to Woolies to buy me a few packs of the chains each December and, even now, the taste of glue takes me right back.

Gerald and Arthur are singing quietly at the bar, practising a tricky part we went over in the rehearsal, but they break off to wave and smile at us. That gives me such a rosy glow – I'm beginning to feel properly accepted in this tiny community, and I don't want anything to spoil it.

'The usual?' yells Kayla, who's already back behind the bar. Roger, the old curmudgeon, doesn't like giving his staff time off and only allows Kayla two hours tops for each rehearsal. When I nod, she shouts, 'Grab a seat and I'll bring them over.'

Josh and I find a table towards the back of the bar and I snuggle into a cosy window nook that's lined with cushions, while he takes a seat opposite me. The pub walls are thick and insulating but draughts are snaking in through the old window frame so I take off my jacket but keep my scarf on.

'No Emily, then?' asks Kayla, carrying a tray with Josh's pint and my gin and tonic.

'She went back with Barry and Storm because her cold's still bad.'

'Tell me about it! Her germs were hitting the back of my neck and are making baby germs in my hair at this very moment.' Kayla takes the tenner proffered by Josh. 'Thanks. I'll bring your change over in a minute. Actually—' she glances at Roger, who's busy at the bar '—are you both around for a while?'

'We're going to have a quick drink and then Josh is coming back to mine.'

'I'm going to be busy all evening by the looks of things but I wanted a quiet word, Annie.'

'Sure. Is it about the being tied down thing?'

Kayla raises her eyebrows as Josh splutters into his pint. 'No, it's not, and Annie isn't talking about my sadomasochistic sexual practices, Josh.'

'I never thought for a moment that she was,' he grins, wiping beer-froth from his chin.

'What it is, is that I'm just a bit worried about you,' says Kayla, indicating that I should squidge up against the bumpy whitewashed wall so she can slip into the window seat next to me.

'Why?'

'It's Barry and Storm.'

'Yeah, I'm sorry about the whole Boozegate thing. Storm was out of order and it won't happen again.'

I take a big slug of gin and reflect on the fact that, even when Barry and Storm don't come to the pub, it seems impossible to escape them. But Kayla waves her hand dismissively.

'Oh, I'm over that. I'm just generally worried that you're being a bit—' She pauses. 'I'm not quite sure how to say this.'

'Just go for it!' I sigh, half-draining my glass. 'Everyone else seems to.'

'OK. I'm worried that you're being a wuss and your new family are taking advantage. 'Cos they're awful,' she adds, for good measure.

Have I mentioned that Kayla is one of the most direct people I've ever met? Even my friend Maura, who once told me that my arse in tight jeans resembled a sack of ferrets, pales in comparison.

'Bit harsh,' mutters Josh, covering my hand with his.

'But it has to be said. Barry and Storm turn up and stay with you for ages and you don't really know who they are.'

'He really is my father, Kayla.'

'Yeah, that's obvious, 'cos of the eyes.' Kayla points at my face, just in case I have any doubts about where my eyes are. 'And also 'cos of the stuff he knows about your mum. And I know they're your family and Alice invited them to stay. But they're stressing you out, Annie, and I don't understand why you can't just ask them to leave.'

Because I'm curious about them? Because, after years of only Mum, it's nice to have a father around – even when that father is Barry? Or because it's true, I am a wuss?

'What do you think, Josh?' asks Kayla, when I don't answer.

'Whoah! Don't bring me into this. They're Annie's family and they seemed all right when we had tea together.' He shakes his head and goes in for another gulp of his beer.

'But you said you were worried too,' insists Kayla, leaning across the table towards him.

Josh flushes slightly and puts down his pint. 'Not worried exactly. I just said that Barry and Storm were making life a bit difficult and it would be easier once they've gone back home.'

He squeezes my hand but I slide it away and place it in my lap. Does he think I'm being a wuss too?

'There's really no need for you both to be concerned,' I say primly. 'I know Barry and Storm are causing ripples in Salt Bay but they're family and I'm not going to make them leave, not like my grandparents did to Mum when she was pregnant with me.'

Aha, lightbulb moment! Is that why I can't bring myself to insist they sling their hook?

'I'm not saying you should ask them to go but this has nothing to do with what happened thirty years ago,' says Josh, brushing a thick strand of black hair from his forehead.

'Maybe not but I want to behave better than my grandparents did. And what about you? You're making huge sacrifices for your family.'

'That's different.'

'It's not that much different. You're working hard to help provide for them, you've taken on private tutoring as well, and you give up what's left of your free time to look after your mum.'

'She's ill!' splutters Josh.

'I know and of course you should stay home and look after her. You're doing the right thing, but I'm just saying that you've given up a lot for your family. Moving back in with them even broke up your relationship with Felicity, for goodness' sake.'

'Here we go.' Josh kicks back his chair and stretches out his long legs. 'I wondered when Felicity would come into this.'

'Felicity? Why is Felicity coming into this?' squeaks Kayla nervously, suddenly realising she's poked a wasps' nest with a very big stick.

'Felicity answered the phone when I rang Josh on Saturday.'

'Ooh, did she?' Kayla's head swivels towards my boyfriend, who's glaring at me.

'Felicity answered the phone because she was visiting my mum.'

'She probably visits a lot but you've never mentioned it.'

'I didn't think it was important.'

Kayla picks up the tray and holds it flat against her chest like a shield. 'Come on, guys, probably best not to talk about this now.'

I ignore her. 'You didn't think it was important to mention that you've been meeting up with the girlfriend you lived with for two years?'

'I've not been meeting her. I've just happened to be around a few times when she's called in.'

'Yeah, funny that.'

'I live there!' Josh is almost shouting now.

'Come on, you two,' says Kayla in an overly bright tone. 'We can chat about this another day when we're not all so sung-out and tired. We'll laugh about it!'

She gives a fake laugh to prove her point. But Josh ignores her too.

'You should trust me. Like I trust you not to do a runner back to London one day when things here get too complicated for you.'

'That's cheap! You know there was a load of stuff going on in my life at the time, and I came back, didn't I? I gave up everything to come back to you and Salt Bay.'

Actually, 'everything' amounted to a lonely life in a rented flat with a dodgy boiler, but that's by the by.

'I'm honoured and just hope you think it was worth it.' Josh stands up so quickly his chair wobbles back and forth on the uneven flagstones. 'There's enough going on in my life right now, Annie, and I can't deal with this. Let's talk about it when we've all calmed down.' As he sweeps past, he pauses to air-kiss me on the cheek. 'I'll ring you tomorrow at work.'

The buzz of conversation in the bar falters when Josh leaves the pub. It's pretty obvious that he and I were arguing – our testy words still seem to hang in the air.

'Well,' says Kayla, folding her arms as the pub door bangs shut. 'It looks like the shag's off then.'

The spell is broken and everyone goes back to their drinks and conversations. Roger gives me a grumpy nod and Jennifer, across the other side of the bar, half-raises her hand at me before looking away.

Sighing, I punch Kayla none too gently on the arm. 'What on earth possessed you to have a go at me in the pub?'

'I wasn't having a go. I was giving some friendly advice because I care about you loads and you're starting to look really stressed.'

'But look what you did!'

'I think you did that all on your own, Sunshine. Mind you, that boyfriend of yours can really go off on one. He's so intense. Actually, I quite fancy him when he gets all glowery. Ollie's never like that.'

'I don't want my boyfriend being glowery, thank you, Kayla, and I'm doing my best with Barry and Storm which isn't easy. I could do with your support, rather than being slagged off.'

It's the first time ever that Kayla and I have had cross words and her cheeks flush bright pink. 'Sorry. I s'pose I didn't handle it very well,' she mumbles.

'No, you didn't. And you're such a hypocrite 'cos you don't get on brilliantly with your family either.'

'That's true,' she concedes, taking a sip of Josh's abandoned pint. 'My smug sisters are a freaking nightmare but we get on great when we're ten thousand miles apart. You should try some distance with Barry and Storm.'

'Or maybe you should try to get to know my family better.'

'Hhmm, maybe,' says Kayla, sounding unconvinced.

She shuffles up close and puts her arm around my shoulder and, although I'm still cross with her, I let myself be hugged for a moment. Why did I overreact and argue with Josh? There's still a faint tang of his aftershave in the air where he leant down to kiss my cheek. But that's all there is of him – minuscule molecules that are fading fast.

Downing the rest of my drink in one, I say goodnight to Kayla and head for home just in case Josh is waiting outside the pub. Perhaps he's had a change of heart and we'll laugh and hug. And he'll come back to Tregavara House and we'll have fabulous – but exceedingly quiet – make-up sex in my double bed, with its swirly metal bedframe that looks like it's wrapped in seaweed. But there's nothing outside apart from a chill wind blowing off a black sea.

Pulling on my gloves, I trudge back to Tregavara House, feeling glum. Summer in Salt Bay was brilliant, with sparkling blue seas, tourists everywhere scoffing ice creams, and glorious blazing sunsets over the cliffs. Josh and I wandered for miles, hand in hand. But now it's *Game of Thrones* in Salt Bay – Winter Is Coming, and even the pretty Christmas lights springing up around the village can't lift my mood.

Chapter Eighteen

Work is a great distraction when I'm feeling low. Chatting about *Line of Duty* with my colleagues, or what Christmas presents we'd buy if money was no object, can keep a low mood at bay. But today, all the chatting isn't helping. I'm too agitated to concentrate on the meeting I'm supposed to be arranging for Celia, and Gayle and Lesley's inane chatter about *Doctor Who* and which Doctor is the best is driving me nuts. Everyone knows it's David Tennant. That's a no-brainer.

The truth is, I'm on tenterhooks waiting for Josh to call. I know I could call him; I'm not some tragic pre-feminist who needs 'her man' to do all the running. But he said he would call and I wonder if he will. Mind you, there's only so long I can hold out before making the first move – I'll give him until one o'clock.

I'm staring unseeingly at my computer screen and trying to block out the chatter when my office phone rings. Snatching up the receiver, it's halfway to my ear before I notice that the displayed number is internal. Balls! It can't be Josh then.

'Anna?' Sonia on Reception insists on calling me Anna, however many times I correct her. 'There's someone here to see you.'

My heart leaps. Josh hasn't rung because he's rushed over in his lunch break instead to take me in his arms and declare his undying love. He is the most wonderful, amazing boyfriend.

But Sonia swiftly stamps on my dreams. 'I'll tell her you'll be right down.'

'Her?'

'Yeah, a pretty young girl. I didn't get her name but she said it was important.'

It might be Emily or Storm with bad news about Alice. Rushing out of the office, I fly down the stairs to Reception, but it's not Storm or Emily waiting for me by the coffee machine. Lucy looks up as I barrel through the door and gives me a nervous smile. She's clasping a polystyrene cup but carefully slides it back into the cup-holder.

'Lucy, is everything all right? It's not your mum, is it?'

'No, Mum's OK. She's got some friends round to cheer her up.'

'And Josh? Is he all right?'

'He's fine, just tired and grumpy. Nothing's wrong really. I just needed to speak to you.'

She glances over at Sonia behind the glass Reception desk. Her head is bent over a laptop and she's clicking away with the mouse but she must be able to make out our conversation.

'It's about Toby,' Lucy mouths at me.

Of course it is. Resignation settles on me like a suffocating blanket as I realise there's no more dodging the conversation I've been avoiding for days. But it can't happen here where we can be overheard.

'Give me a minute to grab my bag and we can go and get a quick coffee.'

Lucy starts zipping up her long, padded coat. 'Thanks, Annie. It won't take long.'

Freezing rain has started falling so Lucy and I head for a small coffee shop just a few doors down from the office. The café smells of wet dog and condensation is running down the plate-glass window facing onto the grey street. But it's noisy and anonymous and perfect for spilling secrets in private.

The place is heaving with mums and fractious babies, but we find a tiny table squeezed into a corner and I negotiate an obstacle course of pushchairs with dripping rain-covers to get to the counter.

'Yes, my darling, what can I get for you?' The skinny man in a Santa hat who's operating the coffee machine winces at an ear-mauling scream. 'The mum and baby group down the road has just chucked out so you might need earplugs with your cappuccinos.'

He grins as he makes me two coffees and places them on a grubby tray. 'Do you want any food with that?'

I shake my head and pay, not wanting to prolong this meeting any more than is necessary. When I wend my way back to the table, Lucy is staring into space, seemingly oblivious to the cacophony around us.

'Thanks.' She takes a sip of the coffee and frowns as the steaming liquid hits her top lip. 'I'm really sorry to interrupt you at work but I needed to talk to you about things. About Toby. And I was in Penzance anyway and thought face to face would be better.' She puts down her cup and starts twisting a silver ring on her middle finger around and around. 'I heard he was staying with you last weekend and I wondered if you'd had a chance to speak to him about—' she checks that no one is listening in '—what we talked about.'

There's really no need for Lucy to talk in vague terms in case of eavesdroppers. I'm directly opposite and can hardly hear her.

'I did mention Freya,' I shout, enunciating extra clearly in case she's lip-reading.

When Lucy swallows hard, it's impossible to tell if she's relieved or nervous. She slides her chair around the table, across the pocked vinyl flooring, until her shiny black hair brushes against my damp, brown frizz.

'And what did he say?'

A young mum in front of me, red-eyed with exhaustion, feeds her daughter morsels of cake as I decide on my next words. I'm at a crossroads and don't know which path to take. Would it be so awful to say Toby doesn't want to meet Freya? Then I could tell Toby that Lucy rejected the idea of a meeting between father and daughter, and things would get back to normal. Freya isn't missing much and Toby probably wouldn't really care.

'What did he say, Annie?' Lucy narrows her eyes as if she can read my mind. 'I know this puts you in a difficult position but I truly think it's best for Freya and all of us, including Josh.'

The paths are still there in front of me, offering a way out of this mess. But I'm too embroiled in this to start telling untruths and influencing life-changing decisions. Plus, I am the world's worst liar. Lucy would see through me in a heartbeat.

'He said he'd be up for meeting Freya. At least once.'

Tension leaches from Lucy's pale face and her shoulders drop. 'That's good. So we just need to set up a meeting and get him more involved in being responsible for his daughter.'

'We can't do something like that without telling Josh.'

'We have to!' Lucy grabs my hand and squeezes really tight. Ouch! She's stronger than she looks. 'If we tell him, he'll go nuclear and the meeting will never happen. How will Freya feel about her uncle when she grows up and finds out he stopped her meeting her father?'

I regard Lucy coolly across our steaming coffees. What do I really know about her, apart from the fact she had a secret relationship at seventeen with Toby, and Freya was the result? Although Lucy and I lived in the same cottage for months, she kept herself to herself and made no effort to make friends. I put it down to my surname bringing up bad memories and a general lack of trust after falling pregnant so young and being abandoned. It must have an effect when your hopes and plans for the future are so irredeemably knocked off course. But though I'm sure that's partly true, there's a determined, manipulative streak to Lucy that I've not seen before.

'So, what do you think, Annie? Will you help me do the best thing for my daughter, so she gets to meet her father a lot earlier than you did?'

Lucy looks younger and kinder when she smiles and it crosses my mind that I'm judging her too harshly. Her life hasn't been easy and, going on the screaming babies in this café, motherhood is absolutely frigging awful.

'I guess so,' I tell her. 'I'll speak to Toby.'

'And you won't tell Josh, at least not until after the first meeting? After that, we can tell him together. When it's a done deal.'

'OK,' I whisper, feeling sick as Lucy pushes her half-finished coffee to one side and starts pushing her arms into her coat.

'My shift starts at two so I'd better make a move. Thanks for the coffee and thank you for helping with the meeting. This is honestly the best thing for Freya, Annie.'

'I know or I wouldn't be doing it.'

Lucy smiles and hesitates after she gets to her feet, as though she's about to kiss me goodbye. But she gives an awkward little wave instead before weaving her way between the pushchairs and out of the door. The window is so steamed up, she's nothing but a navy-blue blur when she hurries past in the direction of the bus station.

I scrape lukewarm froth from my coffee with a teaspoon and shove the spoon into my mouth. The good news is that I'm no longer dithering at the crossroads, wondering which way to go. The bad news is that I may have taken the Road to Hell.

*

Back at work, my concentration is completely shot and I manage to double-book Celia. She's game for packing as much as possible into her working day but a meeting at ten o'clock in Truro followed by another fifteen minutes later in Penzance is beyond even Superwoman. I'm trying to sort out the muddle when my mobile buzzes into life.

It's Josh – hallelujah! Grabbing the phone, I hurry into the corridor before answering. Gayle and Lesley are already curious about my sudden departure to the coffee shop and don't need anything else to gossip about.

'Annie?' Josh sounds anxious when I answer his call. 'Can you talk?'

'Yes, of course.'

There's a pause before we both say 'I'm sorry' at exactly the same time and start laughing. I'm perching on a windowsill and cup the phone to my ear using both hands, as though I'm caressing it. Outside, the rain has stopped and a ray of pale, wintry sunlight shines on the salt-streaked window.

'I am sorry, Annie. I don't want to fight with you and I shouldn't have discussed you with Kayla but we're worried about their effect on you.'

'I know and I didn't mean to be so touchy. I'm just tired out with everything that's going on.' I lower my voice as Gayle wanders past, trying hard not to look as if she's listening in. 'I didn't mean what I said about you looking after your mum. I love Marion and of course you should take care of her. And I know Felicity is only visiting her.'

I leave that hanging in the air, waiting for Josh to offer confirmation, but he moves on without addressing it.

'So are we good, Annabella Sunshine Trebarwith, or is my afternoon going to be as miserable as my morning? Please bear in mind, before you answer, that I'm teaching 8G in half an hour and that's going to be hell enough.'

'Of course we're good and I can't wait to see you.'

'Me too. Let's meet up tomorrow night. Lucy will be around so maybe we can get away from our families for an hour or two and then I can stay at yours.'

'That would be lovely.'

'It's a date. I've got to go because I'm on playground duty but I'll see you tomorrow. And Annie, let's make sure we talk about everything from now on so there aren't any more misunderstandings. Is that a deal?'

'Of course. It's a deal.'

My words sound a bit strangled but I'm not sure Josh heard them anyway because a loud bell is ringing at Trecaldwith School.

'See you tomorrow, Annie,' he yells. 'I can't wait.'

After he's rung off, I sit for a while with my cheek resting against the cold window. Josh called me and he loves me. He didn't actually use the word 'love' but that's what he meant because 'I'm sorry' can be code for 'I love you' sometimes.

Gayle is wandering back along the corridor and does a double take when she spots me with my cheek pressed up against the grimy glass.

'Is everything all right?' She waves an open bag of sweets under my nose. 'I raided the vending machine 'cos I was in urgent need of a sugar rush. I've got shocking PMT.'

I nod, take a sweet and pop it into my mouth. Chocolate starts melting on my tongue and coating my teeth but I'm hardly aware of it. Gayle looks at me closely as she fishes in the bag for another sugar hit.

'Have you sorted things out with your hunky boyfriend then?'

'How did you know that—?'

'I've been around the block a few times, love. Plus, you've been like a bear with a sore head all morning. But if everything's sorted now, that's great. You don't want to break up with someone just before Christmas and miss out on a gift.'

She grins and I reciprocate with a chocolatey smile that doesn't reach my eyes.

My tiff with Josh is resolved with no harm done. However, following my chat with Lucy, there's a bigger problem looming. I'm trying to do what's best for everyone but, as Mum would say after doing something ill-advised, I've got myself into a bit of a pickle.

Chapter Nineteen

Josh comes round on Friday night and is tired so we spend the entire evening in my room – with a chair wedged against the door to thwart Storm's penchant for bursting into rooms without knocking.

But everyone leaves us alone for once which means I'm able to enjoy spending time with the man I love. It's fabulous lying in his arms on the bed, watching a James Bond DVD, laughing and talking about everything, except family. And the make-up sex is so amazing it almost makes falling out worthwhile.

Lucy's on Marion duty the next day, and Josh only has a couple of private tutoring sessions, so he's able to spend much of the weekend at Tregavara House. It's a full house, with Alice, Emily, Barry and Storm around, but we all tiptoe round one another being ultra polite.

That's only derailed when Josh tells Storm that she has a place at his school from Monday. This news tips her into a foul mood and prompts such an eye-rolling extravaganza, I'm seriously worried about long-lasting visual impairment. Plus, there's a lot of door banging until she calms down and slips into a sulky silence.

All in all, it's not the most relaxing of weekends but at least Josh and I get to spend time together and, mostly, I manage to put the Toby/Freya dilemma out of my mind.

I'm getting much better at squashing down guilt and bad feelings – on the plus side, I am getting loads of practice – and when Toby rings me on Monday evening, I bail out completely. Alice shouts for me to come and take his call but I stay cocooned in my room and pretend later that I didn't hear her.

Does that count as being a wuss? Probably. But if something's bothering you, ram your head into the sand right up to your shoulders. That's the life lesson that's working for me right now.

Wednesday evening's choir rehearsal – before judge Mr Kerroway arrives in three days' time – is dreadful. That's the only word for it, apart from appalling. Emily has recovered from her cold and Maureen brings mini Christmas puddings from her tea shop. But everyone is tetchy and nothing goes right – even Jennifer sounds off-key, though I'd never dare tell her that.

I cling grimly to the old adage that a bad dress rehearsal signposts a fabulous performance on the day. That's probably nothing more than wishful thinking from desperate conductors, directors and performers down the ages. But it helps to calm my whirling brain and ease my nightmares. Salt Bay Choral Society *has* to do well, to honour its singers who drowned so many years ago. So no pressure, then.

*

Saturday dawns bright and clear, a crisp day in Salt Bay, and I enjoy the walk from Tregavara House to the church. The few remaining leaves are fluttering from trees in the sea breeze and the sky is a bright china blue.

Cold air hits the bottom of my lungs as I stride along. The air is so fresh here you can almost taste the ozone, and it's a world away from the bad-breath gusts belching from Tube tunnels. That can't be good for you. My skin in London always had a micro-layer coating of grime whereas here my face is soft and glowing. London friend Maura, who visited me a few weeks ago, described my look as '*Countryfile* meets

Charlie Dimmock' and I'll take that, even though I'm not sure she meant it as a compliment.

Quickening my pace through the tumbled-down churchyard, I push open the heavy church door and step inside. I'm alone and the bang of the closing door echoes high into the gloomy rafters. Light is streaming through the stained glass window behind the altar and throwing rainbow patches onto worn flagstones but we're still going to need the lights on so Mr Kerroway can see us. Jeez, I hope he likes us. With my stomach churning, I flick on the lights and arrange chairs from the vestry into a double-rowed semicircle.

'You're bright and early, Sunshine.'

Kayla's voice startles me and the music scores under my arm flutter onto the flagstones.

'Sorry. Didn't mean to make you jump,' she laughs, scooping up the music and dropping it on top of the piano. Her red hair is flying everywhere. Usually she ties it back but, today, rust-red curls are tumbling over her shoulders. 'It's the big day then.'

'Don't say that!'

'OK. It's just a normal Saturday during which it is imperative that we get through to the final of the Kernow Choral Crown. It's life and death!' She spots my expression and pouts. 'Well, maybe life and death is a bit over the top. Honestly, Annie, I'm just joking. We'll either be awful or we won't. It's nothing to get worried about.'

'I guess not. But I'm going to feel as if I've failed if we don't get through.'

'That's daft. It's only a local competition.'

'A competition that the original Salt Bay Choral Society won just before the Great Storm wrecked everything. I don't want to let the old choir down. Or the new choir. Or the community.'

'C'mon mate, you're overthinking. And you're definitely hyperventilating.' Kayla pushes me into a pew and sits beside me. 'I was only joking. It's really not that big a deal.'

'It's big to me.'

There's a cough from the back of the church and, when we both swivel round, Barry is standing near the inscribed stone font. Great, that's all I need when I'm feeling fit to burst with nerves. But at least he's looking surprisingly tidy in dark trousers and a black T-shirt. The T-shirt is plain, without a band logo or rude word in sight.

Leaving Kayla to place music on chairs, I hurry over to Barry, who's shifting uncomfortably from foot to foot.

'You look smart.'

'Yeah, well, that Roger bloke threatened me with GBH if I turned up in jeans and my Homer Simpson top. Does the brewery know he's got anger issues? I wouldn't want him serving me a pint when he's had a few.'

'Smart is good. And please, Barry, if you're planning to sing and be a part of the choir today, you have to behave yourself.'

'What do you mean "behave myself"? I'm not six!'

'What I mean is don't annoy Roger or tell Arthur he's being a pompous prat and, for goodness' sake, please don't compliment Kayla on her arse.'

'It's just banter, babe,' insists Barry.

'Back in the 1980s, it was banter. In the twenty-first century, it's sexual harassment, so rein it in. Please. Just for today.'

'Huh,' grumbles Barry. 'I wouldn't want to let you down.' He undoes the button on the waistband of his trousers and exhales loudly. 'These have shrunk in the wash since I last wore them.'

I eye his not-so-flat belly straining against the cotton of his T-shirt.

'Where's Storm? Isn't she with you?'

'Still in bed,' he calls over his shoulder, wandering off towards the altar. 'Only an earthquake would get her up on a Saturday before midday.'

I send up a silent prayer of thanks to the God of Indolent Teenagers that today's semi-final will be minus Storm's bad vibes percolating through the church.

It's twenty to ten already and people start trickling in while I'm setting up the music stand on the podium-cum-crate. They all look so smart, dressed in combinations of black and white, just as they were for the choir's first ever performance back in the spring. That was a night I'll never forget – not only did the concert go well, Josh declared his true feelings and I decided to stay in Salt Bay. That conversation changed the course of my life.

And now here I am, in charge of this motley crew who have to sing their hearts out this morning if they're to reach the Kernow Choral Crown finals. They're all so different – in age, character, shape – but linked by their love for this choir and the small community around it.

Cyril, wearing an old-fashioned suit with wide lapels, squeezes my arm on his way to his seat and murmurs, 'You go, girl.' He's shaved off his grey bristles and there's a bloodied scrap of tissue on his chin. For him, a partial recluse, the choir has become like family, and doing well in this competition has become a matter of pride. For him and for all of them. So we must do our best.

'Come on, people,' I call, waving at Michaela, who's taken her place at the piano. 'Let's do our warm-up exercises so we can kick some arse when Mr Kerroway gets here.'

We've just finished singing up and down scales when Josh rushes through the door and chucks his battered leather satchel onto a pew. It skids across the polished wood and thunks onto the floor.

'Sorry I'm late,' he puffs. 'Mum isn't so good today so I couldn't get away as early as I meant to. He isn't here already, is he? I drove like the clappers.'

'No, we're still waiting. Is your mum OK?' I ask, giving him a brief hug.

'Yeah, she'll be fine. She gets the results of her scan soon.'

Josh smiles but the tiny crow's feet around his eyes don't move. There are dark circles under his lower lashes and he looks utterly exhausted.

As I'm rubbing his arm through the thin cotton of his white shirt, heads suddenly turn towards the font.

'Here we go,' mutters Roger, pulling down his shirt, which is riding up over his barrel-stomach.

A tall, stick-thin man, in a light grey suit and dark grey waistcoat, has just stepped into the church and is pushing the door to. There's a clipboard under his arm and his shiny black shoes *tap-tap* on the flagstones when he starts walking down the narrow aisle.

'Mr Kerroway?' Hurrying up to him, I hold out my hand. 'I'm Annie Trebarwith. Thank you so much for coming. You found us then.'

Mr Kerroway allows his hand to rest in mine for a moment but makes no attempt to shake it. His skin is cool and slightly damp, like he's just been to the loo and washed his hands.

'You're not the easiest of places to get to,' he barks in clipped tones with no trace of a Cornish accent. He scowls at me as though it's my fault. 'In fact, you're completely in the back of beyond. These little villages are ridiculously remote.'

Which is just what I used to say ten months ago. But times change and his comments put my back up. However, I smile broadly so my annoyance won't show. The last thing I want to do is rile the man who has the power to put us through to the competition final.

'I see your choir is here and ready to begin. That's good,' says Mr Kerroway, glancing at his clipboard. 'You're the Salt Bay Choral Society, which is rather a grand name for a small, amateur choir.' He sniffs and rises up on the balls of his feet, making his shiny shoes squeak.

'It was the name of the original choir, the one that was disbanded after a tragedy.'

'Ah yes, I read about that in the notes somewhere.' He shoots the cuff of his snow-white shirt and peers at his gold watch. 'I suppose we'd better get on with it then. I have another two choirs to see today and the person who organised my judging itinerary appeared to think it was perfectly feasible for me to travel thirty-five miles on Cornish roads within an hour.'

'Gosh, that is rather unrealistic,' I gush, hating myself for sucking up to such a miserable git.

'What *is* ridiculous is the new rule that decrees we must see fledgling choirs in their natural environment at this stage of the competition. Something to do with new choirs being affected by White Coat Syndrome if we put them all together in a competitive environment. But it'll be no holds barred for those that make it to the final so it's all a complete waste of my time.'

Heart sinking, I lead Mr Kerroway to the front of the church and introduce him to the singers. Everyone is sitting upright in their seats, ready to go and looking like a proper choir. I'm so proud of them.

'Would you like us to sing now?' asks Josh who's due to conduct the second of our semi-final songs.

'In a moment. First, I'll have a few words.' Mr Kerroway steps up onto the podium-crate and taps his fingers against his skinny thigh. 'Congratulations, um—' He consults his clipboard again. 'Salt Bay Choral Society on reaching this stage in the competition. You're in the "New Choirs" category, as you know, and getting this far with the digital recording you submitted is an achievement in itself. You wouldn't believe how many new choirs have sprung up in Cornwall over the last twelve months. I blame Gareth Malone.'

A joke! I giggle but he shoots me a straight look. 'No, I really do blame Gareth Malone for making the world and his wife think they can sing. Utterly ridiculous! However, I'm sure that you all *can* sing or you wouldn't be wasting my precious time.'

There's a heavy silence as all eyes turn towards Ollie.

And suddenly I desperately want to laugh. It's the same urge I've had at funerals, when you know that laughing is the very last thing in the whole freaking world that you should do. Terrible things will happen if you laugh. You will become a social pariah, shunned by all normal members of society. But the more you panic, the more hilarious the whole situation becomes.

Ouch! I'm biting my lip so hard it hurts. I try not to catch Josh's eye because the corner of his mouth is twitching, and Kayla doesn't help by grimacing at Mr Kerroway and mouthing 'weirdo'. It's like school assembly all over again, with Susan Bloom making me giggle during prayers when the chairman of governors was visiting. We ended up in detention for a week.

Fortunately, biting my lip plus digging nails into my palm causes enough pain to halt any bubbling hysteria, and Mr Kerroway steps off the podium none the wiser. He marches along the aisle and takes a seat a few pews back.

We're on! The choir stands almost as one on my command – Cyril needs a helping hand to get to his feet – and, giving them a beaming smile, I send a shedload of positive vibes their way. *Please do well today – not for me or to stuff it to Mr creepy Kerroway, but for yourselves.*

You deserve it after working so hard to bring music and joy back into this little village.

On my nod, Michaela plays a short intro and the resurrected Salt Bay Choral Society begins to sing – and, hallelujah, it's not bad. In fact, it's pretty good. Voices soar, bounce off time-smoothed stone and fill the church with sound.

The choir sing their two pieces: the sea shanty and a chorus from Gilbert and Sullivan, and both are a triumph. OK, triumph is probably pushing it. But my fabulous singers are heartfelt and in tune, even Ollie who might actually be miming.

No one says a word as the final note echoes above our heads before dying away to nothing. And a thick, heavy silence descends while Mr Kerroway scribbles on his clipboard as lights glint on his steel-grey hair. When he's finished writing, he carefully unclips the paper and turns it over so we can't sneak a peek. What a spoilsport!

Josh raises his eyebrows and shrugs his shoulders. We've done all we can.

'Is there anything else you need from us?' I ask Mr Kerroway.

Before answering, he takes a spotted red handkerchief from his pocket and carefully wipes it across his nose. The tension is unbearable. 'No thank you, I've heard quite enough.'

He sounds so deadpan, I can't tell if that's good or bad and I suddenly realise quite how out of my depth I am. I'm not a proper choir leader at all and Mr Kerroway must have spotted me just bumbling my way through. I glance at Barry, who's scratching his backside, and Josh, who's chatting quietly to Michaela. I just bumble my way through everything.

'Amy, could I have a quick word?'

We don't have an Amy but Mr Kerroway is looking straight at me so I scurry over. I'll answer to Donald if it helps secure us a place in the Grand Final.

'My sat-nav has inexplicably stopped working and I need to get out of this village and on the road to Penzance without getting lost in some dead-end backwater full of tractors. Perhaps you could point me in the right direction.'

'Hiya, mate.' Barry has crept up behind us and slaps Mr Kerroway loudly on the back. 'What do you think of my daughter then, running a choir like this on her own?'

'Not on my own, Barry,' I say, with a tight grin on my face. 'Josh helps too.'

'But it's mainly you. She's a chip off the old block because I'm a musician too. I used to belong to a band called Va-Voom and the Vikings, back in the day. Have you heard of us?'

Disappointment flits across Barry's face when our adjudicator shakes his head. Mr Kerroway's long, thin nose is wrinkled as though rotten eggs are being wafted under it.

'Never mind. We never quite made the big time, though we came close. Look, why don't I show you out to your car? I can give you directions.'

'I'm sure there's no need, Barry.' My grin is so wide and fixed, it's making my cheeks ache. Josh, who's piling music on top of the piano, glances at me and raises his eyebrows.

'It's not a problem at all. Come on, mate, you've got another choir to get to.'

Barry shoves his hand into the small of Mr Kerroway's back and starts propelling him towards the church door.

'The competition adjudicators will be in touch within the next week. Good day to you all,' calls our adjudicator, over his shoulder.

As he's shoved out of the church, Kayla lets out a long, loud sigh. 'Wow, he's one up-himself bloke.'

'Shush, Kayla, or he'll hear you,' tuts Florence, leaning over to change out of black patent shoes into her usual trainers. She tells me they're ultra comfortable for old feet, which is why I'm working on Alice swapping her usual brogues for Adidas.

'She's right though,' grumbles Roger, who's damp under the armpits. 'That bloke could do with a personality transplant. Pompous prat.'

'That's unkind and uncalled for, Roger.' Jennifer needs to reopen her shop and already has her coat on. 'He's obviously a man of immense musical taste and discernment. The reason you didn't like him is because he's so different from you.'

Roger opens his mouth to answer back but I get in first. 'Come on now. It was a bit stressful but you all did brilliantly well and now we just need to keep our fingers crossed.'

Mary crosses her fingers, waves them above her head and gives me a beaming smile. Why can't everyone in the world be like lovely, gentle Mary? War, conflict and crisis would evaporate in seconds.

'We didn't do too badly,' admits Jennifer grudgingly. And Kayla obviously agrees because, without breaking off from her steamy embrace with Ollie, she gives me a thumbs up behind his back. She's always been expert in multitasking.

'Those two are utterly outrageous with their heavy petting in church,' mutters Jennifer, doing up her buttons. 'And I don't want to worry you but your father is still outside with Mr Kerroway.'

'I expect he's gone on home.'

'You're probably right although he was rather keen to show Mr Kerroway out.'

'Which is exactly what I was thinking,' says Josh, who's wandered over.

Barry *was* keen, wasn't he. With a sense of foreboding, I grab hold of Josh's hand and pull him up the aisle and out of the church.

Mr Kerroway's shiny car is still parked on the road, up close to the churchyard wall. And he and Barry appear to be chatting, or rather... As we watch from the narrow path that runs through the graveyard, Mr Kerroway starts shouting and jabbing his finger at Barry's chest.

'Oh, for f—' Josh rubs his tired eyes and leans against a mossy gravestone. The name has been scoured away by sea winds and rain and all that's left is the faint indentation of a date: *1793*. Whoever it is has been deceased for two hundred years. It must be horrible being dead but at least you don't have to deal with this kind of crap.

'You stay here, Josh,' I say more confidently than I feel. 'I'll handle this.'

By the time I reach Barry, the shouting has stopped but our adjudicator's nostrils are flaring.

'Is everything all right, Mr Kerroway?' I ask sweetly. 'I thought you were on a tight schedule.'

'I am and I'm going to be late now because I have to disqualify you and the paperwork is horrendous.'

'What?' I squeak, glaring at Barry, who's gone a deep shade of puce. 'Why?'

'Because bribery is against the rules.'

'Barry, what have you done?'

'Nothing,' splutters Barry, raising his hands to the heavens.

'This man, who I understand is your father—' Mr Kerroway pauses and draws in his mouth like he's sucking on a lemon '—offered me backstage passes to a concert by someone called Black Saturday.'

'Black Sabbath!' blurts out Barry, appalled. 'They're a brilliant band. All I did was mention a Black Sabbath tribute act and say I know one of their roadies and he could probably get Mr K here backstage passes to the concert of his choice.'

'Which is bribery,' attests Mr Kerroway, flicking through the papers on his clipboard, presumably searching for the Kernow Choral Crown Corruption Form.

'It's not bribery,' whines Barry. 'It's being nice. Aren't people nice to one another in Cornwall, is that against the law? Are you going to charge me with being pleasant with intent?'

'Shut up, Barry,' I hiss out of the corner of my mouth. 'Do you like Black Sabbath, Mr Kerroway?'

'I've never heard of them.'

Barry tuts loudly, shaking his head in disbelief, but I turn my back on him.

'So, it's not really bribery if it's a band you've never heard of and wouldn't dream of going to see. That was never going to influence your decision at all.'

'And it's not the real band anyway,' butts in Barry. 'It's only a tribute act. The drummer looks just like Ozzy and bites the head off a rubber bat every gig.'

Mr Kerroway starts blinking rapidly. 'I'm sorry but I don't understand anything that this strange man is saying.'

'It doesn't really matter. All you need to know is that Barry was just trying to be friendly, in his own cack-handed way.'

'Cack— what?' squeals Barry.

Mr Kerroway stops flicking through his clipboard papers.

'Well, it's very irregular.'

'Please can we just put it down to a misunderstanding and let it go? As you say, the paperwork is horrendous and you'll be late for your next appointment.' I treat Mr Kerroway to the most megawatt smile I can muster. 'To be honest, our remote community rarely has VIP visitors of your musical calibre and, as an inexperienced, fledgling choir, we've truly appreciated you taking the time to listen to us. It would be such a shame to spoil things because of a misunderstanding.'

Mr Kerroway thinks for a moment while seagulls screech overhead and I hold my breath.

Then at last he gives a tight nod. 'All right. I'll let it go this time but I'm not happy. You need to keep your father more under control.'

'I will. Thank you, Mr Kerroway.' Hot relief washes over me. 'Thank you so much.'

'Hhmm. Someone will be in touch.'

There's an overpowering smell of expensive leather when Mr Kerroway opens the door of his posh car, gets in and places his beloved clipboard on the passenger seat. The engine turns over with a low purr and it's a good job Barry and I take a step back as he drives off or his tyres would have squashed our toes.

'What an idiot,' says Barry as the car disappears into the distance.

'You certainly are.'

'What, me?'

'Yes, you. What were you thinking, trying to bribe a competition judge? You're a… a blithering idiot.'

I've never used 'blithering' before. It's an old-school, namby-pamby, rubbish word. But Barry looks aggrieved and, when I shove him hard on the shoulder, he flinches.

'It wasn't bribery. And ouch.' He rubs at his shoulder through his short-sleeved T-shirt.

'What was it then?'

'Oiling the wheels. It happens all the time in London.'

'You're not in London. Though you could be in five hours if you got into your car and put your foot down.'

'Is that what you'd like, then? Me and Storm out of your life?'

I swallow hard and take a deep breath. 'Yes. It's exactly what I'd like. You think you can bowl in here and make up for lost time. Well, you can't. It's too late.'

That wasn't wuss-like! I am strong and confident and in control. I really am. But Barry's hurt expression wrong-foots me completely. I can just about cope with a difficult father appearing out of the blue and turning my life upside down. But I cannot cope with the pain in Barry's eyes. My anger starts to evaporate even though it's his fault I've just had to suck up to the odious Mr Kerroway.

'Oh, you're impossible, Barry, and I don't know what I want at the moment.'

I stomp off towards Josh while Barry sets off for Tregavara House with his head down. His usual swagger has disappeared and, from the back, he's less a wannabe rock star and more a sad, middle-aged man with a tragic ponytail.

'What the hell's going on?' Kayla has just joined Josh in the graveyard and frowns when I get closer. 'Which of these drongos has upset you then – Josh, the judge, or Barry?'

'None of them. It was just a misunderstanding,' I say, giving Josh a 'don't diss my dad' glare. He sighs and does an eye-roll worthy of Storm in a mega-strop.

Kayla tilts her head to one side and puffs out her cheeks. 'If neither of you are going to tell me what's going on, are you at least coming to the tea shop? We're going to eat cake to celebrate surviving this morning.' She licks her lips in anticipation.

'Can't. I need to get home to make sure all's OK and then I've got some tutoring lined up.' Josh steps forward and gives my waist a squeeze. 'Sorry.'

'I should get back anyway to check on Alice. Emily's out for the day and Storm's about as much use as a chocolate teapot when it comes to being a carer. She's usually shut away in her bedroom.'

'Good grief.' Kayla puts her hands on her hips and tuts. 'Look at the two of you! You're in the prime of life, you're mad for each other and it's the weekend – so live a little! If you're not coming to Maureen's, at least nip behind the harbour wall and have a quick shag.'

Josh's mouth twitches in the corner but he replies in his serious voice. 'Unfortunately, Kayla, some of us have responsibilities that we have to attend to.'

'I don't, thank the Lord, and long may it last. So I'm off to eat my own weight in lemon drizzle cake at Maureen's. I would have Christmas cake seeing as it's almost December but I can't stand sultanas – far too squidgy. Come on, Annie.' She nudges my arm. 'Just a quick drink before you get bogged down with all the boring grown-up stuff.'

Sadly, not even Maureen's fat-laced, calorie-crammed hot chocolate, with Cornish cream floating on top, can tempt me today. I'm too annoyed and upset by Barry's ridiculous behaviour.

'Pah! You two are so boring,' moans Kayla when I shake my head. 'You want to try being a bit more irresponsible and fancy-free, like me.'

'You're hardly fancy-free. What about your smitten boyfriend?'

Kayla's face clouds for a moment when she spots Ollie waiting for her by the churchyard gate, but then she grins widely.

'I am totes fancy-free, thank you very much. Ollie's great, we have a brilliant time, and the sex is magnificent, but I'm a free spirit and he knows that, thanks to my wiles.' She taps her nose, gives me a knowing look and heads off to stuff her freckled face.

'What was all that to-do with Barry and Mr Kerroway?' asks Josh quietly when the gate has clanged shut.

'It was a misunderstanding but it's all sorted now. Though I think I might have just told Barry to leave.'

Josh brushes my cheek with the back of his fingers. 'Is that what you really want?'

'To be honest, I don't know what I want. I dreamed of having a dad when I was growing up but Barry's a freaking nightmare.'

'Believe me, compared to some of the parents at my school Barry is a shoo-in for Parent of the Year,' grins Josh. 'But I'll support you in whatever you decide.'

Jeez, he's such a lovely boyfriend. I want to throw myself into his arms and snog him senseless. But Arthur and Fiona have just emerged from the church, so I make do with kissing him on the cheek instead. His skin is chilly in the breeze blowing off the sea.

'Right. I guess we'd better get back to our families,' says Josh, waving back at Fiona, whose earrings are sparkling in the sunshine. She's put on her best bling in honour of Mr Kerroway's visit.

'I guess so,' I gulp, surprised by a sudden longing for London. I'd love to spend the day fighting through Christmas crowds on Oxford Street or wandering along the South Bank with St Paul's in the distance. To be honest, I'd rather be anywhere than in Salt Bay, throwing out my father and half-sister.

Chapter Twenty

The house is quiet when I get back. Alice is resting in her room and Storm must still be in bed, thank goodness. It's best she's semi-conscious and out of the way because Barry and I need to have a few words. Things need to be said, in private. If I can find him.

First I try his bedroom, in case he's packing. But his clothes are still scattered across the floor and there's no one in the sitting room or kitchen. He won't have gone for a stroll because Barry doesn't really do walking.

I eventually throw on my jacket and find him in the back garden, scratching at the hard earth with an ancient hoe he must have found in the cellar. Its wooden handle is stained and the metal tip is encrusted with thick, brown rust.

'Isn't it the wrong time of year for gardening?'

Grey clouds have bubbled up and covered the sun, leaving Alice's garden in shadow. I shiver and pull my jacket tighter around me.

'No idea. I know nothing about it. But I want to do a few jobs today before Storm and I head off.' Barry stops dragging the hoe across dark earth and rests his chin on the end of the handle. 'So we've properly earned our keep. I wouldn't want you to think we were spongers.'

'I never said that you were.'

'I've worked on the house and slipped Alice a few quid here and there, and I've done the shopping a couple of times.'

While it's true he's driven out to Tesco in Penzance and come back with bags of shopping, he never takes a list and his idea of what's needed and mine are very different. Bottles of lager, Pot Noodles and party bags of cheese and onion crisps aren't what I'd call food-cupboard staples. Especially when the only person who eats Pot Noodles is Storm to annoy Emily, when she's cooked a meal.

'I think we need to have a word, Barry.'

'Uh-oh, you sound like my ex-wife.' He wipes a sheen of sweat from his forehead and stares at me with his unnervingly bright eyes. 'Don't worry. I got the message and we will be leaving when Storm's up and about.'

It's great that they're leaving. They've been here far too long. So why do I feel like the bad guy? As if I'm doing something wrong.

'It's just that I'm upset about the bribery,' I tell him, wondering where they'll stay when they get back to London.

'You said it was a misunderstanding.'

'I said that for Mr Kerroway's benefit so he wouldn't disqualify us, but offering backstage passes *is* bribery. Why did you do it? Were you trying to spoil the choir's chances?'

'Of course not,' snorts Barry.

'Were you trying to get at me, then?'

Barry's jaw drops as my accusation hits home. 'Is that what you think? Blimey, what a very low opinion you have of your own father.'

His words spark a memory in me, an echo of something Josh said before we got together, when I got the wrong end of the stick and jumped to all sorts of conclusions. That misunderstanding almost wrecked my chance of a relationship with him. Is that what's happening here?

'Just tell me why you did it, Barry. I want to understand properly.'

Barry fixes me with his piercing stare and says simply, 'I did it for you.'

'How could almost getting us disqualified be for me?'

'I didn't know the silly sod was going to totally overreact. I just thought the prospect of listening to some awesome Black Sabbath might put him in a better frame of mind.' Barry leans the hoe against the house wall and his shoulders drop. 'I can see how much this choir means to you, and this daft competition, and I wanted to make sure you got through.'

'What about us going through on merit?'

Barry sniggers. 'You can put your trust in that if you like.'

'What do you mean? We're good enough.'

'You're fine, if you like weird, old music without a proper beat. But that bloke got on my tits with his la-di-dah voice and the way he spoke to you. He was looking down on us from the minute he arrived and I'm fed up with being looked down on.' He sighs. 'I only wanted to do the best for you, Annie, and I'm sorry if I messed up.'

'Why change the habit of a lifetime, Barry? You've messed up from the very start. You didn't even bother to find out if I existed until a few weeks ago and now you want us to play happy families? You're unbelievable.'

My breathing quickens as the words come tumbling out – words I've wanted to say from the minute he arrived on my doorstep, only I was too busy pussyfooting about and hoping, deep down, that 'happy families' might be something I could have, after all.

'But I did try to find out,' blurts Barry. 'Not straight away, granted. But the rumours played on my mind and a couple of years later I heard where Joanna was living and knocked on her door.'

'No you didn't,' I whisper.

'I did. She was living in a tower block in Hackney and she got really agitated when I turned up. She refused to answer my questions and slammed the door in my face. I went round again a week later but she'd moved on somewhere else. I didn't know where. I sent a letter to her home here in Salt Bay, as a last-ditch effort, but she never replied.' He shrugs. 'So I gave up.'

Barry adjusts his scrappy ponytail while I take in this latest bombshell. If he did try to make contact, maybe he's not quite as feckless as I thought. But would Mum have sent him packing and never breathed a word of it to me? Possibly – because, as I've discovered since her death, she kept secrets as a matter of course.

'If that was true, why haven't you mentioned it before?'

'What's the point? It doesn't change anything. To be honest, I was glad Jo gave me the brush-off because it meant I could go back to gigging with a clear conscience. And I don't blame her for not wanting me in your life. I hadn't exactly been reliable up 'til then, had I?' He shakes his head, face flushed with the cold. 'The irony is that now I'm a single parent and finding it bloody hard. Someone up there is having a right laugh.'

He scuffs his feet into the hard earth while I picture him knocking at the flat in Hackney. I must have been there, too young to realise that my father was just a few metres away. If Mum was unwell when he called round, she probably thought he'd come to take me away from her. She often got paranoid when dark moods smothered her and one of her most persistent fears was the two of us being separated. Like we are now.

I want to know what to do about Barry and Storm. I want to feel more secure in my relationship with Josh. But most of all, right now, I want to see my mum. My infuriating, mixed-up, lovely mum. A tear slides down my cheek and drips onto my neck.

'So what do we do now?' asks Barry.

Tiny flakes of snow start fluttering from a white-grey sky as he wanders over and puts his hands on my shoulders.

'Do you really want me and Storm to go? Only I'm enjoying getting to know you at last, and Storm's grown quite fond of the old lady. Talk of the devil…'

He tilts his head towards the kitchen doorway where Alice is standing, shivering in a light-blue dress and matching cardigan. How long has she been standing there?

'The old lady has grown quite fond of Storm too,' says Alice, holding out her hand to catch a falling snowflake. 'It's wonderful to have young people again at Tregavara House and, in my opinion, it would be a shame if you left so soon. It causes nothing but grief and heartache if families are apart, as Annabella knows more than most.' She spots me dabbing at my wet cheek and gives me a sympathetic smile. 'Some things have to be worked at and you've only been here a short while. But it's up to Annabella.'

Cheers, Alice. Just when I'd love someone else to make a few decisions on my behalf. Barry pushes out his bottom lip, opens his eyes wide and gives a hangdog sigh.

'What do you reckon, Annie? I promise not to bribe anyone else – though I still maintain it wasn't technically a bribe. And it'll be good for Storm to be here a bit longer. She's less stroppy in Cornwall than in London.'

Jeez, I don't even want to imagine what she's like away from Salt Bay.

Barry moves to stand shoulder to shoulder with Alice and I suddenly can't be bothered to argue. I'm far too tired to make them leave. And it's Alice's flipping house anyway.

'Yeah, whatever,' I shrug, channelling my inner Storm. 'But promise me that you'll stay out of trouble.'

'I don't know what you mean, Annie. I'm never any trouble. But thanks.' Barry grins and leans down to plant a smacker on Alice's cheek. 'And thanks, Alice. I always knew you were a fabulous woman. If I was a few years older…'

My father flirting with an eighty-three-year-old makes me feel slightly nauseous but Alice's cheeks redden and, just for a moment, I glimpse the vibrant, giddy young woman she must once have been.

Gardening forgotten, Barry wanders indoors but I stay outside. Tiny snowflakes are melting on the dark soil turned over by the hoe, and the sea is an ice-grey sheet. It's Baltic out here but I need some air.

After a few minutes, I hear the tap of Alice's walking stick and she joins me, now wearing her best coat.

'How did the semi-final go?' she asks, gazing out to sea. 'Did I hear that bribery was involved?'

'Not really. I think Barry was trying to help.'

Alice winces. 'Oh dear. That's probably best avoided.'

'Indeed.' I swing round to face my great-aunt, who's wrapped up in the peacock-blue scarf I knitted for her. 'But are you sure about this, Alice? It's not cheap having two extra mouths to feed.'

'It's fine. I've got a bit stashed away and you're contributing. Plus, Barry's chipping in a little and some of the jobs he's doing are useful. And they're only staying a while longer.'

'But you can't tell me that Door-Slam Storm isn't getting on your nerves.'

'She does find it impossible to leave a room quietly but this house has been quiet for too long. It was built to be full of life, and having your family here is best for you.'

'Are you sure about that? It's taking up a lot of my time and causing problems between me and Josh.'

Alice thinks for a moment and frowns. 'That's a shame. But if you two are meant to be together, you'll weather a storm or two. David and I went through much worse. We had a little boy, you know.' I hold my breath as she studies my face. 'Did you know that already?'

When I nod, she asks, 'Jennifer?' and I nod again. 'I thought she might have let it slip. That's Jennifer for you. But I'm surprised you didn't say anything to me about it.'

'I thought you'd tell me when you were ready.'

'I guess now's as good a time as any,' murmurs Alice, leading the way to the garden bench and slowly sinking onto it. 'His name was Freddie, Frederick George after my grandfather. He was a beautiful boy – dark hair and grey eyes, the colour of the sea on a cloudy day. But he caught measles from a young girl at school. They didn't vaccinate against it then. And within a few days, he'd developed complications and our beautiful boy was gone.'

'Alice, I'm so sorry.' I sit beside her on the bench and stroke her arm to be comforting, though it seems horribly inadequate.

'It was a long time ago and the pain fades, but it's not just the loss of your child. It's the loss of grandchildren too, bringing joy into your life as you get old and decrepit. That's why you've been such a blessing to me, Annabella, and Emily too.' There are tears in her faded eyes when she smiles at me, and my throat tightens.

'So,' she continues, more briskly, 'that's why Storm is welcome here. Yes, she's annoying but she brings teenage noise and vitality into this house which has been lacking for years, ever since your mother left.'

'You really want Storm and Barry to stay, don't you?'

'I do.' Alice puts her age-spotted hand on top of mine. 'Trust me on this one, Annie. Don't forget that I'm ancient and wise.'

Old and wise and far more sentimental than I'd suspected. Storm isn't the only person round here who's sitting on a volcano of buried emotions.

The fluttering flakes are getting larger but still melting as soon as they hit the damp path. The snow won't be sticking around but, unfortunately, the same can't be said for Barry and Storm.

Chapter Twenty-One

Over the next few days I turn into a social media junkie, constantly checking the Kernow Choral Crown Twitter account for news. And finally – after checking my inbox on the hour, every hour at work – the email we're waiting for pings into my inbox.

Eek! For a moment, my finger hovers over the keyboard because no news might be good news. But I'm going in! The email is short but I scan through the words so quickly my brain can't take in what I'm seeing. Are we through? Taking a deep breath, I read it again, more slowly.

Dear Miss Trebarwith,

I'm emailing to inform you that Salt Bay Choral Society has been selected to go through to the Kernow Choral Crown Grand Final in the New Choirs category. Congratulations! Adjudicator Simeon Kerroway was most impressed with your choir's musicality and vigour when he visited you recently. The final will take place at Gwedna Hall in Truro at 3p.m. on Saturday, December 20th. Further details are attached and please don't hesitate to contact me if you have any questions. We look forward to welcoming Salt Bay Choral Society to the Grand Final.

With kind regards,
Emilija Heatherwick-Jones
(Adjudications Officer)

Yippee! It's hard to imagine Mr Kerroway ever being 'most impressed' with anything but at least Barry's bribery attempt didn't scupper our chances. We're through! And with the grand final being on the same day as my thirtieth birthday, winning would be the best birthday present ever.

I could ring people to tell them the news or plaster it across social media – *Woohoo! Through to the finals of the Kernow Choral Crown *bites fingernails and sips champagne** ☺ – but I don't. It's such a relief having a happy secret for once, I hug the news to my heart and don't tell a soul. Instead, I re-read the email until I can quote it word for word and treat myself to a chocolate Father Christmas wrapped in shiny foil. We have a choir rehearsal tonight when I can break the good news to my lovely singers. Ooh, I can't wait!

By ten past seven, I'm in Salt Bay church, chairs set out ready, and pacing up and down. I've hugged this secret to myself for long enough now and need to share the news. Where is everyone?

After walking several circuits of the church to keep calm (aisle: forty-eight paces; vestry: fifteen paces; circling the font: ten paces, tops), the door creaks open and I'm delighted to see that Josh is the first arrival. Before he reaches me for a hug, I blurt out the news and his permanent frown is chased away by a huge smile. I haven't seen him look so happy in ages. He puts his arms around my waist and whirls me off my feet, around and around, until my feet clonk into a pew.

'Oops, sorry. Hilary will kill me if I wreck her church.' He sets me back on my feet, looking flushed and relaxed. 'That's such good news after a rotten few weeks. It's just what we need.'

'I hope so. There's a lot of work to be done, but we're on our way!' The church is still spinning and I grab hold of a pew to steady myself.

'Why don't we wait to say anything until everyone's here?'

'We could. But do you have any idea how difficult it's been not to say anything up to now?'

'You can manage it, Annie,' says Josh, dark eyes crinkling at the corners when he smiles. 'I bet you're brilliant at keeping all sorts of secrets.'

He winks and, just like that, all excitement evaporates and a sickening wave of guilt rushes in to fill the void. Josh is right. I am brilliant at keeping secrets – from him.

Josh is taking off his coat and opening the piano lid and whistling cheerfully but I can hardly hear him. Panic is bubbling up inside me and it's getting harder to breathe. Why did I agree to help arrange the meeting between Toby and Freya? I should never have passed on Toby's mobile number to Lucy. Covering my face with my hands, I try to calm down but my inner voice is in overdrive. *Stupid, stupid, stupid for getting involved. You're trying to do what's best in the long run for Freya and for Josh, but he won't see it that way if he finds out. When he finds out.*

Jeez, I'm not sure I can breathe at all. Is it really so important for Freya that she meets her father right now?

Like an answer from above, the church door creaks open and Barry wanders through it, with Storm in tow. He spots me and gives a little wave. Since our talk in the garden, he's been on his best behaviour.

How different life might have been if Mum hadn't sent him packing all those years ago. Chances are he would have embarrassed me in the playground as much as Mum did, but I wouldn't have spent my childhood wondering and making up ridiculous stories about Scandinavian heritage. At least I'd have known, and Freya needs to know too, and benefit from Toby easing the financial pressure on her family. On Josh.

My inner voice starts to fade into the background as it's smothered with logic and reason. Of course I'm bound to feel awkward about the whole thing but this meeting will probably never take place anyway. And how long have I wasted worrying about terrible events that never actually happen? Years, probably.

Meanwhile, what definitely *is* happening is Salt Bay Choral Society taking part in the Grand Final of the Kernow Choral Crown. Butterflies start fluttering in my stomach again as I imagine giving the choir the good news.

In the end, I manage to keep a lid on it until we've finished our warm-up exercises and are ready to sing.

'I've got something to tell you,' I say, trying to keep a poker face, though Josh is grinning so widely he'll give the game away.

'Are we going to sing something decent?' pipes up Arthur, who's a terrible music snob and fast taking on Roger's mantle of Grumpiest Old Bugger in Cornwall.

'We are, Arthur, and we're going to be singing it in the competition final.' There's a stunned silence. 'We're through! Well done everyone!'

'You told me you didn't know when I came in,' wails Kayla.

'I lied,' I say, hopping from foot to foot. 'I wanted to wait and tell you all together.'

'Not happy about the lying but delighted about the getting through,' yells Kayla, planting a smacker on Tom, who goes bright red. 'Turns out that weirdo Kerroway wasn't such a dipstick, after all.'

Everyone starts beaming and talking at once, except Emily, whose smile fades when Jay makes a beeline for Storm at the piano and throws his arms around her. Storm looks totally unimpressed with his opportunistic hug but the damage is done. Emily sinks onto her chair and sits quietly, twirling a strand of hair between her fingers, while the celebrations go on around her. Poor kid.

'Told you,' calls Barry, catching my eye and giving me a double thumbs up. 'But hey, well done. This stuff isn't really my bag but you're making a good job of it.'

'Yes, very well done, lass,' says Cyril, buttoning up his favourite burgundy cardigan which is littered with cigarette burns. 'I knew you could do it.'

'It was you,' I tell him, feeling close to tears. 'All of you.'

Lovely Mary reaches into her handbag and hands me a small pack of tissues. 'You know what this means, don't you? We're going to put Salt Bay on the map again but for the right reasons this time. For happy reasons.'

'Hallelujah!' Florence grins and claps her hands. 'Your grandad would be proud of you, Annie. And you, Josh – your stepdad took us to the finals sixteen years ago and here you are, doing the same. It's wonderful.'

Echoes of the past ripple around us as the brass plaque to the drowned men of Salt Bay glints under the lights. I shiver when an icy breeze hits the back of my neck – thank goodness I'm a sophisticated twenty-nine-year-old city girl or I might think the church was full of ghosts.

After giving everyone a few minutes to let off steam and celebrate, I wave my arms for quiet.

'Well done, everyone. It's fabulous news but now the hard work begins. We've only got three weeks until the final and, though we can sing the sea shanty and Gilbert and Sullivan chorus we sang in the semis and we've practised "Lamorna" already, we're also required to sing a contemporary song.'

'And they're only telling us now?' huffs Roger.

'Apparently that's so it's a level playing field and all competing choirs have the same amount of time to prepare their fourth song.'

'Never mind that,' sniffs Arthur. 'When you say "contemporary", do you mean a pop song?'

He says 'pop' like it's the worst swear word in the world.

'Or a rock song,' yells Barry, his face lighting up. 'How about something by Led Zep or Whitesnake?'

'I'm definitely not singing about snakes.' Florence folds her arms across her motherly bosom. 'My lovely Bob was bitten by a snake in the Dardanelles and has had a phobia ever since.'

Kayla starts sniggering but skilfully turns it into a cough.

'The rules they sent through say it can be an adaptation of a current song, though I'm not sure Whitesnake is quite what we're looking for. Or it can be an original composition.'

'That's all right then. I'll write one for you,' asserts Barry. He folds his arms and sits back, looking pleased with himself, as Storm theatrically clonks her head down on top of the piano. Ouch, that must have hurt.

Josh leaps in while I'm working out the best way to let my father down lightly in front of the choir. 'That's very kind of you, however there's no need to go to all that trouble.'

But Barry is rubbing his hands together like a man on a mission. 'It's no trouble, Joshie. In fact, it'll be a blast. I've never composed for a proper choir before and it'll look good on the old musical CV. Do you lot like hip-hop?'

There's a collective gasp as fifteen jaws drop in unison, but Barry snorts with laughter. 'Only joking! God, your faces! I thought you were going to have a heart attack on the spot, Arthur, mate.'

Arthur, mate, does not look amused.

'Um, maybe we can get some suggestions for a contemporary song from the choir too.' Josh steps up beside me on the podium-crate and grabs my arm when it wobbles. 'If anyone has any ideas, let me or Annie know and we'll choose a contemporary song before the next rehearsal. We'll need to slot in a few extra rehearsals before the finals.'

'And don't forget we're due to sing carols at the tree lighting ceremony so we need to practise those too,' I add, suddenly feeling overwhelmed. My time, and Josh's, is squeezed at the moment and there's a lot to do. But we'll manage. We have to.

Barry puts up his hand as though he's at school and grins. 'Like I said, it's no trouble at all, what with me being a professional musician. A brand new song will be ready for you next rehearsal.' He rakes his fingers through his long hair and winks at Jennifer. 'It'll be wicked.'

Barry disappears upstairs as soon as we get back from the post-rehearsal pub visit and pretty much stays there for the next couple of days. Which means the house is free from the banging and crashing of his DIY – it's marvellous.

'He's in the zone,' mutters Storm when I ask if her father is OK. 'Doing song-writing and that kind of crap. He thinks he's the next Ed Sheeran. It's totally pathetic.'

She grouches off but, overall, she's much quieter these days. She's in her second week at Trecaldwith School and, boy oh boy, do we know it. The complaining kicks off as she leaves for the early morning bus and continues when she arrives home. But it's low-key whingeing minus door slamming.

I'm pretty sure she'd be bunking off if Josh wasn't keeping an eye on her attendance, which hasn't gone down well. But I can't help picturing her wandering round the school on her own, shunned as a newbie by the bitchy, popular girls.

Josh finally introduces her (reluctantly) to his sister Serena and tells me he's seen them chatting in the school canteen a few times. They're probably bonding over their dislike of formal education and gagging at the thought of me and Josh getting it on.

Knowing she has at least one friend helps to put my mind at rest. It's bad enough having her around the house without having to worry about her as well. But Storm being unhappy at school still niggles at the back of my mind and pops up in my dreams, which are filled with terrifying teachers and cold, dark classrooms.

Chapter Twenty-Two

All in all, home isn't the most relaxing of places right now so I'm delighted to escape on Saturday night to celebrate Kayla's birthday.

Kayla, who's now twenty-four, has been given the night off from the Whistling Wave but has decided she'd like to get birthday-hammered in her workplace; something to do with not having to shell out on taxis and being within fifty metres of her bed. And she's certainly well on the way to being bladdered by the time Josh and I arrive.

That's good because I intend to celebrate her birthday in style with lashings of alcohol. Partly to keep her company – it would be rude to do otherwise – but also to anaesthetise my guilt. Toby rang this afternoon and it turns out he's arranged with Lucy via text to meet Freya at Tregavara House on the morning of the competition final. It's awful timing but he's found out that Alice will be out, staying with Penelope. And it's my job, apparently, to get rid of Emily, Barry and Storm for a couple of hours. Oh, and to keep the whole thing a huge secret from my boyfriend, who would go ballistic if he had even an inkling of what was happening.

There are so many things wrong with this plan, I don't quite know where to start. But Toby is insistent that Tregavara House will give them privacy, he has a right to see his daughter, it's what Lucy wants, and Josh finding out will put the kybosh on everything.

I so wish I'd told Josh when this all began but now I've been sucked in too far. If the plan is quicksand, it's reached my chin and I'm still sinking. Quite frankly, I don't know what to do for the best. Not in the long term anyway. In the short term, I am going to forget my troubles by getting pleasantly rat-arsed this evening.

'Happy birthday, lovely friend!' I shout above the busy bar din. 'Here you go.'

I thrust my presents into Kayla's arms: a bottle of her favourite perfume and a red helium balloon, with a trailing ribbon, that says 'Birthday Bitch' across it in big white letters.

'Classy!' laughs Kayla, green eyes shining. She drops the weighted ribbon onto the floor and the balloon bobs up and down, brushing against her tumbling curls. The khaki-coloured dress she's wearing complements her red hair and pale skin and really suits her. 'Thanks for the presents. You shouldn't have but I'm so glad you did.'

Ripping off the paper, she squeals when she spots the shiny, embossed box. 'That's brilliant, Annie. I'm almost out.' She pulls out the fancy bottle and gives it a sniff.

'That's because you almost bath in the stuff.'

'It's good to be fragrant, especially when so many people around here smell of fish.'

Kayla gives herself a liberal spritz of fragrance under the chin and a waft of gardenias and lemons drifts around my head, making me sneeze.

'Where's Ollie then?' I sniff, searching through my bag for a tissue.

'Up at the bar, getting me another vodka. If you nab him quickly, Josh, he can get your drinks in too.'

Josh heads off, grateful to escape the perfume fug, while I hang my jacket on the back of my chair.

'What's Ollie given you for your birthday then?'

'Nothing yet. He reckons he's got a surprise present for me but won't tell me what it is.'

'That's because it wouldn't be a surprise then.'

'I suppose so but he's usually rubbish at keeping secrets.' Kayla giggles and downs half her vodka and Coke in one huge gulp.

'It's good to see you looking happier, Kayla. You've seemed really stressed recently, what with the whole wanderlust and being stuck in Salt Bay thing.'

'Yeah, I was getting too stressy about all that. Ollie and I are taking things slowly, so there's nothing to get heavy about and, hey, it's my birthday. What's a girl to do but park her worries for the night and get drunk?' She glugs the rest of her drink and settles back in her chair. 'Those boys are taking ages. I know it's busy but they should be more forceful at the bar. Roger always serves the bolshie bastards first.'

The Whistling Wave is super busy tonight and several people have already waved at me which makes me happy. At first I was an outsider here, an oddity with a family link. But now I'm a part of this close-knit community.

'Come on, boys! I'm dying of thirst over here,' yells Kayla. 'What's a girl got to do to get a drink on her birthday?'

Ollie is already on his way with a tray of drinks and Josh beside him. The two of them couldn't be more different – Ollie, pale and blonde with an open, smiley face, and Josh, tall, dark and brooding like a Cornish pirate – but they look fabulous together. Two handsome men in the prime of life and they're here with us. I can hardly believe my luck.

'Hey, Annie.' Ollie puts the tray on the table and places another vodka and Coke in front of Kayla. I'm not sure what's wrong with him but he's shifting from foot to foot as though he's got ants in his pants.

'Where's my present then?' demands Kayla, leaning her head against Ollie's waist. 'How long are you going to keep me waiting?'

Ollie swallows hard and makes a cut-throat gesture towards Roger, who flicks off the sound system, halting Tom Jones mid-'Delilah'.

'What's going on? Oh God, Ollie, you haven't booked me a Tarzan-a-gram, have you? I really don't need some bloke cavorting about in a leopard skin posing pouch, although Annie will be grateful.'

She grins at me but Ollie pulls her to her feet and marches her into the middle of the pub. And suddenly I know. Cold dread slides over me. I should stop this.

'Kayla,' says Ollie, his voice cracking as he drops to one knee.

Too late.

A hush falls over the pub and people put down their drinks.

'What are you doing? Get up!' hisses Kayla.

But Ollie is on a mission and nothing is going to stop him.

'We've been going out for a while now and you are, quite honestly, the love of my life.' A general 'ah' echoes round the pub but Kayla is looking panicked. 'I said I had a birthday surprise for you and here it is.' He fumbles in his jeans pocket and pulls out a tiny box covered in brown velvet as Kayla's eyes open wide. 'Kayla Dorothy Corrigan.' He opens the box and there's a flash as the diamond inside catches the fairy lights strewn around the bar. 'Will you do me the honour of becoming my wife? Will you marry me, Kayla?'

Time stands still as we all hold our breath and wait for what comes next. But Kayla says nothing. Ollie giggles nervously and the brash confidence evaporates from his face. 'Come on, Kayla. Say something.'

Kayla, who's gazing at the ring, suddenly seems to wake up. She starts shaking her head, red curls flying. 'No,' she says in a very loud voice.

Ollie rocks back slightly as if he's been punched in the face. He screws up his eyes and puffs out his cheeks as Josh stands frozen beside me. 'Is that a definite no, then?'

'No. I mean yes. It's a definite no because I can't marry you, Ollie. I'm sorry.'

Kayla turns on her heel, pushes past people and rushes out of the back of the bar.

Ollie snaps the box shut and clambers to his feet, biting his lip. Oh heavens, I think he might be about to cry but I'm frozen to the spot. We all are – united in horror, embarrassment and sympathy. Fortunately, Roger flicks the music back on as Ollie stumbles out of the pub, leaving his jacket behind.

'What just happened?' asks Josh. 'Did she really turn him down, in front of everyone?'

'Did you know he was going to propose like that?'

'Of course not. I'd have told him not to be such a stupid idiot and bare his soul in front of everyone. How could Kayla humiliate the poor bloke like that?'

'She wasn't trying to hurt him but she's been feeling tied down in Salt Bay recently so proposing in the pub wasn't a great idea.'

'Proposing was a terrible idea. Full stop.' Josh seems to be really angry with me though I'm not sure why.

'Ollie loves Kayla and I know she loves him too. They're great together but she's got itchy feet at the moment.'

'Let's hope it isn't catching.'

I stare at Josh. How did this become about me? 'I haven't got itchy feet.'

'Not even for London?' He shakes his head. 'What is it with you women? You give out signals that you want to settle down and then you humiliate a man who professes his love for you in public. Poor Ollie.'

My neck starts prickling because the conversation has veered into dangerous territory. 'I know you're upset for Ollie, and I am too, but ambushing Kayla in the middle of the pub was never going to be a great idea.'

'What would you do?'

'What do you mean?'

'If I asked you to marry me like that in the pub, what would you do?'

Wow, this is getting out of hand.

'For a start, you'd never ask me in the pub in front of everyone even if your life depended on it. You feel uncomfortable enough holding hands in public.'

'But if I did. What would you do?' demands Josh, looking hot and flustered.

'Are you hypothetically asking me to marry you, Mr Pasco?' I'm joking, trying to calm the situation.

'No, of course not. But what would you do if I did ask? Would you humiliate me like that in front of my friends and then run off back to London?'

'Oh, not London again. You have so got to stop feeling insecure about me leaving and going back to London.'

'I don't have to do anything,' hisses Josh, grabbing Ollie's jacket. 'I'd better go after him. I'll see you later.'

He sweeps out of the pub. Again. He's getting to be a serial sweeper. Sighing, I trudge up to the bar and call out to Roger, 'Can I have a double vodka and Coke, please.'

'Is it for Kayla?' When I nod, Roger pours a triple and pushes it into my hands. 'It's on the house.'

Kayla is lying face down on her bed and sobbing so hard into her pillow, her bedframe is bashing against the wall. I have absolutely no idea what to say to someone who's just turned down a proposal, so I sit beside her and gently rub her back.

After a while, she lifts her face off the pillow. Her eyes are swollen and the white pillowcase is splodged with black clumps of mascara.

'This is the worst birthday ever,' says Kayla thickly, giving a huge sniff. 'What did he have to go and do that for?'

'Because he loves you.'

Tears spill out of Kayla's eyes, run down her red cheeks and drip off her chin.

'Yeah, but he didn't have to go so over the top. In front of the whole damn village. Things were fine as they were and I was getting used to the idea of being here for a bit longer, and then he does that.' She rubs viciously at her eyes and blows her nose on the tissue I pass to her. 'Where's Josh?'

'Ollie didn't take his jacket when he left the pub so Josh has gone after him.'

I don't mention the cross words. Or the sweeping.

'Oh. My. God,' squeaks Kayla, 'Ollie will get hypothermia and die and it'll all be my fault.'

'This is Cornwall, not the Arctic Circle, and Josh will catch up with him anyway. He'll be fine.'

'His body might recover but he'll never get over me turning him down in front of everyone. But I can't be tied here forever, like an exotic caged animal,' wails Kayla dramatically.

She sobs into the stained pillow some more until her breath catches in her throat in gulps. Then she lifts her sopping-wet face and says slowly, 'Actually, it's partly his fault.'

'How come?'

Ollie misread the signals big-time but I can't see anyone is at fault here.

Kayla pushes damp hair out of her puffy eyes. 'It's his fault for being so sure I'd say yes in the first place. He must have been absolutely certain that I'd never turn him down. What a cheek!'

'Um…'

I bite my lip. Kayla's reframing the situation in her mind. I get that. She'll have convinced herself that Ollie is a git by the end of the night – it's the only way to ease the awful upset she's feeling. We've all done it, but that doesn't make it right. My heart aches for poor lovesick Ollie, and for Kayla, who's so afraid of being tied down in sleepy Cornwall when there's still a big wide world to explore. But I fear she's just made a huge mistake.

'I guess that's it then,' Kayla says sadly. 'Me and Ollie can't carry on going out after this. He's killed our love by being a cocky bastard. This is worse than my seventeenth birthday party in Sydney when my bitchbag cousin got off with my boyfriend behind the buffet. I only found out when they rocked the food table and got covered in quiche.' She starts sobbing again while I pat her leg and try to force-feed her vodka.

I'm trying to concentrate on my friend's anguish and say the right things but something is niggling me. When Josh was hypothetically asking me to marry him and I hypothetically asked if he meant it, he said 'no, of course not.' That's pretty emphatic. A shake of the head would have done. Or a 'not now' or even just a 'no'.

I can take or leave marriage – I don't think it's a patriarchal conspiracy to keep women in their place and, equally, it's not the be-all and end-all for a woman. But it is rather galling when the man you're in love with, the man you're making love to, dismisses the idea as something totally ridiculous that could never happen. As though I'm just a stopgap until someone better comes along. Or comes back. Pushing thoughts of Felicity out of my mind, I grab the glass from Kayla and down the last of the sickly vodka.

*

After Kayla has eventually cried herself to sleep, I head for home, taking Kayla's birthday balloon with me. It looks so sad bobbing about in the bar – a reminder of a birthday that didn't go to plan – and I don't want her to see it in the morning. 'Birthday Bitch' in huge white letters might tip her over the edge.

I haven't heard from Josh and don't expect to. He'll be busy having a heart-to-heart with Ollie. Though that will probably consist of punching one another playfully on the arm, drinking half a dozen cans of lager and sitting in silence watching telly. The male version of therapy.

It's quite early but I go to bed. Though I seem cursed to keep replaying the entire evening in my head so there's little chance of sleep.

My alarm clock shows it's almost midnight and I'm tossing and turning the bedclothes into a tangle when there's a tap on my window. A sharper rap follows and, when I pull the curtains back, Josh is standing underneath the window, silhouetted in the moonlight, a dark shadow on the frost-encrusted grass. He gestures towards the front door and I creep down the stairs to let him in.

The rest of the house is sleeping so we don't say anything until we're safely ensconced in my bedroom.

'Sorry to chuck stones at your window,' whispers Josh, taking off his jeans and folding them across the chair by the door. 'It was like being sixteen again, after the school disco, but I needed to get your attention.'

'No phone signal?'

'I didn't even bother trying.' He pulls his jumper and T-shirt over his head, drops them in a heap on the floor and jumps into bed, still wearing his tight black boxer shorts. 'This house is always freezing.' He shivers, pulling the blankets up to his chin.

Josh is acting as though our cross words in the pub never happened, and I'm happy with that.

'How's Ollie doing?' I ask, slipping in beside him.

'He's devastated and embarrassed. How's Kayla?'

'Very upset.'

'Hhmm.' Josh leans his heavy body across me and switches off the bedside light. Then he lifts up his legs so I can slip my feet under his thighs to warm up. I've got him well trained.

'You were a long time at Ollie's. Did he want to talk?'

'Not really, but I stayed and watched a *Breaking Bad* repeat. Just to keep him company.' Ha, thought as much! 'Annie?' I can't see Josh in the blackness but his hand feels across the pillows and bumps into my chin. 'Sorry I got a bit antsy in the pub. Mum's op is coming up and I'm rushed off my feet at work and—'

I grab hold of his hand and squeeze it tight. 'That's OK. You're under pressure right now and it was an upsetting evening.'

'It's just a shame that Kayla wasn't more upfront with Ollie and told him she was feeling trapped before he made a total tit of himself.'

'She thought she'd made it clear through the use of her "wiles".'

'Oh God, not Kayla's flaming *wiles* again. I know Kayla's your friend and all but that girl is totally off her head.' Josh gives a loud yawn. 'I suppose we'd better get some sleep before Barry's up with his hammer.' He pauses. 'I don't always show it but you know that I care about you, right?'

'I know.'

I fumble across the bed and aim a kiss towards Josh's mouth but my lips hit earlobe and hair as he rolls over with a sigh.

Before long, Josh is softly snoring and I snuggle up against his broad back. It's lovely lying here with my arm flung across Josh's muscular body. I should be the happiest woman in the world. But instead I'm wide awake, feeling upset for Kayla, and anxious. Kayla wasn't upfront with

Ollie about her feelings, which isn't surprising – feelings are nebulous and changing and often kept under wraps. But I'm being secretive about an actual physical thing, about Toby and Freya's meeting. And, however much I'm starting to think it should go ahead, that's got to be much worse.

Chapter Twenty-Three

I'm sitting at the kitchen table on Monday afternoon, deep in thought, when there's a heavy banging at the front door. It can't be Barry because he's scooted off in the car to buy more screws, having decided that the five hundred in his tool box aren't sufficient.

When the banging carries on, I reluctantly put down my cup of tea and head into the hall. Whoever it is, I wish they'd go away because it's been an exhausting and emotional day. Taking time off work is usually fun but I'd rather have been in the office than standing next to Sheila's grave and then in church with an upset Alice.

It's six months exactly since my grandmother Sheila died of pneumonia, shortly after we'd met for the very first time. At least we found one another before it was too late, but time ran out for her and Mum. They never saw each other again after Samuel threw Mum out for being pregnant with me. All I hope is that Sheila gained some comfort from my visits to the home where she spent the last years of her life.

Sheila's now buried next to Samuel on the cliffs above Salt Bay and convincing Alice that she couldn't get up there to pay her respects was a right palaver. The winding path up from the village isn't particularly steep but it's too much for her these days, even with me giving her a hand. In the end, I visited the grave on my own before joining Alice, who sat quietly in church, lost in thought.

The rapping on the door is getting louder and, when I pull it open, there's Jennifer, red in the face with her hand raised to knock again.

'Is everything all right, Jennifer?' I ask wearily.

'No, everything is most certainly not all right.' Jennifer pushes her way past me and beckons into the darkness outside. 'Come on then. Come inside, now!'

With a loud groan, Storm steps out of the gloom and mooches into the hall. She pulls off her coat and drops it in a heap on the tiles.

'We need a word,' asserts Jennifer, marching into the sitting room as though she owns the place. 'Is Alice around?' She scans the empty room which is gloomy and cold with no fire in the grate.

'She's asleep, upstairs. It's six months to the day since Sheila died so we've been paying our respects and it rather took it out of her.'

'Ah, I'm sorry about that.' Jennifer falters for a moment but then pulls her shoulders back. 'Perhaps it's just as well if it's only you and me, especially if the police are involved.'

'What police?' I switch on the lamp and pull the swirly orange curtains closed.

'Jeez, there's no need to get so stressy about it,' moans Storm, hurling her bag into a corner and collapsing onto the sofa.

'What do you mean by "it"? What on earth has happened?' I ask, looking between furious Jennifer and grumpy Storm.

'I'll tell you what's happened.' Jennifer uses both hands to ram a wodge of blonde backcombed hair into place. 'Your sister is nothing but a common thief. I caught her red-handed, brazenly shovelling goods from my shop into her bag.'

I stare at Storm in horror. 'What things?'

'Pens, chocolate, tissues. It was like Sainsbury's when I tipped out her bag.'

'You're not allowed by law to touch my personal property, and how do you know I didn't get those things from Sainsbury's anyway?' says Storm sullenly. 'You can't prove anything.'

'Maybe not, but my cameras can. Oh, don't look so surprised, Storm. You're not the first outsider to steal my stock and you won't be the last. But I'm fighting back by having CCTV installed… hidden cameras,' she adds when my eyebrows shoot up towards my hairline. I've not noticed any cameras. 'Anyway, I'd better use your landline to call the police.'

'Is that really necessary? I'm sure we can sort this out ourselves. Storm will pay for the goods she took and I know you're a reasonable woman.'

Jennifer folds her arms and glowers. She doesn't have the look of a reasonable woman and who can blame her? She hates shoplifters with a passion, and Storm isn't her favourite person after sniggering at her in choir rehearsals.

'No, I think the police should deal with this. For all we know, your sister has a criminal record and is a serial thief.'

'I don't and I'm not. Please, no police,' whispers Storm before her lower lip wobbles and big fat tears start to track through her make-up and splash onto her knees.

'There's no need to cry,' blusters Jennifer. 'Crocodile tears won't wash with me.' But she shifts uncomfortably as Storm's shoulders shake and she starts sobbing. The make-up on her face melts into streaks as tears stream down her cheeks.

She's so upset I sit beside her on the sofa and put my arm around her shaking shoulders. I'm furious with her for stealing from one of my neighbours but she's inconsolable. The tough-girl façade has finally dissolved in a tsunami of tears.

Jennifer harrumphs as Storm cries on and on and I ferret in my pocket for a tissue to mop up the snot. There's so much snot!

'All right, no police,' blurts Jennifer at last as the snot keeps on coming. 'But this can't just be swept under the carpet. Shoplifters don't think they're doing any damage with a chocolate bar here and a magazine there but it can be devastating for small businesses hanging on by a thread.'

'I do realise how difficult it is, Jennifer, and thank you. But why did you do it, Storm? Can you explain that to both of us? If you didn't have money to buy those things, you could have asked me.'

That's what's really bothering me. The nicking stuff from shops is appalling, obviously. But she could have spoken to me if she was so short of cash. I'd have bunged her a few quid.

Storm gulps an answer, her face almost buried in my chest. 'I didn't even really want the stuff. I just felt upset 'cos school's a pain and I miss London and I'm bored here and I thought taking stuff might be exciting.'

'And was it?' demands Jennifer.

Storm shakes her head miserably, smearing snot across my jumper. 'No, it's just made me feel worse.'

Jennifer sinks into the armchair opposite us. 'I understand it's difficult being the new girl in a new school, but what would your mother think of having a thief in the family?'

'She wouldn't give a toss,' mumbles Storm. 'She's got a different, perfect family so she doesn't care what I'm doing.' She juts out her bottom lip and stares at Jennifer defiantly.

'When did you last see your mother?' Jennifer crosses her chunky ankles and leans forward, hands on her knees.

'What is it to you?'

'Storm,' I say gently. 'Be nice.'

She glances up at me and shrugs. 'I went to stay for a week in the summer but her stupid au pair came back early from visiting her boyfriend so I had to leave after a couple of days. Mum said they didn't have the space for all of us and she wouldn't let me sleep on the sofa 'cos I'd get in the way.'

'I see,' says Jennifer, pursing her lips, 'and you don't want the police called in because…?'

'Because they'll probably take me off Barry 'cos he's a shit dad and then I won't have anyone.' Storm starts sobbing again and I wrap my arms tightly around her. It's horrible not having anyone.

Jennifer pauses for a moment before steepling her fingers under her chin. 'All right, Storm, here's the deal. I won't go to the police if you work off your sentence.'

'She hasn't been sentenced,' I remind Jennifer but she's already on her feet and standing over Storm, whose sobs have turned into shuddering gasps.

'Your sentence is working in my shop for the Saturdays leading up to Christmas, free of charge of course, and then we'll forget it ever happened.'

'Do you really think Storm working in your shop is wise?' I ask, my chin resting on the top of Storm's head.

But Jennifer waves away my concerns. 'My cameras and I will be keeping a good eye on my stock and on you, Storm. So, you can keep your light fingers to yourself. If as much as a Bounty bar goes missing, I'll be calling in the police. But the discipline of having a job – albeit an unpaid one – will be good for you. It's what you need,' she says pointedly, glaring at me like I'm her mother or something. 'Is that agreed?'

Storm sniffs loudly and nods.

'Then I'll see you at eight o'clock sharp on Saturday morning. Until then, you're banned from my shop.'

'Eight o'clock?' gulps Storm, who thinks the weekend starts at noon.

'Yes, eight o'clock on the dot. Don't you dare be late.'

Jennifer gives me a curt nod and hurries out of the room.

'Back in a minute, Storm.' I slide out from underneath my distraught half-sister and scurry into the hall. Jennifer has already reached the front door.

'I'm so sorry, Jennifer. And it's good of you not to hand over the CCTV footage to the police.'

'There is no CCTV footage,' says Jennifer quietly, glancing over her shoulder. 'I can't afford to have hidden cameras in my store. I'm a small shop in a tiny village, Annie, not Tesco.'

Wow, it turns out that Jennifer, stalwart of the local community, is an impressive liar.

'Even if you don't have CCTV, why aren't you going to the police anyway? I know how you feel about shoplifters and Storm, and it's a risk having her working in your store.'

There's a risk I'm talking Jennifer out of her restitution plan but Storm and Jennifer being together in the same space for several hours each week can't possibly end well. They're chalk and cheese.

Jennifer hesitates with her hand on the front door latch. 'What do you see when you look at me, Annie?'

'Um...'

Luckily, she continues before I can answer.

'You see a respectable, successful businesswoman with an amazing singing voice who's held in high esteem by all who know her.' Yeah, that wasn't *exactly* what I was going to say. 'But it hasn't always been that way. Family life when I was growing up was challenging. My mother lacked the maternal gene and I became—' she stumbles over the right word '—troubled. You don't need to know the details but, though Storm would never believe it, we have more in common that she would ever suspect. And hard work will do her good. She could do with some proper discipline.'

She twists the latch and opens the door, letting in a cold draught that snakes past my legs and up the stairs. 'What I've just said remains purely between us, of course.'

'Of course.'

She tilts her head to one side and narrows her eyes, trying to gauge whether I'm trustworthy. Then she gives another tight nod and leaves, slamming the door behind her.

While I'm hanging up Storm's coat, she hurtles out of the sitting room and up the stairs to her bedroom. I should probably follow and try to talk to her because isn't that what a good sister would do? But I head for the kitchen and my lukewarm cup of tea instead. To be honest, I'm floundering. Acting in loco parentis is all very well if you have a good role model to draw on – but I don't. Mum was the epitome of a liberal parent who let me get away with murder, while Barry took hands-off parenting to a whole new extreme.

After an hour in her room, Storm appears in the kitchen for tea and is her usual level of grumpy, as though nothing has happened, though she's pale and shoots me an anguished look when Barry asks how my day has been. When I say, 'Fine, all went well. Nothing to report,' she gets up from the table, unbidden, to make me a cup of coffee.

This is the first time Storm has ever voluntarily made a hot beverage for anyone and Alice and Emily exchange puzzled looks. But they'll have to remain none the wiser about the reason behind Storm's spontaneous burst of goodwill. The situation with Jennifer has been dealt with and I'm not about to grass on her.

This does mean that I'm keeping yet another damn secret but I'm getting pretty skilled at keeping my gob shut.

Chapter Twenty-Four

Barry has been secretive about the song he's composing for the choir. But tonight's the night, apparently, according to his announcement when he arrives at the church on Wednesday evening. He's brought his guitar along specially.

'Don't be a dick, Barry,' mutters Storm, who claims she's only come along because she's dying of boredom. Although I overheard her humming one of our competition songs this morning. She blanches when Jennifer bustles in through the door and rushes off to sit at the piano, hidden behind Michaela.

'Are you quite sure about this, Barry?' I murmur so no one can hear while they're taking their seats. 'I don't want you to be upset if the choir decides the song isn't for them. They're quite old fashioned and your creative genius might be a little too, um, avant-garde for their conservative tastes.'

'Don't worry, babe. They'll love it,' says Barry, tuning his guitar. It's a glorious chestnut colour and covered in stickers from various bands.

'Love what?'

Kayla has crept up without me noticing. Usually, she's hard to miss on account of her being one of the loudest people I've ever known. She also loves wearing bright colours and short skirts that Roger describes as belts. But tonight her look can best be described as subdued. The plain, grey jumper she's wearing has a polo neck and if her light-brown trousers have an elasticated waist, it wouldn't surprise me. They're hideously frumpy. Her pale face is make-up free, which looks fine actually because the freckles across the bridge of her nose are cute. But there are dark, puffy shadows under her green eyes.

'How are you doing?' When I give her a hug, she's more bony than usual – I'm sure she's lost a pound or two since Saturday night. 'I've called into the pub to see you a few times but you were either hard at work or Roger said you were asleep.'

'Yeah, I've been sleeping a lot and didn't really feel up to talking about stuff. But I'm fine now.' She bares her teeth in what I presume is meant to be a smile. 'Don't look at me like that. I really am fine. I've had a lucky escape actually. Ollie's a nice bloke but I'm not ready to settle down with him in Salt Bay. So it's for the best.'

Her face tightens as she spots Ollie sidling into the church and she turns her head before he sees her. He looks miserable as sin.

'You two still aren't speaking then?'

'Nope,' says Kayla in a grating, overly cheery voice. 'Not since we had a few words on the phone on Sunday and he said it was best if we forget the whole affair. He's absolutely right 'cos we want different things and I'll be off on my travels again soon. Plus, he's an arse and I never really liked him anyway. I was only using him for sex.'

'Of course you were, Kayla. He was your Salt Bay sex slave.'

She grins but her eyes are watering. 'Stupid hay fever,' she exclaims, pulling a tissue from her pocket and sniffing into it.

Yeah, stupid hay fever. In December.

Kayla takes a seat as far away from Ollie as possible while I get the rehearsal underway. It's just me tonight because Josh has arranged an extra rehearsal for his school's Christmas play, which is driving him demented.

His students won't learn their lines and, with opening night approaching, it's yet another pressure on my poor, overwhelmed boyfriend.

We start the rehearsal by singing the carols we'll be performing at the tree lighting – 'Ding Dong Merrily On High', 'Silent Night', 'O Little Town of Bethlehem' and, my favourite, 'Good King Wenceslas'. Then we go through the traditional Cornish songs we'll be singing in the final. Both were pretty much nailed last week but tonight they sound lifeless and dull. Notes are in tune and harmonies merge but the singing is lacklustre.

Usually, rehearsals are fun. We enjoy making music together and having a laugh. But tonight the choir's *joie de vivre* is being strangled by thick strands of tension that are twisting and turning around us. Jennifer and Storm are glaring at one another, Ollie and Kayla are studiously ignoring each other, Emily is mooning over Jay while he's winking at Storm, and everyone is giving Barry the evil eye.

'Come on, people, where's the spark gone? Just sing out loud and proud and enjoy yourselves,' I implore them. But it does no good so we stagger on, murdering perfectly good music.

Just before the half-time break, Fiona raises her hand with a question. 'What about the contemporary song we have to sing? Did anyone send in suggestions?'

'I've had a couple. Maureen suggested a Take That medley because she *lurves* Gary Barlow.' I grin at Maureen who, beneath her staid tea shop owner exterior, is a Gazza super-fan. 'And Charlie thought a David Bowie tribute might be a nice idea. I've got a few suggestions too and Michaela can play through those after the break.'

'I've told you before that I'm not singing popular music,' pipes up Arthur. 'You'll be asking us to rap like Kanye next. Ridiculous! This is a serious choir.'

I'm quite impressed that Arthur knows who Kanye is, seeing as his knowledge of music stops at around 1850.

'I promise no rapping, Arthur,' I reassure him. 'But what about a David Bowie tribute?'

'Totally unoriginal,' calls Barry. 'Everyone will be doing Bowie.'

Great. Even my own father is now dissing me in public.

'Can you do better then?' retorts Jennifer.

'Funny you should say that, Jenny.' Barry pulls a sheaf of hand-written music from his jacket pocket with a flourish. 'You should sing something new, something fresh, something fabulous, with no copyright red tape to get your knickers in a knot. In fact, something I've written just for you.'

'I'm not sure about this, Barry,' I say as Jennifer groans and stretches her neck towards the rafters. But uber-keen Barry has already scrambled out of his chair and picked up his guitar.

He perches on the end of a pew facing the choir and flicks his long hair from his shoulders. 'I've called this song "The Great Storm".'

There's a murmur of discontent from the choir and I go hot and cold as the plaque to the men who died in the Great Storm shines behind Barry's head. My father is about to sing some dreadful song about the village tragedy in front of Cyril, who lost two grandsons when their boat was submerged by towering waves.

'I'm not sure that's appropriate,' I hiss, but there's no stopping Barry, who's already strumming his guitar with calloused fingers. At least it sounds quite gentle, with no hint of heavy metal.

Swallowing hard, I sit down on the edge of the podium as guitar chords fill the church and Barry starts to sing.

Ed Sheeran has nothing to worry about. Barry's voice is in tune but thin and unremarkable. He basically sounds like a middle-aged bloke singing karaoke in the local after a few pints. But as the song gets into its swing, the murmur of discontent settles and people start listening properly.

Blimey, I can't believe it! Barry's song is tuneful and the words are beautiful, like a poem. He's also pretty good on the guitar.

His song tells of the cataclysmic storm that wrought havoc but mostly it's about the men who died, the families they left behind, and their small community ripped apart. The chorus brings tears to my eyes, and I'm not the only one.

Waves forever wash upon the shore
As mothers mourn Salt Bay sons
Who sail no more.

As the last strum of Barry's guitar fades away, there's a stunned silence and a flicker of uncertainty crosses his face. Then Arthur gets to his feet and slowly begins to applaud. His sharp claps bounce off the worn stone and become a wave of applause as the whole choir joins in. Even Jennifer taps her hand against her skirt, too conflicted to applaud properly. Storm doesn't join in but treats me to a rare smile.

'Cheers! It's nice to know I've still got it!' Barry grins and takes a bow. 'I've written harmonies so you can sing the song together in your different parts and I can accompany on guitar. It'll make a nice change from that plinky-plonky piano. No offence, Michaela love.'

Michaela shrugs and pushes her heavy-framed glasses further up her nose.

Stepping back onto my podium, I face the choir. 'What do you reckon then?'

'I never thought I'd say this but I think we should sing Barry's song,' says Jennifer, giving the composer a grudging nod. 'It's unique, relatively tuneful, and it speaks about Salt Bay and what happened here. It's the story of Salt Bay Choral Society.'

When there's a murmur of assent, Barry pulls a sheaf of folded music from his inner jacket pocket and starts handing the sheets around. 'That's sorted then. Let's go through it now. Bugger the break!'

Barry has written a four-part harmony and he plays through and sings each part. Then he lets me take over and, by the end of the rehearsal, 'The Great Storm' is sounding fairly decent. There's still a way to go before we're ready for a public performance but there are still some rehearsals before the final and we can slot in extra practice, if need be.

Barry's song has given everyone a boost and the choir is far more cheerful when we break up to go home. Even Ollie makes jokes with Tom and Jay, though his voice is overly loud and he keeps glancing at Kayla, who's swapping hair-care tips with Michaela at the piano. Storm has already sloped off home after first checking that Jennifer didn't accost Barry with tales of his light-fingered daughter.

It takes me five minutes to sort out the chairs that Roger has returned to the vestry – he has a habit of piling them up too close to the door – and by then there's no one left in the church except for me and Barry.

He's crouched over, placing his guitar into its case when I give a slight cough to warn him I'm approaching.

'Thank you, Barry, for composing a song for the choir. It's really good.'

Barry glances up from fastening the silver catches on the scuffed case. 'You thought it would be awful, didn't you?'

'Of course not,' I say quickly, my face flushing.

'It's all right. Storm thinks it's rubbish.' Barry stands up and swings the case up and over his shoulder. 'Mind you, she thinks that about everything I do. But that's daughters for you.'

His blue eyes lock onto mine. Usually they're sparking with vitality and mischief but tonight they look sad. If I didn't know any better, I'd say that my father's feelings were hurt.

'The words were really beautiful, Barry,' I gabble, overcome by an annoying urge to make him feel better. 'How did you find out so much about what happened sixteen years ago?'

'I asked Alice and she told me all about it.'

'Alice! Really?'

When I first arrived in Salt Bay, no one spoke about the tragedy. It was a sorrowful secret that sucked the joy out of this community. But people have changed since the choir was resurrected and brought new life to the village. Alice has changed.

'Have you played the song to her?'

'Not yet but I will. I wanted you to hear it first.'

Barry drops his piercing, hypnotic gaze that's making me uncomfortable and zips up his jacket.

'I'm not as horribly insensitive as you think, Annie.'

'I don't think that at—' I stop. What's the point in pretending? I've had Barry pegged as an insensitive, tactless fool but that's not what his beautiful song suggests. 'Why did you write the song?'

'For you,' says Barry simply. 'Because I've been such a rubbish dad. I don't suppose it makes up for not being around for twenty-nine years but it's better than nothing. And it might help you to win that daft competition. Anyway—' he trots over to the church door with the guitar case bouncing up and down on his back '—are you coming to the pub?'

'I don't think so. I'm really tired and Josh isn't here so I'll get an early night.'

Barry pauses, framed in the doorway. 'I'll be up early sorting out the attic tomorrow so I'll give the pub a miss too and walk back to Tregavara House with you.'

He steps into the church porch, holding the door open for me, while I wonder when Barry Stubbs, Worst Dad in the World, was switched for a normal human being.

Chapter Twenty-Five

One reason I'm so godawful tired all the time is heavy, corrosive guilt that's sapping my soul. I keep squashing it down but it turns out that guilt is the bad penny of unwanted emotions.

It's extra soul-sappy at the moment because Lucy and Toby have been in touch and I'm now a co-conspirator regarding the meeting. This will take place at ten o'clock on the same day as the competition Grand Final, which is also my birthday. Yay for me! Two weeks on Saturday, Toby will meet his daughter for the very first time and I will begin a new decade of life by… cheating on my boyfriend. That's how it's starting to feel. I may not be shagging someone else behind Josh's back but I'm still screwing him over big-time.

Clearing Tregavara House on the day shouldn't be a problem: Alice will be with Penelope for their traditional festive lunch at a posh hotel, Emily's arranged to go Christmas shopping with her mum, Storm will be working off her sentence in Jennifer's shop, if she and Barry are still around. And I can always send Barry out on some spurious errand. If only clearing my conscience was as easy.

I've tried logic, meditation, striding across cliffs and remembering the reality of being a fatherless child until it made me cry. But I can't shift gut-wrenching guilt that's stickier than superglue.

Everything comes to a head on Friday evening as I'm standing in a gale on the harbour wall, watching tethered boats dip and sway. That's where you'll often find me when a storm hits Salt Bay.

Seagulls are white specks in the lights from Tregavara House, buffeted by air currents sucking them high into the sky. And the blustery wind is so strong it keeps pushing me along the stone wall. But I love it out here.

There's something primal about Cornwall when waves are smashing into stone and salt spray is wet on my face. It strips away the self-imposed layers that blanket our lives and gets to the nub of what's important. Or maybe that's just me being a bit of a tree-hugger.

Either way, the fug in my brain lifts as the storm sets in and suddenly the way ahead becomes clear: *Doing the wrong thing for the right reasons makes no difference at all. It's still the wrong thing.*

I simply have to tell Josh. It'll cause ructions with Lucy and Toby, and I still believe Freya will lose out if the meeting doesn't go ahead. But secrets and guilt have built a wall between me and my lovely boyfriend and I need to knock it down. I have to tell him, face to face, when we meet up tomorrow.

However, first I have to call Toby. Telling my cousin I'm about to blab doesn't fill me with joy but I owe him that much. He's expecting to meet his daughter in a fortnight and I was the person who set things in motion. Oh boy, if Toby disliked me before, he's going to hate my guts after this.

While his phone rings in London, I tap my fingers nervously on the smeared glass of the village phone box. Please don't pick up! Delivering my news to a soulless answerphone will be so much easier. The phone continues to ring as I *tap-tap-tap* until – hooray! – Toby's voicemail clicks into life and I leave a carefully rehearsed message. Toby will be furious and I'll have to face Lucy once I see how Josh reacts to my confession. But I feel lighter as I walk back to Tregavara House.

*

Saturday dawns bright and clear. The storm has blown itself out, leaving one of those gorgeous early December days when people's breath hangs white in the crisp, cold air. Josh and I have plans to go shopping in Penzance later, now I've persuaded him that panic-buying on Christmas Eve is a Bad Idea – but first of all I need to confess what's been going on. I'm not looking forward to it.

Josh arrives much earlier than expected, as I'm washing up after my breakfast, and barges in through the kitchen door without knocking. There's a flush on his cheeks and a dark shadow of stubble on his strong jaw. He hasn't shaved since yesterday.

'Is everything OK? Is your mum all right?'

Josh nods but doesn't catch my eye.

He knows, whispers my inner voice. But how can he? Lucy won't have said anything.

'Good morning, Josh,' calls Alice, who's still shuffling around in her dressing gown. She gets dressed later and later these days. 'How is your mother doing?'

'Mum's having a pacemaker fitted next week. We've just heard it's scheduled for Tuesday morning at the hospital. There's been a cancellation.'

That's why he's so stressed! Stripping off my rubber gloves, I wander over to stroke his arm but Josh moves to close the door and my hand falls back to my side.

'Do send Marion our best wishes.' Alice gives a slight shake of the head. 'This heart business is such a shame but she's a relatively young woman and I'm sure she'll be fine after the operation. Having a pacemaker fitted is fairly routine these days.'

'So I've been told. We can't help worrying about it though and Mum's nervous.' Josh glances at the glistening wet bowls on the draining board. 'If you've finished washing up, Annie, let's go for a walk on the cliffs. I'll meet you outside. See you later, Alice.'

He rushes back out into the garden, banging the door closed behind him, before I can point out the dirty tea cups still in the sink.

Alice shrugs. 'I can manage those. Give him some leeway, Annabella. He's exhausted from looking after his family and worried sick about his mother.'

'Don't worry, Alice. I'll be understanding and supportive. I know what it's like to be sick with anxiety about your mum.'

'Of course you do, dear,' murmurs Alice, before biting into a thick slice of toast. 'And wear a hat if you're going up on the cliffs. It's freezing out there.'

Josh is pacing back and forth by the garden gate when I get outside and, without a word, he heads for the cliffs with me scampering after him. It's hard to keep up and he doesn't break his long stride, even when I grab hold of his arm to try to slow him down.

He knows, says my inner voice again but I ignore it. He's worried about his mum, that's all.

Eventually I give up and let Josh go ahead and he reaches the top of the cliffs a couple of minutes before me.

'Blimey,' I puff towards him, very aware that my face is glowing pillar-box red. 'You've got to remember that my legs are much shorter than yours. Plus I'm not as fit as—' I was going to say Felicity but decide not to '—as other people.'

I turn full on into the breeze to cool my cheeks and look out across the sea towards the horizon. The water is a deep indigo today with darker shadows where rocks are lurking beneath white crested waves. It's beautiful.

'I'm really sorry about your mum, Josh. You must be worried but the operation will give her a whole new lease of life.'

'I know that and the sooner it's done, the better.'

Josh stares along the jagged coastline bathed in wintry sunlight. He looks moody and troubled and absolutely gorgeous and I'm so tempted to give him a hug. But first I need to talk to him about Toby and Freya, the meeting that's weighing so heavily on my mind. I feel mean adding to his troubles but he needs to know.

'Josh.'

When he doesn't move, I call his name again and, when he turns towards me, I'm shocked by how haggard he looks.

'Is there something you need to tell me?' he says, slowly. 'Or is everything in your life a secret?'

I'm suddenly aware of my own heartbeat pounding in my ears. The pulse is so loud it partly masks the thunder of waves hitting rock far below us.

'What do you mean?'

'Surely you've got something to tell me about your cousin. And Lucy.'

He damn well knows, screams my inner voice. *I told you so.* My chest tightens and I'm finding it hard to breathe.

'How could you, Annie? You know how I feel about Toby and the way he's treated Lucy and Freya. How could you arrange for them to meet without telling me?'

Confusion is etched across his handsome face and I could cry.

'I'm so sorry. I shouldn't have arranged a meeting without telling you but Lucy and I were so worried about you.'

'About me?'

'Yes, you. You're so tired all the time, working and doing private tutoring to scrape money together and it's not fair. Toby should be paying towards Freya.'

'But that's not your decision,' Josh is almost shouting but his words are whipped away by the wind.

'And it's not yours. It's Lucy's, and she wants the meeting to go ahead. Did she tell you about it?'

'Only when I confronted her this morning about what was going on. I could tell something was up. I know my sister very well, far better than I know you, apparently.' He shakes his head and grimaces. 'I don't want Freya meeting that awful man.'

'That awful man is her father, Josh, and, however much you don't like the idea, he has a right to see his daughter. And, more importantly, she needs to know who her father is. That's the main reason why I got involved.'

Josh runs his hands through his thick, black hair and takes a deep breath.

'I can kind of understand that. You grew up without a dad which wasn't easy and you don't want Freya to suffer in the same way. I get it. I really do. But Freya has nothing in common with Toby. And I don't want my lovely, innocent niece polluted by your dreadful family.'

His words strike me like a blow.

'Is that how you see my family, as pollution? Is that how you see me?'

It's hard to get my words out and they tumble over one another as the waves boom into granite rocks far below us. I've so badly mishandled this whole thing and hurt Josh and now he's hurting me, which I guess is only fair.

'I thought you were different,' says Josh, the muscles in his jaw so taut his face is like a mask. 'But you organised this behind my back, without saying a word.'

'It was Toby and Lucy who organised the meeting but I agreed to keep it a secret. I'm sorry. That was wrong and it's been eating me up.

I actually rang Toby last night to tell him I couldn't keep it from you any longer. I was going to tell you about it today.'

'Of course you were,' says Josh, as a squawking seagull swoops over our heads and out to sea. He closes his eyes for a moment before pulling himself up tall. 'I cared so much about you, Annie, but we can't have a relationship that's built on secrets and lies.'

Cared? Josh is using the past tense. I grab his arm and curl my fingers around the heavy fabric of his coat.

'I didn't lie, and it was only one secret. A big one, I know that, but I thought I was doing what's best for you and Freya. I'm so sorry and I was going to tell you.'

'Lying by omission is still lying. And I can't cope with all of this right now.'

Josh shakes off my hand and strides back the way we came, with his long black coat flapping behind him.

'So, is that it?' I yell after him.

'Yes, that's it,' he shouts without breaking his stride. 'I can't be in a relationship with someone I can't trust.'

'You can trust me,' I call, scampering after him.

Warm tears are sliding down my cheeks but Josh shakes his head and keeps on walking.

'What about the choir?' I yell, desperate to come up with anything that will make him stay and talk to me.

'I'll help out until the final so I don't let people down. And after that, it's all yours – if you're still here, that is, and not back in your precious London. Goodbye, Annie.'

And he leaves me there, with the cliffs and the deep blue sea that matches my mood.

Chapter Twenty-Six

I slip in through the back door but, just my luck, Alice is still in the kitchen, pottering about in her dressing gown. Doesn't she ever get dressed these days?

'Hello, that was quick. I was just about to make another cup of tea. Would you—?' She catches sight of my face and pauses with one hand on the kettle. 'Oh, Annabella, what's happened? Are you all right?'

'I'm fine,' I sniff, patently lying because I've been sobbing for ten minutes and my eyes are puffy slits. Any make-up I had on is now plastered across the tissue I've been using to scrub tears from my cheeks.

'Is it Marion? Is she worse than we thought?'

'No,' I gulp. 'Josh and I have decided to call it a day. We broke up.'

My lips are wobbling but, surely to goodness, I can't have any tears left. The human body is about fifty per cent water but it was like Niagara Falls up on the cliffs and my tear ducts must be spent.

'But why, Annabella? You're so good together. Is it because Barry and Storm are here?'

I shake my head, very tempted to tell Alice the real reason, because it was keeping secrets that got me into this mess in the first place. But Lucy's secret is not mine to tell and I've already upset Josh enough.

'It just isn't working, Alice,' I say resolutely, pinching the back of my hand to make sure my tear ducts stay dry. 'These things happen.'

'Do you want to talk about it?'

Alice holds onto the table and lowers herself into a chair. She's ready for me to open my heart which is so sweet of her. Mum was always the one needing comfort when I was growing up so I'm not used to being listened to – and sympathy and support from Alice would be wonderful right now when my heart is breaking. But I can only tell her half the story.

'I'll be OK, thanks, Alice. I think I'll just go and have a little lie down for a while.'

Alice reaches out and pats my waist as I walk past, and there's a waft of her lily of the valley talcum powder.

'I hope you realise how very dear you are to me, Annabella.'

I nod mutely, aware that if I say anything at all I will erupt into heaving, snotty sobs. Again.

'This doesn't mean you'll be leaving Cornwall, does it?' asks Alice when I reach the door. The deep lines on her face are more pronounced under the bright kitchen light that no one's got around to turning off.

I shake my head to reassure her but the truth is that I don't know. My life has been upended within the space of half an hour. I let someone get too close and I messed up and now I'm paying the price. I've grown to love Salt Bay and its ragbag of weird and wonderful inhabitants. But how can I stay and watch Josh move on from me? He'll probably end up marrying Felicity and having super shiny children. Ugh.

After making it to my bedroom without bumping into Barry, I throw myself down on top of the counterpane, with my shoes still on. What's a little mud when your heart has been shattered?

It's all your own fault, whines my inner voice that *really* hates me. *You've messed up hideously. And now you'll die alone or end up settling for some bloke who sweats and has halitosis but you'll be super grateful*

because at least he puts up with your dreadful, man-repellent family. Like
I've said, my inner voice is a total bitch.

I lie on the bed for ages as the sun tracks its beams across the uneven
bedroom wall. Outside, children wrapped up in coats and hats are
shouting as they head to the harbour, and there's a low drone of boats
motoring towards shore. But I'm cocooned in my Bedroom of Misery.

I'm just nodding off into an exhausted sleep when the door is flung
open and Storm stomps in.

'I can't stand working for that slave-driver any longer,' she yells as
the door bangs into the wall and bits of paint flake onto the carpet.

Oh, great! It's going well, then.

'That woman has had me cleaning out her ice-cream fridge for the
last hour and it's full of crud. My fingers have got frostbite. Look!'
She waves grubby fingers in my face. 'And she's only given me a lunch
break because I threatened to call ChildLine. It's totally out of order.
She's a proper cow.'

I raise my head wearily from the pillow. 'Work in the shop or be
reported for shoplifting. It's your choice and to be honest, Storm, I
don't give a monkey's what you do. You can spend the night in Penzance
jail for all I care.'

Storm looks puzzled. Like most people who dish it out, she's not
so good at taking it.

'What's up with you?' She peers at my face. 'You've gone all blotchy.'

'Josh and I broke up,' I say flatly.

'Oh.' Storm plonks herself down on the bed. 'Well, I always thought
he was a loser if that helps.'

'It doesn't.'

Storm huffs, apparently offended that rubbishing my boyfriend – my
ex-boyfriend – isn't more comforting.

'Why did he dump you then?'

'He didn't.'

'You wouldn't have been crying so much if it was your idea.' She lightly touches my arm. 'But don't get so upset 'cos he obviously is a loser if he's decided you aren't good enough for him and he doesn't love you any more.'

I wish with all my heart that Storm would just stop talking. She's not going to get a job as a counsellor any time soon.

'Anyway, sorry,' she mumbles, standing up, shaking out her legs and heading for the door. 'I'd better go.'

Hallelujah! But she suddenly swings round and plonks herself back down on the bed.

'My mum doesn't want me either,' she says in a rush, picking at threads on the faded yellow counterpane. 'What I mean is, you're not the only one who isn't wanted.' She bites her lip. 'Mum says she loves me and I'm still her daughter and all that crap, but apparently I'm a bad influence on Poppy and Eugenie – that's her new children. They go to private school and talk funny and they're dead posh.'

'That must be difficult for you.' I pull myself up and sit back against the soft pillows.

'I see Mum every now and again and life's all right with Barry. He just got landed with me, like you and Alice have. He's a dork and I've never known anyone who farts so much. There is something seriously wrong with his digestive system. But he looks after me – in his own special way.'

'Barry's very special, but he grows on you – a bit like a fungal infection.'

Storm and I share a smile, united in exasperation with our father.

'And you're not as snobby as I expected. At first I thought you were right up your own arse but you've chilled out. A bit. We came looking for you because Barry thought you might be loaded, but you're not and he's still stayed so he must like you too.'

'Hang on.' Suddenly I'm wide awake. 'Is that the only reason Barry came looking for me, because he thought I had money?'

'No, not really.' Storm starts twisting yellow threads around her fingers. 'Don't tell Barry I said anything or he'll go off on one.'

'So when you were both leaving and the car wouldn't start...'

'That was Barry,' she sighs. 'He unhooked the something or other so the engine wouldn't work and we could stay a bit longer. He only told me later and I was well annoyed. It was so he could get to know you better.'

'Me and my bank account.'

'No, honestly, it's not that. He knows you're skint. You won't make us leave, will you, not before Christmas?'

'Why would you want to stay? You hate school and Salt Bay and everyone in it.'

'Yeah, it's so boring here and London is so much better. Only—' she stops, swallowing hard '—there's no one there who gives much of a toss about me. Barry's friends ignore me and he usually works over Christmas, doing hotel work if there's nothing happening with his band, so I'm dumped on someone. Last year it was his mate Rodney who spent the day playing *Street Fighter*. I thought Christmas here might be a bit different.'

'Don't you ever go to your mum's at Christmas?'

'No, I told you, bad influence. I swear too much.'

'Which you bloody well do.'

Storm laughs. Properly laughs!

She glances at the huge, black rubber watch on her wrist. 'Balls! The old witch will be on the phone to the police if I'm not back in five minutes. She's such a grass.'

After she's finally, blessedly, left the room, I lie back down and stare at the cracked ceiling. What a perfectly rubbish morning! Dumped by the man I love and then discovering that my father only came calling because he thought I might be worth a bob or two. And just when I was starting to think that having a long-lost father might not be so awful after all.

Kicking off my shoes, I crawl under the counterpane and imagine I'm standing high on Hampstead Heath, looking across London. The pull of the city has never fully gone away and, right now, it's a ginormous magnet drawing me back.

It would be so easy to walk away from Salt Bay complications and heartbreak, like my mum did thirty years ago. A new flat, a new job and Bob's your uncle – I'd soon be back in the swing of the cosmopolitan city with Cornwall far behind me and Josh just a distant memory. Give it a couple of decades and a shedload of therapy and I might even start dating again. Pulling the covers over my head, I close my eyes and pretend that none of this is happening to me.

Chapter Twenty-Seven

It's Saturday night and I'm spending it with Kayla, who's blagged the evening off after telling Roger I've been dumped (which I have) and am suicidal (which I'm not). So here we are, two lovelorn saddos together. And we're both pretty wasted.

'Tell me again why that glowering Cornish git dumped you?' says Kayla, slumping across a table in the Growling Owl.

We've ventured out of the sticks into hip and happening Penzance – woohoo! – because we want to avoid pitying looks in the Whistling Wave. But Growling Owl? Whoever thinks up pub names around here must have imbibed rather too much of the product.

'As I've told you many times already, Ms Corrigan, we argued and he said that our relationship wasn't working.'

I'm not so drunk that I'm going to start blabbing about Lucy's secret.

'Hhmm, that is the most ridiculous reason I've ever heard. No one's relationship "works". It's all lies and deceit and passive-aggressive comments but that's what love is and you've just got to put up with it.'

Kayla downs a huge slug of her gin and tonic and wobbles the glass in front of my face. The liquid inside twinkles as it reflects the fairy lights on the pub's Christmas tree.

'Anyway, you two are made for each other,' asserts Kayla, 'unlike me and Ollie. I didn't like Ollie much anyway, with his Greek god good looks and his chunky thighs. And who the hell does he think he is asking me to marry him?'

'I know,' I slur. 'What a total liberty!'

The branches of the plastic tree are starting to smudge and blur into one another. Maybe a fourth vodka and cranberry juice on an empty stomach wasn't such a good idea.

'I mean – oops—' Kayla's chair wobbles on two legs as she leans back too far '—I mean, he must have known I'd say no, so it's all his fault for asking me such a stupid question in front of so many people.'

'An incredibly stupid question.'

'But you and Josh can sort things out. He's a grumpy sod – absolutely no offence meant – but he's crazy about you. That's obvious.'

'Not any more. He's made his decision and Josh is very straight down the line, like an arrow.' I shoot out my arm in arrow-like fashion, almost hitting Kayla in the face. 'He's very black and white about everything and all I did was introduce some grey into his life for a while.' A horrible thought strikes my fuddled brain. 'Perhaps that's all I am, grey and boring. A big, grey, useless blob. A glob.'

'What on earth are you talking about, you drongo?' laughs Kayla, knocking over the last of my vodka and cranberry and watching as it pools on the table, like a blood stain.

'I dunno, but Josh and I are finished. Finito. End of the line.'

'Well, I think that's a shame.' Kayla glances at the empty glasses lined up along the edge of our table. 'What the fuck? Who drank all those?'

'I think we did.' I giggle but tears are pricking at the corners of my eyes. 'Hey, Kayla, here's some news for you. I've been thinking about going back to London.'

'Nooo,' wails Kayla so loudly people at the bar turn and look at us. 'You can't leave us.'

'Why not? You're thinking of moving on from Salt Bay.'

'Yeah but that's different. I'm an alien here, a nomad, a traveller, a woman out of time and place.'

'You're a drunk Aussie in Cornwall on a never-ending gap year.'

'Yeah, yeah.' Kayla bats my words away. 'But you belong here, Annie. You're one of them. Your family's been in Salt Bay for, like, thousands of years, and people need you.'

'Josh doesn't.'

'Josh, shmosh, he's a dickhead.' She starts ticking things off on her fingers. 'Alice needs you, and Emily, and your awful sister, and your dreadful dad, and I need you, and Salt Bay needs you, and the choir definitely needs you. Which all means you can't just leave before the competition and Christmas and your special birthday.'

Balls. In all the upset, I've forgotten my thirtieth birthday. What a doozie of a birthday that's going to be – spending all afternoon at the competition with Josh, who now hates me, and trying to get Salt Bay Choral Society to do the village proud. I bet we'll come last and be humiliated. Barry will probably do one of his legendary farts in front of the judges.

I clonk my head down onto the sticky table and sigh while Kayla pats my hair.

Running away is tempting. So tempting. But who am I kidding? I'm not my mother and it's not my way. I can't abandon Alice or leave the choir in the lurch. Not after they've done so much for me and made me feel part of this weirdly wonderful community.

Nope, I just have to come to terms with the fact that I'll always be sad. And, as I get older and Josh and Felicity have lots of children and grandchildren, I'll become bitter – the bitter mad old lady of Salt Bay. And then I'll die.

I close my eyes and doze slightly as Kayla finishes off her drink and lurches to the bar for another.

*

People tiptoe round me at Tregavara House the next morning. I'm not sure whether it's because they feel sorry for a sad loser who's been dumped or because I have the stonking hangover from hell.

'The whites of your eyes are pink, like a rabbit's,' says Emily, gazing at me in awe.

'Oh my days, you look terrible,' adds Storm in a very loud voice that makes my poor dehydrated brain rattle in my skull.

Alice stays quiet but places a large, steaming mug of tea in front of me and tells me to drink up. I sip at it gingerly while trying not to heave. Damn alcohol! I resolve never to drink again though that's a resolution I've made several times before.

When I've had a bath, and am feeling slightly less deceased, I walk very, very slowly to the phone box so I can make a private call. Toby picks up on the third ring.

'Hey Toby, that was quick,' I mumble. My lips are desert-dry and my tongue feels too big for my mouth.

'Annie, it's you.' He sounds disappointed but then Toby often does when speaking to me. 'Why are you calling me on a Sunday morning? You don't want the painting back yet, do you? We need to get the house properly secured first, with a burglar alarm and window locks.'

'Alice hasn't mentioned the painting.' I gather my scattered thoughts. 'I'm calling about the meeting with Freya. I'm afraid it's not likely to happen.'

'Why not?' splutters Toby. 'You didn't really tell Josh Pasco about it, did you, like you threatened in your voicemail?'

'I wasn't threatening, and Josh found out before I said anything anyway and he isn't happy about the meeting.'

'Marvellous!' drawls Toby from his plush, gazillion-pound apartment on the riverside in Chelsea. 'So Josh says no and we all have to dance to his tune, even though she's my daughter.'

'This is Josh who's been working all hours to support your daughter because you've never contributed a penny.'

'I certainly don't need a lecture from the likes of you,' retorts Toby as I rest my hot forehead against the cool glass of the phone box. Ugh. A blob of grey chewing gum has attached itself to my skin and stretches into a long strand when I pull my head back. Picking off the gum, I drop it onto the floor, feeling even more nauseous.

'Are you still there? Can't you persuade Josh stupid Pasco to stop poking his nose in? You are his girlfriend after all.'

'Not any more.'

There's a slight pause on the crackly line. 'You've come to your senses at last and told him to get lost, then.'

'No, Josh broke up with me because I kept your meeting with Freya a secret from him. He doesn't trust me and, quite frankly, I don't blame him.'

I'm almost crying because I'm not sure what hurts the most – my rattling, hungover head or my trampled, battered heart. There's silence from Toby while I snivel pathetically down the line, then he clears his throat.

'Has Lucy said that the meeting is off? She hasn't texted me.'

What a charmer! My heart is in shards and all he cares about is seeing the daughter he's never taken the slightest bit of interest in before now.

'I haven't spoken to Lucy but I'm sure she'll be led by her brother.'

'No doubt. I'm disappointed but I doubt whether it would have come to any good anyway. It's probably just as well that the meeting has been aborted. I tried but it's not to be.'

There's relief in his voice, the hint of a guilty conscience being eased.

'You could still think about paying something towards her maintenance. It costs a fortune to bring up a child.'

Toby ignores me. He's the richest person I know, and also the tightest. 'Must go. Thanks for your call, Annie, and, um, chin up about breaking up with Josh Pasco. If it helps he's a complete bastard.'

'It doesn't,' I say wearily as Toby puts the phone down.

After staring at the receiver for a while, I place it back into its cradle. I should call Lucy about the meeting but Josh might be nearby and overhear us talking. Plus, Lucy didn't even try to warn me that Josh had found out which was pretty mean. And I'm not sure I can string that many words together at the moment anyway.

I'll text Lucy tomorrow from work, I decide, wondering if Jennifer is open this morning and selling fizzy pop. The only thing I can stomach right now is coloured water with a shedload of sugar in it.

Chapter Twenty-Eight

I usually enjoy choir rehearsals because I've grown so fond of my ragbag of singers: Roger grumbling, Tom pulling up his jeans, Mary smiling serenely like Mother Teresa and newlyweds Charlie and Pippa canoodling in the break as though they can't bear to be apart.

But I'm dreading the next rehearsal and hoping it just won't happen. Maybe a freak blizzard will dump tons of snow on the village, or there'll be a nuclear apocalypse – just a minor one, obviously, with no casualties; I can't expect others to suffer on my behalf. But Wednesday evening rolls around with no hint of snow or Armageddon in our peaceful corner of Cornwall.

I don't want to see Josh because I have no idea how to react, not being au fait with relationship etiquette regarding dumpers and dumpees. When past relationships have come to an end, it's all been very civilized; I've shed a few tears because that's kind of expected but, really, I've been relieved and have rarely seen ex-boyfriends again. But then I wasn't properly in love with them.

Kayla copes by convincing herself that she hates Ollie – but I can't do that. Josh Pasco, vulnerable Cornish pirate, has a place in my heart, which is in pieces now we've split up. But I can't blame him for ditching me and my dysfunctional family. His life is stressful and complicated enough.

I was only kidding myself that happy ever after was possible with a decent man like Josh. My shiny, new life in Salt Bay made me believe it for a while, but it was all fantasy.

Josh is already in the church and chatting to Jay when I arrive just before seven-thirty. My stomach does a weird lurch when he catches my eye and immediately looks away, without even the hint of a smile. Ooh, this is going to be awful but it can't be put off any longer. Josh and I need to have a civilised break-up if the choir is to stand any chance of doing well in the competition.

Taking a deep breath to calm my nerves, I march up the aisle. 'Hi, Jay, and hello, Josh.'

'Hey, Annie. Wha's happenin'?' says Jay brushing boyband hair off his forehead. He treats me to his glaringly white smile before he wanders off, leaving me and Josh alone.

For one horrible moment, I think Josh is going to ignore me, but he gives a wan smile and says hello.

'How's Marion doing?' I ask, keen to find out how she is, as well as keep the conversation going.

'She had the op yesterday and all went well. She came home last night.'

'That's brilliant. Give her my love and I hope she's soon feeling much better.'

'I will, thanks.'

'It must be a weight off your shoulders.'

'It is.'

And then we stand there, like ill-at-ease strangers who'd far rather be somewhere else. The fitted navy jumper Josh is wearing makes him appear thinner than usual, and the lovely face I've kissed so many times is pinched and pale.

'Hey, guys. It's so good to see that you two morons are talking,' gushes Kayla, rushing up behind me. She puts her arms round my waist and gives me a squeeze.

'We're both adults so why wouldn't we be?' says Josh. 'Although we're not together any more, we still like each other.'

Like! One of the blandest words in the English language. He'll be saying I'm nice next. My heart sinks into my scuffed boots. Josh Pasco doesn't love me any more. But at least he likes me. Hoo-feckin-ray!

Any further awkwardness is postponed by Jennifer, who's tapping her foot impatiently on the worn flagstones.

'Come along, people. There's an awful lot of work to be done before this choir attains an acceptable standard for the final and everyone is standing around, chatting. It's not professional.'

She points at Ollie, who's talking to Tom and studiously avoiding Kayla, who's staring at him. Pale Emily is in the corner mooning over Jay, who's leaning against the piano chatting up Storm. This ancient church must have soaked up so much sorrow over the centuries, and tonight it's full of unrequited love, longing and loss.

Feeling unutterably sad, I tap the edge of my music stand with the baton that belonged to Josh's stepdad.

'Right, let's crack on with making some music. The final is just around the corner and we've got the tree lighting ceremony next Saturday. Christmas is coming!'

Cyril gives me a thumbs up, bless him, but everyone else seems unimpressed at the prospect of carols and wassailing. Christmas is coming and I've never felt less festive in my whole life.

The first half of the rehearsal goes pretty well, considering. People have been practising Barry's song at home and it's starting to come together. There's one soaring section, where everyone's singing in harmony and the key changes from minor to major, that makes the hair on the back of my neck stand up. And Jennifer's solo that starts the song is particularly magnificent.

She bagged the solo at once but was the obvious choice anyway with her crystal-clear soprano voice which, she never tires of telling us, was classically trained in Paris. Quite why she ditched the chic French capital for unreconstructed Salt Bay remains a mystery. In fact, the more I get to know Jennifer, the more I realise that I don't really know her at all.

Maureen has brought in Christmas cupcakes and people descend on them during the break. They're fabulous creations, piled high with rich, yellow buttercream and topped with Santas made from red icing. My appetite has disappeared but Alice will appreciate a sugar rush if I take one home for her.

I'm in the cake queue, hoping the gannets in front of me won't scoff the lot, when Florence sidles up, ruddy cheeks glowing under her grey perm. She always looks as if she's spent the day outdoors, ploughing.

'Is everything all right, Annie?' she asks quietly, placing her rough, red hand on my arm. 'Only you and Josh seem a little... out of sorts this evening.'

'We're fine, thanks, Florence. It's nothing. Just a bit of an argument.'

'Don't worry,' says Pippa, who's behind me in the cake queue.

She was off carbs before the wedding but has made up for it since, and a tiny pot belly is just showing over the top of her skinny jeans. It's weird because the rest of her is as skinny as ever and... oh, wow! My mouth drops open as the pregnancy penny drops.

Pippa puts a finger on her lips and grins, before linking her arm through mine. 'It'll just be a lover's tiff between you and Josh, and believe me—' she lowers her voice '—the make-up sex will be fantastic.' Then she blushes furiously.

'Thanks, Pippa, but we broke up for good. It's for the best really.' I glance around to make sure Josh is out of earshot. He's sitting on his own at the back of the church, drinking orange squash from a plastic cup and staring into space.

'Ah, that's a shame but I'm sure you can work things out.' Florence steps in front of me and grabs a squidgy cake. 'Me and Bob have had our ups and downs, and life's not easy now he's ill all the blessed time, but things always work out.'

'Not this time, I'm afraid. It's really over but I'd rather not talk about it.'

Florence isn't keen to let the subject drop, even though buttercream is oozing through her fingers.

'But you two are so good together. Whose daft idea was it to split up?'

'It's what Josh wanted but he had his reasons.'

'I can't think of any reason why Joshua Pasco would break up with a lovely little thing like you,' says Florence in her soft Cornish accent.

And she sounds so maternal, I suddenly ache with longing to see my mum. She'd look after me and show me how to get over a broken heart. Actually, she probably wouldn't but I'd love to see her, all the same.

My lower lip starts to wobble and, to my amazement, Jennifer marches over in a cloud of Diorissimo and slips her arm around my shoulders. I didn't realise she was listening.

'Men can be thoughtlessly cruel, Annie,' she says in a loud voice that carries across the church. 'They're self-centred creatures and not all they're cracked up to be.'

'That's true,' pipes up Mary, 'which is why I've always preferred women anyway.'

Did Mary just come out in the middle of a Salt Bay Choral Society rehearsal? I glance at Kayla, who opens her eyes wide and shrugs her shoulders. No one else bats an eyelid so we've either got the wrong end of the stick or Mary's sexual preferences are old news around here.

I'm surrounded by women now and Josh will realise that I'm talking about him. He'll hate that. Though he's now in a huddle with Ollie and Gerald and they seem to be having an intense conversation. Gerald suddenly looks at me and shakes his head. Oh great, my tragic love life will be all over the village by tomorrow. Kayla and Roger have kept schtum so far after I threatened to get hysterical in the pub if they blabbed. But very little stays a secret for long in Salt Bay, I realise, suddenly longing for the anonymity of London where heartbreaks can be buried.

By the time we crack on with the second half of the rehearsal, everyone knows my business and the choir starts to split along gender lines. The women are on my side, although they know nothing about the circumstances of our break-up. They keep smiling at me and scowling at Josh, who shifts uncomfortably under their hostile glares and loosens the collar of his snow-white work shirt. Even lovely Mary gives him a straight look.

Meanwhile, in a display of masculine solidarity, all the men (apart from Barry and Cyril) laugh overly loudly at Josh's attempts at humour and, once the rehearsal is over, they crowd around him, inviting him to drown his sorrows in the pub. Josh declines and is leaving the church, after giving me a nod goodbye, when I spot Barry following him. Oh, this can't be good.

Throwing on my coat, I lock up quickly and hurry towards Barry and Josh, who are deep in conversation by the churchyard gate. Snippets of their conversation carry through the cold, damp air but, as I get closer, Josh hunches his shoulders and walks off briskly towards the pub where he must have parked his car. Barry kicks at the low wall around the graveyard before sauntering off towards Tregavara House.

I follow Barry back home, where he walks straight past the front door and round the side of the house into the back garden. It's freezing cold but he stands there, staring unseeingly at the black cliffs that are towering above him.

'Barry, what are you doing back here?'

He jumps at the sound of my voice and turns to face me. 'Crikey, Annie. Are you trying to make me keel over? All I'm doing is getting some air and having a think.'

'And what was that with Josh just now?'

'I don't know what you mean.'

'What I mean is, I just heard you calling Josh a wanker outside the church. You're addicted to being rude to people in the churchyard!'

'I did not call him a wanker. I dispute the fact that word ever left my lips. However, I may have called him a tosser – and with very good reason. No one upsets my little girl and gets away with it.'

'I'm not your little girl, Barry, and I don't need you to fight my battles.'

'Maybe not, but I can't bear to see you hurt by some fly-by-night Cornish plonker who thinks he's the bees knees just because he looks a bit like that Poldark bloke off the telly. Glowering great arse!'

Oh, Lord. I sigh and rub at my tired eyes. 'Josh is a decent man, Barry, and you have no idea what this is all about. It's my fault so you need to keep out of it. Heaven knows what he thinks of all of us now.'

'I'm your dad, Annie, so I've got every right to be involved.'

'Why? You weren't involved when I was growing up. Or when Mum and I were doing midnight runners from flats when I was a kid because she couldn't afford the rent.'

'I've already apologised for that and explained what happened,' mutters Barry, his face in deep shadow but his breath white in the winter air. 'I'm here now and that's what counts.'

'You're only here because you thought I had money.'

'Says who? That's a wicked slur on my character,' blusters Barry. 'You, um, haven't been talking to Storm, have you?'

When I nod, I hear him suck his lower lip between his teeth.

'I see. I do love my younger daughter but she's got an almighty gob on her. Just like her mother.' He steps farther away from the cliffs that are looming over us like dark spectres, and sighs. 'I Googled you 'cos I'm getting on a bit and was curious to see if I did have another kid out there somewhere. Approaching fifty and the Grim Reaper getting closer gives you a different perspective on life. And then I saw a photo of you with this big house and it's true that I was broke and thought you might be worth a few bob. Yeah—' he gives a short laugh '—I can see that doesn't cast me in a particularly positive parental light.'

'You're not the dad of my dreams,' I say drily, wriggling my toes which have gone numb. 'Um, shall we continue this conversation indoors?'

'No,' puffs Barry. 'I need to say this now. Right.' He takes a couple of deep breaths and ploughs on. 'I soon realised that you're almost as skint as I am, although the old lady is worth a bob or two. But even though you can't help with bailing me out financially, I still stayed, didn't I?'

'Yes, because you thought you might eventually get your hands on some of Alice's money.'

'No, that's not why I stayed. That's not it at all. Oh, it's so ridiculously dark in this stupid village. Hasn't Cornwall heard of street lights? Come with me.'

He pushes his arm through mine and pulls me round to the front of the house where the porch light is shining across the garden.

'That's better. I can actually see you. Good grief, is that a bat?' He ducks as a black shape dive-bombs his bald patch. 'Look, I stayed because you're my daughter and you're impressive. Giving up London to build a new life in the sticks and set up the choir takes balls. Huge balls. I can't take any credit for the woman you've become but I really like you and I'm proud of you. And the day you call me "Dad" will be one of the happiest of my life.'

Well, isn't that flaming typical! I've waited a lifetime for a father to say nice things about me and then, when he does, it's after he's confessed to seeing me initially as a cash cow.

Barry stands in silhouette, waiting for me to speak, but what can I say? *I don't know if I really like you, calling you Dad would be too weird, and I have no idea what kind of balls you have.* Hhmm, probably best to leave out any mention of balls.

In the end, all I say is 'thank you', because it's hard to dislike someone who just called out a bloke for ditching me. Even if he has got the whole thing arse about face.

'OK. So long as you know I'm not here on the make. I'm just making up for lost time and trying to do what's best for Storm. She's back at school and working in Jenny's shop now which is a miracle. You're a good influence on her, Annie. Much better than me, and I can't bear to see you hurt. That's why I had a go at that bloke of yours.' He pushes his hands deep into his jacket pockets. 'Anyway, if you could just let us stay until after Christmas, I'd appreciate it.'

'What is it with you two and Christmas?'

'Christmas has never been a big deal for us. But I think it might be different here. Salt Bay is more of a Christmassy place. You've got a tree and everything.' He points in the vague direction of the fir tree on the village green. 'We've never had a tree.'

'What, never ever?'

'Not since Amanda left me and ran off with a merchant banker or, as I prefer to call him, a merchant wa—'

'OK, stay for Christmas,' I say quickly, cutting him off. 'But then the two of you will have to get back to your real lives. You can't stay here much longer.'

'I know. And thank you.'

Barry grabs hold of my hand and I let it rest in his for a moment before heading inside for the warmth of Tregavara House.

When I peep through the curtains, after making myself a hot chocolate, Barry is standing on the harbour wall looking out to sea, like a Salt Bay sentry.

I sip the sickly sweet chocolate and try not to cry. I've managed to impress the man I want to get rid of, and disappoint the man I love. That really is arse about face.

Chapter Twenty-Nine

The temperature continues to drop over the next few days and something is different when I open my eyes on Saturday morning. It's quiet. Too quiet. Usually I wake up to a chorus of screeching seagulls but they're muted this morning and the light snaking under my curtains has a strange bleached hue.

Walking barefoot to the heavy brocade curtains, I peep outside and do a double take. Wow, there's been a change while I slept and everything is so pretty!

Overnight, a soft blanket of snow has fallen and the paths and garden are coated. There's even a sprinkling on the harbour sand and the cliffs are stark white mountains, falling into a milk-white sea.

Tonight's tree lighting ceremony will be extra Christmassy if the village still has an Alpine vibe going on!

In spite of my broken heart, excitement fizzes up from my toes because I *love* snow. It's one of my favourite things in life – along with free Wi-Fi, actor Richard Armitage, and the skin on top of custard. Most people hate the wrinkled membrane on custard but I love the texture of it as it coats my mouth. And don't even get me started on blancmange.

Mum loved it too – snow, not blancmange – and, on the rare occasions it snowed in London, we'd take a cheap toboggan to the top of Primrose Hill and slide all the way down. Mum would yell with delight, louder than the kids, and I can still picture her with glowing cheeks and her long brown hair flowing behind her. They were good times.

As I'm opening the window a crack to see how cold it is, the front door slams below me and Storm bowls out with her head down. Oops, it's almost ten past eight – Jennifer will have her guts for garters.

Storm takes a few strides along the path before stopping and turning back towards the front door with a frown on her face. She kicks at the snow under her feet and swears loudly, just as Emily appears around the corner of the house, carrying the garden broom.

They'll probably do the usual and pretend they haven't seen each other but, nope, they're too close. Emily hesitates, then nods at Storm and starts sweeping snow from the path onto the garden. She really is a little Christmas angel, clearing the path so it's safer for Alice, bless her. Not for the first time, I thank my lucky stars that Alice took a punt on Emily as her live-in helper. She's young but she's capable and has a heart of gold.

'Oy, watch what you're doing with that broom,' yells Storm, jumping back when a flurry of snow lands on her foot. When she shakes her shoe, snow scatters in fluttery flakes. 'My feet will be soaking by the time I get to the shop. Why did it have to stupid snow anyway?'

Emily stops sweeping and leans on the broom. 'Don't you like snow? We don't often get any round here so, when it does snow, I think it's brilliant.'

'Yeah, but you think Salt Bay is brilliant.' Storm shivers, pulls up the collar of her jacket and buries her neck in it. 'Have you ever even been to Oxford Street?'

'Of course I have,' says Emily, indignantly, going red beneath her woolly hat which has stripy ear flaps and a bobble on top.

'How many times?'

'Twice.'

'Twice! In your whole life! That's sad!'

'London is a long way from here,' huffs Emily.

'Tell me about it.' Storm glances at her watch. 'I'd better go or I'll be even later and Jennifer will give me a right rollicking, like she's the Time Police or something.' She winces as her foot squelches down and snow snakes inside her canvas trainers.

'Do you want to borrow some wellies?'

'Wellies?' Storm gives a you-must-be-joking snort. 'I don't do wellies. At least, not wellies like yours.'

She grimaces at the acid-yellow rubber that's encasing Emily's feet.

Ignoring her, Emily fishes in the pocket of her sensible brown coat and pulls out a small white envelope.

'Before you go, this came for you. It was on the front door mat this morning but there weren't any footsteps. Someone must have put it through the door last night before the snow came.'

Storm takes the envelope and turns it over in her hands before tearing it open and pulling out a brightly coloured card. What the hell is it? I stand on tiptoe trying to read it but the card is nothing but a jumble of colours from here.

Storm gives the card a cursory glance and thrusts it into her jacket pocket before tiptoeing through the snow towards the garden gate. The wind has piled up sparkling mini-drifts against the wood and, though Storm gives the gate a sharp shove, it only opens partway. As she flattens herself against the gate post and squeezes through, the latch catches on the card poking out of her pocket and it flutters down into the snow. But by the time Emily has noticed, my half-sister is a navy-blue smudge in the distance.

Emily picks up the damp card and waves it at Storm before shoving it into her coat pocket. Wow, she's a much better person than me.

Although it's unethical and unfair and lots of other un-things, there's no way I'd have resisted having a quick peek.

Oh, hang on. Emily is fishing about in her pocket and, with a quick look to make sure no one's about, she pulls out the card and studies it for a few moments. Her shoulders slump and she hangs her head before carefully putting the card back into her pocket and going back to sweeping the garden path of snow. Now I'm even more curious.

*

By the time I've had a quick shower and got dressed, Emily is in the kitchen with Alice. There's a low murmur of voices as I come down the stairs and I'm about to join them when my eye is caught by the card drying out on the cast-iron radiator in the hallway.

I know I shouldn't – it's like reading someone's mail or checking their web history – but Emily's already had a look so my peeping won't count. Not really. And it's sisterly to find out who's contacting Storm in Salt Bay. She's only sixteen, after all.

Conscience settled, I pick up the thick, soggy card and scan it. It's an invitation to a nightclub in Penzance, to something called a Festive Fusion and Funk Night. Good grief, I must be getting old because that sounds awful. The words scrawled across the top of the card have smudged but are still legible: *Hope to see you there, gorgeous – Jay x*

Oh dear. No wonder lovelorn Emily was upset and, to be honest, I'm not overjoyed at the thought of Storm funking it up with cocky Jay. Sighing, I place the card back on the radiator and adjust it carefully until it's in exactly the same place as before.

Alice spends all of breakfast moaning about the snow, which I get because it means she's pretty much housebound. She can't risk slipping when she often loses her balance anyway. But the festive covering has lifted my spirits and, immediately the breakfast things have been washed and put away, I get wrapped up and slip outside.

It's another world out here. The sun has appeared from behind thick white clouds and is glinting on the snow which sparkles like tiny diamonds as I wander away from the harbour and up onto the cliffs. My wellies have a good grip and the snow is still soft so I don't slip and slide too much.

Wow, it's even more beautiful up here. Behind me, the roofs of the village are white and the branches of the village Christmas tree are brushed with snow. The clifftop cemetery is blanketed in white and snow piled up on top of each gravestone is bright against the black granite. Right now, there's nowhere in the world that I'd rather be.

Treading towards the edge of the cliff very carefully – because now would be a *really* bad time to slip – I peer over at Salt Bay beach far below me. The hair-raising Path of Doom that winds down the cliff is sprinkled and the two rock stacks standing tall and proud a little way out to sea are crowned with white. But the beach itself – the sand and huge boulders edged with rock pools – is clear. The tide must have been in and the beach submerged when snow started falling. The flakes floated into salt water and dissolved as quickly as they tumbled from the sky.

There's nowhere to sit without risking a numb bum so I brush snow from the top of Samuel's gravestone and lean against it, breathing in the bracing air. I like to think that my grandfather wouldn't mind.

After a while, I start to lose feeling in my toes so I head down the cliffs and march briskly into the village to keep warm. The snow is marked with footprints when I get closer to the houses and there are deep tyre tracks on the narrow road.

A group of youngsters are running around in delight on the blanketed village green. One little boy is patting the belly of a snowman near the fir tree that's festooned in lights, ready for tonight's switch-on.

It's a picture-perfect scene from a traditional English Christmas card. Americans would go mad for it, and seeing the youngsters having such fun almost makes me want to have kids.

As I stop to watch, one little girl rolls a perfect snowball, takes aim and throws it at the boy's head. It smashes and shatters onto the back of his neck and he starts grizzling as ice-cold snow slides inside the neck of his jacket.

Maybe kids aren't such a great idea after all, which is just as well now that the only man I'd contemplate procreating with doesn't want to spend time with me. I wonder if he's making babies right now with Felicity. Practically Perfect Felicity who probably loves snow and is a ski champion on the quiet.

Cupping a warm hand over my frozen nose, I trudge on towards Jennifer's shop. I intend to pick up Alice's paper and buy myself the most mahoosive bar of chocolate Jennifer has in stock. Then I'll head home for a chocolate binge – scientifically proven to help heal a broken heart. I bet Felicity never eats chocolate. Sugar, fat and carbs probably never pass her perfect plumped-up lips. Ugh. I'm not sure but I think that I might be a teensy, tiny bit obsessed with her.

It's minus two degrees in December but the display outside Jennifer's shop still includes a couple of blow-up beach balls and a garish striped windbreak for the beach.

'You could do with selling toboggans today, Jennifer,' I tell her, picking up a ginormous bar of Cadbury's Dairy Milk and wondering how many calories it contains.

'Not much call for them round here, thanks to the microclimate.'

'Micro-what?' I reluctantly put the Dairy Milk back and, for the sake of my hips, pick up a sensible packet of chocolate buttons.

'Microclimate. Parts of Cornwall are in a little bubble, something to do with the Gulf Stream. And it means that our climate is the mildest and sunniest in the country.'

'Blimey, are you sure?'

There was nothing but endless drizzle during my first few weeks in Salt Bay. Though to be fair, we've had a decent summer and the village was awash with sunburned tourists for weeks.

'I'm absolutely sure,' harrumphs Jennifer, who's wearing a thick grey sweater dress over what must be an industrial-grade girdle. 'We can grow plants here you'd never get in London gardens.' She winces when she says 'London' as thought the capital is a barren wasteland. 'Are you going to pay me for those chocolate buttons?'

As I'm rooting through my pockets for change, Jennifer serves a tall woman with jangly earrings who buys a copy of *Woman and Home* magazine.

'That's Linda from Perrigan Bay who's had work done on her face,' whispers Jennifer very loudly as Linda leaves the shop. 'She claims she hasn't but it's obvious when you go on an extended holiday and come back looking like you've spent a week in a wind tunnel.' Pulling back the skin on her cheeks, she purses her lips into a pout. She looks dreadful. 'Have you ever had Botox for the lines around your eyes?' she enquires, peering closely at my face.

Cheers, Jennifer. I self-consciously brush my fingers over the skin under my eyes and determine to raid Boots in Penzance for a vat of anti-wrinkle cream. No boyfriend, nightmare family, and now craggy crow's-feet too. I'm living the dream!

'I'm not saying you need it,' backpedals Jennifer. 'But maybe it's good to start early before the rot really sets in.'

'Where's Storm?' I ask, keen to move the subject on from my ravaged face.

'She's out the back, painting my storeroom. I'm keeping her away from customers for a while because she can be a bit bad-tempered with them,' grumps Jennifer, moving to close the shop door which Linda left open. 'She was late this morning, by the way.'

'Sorry,' I mutter, not sure why I'm apologizing for Storm's appalling timekeeping. 'I think the snow threw her a bit.'

'Talking of which, she turned up with sopping feet in ridiculous shoes. I've had to lend her a pair of my old boots to do the painting. You'll need to talk to her about dressing sensibly for the weather.'

'I'm not her mother, Jennifer,' I say wearily, pulling open the packet of buttons and shoving several into my mouth. The sweet chocolate starts melting on my tongue and instantly makes me feel better. Wouldn't it be great if we could mainline chocolate? Everything would seem more manageable with a chocolate drip constantly feeding atoms of deliciousness into your venous system.

'What's the situation with her real mother then?' asks Jennifer, settling down on the stool behind the counter. 'And why is Storm roaming round the country with an oaf like Barry? Oh, I know he's your father, Annie—' she waves her arm dismissively '—but he is an oaf, you must admit.'

Admitting nothing, I deliberate whether to give Jennifer any information or not. On the one hand, she's a dreadful gossip. But on the other, I'm sick and tired of keeping everyone's secrets.

'Storm's mother lives in London with her new husband and two young daughters and she doesn't seem to want much to do with Storm. So Barry's looking after her and bringing her up, as best he can.'

'Hhmm.' Jennifer gazes into the distance and thinks for a moment. 'Well, that puts Barry in a better light. It's not easy being a single parent, especially to someone like Storm, and at least he's not shirking his responsibilities. I don't like the sound of Storm's mother at all. I don't like to speak ill of people, but she sounds like a total bitch.'

'Jennifer!' I start laughing and she chuckles along with me.

'Well, she does. Did you want to see Storm?'

Not really but I follow Jennifer as she takes me through a low door behind the counter. I've never been back here before. Cardboard boxes are piled up along the sides of a narrow corridor and we have to pick our way along carefully.

'That's the problem with painting the storeroom. We had to empty it first,' explains Jennifer, pushing open a heavy black door. A strong smell of paint hits my nose as we step into the room which has high, narrow windows across one wall. They're open to let out some of the smell so it's absolutely freezing in here. Half of the room is a dingy nicotine colour but the other half is glowing a brilliant white. Storm has been busy with her paintbrush and is doing a good job, by the looks of things.

She's standing with her back to us in the farthest corner, slapping paint onto a wall and moving the paintbrush easily up and down in broad strokes. And she's singing. Storm is singing the song that Barry wrote for the choir. And it's beautiful.

Jennifer comes to an abrupt halt and puts out her arm to bar me from going any further into the room. 'Wait,' she whispers. 'Listen.'

So we listen while Storm's rich voice fills a tiny Cornish storeroom and she sings of the loss suffered by this small community long ago.

When she's finished, Jennifer claps and Storm swings round, arcing paint across the concrete floor.

'Bravo,' calls Jennifer, her cheeks flushed. 'Where have you been hiding that voice?'

'I didn't know you were listening,' scowls Storm. She's wearing huge white overalls and her feet are encased in scuffed black boots scattered with pimples of paint.

'Your singing was lovely,' I tell Storm but she shakes her head.

'Mum says I sound like a strangled cat.'

'Then your mother obviously has a cloth ear,' says Jennifer giving me a sharp look. 'Carry on singing, by all means, but make sure you don't slack on the painting. There's still a long way to go.'

Rolling her eyes, Storm slaps her brush into the paint pot and steps back as splashing paint starts dripping down the side of the tin.

'Do try to get more paint on the walls than on the floor,' sighs Jennifer, ushering me out of the room and closing the door behind her.

'We have to get that girl into the choir,' she tells me the moment the door clicks shut. 'Haven't you noticed her voice before?'

'Not really. She hums a bit at home and sings along next to Michaela at choir.'

I blush, feeling very much on the back foot. Jennifer's right. I'm living in the same house, I'm her sister, for goodness' sake, and should have realised that she's a talented singer. Music has been my salvation more than once and it could be Storm's too.

There's a crash from inside the storeroom and I give Jennifer an apologetic smile when a volley of swear words punch through the door. It's going to take more than a bit of communal crooning to calm her down but it might help. Being hands-off and waiting for Storm to adapt to Salt Bay isn't working – she needs a push in the right direction.

There's a rabble of people waiting at the counter to pay for newspapers when we emerge back into the shop. Well, there's Florence,

Maureen and a woman I don't recognise, but that counts as a rabble in sleepy Salt Bay.

'Morning, Annie,' says Maureen, whose boots have tracked clumps of snow across the shop floor. 'All set for tonight's tree ceremony? It's the perfect Christmas weather for it. I'm opening up the tea room afterwards to sell mince pies and mulled wine, and you'll come along, won't you?'

'If there's wine, I'll be there,' I assure her, dodging Jennifer as she mops puddles off the floor with ill-concealed annoyance.

Mopping done, she slides back behind the counter and starts totting up how much Florence owes for a *Woman's Weekly*, two rolls of glittery wrapping paper and a large packet of Quavers.

I've reached the door when she shouts over the heads of her customers, 'I've banned him, by the way.'

'Banned who?'

'Josh Pasco. I've banned him from my shop for upsetting you. We women have to stick together against fickle men.'

Maureen, Florence and the woman I've never seen before fold their arms and nod at me in sisterly solidarity.

'Honestly, Jennifer, there's no need to do that.' A thought suddenly strikes me. 'Does Josh ever come in here anyway?'

Jennifer pauses and hoists up her large bosom. 'No, but if he does come in, he's banned.'

Chapter Thirty

A crescent moon is shining from a dark sky when we gather around the huge fir tree that marks the centre of Salt Bay. The branches are dusted with snow and strung with lights.

'Of course, by rights I should be performing the switching-on ceremony,' says Jennifer, snuggling into the fox-fur collar of her coat. 'I'm the closest thing to a Mayor this village has.'

'Are you really the Mayor?' asks Emily, wide-eyed, pulling her hat further down over her ears.

'Not officially, though I was once referred to by the local paper as Salt Bay's First Lady. However, they're getting Enid to do the switch-on for some strange reason.'

'That's because she's the oldest person in the village,' butts in Alice, who's looking very smart this evening in a felt hat that matches her black coat and wellies. The wellies aren't terribly chic but they're helping her to stay upright which is all that matters.

'I thought you must be the oldest person in Salt Bay.' Emily scans the crowd on the snow-blanketed grass, searching for Jay.

'Enid pips me by about six weeks.'

'It'll be your job when she pops her clogs then, Alice,' says Barry, who's supposed to be rounding up the choir but has just appeared with a neon Frisbee in his hand after having a chuckabout with some local kids. 'Ooh, look! It's show time.'

The choir are gathering together in front of the tree, all wrapped up in scarves and hats and stamping their feet to keep warm. Jennifer, Emily and Barry wander over to join them but I hang back.

'Are you going to come and sing with us?'

Storm shakes her head but stops kicking up snow in the borrowed wellies she's only wearing because it's dark and no one will see them. 'Music is Barry's thing.'

'It could be your thing too. You obviously like music and you can certainly sing.'

'Hhmm.' Storm wrinkles her nose, which is smudged with paint from this morning's work. 'I don't want to be in your choir.'

'I'm not asking you to join the choir, I'm merely seeing if you'd like to sing some carols with us as a one-off with no obligation. You can stand by me if you like.'

Storm hesitates and tilts her head at Alice. 'I'd better stay and keep the old lady upright.'

'The old lady can manage to stay on her feet unaided for four carols,' says Alice sharply. 'Go and sing!'

Grumbling gently under her breath, Storm follows me to the tree and stands next to Kayla, who does a double take but pushes her word sheet under Storm's nose. Josh sings the note we'll be starting on and the choir launches into 'Good King Wenceslas'.

It's fabulously Christmassy singing carols in the snow, and the crowd seem to be enjoying it, but I hate it. Josh is leading the carols which means he's directly in front of me and I have to look at him. All the blessed time – as he's swaying to the music and beating time and biting his lip because he's concentrating. And the more Christmassy it gets, the more it's hammered home that I'll be spending this festive season without him. Every festive season without him until I'm as old as Enid. I mouth the words, too choked to sing.

Never have four songs lasted as long. But finally, we're done, our audience applauds and the choir scatters, ready for Enid to flick a switch.

'Did you enjoy it?' I ask Storm when she wanders back to Alice, who's still standing.

'It was all right.'

'You did well.' Kayla pushes her arm through mine and huddles close for warmth. 'And you've got a good voice. I wasn't expecting that.'

When Storm frowns, not sure whether she's being complimented or insulted, Kayla laughs. 'What I mean is, you haven't joined in before so I thought you might sound like Ollie, who's got an awful voice. Yes, Annie, the scales have finally fallen from my eyes.'

'And your ears?'

'Yep, those too.' Kayla gestures towards Ollie, who's chatting with Josh on the other side of the tree. 'We finally see our former lovers for what they really are. Yay, it's time for the switch-on.'

Enid, in a fancy blue hat she must have once worn to a wedding, is being escorted to a small black box.

'Just flick that switch,' says Roger, who starts leading a countdown from ten with the crowd. Three, two one… 'Flick it, Enid!'

'Ooh!' There's a collective gasp as the tree lights up, a riot of silver and blue from its lowest branches to the tip, crowned with a silver star. It's absolutely beautiful.

'Wow!' breathes Storm next to me. She smiles, her face upturned to the tree and illuminated by the Christmas glow. She looks so young.

The back of my neck is prickling and, when I turn away from the tree, Josh is staring straight at me. He dips his head but doesn't move when I stride purposefully towards him. There's something I have to do.

'Hi there.'

'Hello, Annie. How are you?' he says in his deep voice. He's so formal, it breaks my already-broken heart.

'I wanted to say sorry that Barry accosted you after the rehearsal. It was nothing to do with me and I've told him off for calling you a tosser. Sorry.'

'I actually think he called me a wanker.' I knew it! 'But let's forget the whole thing. It was just Barry sticking up for you which is what fathers do.'

'I guess so. It's not something I'm used to.'

A neon Frisbee suddenly flashes past us and heads for the tree, with Barry scooting after it. His face is flushed and sweating and he's not looking where he's going. All concentration is focused on a piece of cheap plastic thrown by some kid by the river.

There's another collective gasp as Barry suddenly spots the tree ahead of him, tries to stop and starts sliding. His arms windmill as he attempts to slow down but he hits the tree full-on with a sickening crunch and falls backwards onto his backside.

For a moment, nothing happens and then the tree begins to wobble – and the lights go out.

It takes twenty minutes for Barry and Roger to find the wire that's come loose and get the lights working again. Twenty long minutes spent standing in the cold, apologising for my father over and over again every time someone new comes up to have a moan.

But the strange thing is that I'm not angry. It was an accident, the damage has been fixed and my first thought, as Barry's face whammed into hundreds of pine needles, was *I hope he's not hurt*. Maybe I'm starting to quite like him after all.

Chapter Thirty-One

I can hear shouting as I pick my way along the garden path after work on Monday. Jeez, it's slippery out here. Thawing snow is freezing over as the temperature drops and the path is an ice rink, but I pick up speed. I'm one slip away from a thigh-high plaster cast but, on the other hand, someone is being murdered in Tregavara House.

Bambi-sliding to the front door, I hurtle inside to discover Alice standing in the hallway with her ear against the sitting room door.

'What the hell's going on?'

The shouting was loud from outside but it's deafening in here – two female voices, high-pitched and out of control.

Alice shrugs. 'I have absolutely no idea.' It's almost impossible to hear what she's saying above the din and I move closer. 'One minute I was reading *The People's Friend* in peace and the next, I'm jumping out of my skin. To be honest, I'm surprised at Emily.'

'One of the people shouting is Emily?'

I can't believe it. Gentle, mild Emily never raises her voice. She yelled after Barry last week when he was about to drive off without the shopping list and then spent five minutes apologising to him. But she's really going for it now – hammer, tongs, kitchen sink, the lot.

'It's Emily and Storm.' Alice leans against the wall for support. 'They've been ignoring one another for weeks so I suppose this has been brewing. What do we do now?'

'I guess we'd better get in there and sort things out.'

'That sounds like a very good idea,' says Alice, shuffling towards the kitchen. 'Good luck, dear.'

Thank you so much, Alice. Top of my list after getting home was having a heartbroken sobbing session in a lovely, hot bath, not refereeing a slanging match between two hysterical teenagers. But I'm going in. With a deep breath, I push open the sitting room door and ram my fingers into my ears.

Storm and Emily don't notice me at first. They're too busy standing nose to nose and yelling into one another's faces. It's hard to make out what they're saying because they're both shouting at once.

'Will you two stop yelling and start behaving like civilised adults!'

Crikey, I sound like a mother. Not *my* mother, obviously, because she'd never tell anyone to behave; she was usually the one getting into trouble. But raising my voice does the trick. Both girls stop mid-rant and stare at me, eyes bright with fury.

'What on earth is going on in here? I thought someone was being murdered.'

'Someone will be in a minute and I know how 'cos I watched *The Sopranos*,' mutters Storm, looking mutinous. 'It was her fault anyway, reading my private mail.'

Oops, I know what this is about, and there's only one thing for it.

'Reading someone else's mail is not on, Emily.' I adopt an appropriate expression that indicates both surprise and disappointment. 'Why on earth did you do that?'

I know, I know. I'm a hideous hypocrite and a terrible person.

Emily hangs her head, her long, thick plait swinging in front of her. 'Storm dropped an invitation and I picked it up and couldn't help seeing what it said.'

'Pah!' snorts Storm before being silenced by a glare from me.

'So how does Storm know that you read the invitation?'

'I asked her if she was going to the event. I was only being friendly.'

'Nosy, more like. The invitation was from Jay in the choir. I didn't realise that Emily *luurved* him.'

'Stop it!' scowls Emily, yanking off her smeary glasses and furiously polishing the lenses on her cardigan.

'Why should I stop it? You read something that wasn't addressed to you. That's like invading part of my life.'

'Like you've invaded my life since the moment you got here, you… you…'

Gentle Emily is out of insults and Storm opens her mouth to leap in.

'Both of you stop it!' I yell. 'I can't cope with this right now, not while my life is going to hell.' I must sound a tad deranged because both girls survey me anxiously from beneath their lashes. 'Why can't you girls just get on? You're almost the same age. You could be friends.'

'She won't be friends with me,' spits Emily. 'She's one of the cool girls.'

Storm's nose wrinkles and she shakes her head. 'I'm not one of the cool girls, you daft cow. I'm odd.'

'No you're not. I'm odd and you're nothing like me.' Emily puts her glasses back on and blinks at Storm through the still smeary lenses.

'I'm a different odd. I mean, for God's sake, my dad was in a band called Va-Voom and the freaking Vikings, we sleep on people's sofas and my mum would rather live with a boring banker and two poncey little rich kids than with me.'

'That's harsh,' says Emily slowly, the angry flush on her cheeks fading. 'But at least Jay likes you.'

'He's a dick and I'm not that keen on him anyway.'

'That makes it even worse,' wails Emily, tears trickling down her face. 'No one I like ever likes me.'

'We like you,' I say, totally ineffectually because Emily's self-esteem needs a boost from a fit, testosterone-fuelled hunk, not from an overwhelmed woman whose own love life is a total shambles.

'Yeah, we like you,' mumbles Storm, looking rather shamefaced. 'If you really like Jay – though you're totally deluded 'cos he's an idiot – maybe I could help you get off with him.'

'You. Can't. Say. Anything. To. Him!' Emily grabs Storm's mustard-yellow jumper in panic and hangs on tight.

'OK, no need to get so stressy and strangly.' Storm pulls away from Emily's clutches and adjusts her clothing. 'Saying something to him would be, like, so amateur. Jeez, Emily, you have got so much to learn, though it's not your fault 'cos you've lived in this backwater all your life. But Barry always says there's more than one way to skin a cat so let me have a think about it.'

Blimey, I don't rate Jay's chances too highly if he's the cat.

Emily folds her arms and pouts. 'All right. Thanks, then.'

'You're welcome,' mutters Storm, kicking at fluff on the carpet.

Both girls shuffle self-consciously from foot to foot as the clock on the mantelpiece strikes six o'clock. The chimes die away but both girls continue their awkward shuffle-dance in silence.

'Storm, haven't you got any homework to do?'

'No,' huffs Storm as if it's the most ridiculous question in the world. 'But I might go up the Whistling Wave and use their Wi-Fi, just so long as that Kayla keeps out of my face. She didn't seem so bad at that tree thing.'

'And I need to go and check on Alice,' says Emily, heading for the door.

'She was rather alarmed by all the shouting.'

'Yeah, sorry about that. Things just got a bit... out of hand. It was my fault really. I shouldn't have read that invitation. Sorry, Storm.'

'Yeah, you're all right,' says Storm, following Emily into the hall. 'And I'll let you know about that skinning a cat thing.'

And just like that the feud between them is over, all shouted out in Alice's elegant sitting room. Both girls are odd, let's face it, which is why they should be friends. Maybe Storm will take on a little of Emily's gentleness, and Emily can learn from Storm's fierce attitude to life. And they'll both be better equipped to face life's 'cool people' who so often turn out to be total pains.

Witnessing the tentative beginnings of a friendship between Emily and Storm was rather sweet and I'm feeling all warm and fuzzy right now. Until I remember that the boyfriend I love probably hates me, the father I'm a bit *meh* about has gone all paternal, I'll hit the big three-oh at the end of the week, and Salt Bay Choral Society has to prove itself in a big, scary competition.

After hanging up my coat, I head for the bathroom, turn on the taps full pelt and lock the door. There's half a bottle of bubble bath under the sink and I upend it into the tub while steam curls towards the ceiling. I'm going to soak and sob until I look like a prune.

Chapter Thirty-Two

Happy Birthday to me! Sitting up in bed, I pull the covers around my shoulders and lean back against the soft pillows. Thirty years ago today, my mum gave birth to me in a cramped flat off Ealing High Street. My swift arrival took her by surprise and a neighbour ended up delivering me on the bathroom floor. I drew my first breath wedged between a chipped bath and a dodgy toilet, which wasn't the most auspicious of starts.

Mum often told me all about it, and I mean *all*. Her waters breaking over the living room carpet, searing contraction pains, the placenta getting stuck – the lot. No wonder I'm so ambivalent about having kids of my own. Though if I do decide motherhood's for me, I'd better get a move on now I've hit the big three-oh and my ovaries are shrivelling.

It's early but there are muffled voices outside my door and I hear Emily stifling a giggle. Something's definitely up because she and Alice were huddled together in corners yesterday and changed the subject whenever I came into the room. I'm so lucky to be celebrating my birthday with them.

Stretching my arms above my head, I give a huge yawn. It's been a funny old life so far and today isn't going to be how I imagined it.

In my fantasy life – the one that runs in my head alongside reality – Salt Bay Choral Society wins the Kernow Choral Crown and Josh and

I go out to celebrate. He lifts my hand to his lips and kisses it before wishing me a happy birthday and telling me that he loves me. Then he takes me to a posh hotel and ravishes me senseless.

Well, that's not going to happen now I've messed everything up, and I really miss him. A tear slides down my cheek but I furiously brush it away. There's no way I'm crying on my thirtieth birthday. Tears on such a significant day might herald a decade of bad luck which would be the ultimate in unwanted gifts.

Slipping out of bed, I nip across the landing and into the steamy bathroom which shows signs of having been Stormed. Water is pooled on every surface and there's a pile of sodden towels next to the vintage enamel sink that has delicate forget-me-nots picked out across its surface.

I fight the urge to tidy up and shiver instead under the shower which is only lukewarm this morning. Is having a bit of hot water on your birthday too much to ask? My bedroom is cold too so I dress in a hurry, choosing a warm, red wool dress because jeans on such a special day seems wrong. Then I add a smart black cardi to make me feel extra cosy.

Tregavara House never feels properly warm because draughts are constantly snaking through the cracks in this old building. It took me a while to get used to the drop in temperature because my Stratford flat was always toasty, with hot air rising from the flats below.

Just for a moment, I let myself imagine spending my special birthday in London. Maura and I could sip cocktails in some trendy hipster bar before lunching at The Shard and marvelling at the city laid out before us. It sounds wonderful, but not really like me any more. I've become provincial.

Dressed and warm, I head for the kitchen in search of breakfast. I'm not really hungry – I've lost weight since Josh and I broke up because my stomach is in knots – but the choir has a big day ahead so I need to be sensible and pace myself.

When I push open the kitchen door, Alice, Emily, Storm and Barry are sitting around the kitchen table. And they're all fully dressed – no wonder the shower was almost cold.

'At last,' moans Storm while the other three burst into a chorus of 'Happy Birthday'. They start off much too high and it's so terrible Storm puts her fingers in her ears, but I'm touched by their impromptu performance.

They've gone to a lot of trouble: the table is laid with a pretty cloth; someone (probably Emily) has made a table decoration out of Christmas tree baubles, birthday candles and fir cones; and there's a bottle of Buck's Fizz next to it. Mingling with a sharp tang of pine is a mouthwatering smell of bacon. And is that pancakes?

'We made you a special breakfast,' declares Emily, placing a plate of food in front of me. 'Sit and eat and then you can open your cards and presents. Um, if that's OK with you.'

'That's absolutely fine with me.' I laugh as Emily grins and points excitedly at a small pile of gifts wrapped in shiny paper on the dresser. 'This food smells delicious. Thank you so much.'

It's quite hard eating when everyone's staring at you but the pancakes are so delicious, I get stuck in. Emily has bought real maple syrup and laced the pancakes liberally so they're islands in a sea of amber gloop. Ooh, I was more hungry than I thought.

Dipping the final piece of pancake into the gooey liquid, I rub it round the plate before popping it into my mouth. The syrup coats my teeth before slipping down my throat. That was absolutely lovely – though now I feel sick as a dog.

When I pat my stomach and lean back, Emily removes my plate, grabs my presents and piles them on the table in front of me.

'Open them.' She grins, bouncing up and down behind me.

Heaven knows what she'll be like when Christmas Day arrives.

'Can I go now?' asks Storm, scraping her chair across the tiles and getting to her feet. 'Jennifer will go ape if I'm late again. She's gone all weird and keeps talking to me about breathing exercises that improve the voice. Menopausal women are, like, totally mental.' She nods at the present pile. 'There's a card from me in there.' Then she turns towards Emily. 'Jennifer's shutting up shop at lunchtime 'cos of getting ready for the competition so I'll be back in plenty of time to… you know.'

'To what?' asks Barry.

'Girl stuff,' says Storm, wrenching open the back door and slamming it behind her.

'Come. On!' Emily thrusts a small parcel into my hands. 'Start with this one.'

The gift is beautifully wrapped in gold paper with silver ribbon and there's pink tissue paper inside. Nestled inside the tissue is a pair of pretty turquoise and silver earrings.

'They're gorgeous, Emily. Thank you so much.' I lean across the table and give her hand a squeeze before pushing the silver posts into my ears. The turquoise bangs gently against my neck. 'How do they look?'

'Lovely.' She smiles. 'They're only from a little shop in Penzance but they look really pretty next to your hair.'

'And this is from me,' says Barry, thrusting an envelope into my hands. 'Though I can't quite believe I'm old enough to have a thirty-year-old daughter. How the hell did that happen?'

'You'll get used to it,' murmurs Alice, patting his hand. She looks older today and tired and I hope she didn't get up too early just for me.

Inside Barry's envelope is a birthday card that says 'To a special daughter' across the top and, inside, there's a piece of paper.

'I didn't know what to get you and I'm a bit skint right now so…' Barry shrugs. 'I hope you like it.'

When I unfold the paper, it says in Barry's untidy scrawl: *I owe you one special song.*

'It's called "Annie" – not very original, I know – and it's not quite finished. The chorus is proving to be an absolute pain and you can't rush the creative process. But it'll be done soon. I hope that's OK.' He suddenly seems unsure.

'Wow, no one's ever written a song just for me before. It's a lovely idea, Barry. Thank you.'

Before I can change my mind, I lean across the table and give him a brief hug.

Next I open Storm's card which looks very much like one I spotted in Jennifer's shop last week. I ignore my inner voice which is questioning whether Storm paid for it. Of course she did and it was kind of her.

'There's still Alice's present. Open that before your other cards.'

Emily pushes forward a small rectangular parcel. The wrapping is a little haphazard – Alice must have done it herself – and inside is a square black velvet box with an old-fashioned gold clasp.

'Go on, open it,' urges Alice gently.

The box feels soft when my fingers press on the catch and the lid swings open. Inside, resting on ruched black satin, is the most beautiful bangle I've ever seen. It's made of yellow gold with tiny sparkling stars pricked out all around the band in diamond chips.

'Wow,' breathes Emily, her eyes opening wide. 'That is lush.'

'It belonged to my mother. It was a present on her twenty-fifth birthday from my father,' says Alice.

'It's beautiful, Alice, but I'm not sure I can accept it when it must mean such a lot to you.'

'I want you to have it,' says Alice in her firm voice, 'because you mean a lot to me too and it's good to keep it in the family. Try it on.'

When I slip my hand through the bangle and fasten the clasp, it lies heavy on my wrist, sparkling under the kitchen lights. It really is the most gorgeous thing I've ever owned.

Moving to where Alice is sitting, I kneel down and give her a huge hug. She feels fragile in my arms and I experience a flash of sorrow as I imagine the gap she'll leave in my life when she's gone.

Oh, get a grip, Annie. Alice is practically immortal and you're not supposed to cry on your birthday, you dork.

I sniff back tears and have just got to my feet when there's a hammering on the front door.

'Who on earth is that trying to knock my door down?'

Alice starts pulling herself to her feet but sinks back down when I put my hand on her shoulder. The gold bangle rests lightly against her sensible grey cardigan.

'You stay there, Alice. I'll go and see who it is.'

Blimey, whoever's knocking is ultra keen to get in. Maybe it's Josh, desperate to wish me a happy birthday and say he's forgiven me. I quicken my pace, as the bangs get louder, and yank open the door.

'Thank goodness. I thought you'd gone deaf. I forgot my damn key.'

It's not Josh. Did I really think it would be? I try not to look too disappointed that the man standing on Alice's doorstep is Toby. When I don't speak, he brushes past me and drops his overnight bag onto the tiles with a thud.

'Nice to see you too, Annie. Is she here already?'

When I look at him blankly, Toby gives a hiss of irritation.

'Is Lucy here? She emailed me yesterday and said she'd bring Freya over this morning if I wanted to meet her.'

'Does Josh know?' I blurt out.

'I damn well hope not. The last thing we need is prudish Pasco getting involved. What time is Alice due back?'

'She's here, in the kitchen.'

'What? She's here now?' Toby runs a hand over his tidy goatee beard. 'She's supposed to be out with her friend Patsy or Polly or something. She said she was being picked up early.'

'Penelope. Her friend is called Penelope and the Christmas celebrations have been postponed until tomorrow.' I don't bother explaining that the postponement is due to my birthday because Alice wanted to be here on my special day.

'Well, that's inconvenient,' huffs Toby. 'Is that weird Emily girl here too? And please tell me that your dreadful father and sister are back in London.'

When I shake my head, Toby whistles through his teeth. 'Jeez, this place is turning into a refuge for the lost and hopeless.'

I get the feeling that Toby includes me in that assessment but, ignoring the jibe, I push him into the sitting room and close the door.

'What are we going to do? And how come the meeting is still on?' I ask him.

'You didn't know?' Toby shakes his head and sinks slowly onto the sofa. 'This is a total mess. Lucy emailed me late yesterday to see if I still wanted to meet my daughter. She said if I did, it was on for this morning. Talk about last minute. She's terribly fickle. Typical bloody woman.'

'So you rushed down here? I'm surprised. I didn't think you were that bothered about seeing Freya.'

Toby shuffles his feet and stares at the carpet.

'Yes, well, I've been thinking about her and I'm curious, I suppose. Like you were curious about meeting up with Alice. I hadn't even seen a picture of the girl until you showed me that one on your phone. And I know it's my fault but you've no idea of the pressure I was under from my parents during the whole pregnancy thing.'

Toby's parents have been dead for some time but I let it go because I'm too busy panicking inside. If Lucy does turn up and the meeting goes ahead, Josh will hate me forever if he finds out. Oh, who am I kidding? *When* he finds out. It'll be all over the Salt Bay grapevine within hours. Someone will spot them.

'What are we going to do?' whines Toby, as though I've got all the answers. 'Alice, Emily and your family – you've got to get rid of them. Immediately.'

'What would you suggest? Homicide?'

'There's no need for sarcasm, Annie, it doesn't suit you.' Toby narrows his pale grey eyes and stretches his legs out across the thick rug. 'I don't want Alice finding out about all this and I especially want to keep it quiet from your dreadful family.'

More damn secrets. Sighing, I leave Toby to stew in the sitting room and he rests his head against the back of the sofa and closes his eyes when I pull the door to. He must have left London in the small hours to get here so early.

Alice, Emily and Barry are still sitting at the table when I slope back into the kitchen. Somehow, I'm supposed to get them out of the house, but I really don't know if I can be arsed, not when it's only going to lead to even more deceit.

'Who was that?' enquires Alice.

'It was Toby,' I say flatly, brain still whirring about how I'm going to deal with this.

'How marvellous,' she says, turning towards the back door as it opens. 'Lucy, is that you? And you've brought Freya to visit.' Alice sounds pleased but puzzled. 'Come in both of you or you'll freeze out there.'

Lucy and Freya, both pink-cheeked from the cold, step into the kitchen, holding hands. The young girl steps behind her mother and peeps out at us around Lucy's long, navy-blue Puffa coat.

Emily smiles at her and holds out a biscuit which Freya darts out and takes after getting the nod from her mum.

'Is he here already?' Lucy glances at Barry, who's eating pancakes, oblivious to the strange atmosphere swirling around him. 'I thought that might be his car outside so I nipped round the back.'

What do I do now? Everyone's looking at me but I haven't got a clue. I'm so muddled about who knows what and who's allowed to know what. The rules appear to be changing all the time.

You know when you think things can't possibly get any worse and then they nosedive into super-fuckity shite? The back door is suddenly pushed wide open and in strides Josh, all flushed and handsome with dark hair flopping over his eyes.

'Oh, my God.' Lucy's chin drops to her chest. 'Are you seriously following me now?'

'Don't be ridiculous, Lucy.' Josh doesn't even register that I'm in the room. 'Mrs Carter told Mum she saw you getting on the Salt Bay bus with Freya and I guessed what was happening. I see Toby's car is outside. Where is he?'

'In the sitting room,' I say, stepping forward. It's time to get this situation under control. 'Alice and Emily, do you think you could take Freya upstairs for a while? And Barry, you need to go to B&Q to get some—' what do people buy in B&Q? '—widgets.'

'What sort of widgets?' asks Barry, looking perplexed.

There's more than one type of widget? What the hell is a freaking widget anyway?

'Just go, please, Barry,' murmurs Alice with her eyes on my face. 'Any sort of widget will do. Get a selection.'

'OK,' huffs Barry, getting to his feet and pulling car keys from his pocket. 'Widgets it is. I sometimes think Storm is right and you Cornish folk really are all barking. I'll see you in half an hour then.'

'Make it an hour,' says Alice, walking up to Freya and holding out her hand. 'Why don't you come with me and Emily? You can see lots of seagulls on the cliffs from my bedroom window.'

Freya is hesitant but takes Alice's hand and is led out of the kitchen, with Emily following. Barry goes with them so it's just me, Lucy and Josh in the kitchen. We stand there in silence for a moment until I can't bear the tension any longer.

'Right,' I bark, 'let's get this over with.'

Beckoning for Josh and Lucy to follow me, I lead them into the hall and towards the sitting room. Some special birthday this is turning out to be.

Toby gets to his feet when we all bowl into the room. 'So, you came. Oh, balls. You came too!'

'It's nothing to do with me. Josh followed me from Trecaldwith,' whines Lucy.

'Unbelievable.' Toby tucks his designer shirt into his trendy designer trousers. 'You're obsessed, Pasco.'

Josh's chocolate-brown eyes narrow. 'Just concerned that you're going to manipulate Lucy, like you did six years ago.'

'Manipulate?' Lucy sighs heavily. 'I'm not seventeen any more, Josh. I don't need you to run my life.'

'That's not what I'm trying to do, but this man is heartless and not the sort of person I want in Freya's life.'

'That's great but it's not your decision. I'm her mother and I know what's best for my daughter.'

'Exactly,' interrupts Toby as Josh's jaw tightens. 'And what exactly are you going to do about it, Pasco, hit me again? Are you?'

The two of them start squaring up and that's when something snaps. Today is my pigging birthday, people!

'There's not going to be any violence,' I yell, standing between Josh and Toby and feeling as if my head is about to burst. 'Both of you, grow up, and everyone sit down. Now!'

Crikey, that felt good. Toby's mouth drops open but he sits obediently on the sofa while Josh and Lucy take a seat in the chairs either side of the fireplace.

'Right, Lucy first. Why do you want Toby and Freya to have this meeting?'

'He's her father,' says Lucy, sullenly.

'Indeed, but he's hardly a good role model.'

'Um,' squeaks Toby, shifting in his seat.

He shuts up when I wave my arm at him. 'It's true, Toby. You abandoned Lucy and left her family, including Josh, to bring up Freya.'

'Fair enough,' mutters Toby, sinking lower into the sofa.

I point at Lucy, who's chewing her lip. 'So why now, Lucy?'

'Yes, why now?' echoes Josh.

'Partly because of you, Josh. You're tired and grumpy all the time because you're working all hours to support us, and you're even more bad-tempered since you split up with Annie, which was because of all this. And it's not fair that Toby has no responsibilities and doesn't pay anything towards his daughter's upbringing. But it's not really about the money.'

She turns to me, all hot and flustered. 'I want Freya to grow up knowing her father, even if that father is someone like Toby. You didn't know your dad until he turned up on your doorstep a few weeks ago, Annie, and look how that's turned out. It's not healthy.'

She's got a point, though I'm still not convinced that having Barry in my life throughout childhood would have radically improved things. But it's true that turning up like he did, with Storm in tow, has sent shock waves reverberating through my adult life.

'So, Josh.' I ignore the urge to sit on his lap and put my head against his chest so I can hear his heart beating. 'Why don't you want Toby to be a part of Freya's life?'

'Because he's a shit,' splutters Josh.

Toby's getting to his feet again. I put my hand on his shoulder and, none too gently, shove him back down.

'If you could explain without being rude about Toby, that would be helpful, though I appreciate that not being rude about Toby is immensely difficult.'

Wow, this is brilliant! Being thirty appears to grant you permission to say what you really think, rather than pussyfooting about, pleasing people all the time.

'OK. I was very—' Josh pauses '—disappointed that Toby didn't face up to his responsibilities when Lucy got pregnant. It was a terribly difficult time for her and for the whole family. But we wouldn't be without Freya because we all love her to pieces. She's a wonderful little girl.' He fixes Toby with a hard stare. 'I feel sorry for you because you have no idea what you've missed. And it's because we love Freya so much that I don't want you in her life, polluting her with your lack of moral fibre.' He glances at me and shrugs. 'It's impossible to do this without being a bit rude about him.'

'I know. Carry on.'

'That's it really. Toby has never wanted to know Freya, so why is he so interested now?'

'That's a good question. What do you say to that, Toby?'

Ooh, I feel like David Dimbleby on *Question Time*. In charge, in control, invincible.

Toby sits forward, his usual swagger gone. 'I didn't want to see her. The whole thing was a complication I didn't need and I don't do complicated. So I kept her at arm's length.'

That chimes with how I lived in London, always pushing people away to keep my life simple. Perhaps my cousin and I have more in common than I imagined. Deep in my heart there are tiny stirrings of sympathy for him.

Toby exhales loudly and continues, 'It began to feel like I'd imagined it and I didn't really have a daughter at all. But then Annie arrived and everything got stirred up.' Oh great, suddenly it's all my fault! He swallows hard. 'I started thinking about her. About Freya. I tried to ignore it but I've realised that I would like to meet her and perhaps be a bigger part of her life than I have been.'

'That wouldn't be difficult,' mutters Josh but he's silenced by my Dimbleby glare.

'So what happens now?' demands Toby. 'Surely it depends on Lucy.'

Lucy puts her elbows on her knees and her head in her hands. 'I don't know what's best any more. I'm stuck in the middle.' When she looks up at me, her eyes are wet. 'You decide.'

What, me? Lucy has got to be joking. 'No way. It's not my decision.'

'It should be you who decides,' says Lucy. 'You're not directly involved in all of this but you know Toby and you care about Freya and Josh. Plus, you know what it's like growing up without a father and having him turn up when you're really old.'

Whoah, I've only just reached thirty! Literally today, if anyone actually cared.

Lucy turns to her brother, who's staring at me intently. There's a strange whooshing sound in my ears and I contemplate whether a brief fainting spell might be in order right now.

'That's not fair,' whines Toby. 'Annie is obviously going to side with lover boy who hates me.'

'The hate goes both ways,' hisses Josh.

Toby sinks so low on the sofa, he appears to deflate. 'I don't hate you, you pompous prat. I envy you.'

'Yeah, of course you do,' splutters Josh. 'You really envy me from your penthouse apartment while earning megabucks and doing whatever you want, whenever you want. Of course, the great Toby Trebarwith envies me – a teacher who's living with his mother, working all the hours God sends, and spending every penny on supporting his family.'

'When you put it like that, your life sounds dreadful and I don't envy you any of that. What I do envy is the fact that you've got people who care about you. My life is totally devoid of anyone who's half bothered about me.' Toby gives a hollow laugh. 'You're surrounded by people who love you. I've got Alice, who doesn't really know me and is likely to keel over soon anyway, and there's Annie, who merely tolerates me and is more accepted in Salt Bay than I've ever been. And I was born here.'

He shifts in his seat and shakes his head. 'That's why I want to see Freya and be a part of her life. I'm lonely. There you go, Josh. That'll cheer you up. Successful Toby Trebarwith is lonely and wants to do the right thing for once. So, what do you say, Annie? Can I see Freya or not, because if it's a no I'll head back to London right now.'

When Lucy gives an 'I don't know' shrug, I could shake her. She's washing her hands of the whole thing and putting a huge decision on my shoulders. And if I refuse to choose, the whole thing is likely to degenerate into more mud-slinging.

Toby's declaration of loneliness has really thrown me. It's a heartfelt confession from a man who'd usually rather stick pins in his eyes than admit his life isn't perfect. And then there's Freya, whose future with or without her father appears to be resting on what I say next. An image of Barry trudging away from our Hackney flat, after Mum sent him packing, floats into my mind.

'I think…' I look at Josh, the man I love, who's sitting back in his chair with his eyes closed. 'I think that Toby should meet Freya and we'll see where it goes from there.'

Even as the words leave my mouth, I know they're the final nail in the coffin for me and Josh. He'll never forgive me for not backing him. He'll see it as a betrayal; that time I chose my family over him. I feel so sad I could cry, but I don't want to change my mind. It's time to do what I think is right for Freya.

Thirty years ago, Mum decided that her family would never be a part of our lives, and look what I missed out on – my grandparents Sheila and Samuel, lovely Alice, beautiful Salt Bay. I don't want that for Freya. Chances are she'll realise in the future that Toby is a prize prat and will distance herself from him. But that's her decision to make, not anyone else's.

I walk over to where Josh is sitting and brush my fingers across his broad shoulders.

'I'm sorry Josh. I'm trying to do what's best.'

But he shakes me off. Yep, Josh and me – us – is over forever.

There's a small squeak from the doorway and, when we look round, Alice is standing there, holding Freya's hand. 'I thought it was about time we came downstairs,' she says.

It feels as though the air has been sucked from the room. All I can hear is the clock on the mantelpiece which has a very loud tick I've never noticed before. Alice steps into the room and Freya follows.

'Freya, you know everyone here except Toby. Though I'm beginning to think he's someone you should have met a long time ago.'

Alice frowns at Toby but he doesn't notice. He's too busy staring at Freya, whose pale, soulful eyes are darting around the room. Her long dark hair is caught up in a plait down her back and she's wearing shiny black shoes that look new. Party shoes to meet her father for the very first time. There's a lump in my throat.

'Freya—' Alice gently pushes the young girl forward '—say hello to Toby.'

'Hello,' says Freya seriously, stretching out her chubby little hand.

'Hello Freya.' Toby slowly reaches out and takes her hand in his. 'You're so grown up. It's lovely to meet you at long last.'

His bottom lip wobbles but Freya has snatched back her hand and run to her mother as a single tear snakes its way down Toby's cheek and into his beard.

Josh stands up suddenly without a word, brushes past me and rushes out of the room.

I leave them to it and wander into the kitchen where my cards are waiting in a sad little pile. Josh has already jumped into his car and screeched off out of my life. Any tiny hope I had that we might make up and get back together has been stomped on. By giving Toby the chance to see his daughter, I've cleared the way for Felicity to get her hooks back into the man I love. Kayla would say I'm a moron, and she wouldn't be wrong.

Feeling thoroughly fed up, I open my cards and stand them up on the kitchen table. They're all from friends, including one with a naked man on the front from Maura, and an old-fashioned card from my ex-flatmate Amber. It's the kind of card you'd buy from a garage for your granny. But it was kind of her to remember.

Once the cards are done, I make myself a cup of tea and sit for a while in the silent kitchen. It's very quiet in the sitting room but I don't go and investigate what's going on. I don't want to know. Family matters can wound and scar, and I've got far too mixed up in them for my own good. For a moment, I think back fondly to my life in London. Before Salt Bay. Before family complications. Before heartbreak.

But, sipping at my tea, I realise that I wouldn't change things. It would be awful never to have met Alice and, though I can take or leave Toby, I can't regret my time with Josh. He's the man who finally opened my heart. Which is fabulous, though I could have done without the jumping on it and smashing it to pieces.

I'm running my finger round my pancake plate and licking off maple syrup when the front door slams. And a minute later, Alice shuffles into the kitchen.

'Are you all right? Here, sit down.'

Alice's face is grey with exhaustion. She sinks onto a chair with a weary 'oof' and rests her wrinkled cheek on the cool oak of the table.

'I should have known,' she says, her words muffled.

'Known what?'

'That Toby is Freya's father, of course.' She lifts her head and looks at me with sad eyes. 'I can't work out if I was stupidly dense or if I deliberately refused to acknowledge the truth of it to myself.'

'Don't be so hard on yourself, Alice.' I stroke her thin arm through her woolly cardigan. 'Hardly anyone knows and it's not as if Toby was living here.'

'You knew.'

'Only because Josh told me, because he had to, really.'

There's no point in telling Alice about all the lies that Toby told me before the truth came out. Lies that eventually forced Josh to tell me the truth.

'Why didn't you tell me, Annie?'

'Josh asked me not to. It was a secret and I didn't see that it would help if you knew that…' I peter off.

'If I knew that Toby, a Trebarwith, had behaved like the most dreadful cad.' Alice's breath catches in her throat. 'What must Marion Pawley think of this family? What must she think of me?'

'Josh's mum doesn't blame anyone except Toby. And it took two – Lucy was involved as well.'

'But it was Toby who fled from his responsibilities. Oh, how his parents must have hated it when he took up with Lucy Pawley from Trecaldwith. Patrick and Fenella always had high ambitions for their son and were the most appalling snobs.' She blinks rapidly as her brown eyes fill with tears. 'And Freya is such a lovely child. What an awful mess.'

'Do you need a cuppa? I've just boiled the kettle.' When Alice nods, I fetch a clean mug from the cupboard. 'So where is everyone now?'

'Toby has given Lucy and Freya a lift home. Is this whole sorry affair what put paid to your relationship with Josh?'

'Yes, indirectly. It was my fault, really, for not being straight with him.'

Alice closes her eyes and draws her mouth into a tight line.

'I'm so terribly sorry, Annie, that you got dragged into all of this. Maybe you were right to live in London on your own. Families can be more trouble than they're worth.'

'I don't know. You're not so bad.' I smile, pouring milk into Alice's tea and putting the steaming mug in front of her. Alice usually insists on a china tea cup but I'm hoping she won't notice today. My hand knocks into the naked-man card which goes flying onto the tiles.

'And it's your birthday, too,' wails Alice. 'I'd completely forgotten in all the hoo-hah.'

'It doesn't matter, Alice. Really. It's just another day that's probably best forgotten anyway.'

I hope I can forget it but I fear it will be imprinted on my memory forever. Most people remember their thirtieth birthday for happy reasons – parties, presents, time with loved ones. But I'll always remember the look on Josh's face when I put my family first and betrayed him.

Chapter Thirty-Three

'Come on, girls. What are you doing in there? We've got to go.' I'm standing outside Storm's bedroom and shouting through the door, having been threatened with death if I dare to open it. 'The minibus leaves in ten minutes and we have to be on it.'

I don't suppose the bus will go without us, seeing as I'm conducting two of the competition songs this afternoon. But my luck so far today has been awful, so best not take any chances.

'We're just coming,' yells Emily, who's been shut in the bedroom with Storm for the last two hours. 'Don't come in!'

She giggles and, in spite of my traumatic morning, I smile. It's so lovely to hear serious Emily laughing, and for Storm and Emily to be chatting, rather than circling each other like wild animals.

I'm checking my watch for the tenth time when the bedroom door is suddenly wrenched open.

'Ta-dah!'

Emily is standing in front of me, dressed sensibly in black trousers and a plain black jumper – the choir's uniform. But her long, brown hair, usually pulled into a plait down her back, is falling in gentle waves around her face. And she's wearing make-up. Rather a lot of make-up, which accentuates the almond shape of her pale blue eyes and her high cheekbones.

'Wow, Emily, you look flipping amazing!'

'Do I?' she asks shyly, twirling round to look at herself in the mirror on Storm's wall.

'Where are your glasses?'

'In my pocket. I'll put them on for the performance so I can see you and Josh, but I can do without them until then. Everything's blurry but it's quite nice, actually. The seagulls on the cliff look like little white specks on a fuzzy green carpet.'

'Emily should so get contact lenses,' says Storm, poking her head around the door. She appears to have dyed her fringe pink for the competition. 'Do you like my mega makeover then? It took a while, on account of Emily having some issues. Her hair has, like, never been conditioned, not ever, and it went frizzy at first with the curling tongs. But we managed.'

'I think Emily looks absolutely fabulous but we really need to get a move on so grab your things.'

Barry does a double take when he spots us barrelling down the stairs.

'Bloody hell. Oops, sorry Alice.' He winces. 'I didn't mean to swear but you look so different, Emily.'

'I know,' beams Emily, doing a twirl for Alice, who seems bemused by her carer's transformation. 'I didn't realise I could look like this. Do you think people will be surprised?'

Surprised isn't the word. Gobsmacked is more like it. Within seconds of us boarding the minibus, Emily's transformation from meek mouse to glamour goddess is all that anyone is talking about. Roger's face, in particular, is a picture when he spots 'odd Emily', which is what he usually calls her. Not to her face, obviously.

But the best reaction comes from Jay, who's even later than us and leaps on the bus just before it pulls out. He wanders to an empty seat in front of Emily and Storm and plonks himself down. Emily is chatting to Mary and has her back to him.

'Who's your friend?' he asks Storm, staring at Emily's thick hair, falling in soft waves past her shoulder blades.

'It's Emily, you dipstick,' snorts Storm. 'You know, that girl you've been almost standing next to in this dorky choir, like, forever.'

'Huh?' says Jay with a 'does not compute' frown, just as Emily turns around in her seat and he gets the full force of the megawatt makeover. She smiles at him coquettishly. Wow, meek little Emily is learning fast.

Across the aisle from me, Tom gives Jay a filthy look and spends the rest of the journey staring steadfastly out of the window as we leave the jagged Cornish coast and head inland for the bright lights of Truro.

Josh is sitting right at the back of the bus, chatting to Arthur and Cyril, and gives me a slight nod when I glance his way. Which is surprising as he'd be totally within his rights to ignore me completely, seeing as I've just kicked him in the balls. Metaphorically speaking.

But the afternoon will go so much better if we can be civil and then, once the competition is over, we won't have to see each other ever again. Except for when our paths cross in the pub and I'm dignified and friendly to his face before sobbing myself to sleep later in my lonely bed. Yay, my thirties are going to be fab!

Compared to Salt Bay, Truro is a massive metropolis and it takes ages for Colin, our minibus driver, to find Gwedna Hall. We chug along various side streets and execute illegal U-turns while the minutes tick by and my throat gets tighter. But at last we arrive, twenty-five minutes before the competition is due to start, and all pile off the bus into a grey, Cornish afternoon.

'Crikey, they could use this place in a horror film. Was the architect on crack?'

Kayla, who's staring open-mouthed at the competition venue, has a point. Gwedna Hall is the stuff of nightmares – a riot of towers and turrets in dark brown stone, and inside it's not much better. A wide, stone staircase at the back of the entrance hall winds up to the first floor, and everywhere you look there are stone columns and twiddly bits, though I doubt that's the architectural term.

'Are you Salt Bay Choral Society?' gasps an overweight lady in emerald green who comes huffing up with a sheet of paper in her hand. She calms down when I confirm that we are, and ticks us off her list. 'Thank goodness for that. We thought we'd have to disqualify you for late arrival.'

What is it with these people and disqualification? They seem determined that Salt Bay Choral Society will crash and burn but we'll show them. We'll deliver a performance that takes their breath away. We'll be loud and proud and wonderful! Beside me, Jennifer begins to cough, Roger scratches his large belly and Jay stares at his pretty face in the huge mirror covering one wall. Hhmm. Fingers crossed that we'll take their breath away for the right reasons.

Forty minutes later, we're waiting backstage and listening to live performances onstage via the backstage speaker system. The other choirs sound good. Really good. I mouth 'eek!' at Josh, who's chatting with Arthur but he doesn't see me. Or he pretends not to.

'Cheer up, love. Isn't it your birthday? A little bird told me that you're thirty today,' says Cyril while I'm helping him secure his bow tie. It's an old-fashioned one that needs proper tying and it's a nightmare. I'm going to buy him a newfangled one attached to elastic before our next concert.

'Don't remind me,' I murmur as other members of the choir join in with happy birthday wishes. Most of them have hardly mentioned it until now and that's fine by me. The sooner today is over, the better.

Jennifer starts wishing me a happy birthday but only gets a couple of words out before she gives a mega cough followed by a dramatic gasp.

'Is everything all right?' asks Arthur, adjusting the collar on Fiona's blouse.

'I think so,' croaks Jennifer, clasping her throat.

Croaks? Our star soprano, whose soaring, crystal-clear voice is Salt Bay Choral Society's secret weapon, is coughing and croaking fifteen minutes before we go onstage. My stomach does a huge lurch and I start to feel sick.

'It's nothing really – just a bit of a cough and a sore throat,' whispers Jennifer. Jeez, now she's whispering! 'I'm trying to conserve my voice, so you'd better not be about to light up, Gerald. I'm sure it's non-smoking in here anyway.'

Gerald grabs the cigarette that's balanced between his lips and shoves it back into the packet.

'Are you going to be all right to sing this afternoon?' asks Josh, a deep furrow appearing between his eyebrows.

'Oh yes, I'll be fine. It's not a problem,' whispers Jennifer as my worry-brain goes into overdrive. If she can't sing her solo, we're well and truly screwed.

Talking of which, Ollie, who's had a face like a smacked arse all afternoon, has just grabbed hold of Kayla's arm and dragged her out into the corridor. Sending up a quick prayer to the God of Birthdays to give me a chuffing break, I scurry after them. With one singer ailing, we can't afford to have another two indulging in a domestic.

A couple of minutes later, I track them down, tucked away behind a huge brown stone pillar near the caretaker's office.

'So what I'm saying, Kayla,' says Ollie as I get closer, 'is that you don't need to worry because you are definitely, absolutely the last woman in the whole world that I would ever want to marry. I'd rather marry my own mother, which would be weird, or even… Jennifer.'

He winces and rakes his fingers through his straw-blonde hair until it's standing on end like a bog brush.

'OK. Thanks for passing on that very important information,' says Kayla, spotting me and raising her eyebrows. She tries to move past him but Ollie isn't budging.

'Quite frankly, Kayla, proposing to you was a huge mistake because I've since realised that you're terrible wife material. You're headstrong and rude and insensitive.'

'Is that right, mate?'

Kayla puts her hands on her hips and pushes her boobs forward. I know that move! She'd never admit it but she's turned on by Ollie's un-proposal.

'Yes, it is right,' splutters Ollie. 'There's no way I'd get tied down with you. Not ever. You're loud and vulgar and, on top of everything else, you're horribly capricious.'

'What does "capricious" mean?' Kayla mutters to me out of the corner of her mouth. 'Is that good?'

'Absolutely. It means Ollie won't be asking you to marry him in a month of Sundays.'

'That's brilliant. What else am I then, Oliver Simpson?' Kayla moves so close to Ollie, her red hair brushes against his black shirt.

'You're unkind and only an average singer.' Ollie's nostrils flare and his breathing quickens. 'Your driving is, frankly, appalling. You can't pull a decent pint to save your life, and… and you're utterly egotistical.'

'Egotistical! Bloody hell, Ollie. Snog the life out of me!'

Kayla flings her arms around Ollie's neck and the two of them start kissing passionately while I stand there like an oversized gooseberry.

'Oh, Ollie,' murmurs Kayla, pressing herself against Ollie's hard thighs.

'Kayla,' mumbles Ollie, putting his hand into the small of her back and pulling her in tight as their lips meet again in a crescendo of slurps.

Flaming heck! I'm going to need a bucket of water in a minute or Kayla and Ollie will be doing it behind a pillar in Gwedna Hall while Salt Bay Choral Society is singing onstage.

'Break it up, you two,' I hiss, pushing between them in a bid to prise them apart. 'Can you please save your make-up sex until after the competition.'

'Yeah, of course,' puffs Kayla, pupils dilated as she wipes the back of her hand across her red lips. 'The choir must come first. But just remember all those words, Ollie. For later.'

Ollie gulps, his chest moving swiftly up and down. 'Righty-oh. I might have some more insults for you by then, as well, you Australian hussy.'

'Super!' breathes Kayla, loosening the collar of her blouse.

Josh is pacing up and down the corridor in rolled-up shirtsleeves when we get back to the waiting room. The white cotton skims his chest and complements his skin tone – he still has the faint trace of a tan. Phew, I'm feeling really hot after witnessing the Kayla-Ollie clinch and this isn't helping.

'Where the hell have you been?' demands Josh. 'They've given us a five minute warning and we've got a problem. Come with me.'

Grabbing my arm, he pulls me into the room where everyone is huddled around Jennifer, who's sitting on a chair with a scarf wrapped around her throat.

'She can't sing,' Barry informs me. 'Her throat's knackered.'

'That's not what I said, Barry,' croaks Jennifer, adding a cough for good measure. 'I'm sure I can manage to sing as part of the whole choir but I can't hit the high notes in the solo. So someone else is going to have to do it.'

'Don't look at me,' huffs Kayla. 'I'm an alto. If I try to sing that high, I'll wet myself.'

'And none of us knows the solo part well enough,' says Fiona. 'What happens now?'

'We're royally screwed, that's what happens.'

You can always count on Roger to give a pessimistic answer but, this time, he might be right. Barry's song is the centrepiece of our performance and, without it, we won't meet the competition criteria which means we'll be disqualified. They're going to disqualify us after all.

'Although…' croaks Jennifer, feebly. 'There is someone who can sing the part.'

'Who?' demands Roger, anxiously scratching his belly with both hands.

'Her.'

Jennifer's gaze settles on Storm, who's sitting quietly in the corner, playing with her mobile phone.

'What, Storm?' laughs Jay, who's sitting thigh to thigh with Emily on a long, vinyl bench seat.

'Yes. Storm,' replies Jennifer, in a stronger voice. 'She's a marvellous singer and, fortuitously, I've been teaching her how to sing the song to the best of her ability. She's the one you need.'

'Nope,' says Storm, putting her phone into her pocket and getting to her feet. 'There's no way on earth that I'm singing with your stupid choir in front of people. You don't want me anyway. No one wants me.'

Jennifer raises a single eyebrow, daring me to get this wrong.

'We want you, Storm. I've heard you sing and, Jennifer is right, you have a beautiful voice.'

'Really? Are you sure?' huffs Arthur, but a volley of coughs from Jennifer shuts him up.

'What's the alternative?' I say, addressing the choir, who are still grouped together in a concerned huddle. 'Jennifer is adamant that she can't sing the solo. You're absolutely sure about that, are you, Jennifer?' Jennifer rubs her throat and nods. 'And the only other person who knows the part and can sing it is Storm and, if we don't perform Barry's song, we'll be disqualified. Do you want to go back to Salt Bay empty-handed? Do you want to return to your wonderful community without having tried?'

Jennifer gives me a slight smile followed by a tiny cough.

'Do I get any sort of a say in all of this?' mutters Storm. 'It is my voice, after all.'

'Storm, please.' Her hands are soft and cool when I grab hold of them. 'I know you don't like Salt Bay very much and you're probably not that keen on any of us. But you would be doing us a huge favour if you sang the solo part. You don't have to join in any of the other songs. We can say you're our guest soloist.'

Storm's eyes dart round the room, taking in the choir collectively holding their breath. She leans forward until our heads are touching.

'I'm too scared to sing in front of an audience,' she whispers. 'Everyone will laugh at me 'cos I'm no good. I'm not good at anything.'

And she looks so panicky, I just can't do it. She's a damaged kid who needs support, not more pressure.

'It's OK, Storm. I shouldn't have put you in such a difficult position. We'll speak to the organisers about Jennifer and see what can be worked out. Honestly, don't worry about it.'

'Maybe Barry can sing the solo bit?'

She looks at her dad, who nods but says nothing. Barry *could* sing the solo. He'd probably jump at the chance to take centre stage but he's a touch too karaoke to do the song justice.

Storm is biting down hard on her bottom lip. 'I'll do it if I know for sure they won't laugh at me.'

'It's up to you but they honestly won't laugh because you have a lovely voice. And I'll be there with you onstage. You can look at me when you're singing and forget that anyone else is in the room.'

'You really, honestly think I can do it without people wetting themselves laughing?'

'I know you can do it. Trust me, every pair of pants in Gwedna Hall will be bone dry.'

When Storm sniggers, her soft cheek brushes against mine.

'Go on then,' she huffs. 'This is so out of order.'

'That's brilliant!' yells Barry, enveloping his daughter in a huge bear hug, then backing off quickly when she tells him to get the hell away or she'll change her mind.

The choir that's performing before us has just finished. We can hear their applause over the speakers, and a young girl with a clipboard pokes her head around the door to tell us we're next and should follow her. We're on.

The auditorium is full when we troop onstage and take our places, though the lights shining in our eyes are so bright, the audience is a hazy blur. Storm settles down at the piano, next to Michaela, and I stand by her for moral support while Josh conducts first the sea shanty and then the old Cornish song 'Lamorna'. After a slightly nervous start, the choir get into their stride and do the songs proud.

Next it's my turn to conduct and I take Josh's place at the front of the stage. My legs are shaking and wobble even more when Josh gives me a polite smile while we're passing one another.

But the Gilbert and Sullivan sounds great. It's the best we've ever sung it and I'm so proud of our fledgling choir, who are peaking at just the right moment.

As the applause dies away, I beckon for Storm to come forward and cross my fingers that she's not about to do a runner. But she clumps across the stage in her heavy shoes, head down, and takes her place next to Jennifer. As Barry starts strumming his guitar, Jennifer squeezes her arm for courage, and Storm's eyes lock on to mine.

Her face is rigid with fear and I realise how much we're asking of her. Storm makes a lot of noise. She moans and complains from the sidelines but never pushes herself centre stage because she doesn't think she's worth it. That's what being abandoned by your mum and pushed from pillar to post with Barry will do for you.

'You can do it,' I mouth at her, and she opens her mouth to sing.

The choir aren't expecting much, to be honest. Storm is a bit of a nuisance; a stopgap; a second-best because Jennifer is indisposed. But my terrified, amazing sister absolutely smashes it.

Her haunting voice is slightly wavery at first but soars as she becomes more confident with every note. And I live every note with her, willing her on, as her father plays guitar and the audience are reminded of the tragedy that devastated the tiny community of Salt Bay.

The choir seem inspired and energised by Storm's solo when it's their turn to sing and the whole of Barry's song is truly beautiful. At the risk of sounding like pretentious Mr Kerroway, I'd say that we make magic as well as music when voices blend and Barry's words of love and loss float to the back of the hall.

At the end of the song, the choir seem dazed and there's a beat of silence before the hall erupts into loud applause. I even catch a shout of 'Bravo' on the air, and Kayla darts out from the altos to pat Storm on the back.

Without thinking, I step forward and give Storm a huge hug. 'See, I told you. No one laughed – it's dry pants all round. And you were really brave.'

'Well, I wasn't really scared. I was just saying that,' she murmurs in my ear, her hair tickling my face. But I can feel her trembling as she hugs me tightly back.

I'm so proud of my lovely choir and my fabulous sister who didn't let us down, it doesn't really matter if we win at all.

Except it does, of course, and we sit at the side of the stage in nervous silence, waiting for the judges to read out the results. The other choirs in our category are seated around us and seem far more confident and assured than we are. We were too busy sorting out various emergencies to listen properly to their performances so maybe they smashed Salt Bay's resurrected choir out of the park. We'll soon find out.

After an age, three judges walk onto the stage, and my hopes sink when I spot that one of them is Mr Kerroway. Just what we need; a judge whom my father attempted cack-handedly to bribe. Mary, who's sitting next to me, laces her fingers through mine and holds on tight.

Mr Kerroway, looking dapper in a grey suit and red spotted tie, steps up to the microphone and clears his throat.

'Thank you for bearing with us, ladies and gentlemen. We had a lot to discuss and it took some time to come to a decision but we have decided on a winner. All of the participants in this "New Choirs" category did themselves proud and that's why it was so hard to choose between them.'

He takes a piece of paper from his waistcoat pocket and studies it for a moment, building up the tension. 'In third place… are the Conellwick Choir.'

To loud whoops from the audience, the choir troop up to collect their certificates. They seem quite disappointed, though third place sounds good to me.

'In second place, we have—' Mr Kerroway pauses as everyone holds their breath '—the Salbarth Singers.'

'Aah.' Roger lets out a long sigh that's almost a shout.

That was cruel. When Mr Kerroway said 'Sal', my heart leapt, but soon came crashing down again when he got to the 'barth' bit. Roger has gone bright red as though his blood pressure is through the roof, and we all know how he feels. Even Josh, who's staring impassively at Mr Kerroway, is feeling the tension. A muscle in his jaw is twitching and there's a bead of sweat on his forehead, where his thick, dark hair touches his skin.

The Salbarth Singers have trooped on and off and now it's the moment Mr Kerroway has been waiting for. He certainly milks it, gazing into the crowd for a few moments before bending his head over his piece of paper.

'Get on with it, you utter knob,' says Barry quietly and, to be honest, I couldn't have put it better myself.

'Ladies and gentlemen, it's my job now to announce the winner of the "New Choirs" section.' Mr Kerroway sniffs. 'This choir's traditional songs were on a par with the other participants, but their contemporary offering stood apart. It had impressive depth and musicality and was excellent in all respects, particularly in the clarity and haunting quality of the solo. The winner of the Kernow Choral Crown New Choirs section for this year is—' he hesitates as though he can't bear to pass on the information '—the Salt Bay Choral Society!'

'Bugger me backwards!' roars Roger, leaping to his feet. 'We did it!'

He hurries across the stage with the rest of us trying to keep up, still stunned and expecting Mr Kerroway to change his mind at any moment. Josh waits for me to go past him before following me into the spotlight.

'Well done,' says Mr Kerroway, thrusting a handsome glass trophy into Roger's hands. It looks like a thick wedge of transparent cheese with writing etched across it in frosty white. 'Your contemporary song was outstanding.'

'I wrote that!' says Barry, loudly.

'Really? Well, that certainly does surprise me.'

Mr Kerroway makes his way off stage and leaves us to soak up the applause from the audience.

Storm is standing at the edge of the choir, one foot turned towards the stage exit as though she wants to escape. But Roger is having none of it. Striding up to her, as the applause continues, he thrusts the trophy into her hands and plants a smacking kiss on her cheek.

'There you go, me 'andsome. You deserve that for saving our arses.'

And the rest of the choir applauds while Storm goes bright red and a huge smile creeps across her face.

*

It's early evening when we get back to Salt Bay, exhausted from reliving over and over again the moment when Mr Kerroway said our name.

'Did you see his smarmy face when he heard I wrote the song,' crows Barry, who's feeling very pleased with himself.

He and Storm are the toast of the bus and Barry has taken advantage of the goodwill to secure several job offers from choir members who have odd jobs around their houses that need doing. My father, wheeler-dealer extraordinaire, will never starve and I quite admire him for that.

I fancy going to the pub for a quick drink when we get back, to toast our success and maybe even my birthday? But everyone cries off.

Jennifer says she's still feeling unwell, Barry's nipping round to Cyril's to sort out his dodgy boiler, Emily and Storm are getting a lift into Penzance with Josh to go to the pictures, Ollie and Kayla are desperate to nip off for a shag, and everyone else has somewhere they need to be that's not with me.

'Why don't you take the trophy home to show Alice?' suggests Florence. 'She'll be delighted to see it and you can celebrate with her.'

'That's a lovely idea, Florence. I'll do that.'

Though I'm keen to see Alice and tell her the good news, I can't help being disappointed that my birthday, trophy-winning aside, has been such a bust. But I give myself a stern talking to because Alice will be delighted to see the trophy and spend the evening with me. And having someone who truly cares about you is the best birthday present of all.

Chapter Thirty-Four

Tregavara House is in darkness when I get back, with only the porch light on, scattering its beams across the garden and towards the harbour and black sea. Where's Alice?

I let myself in and stand in silence in the hallway. These days, the house is normally full of voices and door-slamming but, this evening, it's far too quiet. There are no TV sounds drifting from the sitting room and no sign of Alice. We shouldn't have left her on her own for so long. What if she's had another fall?

Turning on lights as I go, I run from room to room, terrified of discovering Alice in a heap on the floor. But the house appears to be empty. The mystery is solved when I rush into the kitchen and spot a note on the worktop in Alice's shaky handwriting: *Am spending the night at Penelope's. See you tomorrow.*

Phew. It's good news that Alice is fine but her outing means I'll be spending the evening on my own, like I often used to in London. Though it's worse here because there's nothing going on outside my window. No shouts from drunken people heading home from the pub or cars zooming past.

Sighing, I place the choir's glass trophy next to the Aga where it refracts the overhead light, sending rainbow beams across the birthday cards on the table. Salt Bay Choral Society has just kicked arse in the

Kernow Choral Crown but I feel really miserable. I'm so disappointed that Alice isn't here to share my good news. She *is* Tregavara House and it doesn't feel like a home without her in it. I've grown so fond of her and I thought she might want to spend some time with me on my special birthday.

It's terribly self-indulgent, and I've been putting it off all day, but I think I might have a bit of a cry. Let's call it my birthday present to myself.

I'm thinking of Josh and snivelling pathetically when a loud knock on the back door makes me jump. What the hell? When I peer through the window, Kayla is shivering in the garden, wearing far too few clothes. She's changed into a short dress and angora cardigan but doesn't have a coat on.

'Stop messing about and let me in,' she shouts, hugging herself and stamping her feet to keep warm.

'Jeez,' she moans, stepping into the bright kitchen. 'It's stupidly cold out there. I went to Reykjavik once and it was warmer. Mind you, I went in July and they were having a heatwave.' She peers at me closely. 'Have you been crying?'

'Not really. Only a little bit.' I wipe my nose with a tissue while Kayla picks up my cards and starts reading them. 'Alice is out at Penelope's and I was feeling a bit lonely.'

'Which is why I'm here to take you to the pub for a birthday drink.'

'What about your, um, rendezvous with Ollie?'

'Oh, that can wait,' says Kayla airily. 'So, go and put on your glad rags and come with me.'

'I can come as I am.'

'In your choir stuff?' sniffs Kayla. 'I don't think so. I know you're thirty now, Annie, but if you start letting yourself go from day one you'll have Crimplene slacks flapping round your ankles before you know it. Go on, make an effort, put your sexy blue dress on and be back down here in five minutes. In the meantime, I can finish reading your cards. I love the one with the hot naked man on it, by the way. That Maura knows you well.'

She glances up at me and points towards the kitchen door. 'Go on! Get changed, now!'

'Yes, miss!' I give Kayla a mock salute before heading upstairs, feeling more cheerful already. A few drinks in the pub could be just what I need to shake me out of the doldrums.

'That was more like ten minutes,' grumps Kayla when I reappear, but she gives me an approving nod. I'm wearing the fitted periwinkle-blue dress that matches my eyes, and a touch of make-up. Just a slick of mascara and some lip gloss but it makes me look much better. 'Right, get your coat on and let's go get the gins in. I told Roger to get them lined up.'

It's absolutely freezing outside and we walk briskly past the Christmas tree on the frosty green towards the welcoming lights of the Whistling Wave. The pub is very quiet as we get closer. Roger often has music playing in the bar these days and Saturday nights are usually noisy but it all seems very subdued.

'You go first,' orders Kayla, pushing open the pub door. I've lent her a coat but her teeth are still chattering in the crisp December air. 'Go on.' She pushes the door wider and gives me a shove inside.

'Yay! She's here!'

A wall of sound hits me as I step, blinking, into the bright, warm bar. There are people everywhere, including what looks like the whole choir. I can see Barry, Tom and Mary at the bar, Gerald talking to Arthur in the corner, and Maureen and Cyril chatting at a table. And there in front of me, in her best silk tea dress, is Alice, who smiles as I look around me in confusion.

'Happy birthday!' yells Roger from behind the bar. 'Shut the door, Kayla, or we'll all freeze to death.'

The door bangs shut behind me as I take in the plastic birthday banner tacked up above the bar and the huge chocolate cake covered in neon-pink candles. Everyone is grinning and raising their glasses.

'Is this all for me?' I hiss out of the corner of my mouth to Kayla.

'Of course it is, you drongo. Are you pleased? We sent you home so we could get the pub ready, and we kept the whole thing a secret. Even me, and I tell everyone almost everything!'

'It's wonderful,' I splutter, as Alice steps forward and plants a kiss on my cheek. She's styled her white hair which is party-flicky around her ears.

'I'm so sorry about the subterfuge, Annie, but we all wanted to surprise you. And congratulations on the choir's success. Your grandfather would be very proud of what you've achieved.'

'You're a dark horse, Alice. I thought you'd gone to Penelope's.'

'As if I'd go out and leave you alone on the evening of your thirtieth birthday. I wouldn't have missed your party for the world. None of us would have.'

I nod, too emotional to speak. All these people are here for me. My throat feels tight as Roger lumbers over and presses a drink into my hand.

'Here you go, it's a freebie and there won't be any more, so don't get used to it. But happy birthday. You're not so bad for an outsider.'

'She's not an outsider,' says Alice, with a disapproving frown at Roger. 'Annie is one of us.'

'Hear, hear,' calls Cyril, holding up his half pint. 'She's a Trebarwith and a part of Salt Bay.' He blushes bright red when everyone looks at him and bends his head over his drink. He's such a sweetie.

'We wanted to have a celebration to wish you a happy birthday and to say thank you,' says Mary, while Tom nods beside her. 'Thank you for reviving the Salt Bay Choral Society and bringing life back into the village. And for leading us, with Josh, to victory at the Kernow Choral Crown.'

'That's my girl!' yells Barry, holding his pint aloft.

When everyone cheers and starts singing 'Happy Birthday', my eyes fill with happy tears. This is so much better than a soulless bar in London's West End with friends who like me well enough but have other things in their life which matter more than me. Who'd have thought, when I first left the capital and travelled to this tiny Cornish backwater, that I'd end up feeling I belong here more than anywhere else in the whole world.

Suddenly I spot Josh in the far corner of the pub, with a drink in his hand. He came to my party which is the best birthday present of all. But, as I give him a shy smile, the blonde woman close to him swings around and my stomach lurches. Josh is at my birthday celebration with Felicity.

I'll need to get used to the two of them together if I'm staying in Salt Bay and now's a good time to start, seeing as I'm thirty and wonderfully mature. With a gulp, I down my gin and tonic in one go. I'm going to need all the help I can get.

'It's the first time Cyril has been in here since his wife died,' says Jennifer, wandering over and breaking my train of thought. The apples of her cheeks are red and I wonder how many drinks she's had since getting off the minibus. Her voice sounds fine though and there's no hint of the hacking cough she had earlier.

'Did you really have a sore throat this afternoon, Jennifer?' I ask quietly while conversations buzz around us.

'Of course I did. It was red raw.'

She gives a pathetic cough and glances at Arthur, who's loudly thanking Storm for 'saving the day' while Storm blushes. Jennifer grins. 'Why on earth would I lie?'

Without thinking, I step forward and give Jennifer a hug. At first, she's stiff in my arms but then she softens.

'Thank you. That was very kind of you,' I murmur, breathing in acrid hairspray fumes that sting the inside of my nose. 'Being the hero of the hour will do wonders for her self-esteem.'

'I don't know what you're talking about,' she harrumphs, pulling away from me, but she winks before heading off to scold Gerald, who's telling a rude joke.

Serena is standing near Storm but I can't spot Emily anywhere. I start scanning the pub, hoping that she hasn't sneaked off home on her own. It would be awful if she was sitting at Tregavara House in the dark. There's Tom, sitting on a barstool and looking miserable and I follow his line of sight… ah, there's Emily. Blimey! She's in a gloomy corner of the bar and appears to be snogging the life out of Jay.

Typical. One quick makeover and Jay, the shallow little shit, is all over the girl he's totally ignored for the last few months. I doubt the relationship will last and I hope Emily won't get hurt, but with any luck she'll have a lot of fun along the way. She deserves it, though my heart aches for poor Tom, who's necking beer like there's no tomorrow.

There's a sudden draught on my neck as the pub door swings open and in walks Toby. Perhaps I'm imagining it but there's a beat of silence before the buzz of conversation continues.

'Hello, Annie.' Toby makes a beeline for me and thrusts a card into my hands. 'Happy birthday, and sorry for spoiling your morning. I must admit I forgot it was your special day until Alice reminded me.'

'How did things go, with…?'

I don't say Lucy's or Freya's name just in case anyone is listening in. I don't suppose it'll stay a secret for much longer, not now things are changing, but I'm not going to blurt it out in the pub.

'Yeah, OK. Quite well, really. We had a good chat and I'm going to be a bit more involved, financially and personally.' He looks around him. 'You've got a good turnout. Half of these people would leg it across a busy motorway rather than come to a party for me. Which is just as well because they're mostly morons.'

When I frown at Toby, he looks sheepish and starts rising up and down on the balls of his feet.

'I'm not staying anyway – I can't wait to get back to London and we've got a big auction next week that I have to prepare for – but I just wanted to say thank you for taking my side and letting me meet my daughter. It was more emotional than I expected, to be honest.' A flicker of pain crosses his face and is gone. 'Anyway, I hope it hasn't caused you too many problems with, um…'

He points towards Josh, who's got his back to us. Felicity is talking with a girl next to him and, as I watch, she gives a tinkly laugh. She's looking particularly gorgeous tonight – all smoky eyes above full, pink lips, and wearing a figure-hugging body-con dress in pillar-box red that's cut low to show off her magnificent cleavage. How did I think for even one minute that I could compete with what Felicity has to offer?

I shake my head sadly.

'That was always a no-go, what with me being a Trebarwith. Not surprisingly, Josh doesn't have too high an opinion of us, and me keeping your meeting with Freya a secret was the final straw.'

Toby pauses for a moment and puffs out his cheeks. 'Do you want a drink? What are you on, G&T? I'll go and get you another before I head off.'

He marches off towards the packed bar, weaving in and out of my partygoers, who don't try to engage him in conversation. I should have known better than to start opening my heart to Toby.

I'm chatting with Maureen a few minutes later and deliberately not looking Josh's way when a gorgeous smell of fresh flowers suddenly wafts over me.

'Annie, can I have a quick word?' Felicity is standing behind me – trust her to be so fragrant. 'Sorry, I don't mean to interrupt,' she says sweetly, giving Maureen a dazzling smile.

'That's fine. I really ought to stop monopolising the birthday girl anyway. See you later, Annie. Come into the tea shop on Monday for a free hot chocolate.'

'I just wanted to say happy birthday, Annie, and I'm so sorry that things haven't worked out with Josh.' Felicity pouts but doesn't look terribly sorry. 'He's a complicated man who doesn't deal well with complication.'

She stares at me with her freaky yellow-brown eyes while I wonder how to reply. I don't feel comfortable discussing Josh with his ex-girlfriend.

'Is everything all right?' Barry is suddenly by my side, giving Felicity a quick once-over.

'Absolutely fine,' trills Felicity, tapping her tiny foot on the flagstones. 'I just came over to wish Annie a happy birthday and very many happy returns, hopefully. Are you a member of the choir?'

'He's my father.'

'Golly.' Felicity takes in Barry's ponytail and the ripped jeans and Metallica T-shirt he's changed into.

'And that girl over there, the one with a pink fringe who's talking to Serena, is my sister. They're staying with me for a while.' Storm spots us looking at her and gives us a wave from the bar.

'That's nice. Well, I'd better get back to Josh.'

Felicity gives Barry a faint smile, turns swiftly and walks away. Her silver shoes are covered in diamante and catch the light from the Christmas tree – they look like fairy shoes. I glance down at my boring, black ballet pumps and sigh.

'What was that all about?' Barry watches Felicity disappearing into the throng and frowns. 'She's a strange one.'

'I'm not sure but thanks for rescuing me.'

'Any time. That's what family do – look out for each other.' Barry winks and wanders off to blag a pint from another member of the choir.

Chapter Thirty-Five

After an hour or so, I start to feel overwhelmed. In a good way, but overwhelmed nonetheless. There's so much noise, and it's so hot, and there are so many people and they all want to talk to me. I'm an introvert at heart, and there's only so much being the centre of attention I can cope with before I need an escape to recharge my batteries.

That's why, on probably the coldest night in Salt Bay since the last Ice Age, I end up standing outside the back door of the pub on my own. It's peaceful out here next to the kitchen and the night sky is amazing.

I pull Roger's borrowed fleece tighter around me and lean my head back as far as it will go. I've never seen stars like it. Kayla assures me this is nothing compared to the glittering panoply above the Australian outback. But compared to London's light-polluted skies, Salt Bay's carpet of pinprick stars is outstanding.

Experts say there are more stars in the universe than grains of sand on all of the world's beaches. That's a shedload of stars but, when I look up in Salt Bay on a clear night like tonight, I can easily believe it because every patch of sky is littered with pricks of light.

I'm still gazing upwards and getting a crick in my neck when I'm startled by the footsteps of someone approaching.

'They're beautiful, aren't they?' Josh's low, deep voice makes me catch my breath. When I look round, he's silhouetted in faint light from the kitchen window. 'They're even more brilliant when you're out at sea and there's no light for miles.'

'What are you doing out here? You'll freeze in just a jumper. It must be minus five.'

'I could say the same to you. Is that Roger's fleece?'

'It is. That's why it's about ten sizes too big.'

It's also covered in dog hair because Roger's on-off girlfriend keeps Labradors, and there are lots of crumpled-up, used tissues in the pocket. But it was kind of him to let me borrow it.

'Look, Annie, I wanted to wish you happy birthday and speak to you.'

'You spoke to me this afternoon.'

I'm surprised that my voice sounds as cold as my toes are right now. I'm not meaning to be frosty but I'm tired, it's been an emotional day and, to be honest, I feel like I've been hollowed out. As though everything's been scooped out of my insides with a spoon.

'I know we were together earlier, but there were lots of people around and I didn't want them knowing my business.' Josh takes a deep breath. 'First things first, is it true or not that you're moving back to London?'

'Not this again! No, I'm not going back to London. Who told you that?'

'Kayla. She told me in no uncertain terms this afternoon that you were heading off after Christmas.'

'I might have mentioned it in passing, when I was tipsy, but honestly, Josh, how can I leave this place?' I think about the people in the pub and my lovely, clever, prize-winning choir. 'Whatever's happened between you and me, I'm staying in Salt Bay because it's my home.'

'What about Barry and Storm?'

'They'll go back to London one day, and we'll keep in touch, but I'm not going with them.'

Josh exhales deeply and hugs his arms across his chest to keep warm. 'OK, that's good to know. But that isn't what I really wanted to speak to you about.'

'Go on then,' I sigh. 'I know you've got lots to say about what happened this morning. So, go ahead – tell me off for betraying you and letting you down.'

'I'm not going to tell you off. You're not one of my students, Annie, and that's not what I was going to say. Why do you always presume you know what I'm thinking?'

'Because you are thinking it.' I huddle further into the oversized fleece and try to relax my tense shoulders. 'I'm sorry but I was only trying to do what's best for Freya. I wasn't taking sides with Toby or siding against you. I truly wasn't. There's just something about Freya's situation that chimed with me. She needs to know who her father is, even if he is a pompous prat.'

I close my eyes, waiting for the final onslaught from Josh. The perfect end to an imperfect birthday.

But all he says is, 'I know that, Annie. I'm not a complete idiot.'

'You what?' I open one eye and peer at him through the gloom.

'You're a kind person and I know you were trying to do your best for Freya, even if you didn't go about it in the right way. We were close, Annie, and you should have told me what was going on. We were sleeping together, for God's sake – you can't get much closer than that.'

He stops talking as Roger bustles into the kitchen and grabs a handful of glasses. Not realising we can see him, Roger scratches his backside through his trousers before heading back to the bar.

'But,' continues Josh quietly, 'I guess Lucy put you in a difficult position. We had words about it actually, just before I came out this evening, and now I don't think she's speaking to me. Oh well, such is life.' He shrugs his shoulders and shivers. 'Jeez, it's absolutely freezing out here. Maybe we could talk in the kitchen?'

'Here's fine,' I say distractedly. 'So why aren't you furious about this morning's meeting?'

'I don't know.' Josh raises his hands to the starry heavens and shakes his head. 'Maybe it was seeing Toby's face when he spotted Freya for the first time. He seemed really moved, as though for once he wasn't putting on an act or being a git. And he admitted that he's lonely. He showed his emotions, and I didn't think until then that the man had a heart. And then he had a word with me earlier.'

'When?'

'An hour or so ago, at the party. He sneaked up on me while Felicity was wishing you happy birthday and told me that you rang him to say you were going to call the meeting off and tell me about it.'

'Which is exactly what I said when we argued on the cliffs.'

'I know, but I was too upset at the time to take it all in.'

A thought suddenly strikes me. 'Why would Toby bother to speak to you at the party and tell you that?'

'He said, and I quote, "I still think you're a wanker, Pasco, but Annie seems to like you for some unfathomable reason and I don't like seeing her unhappy." Then he told me to get my act together or I'd lose you.'

'Gosh, Toby said that?'

'He did, though it came out through gritted teeth. And I still hate him, obviously.'

'Obviously,' I murmur, blowing on my hands in a vain attempt to warm them up.

'But Toby was right for once – though if you ever tell him I said that I will have to kill you.' Josh laughs, his breath a white mist. 'I do care about you, Annie, and I was thinking that maybe things can be OK between us again?'

'Things will always be OK between us, Josh. We'll always be friends.'

'Just friends?'

There's disappointment in Josh's voice and a flicker of hope in my heart until I stamp on it, pronto. Maybe it's the cold, or the excitement of this afternoon, or the heartbreak that's been eating me up, but I don't think I can do this. I can't risk my heart again.

'I think friends is good enough for now, don't you? The way we approached our relationship was too different. We're too different.'

Josh shakes his head. 'I don't understand.'

'Felicity hit the nail on the head when she described you as a complicated man who doesn't do complication.'

'Oh God, what has she been saying?'

'Just the truth because she knows you well, maybe better than I ever did. I took a chance on you, Josh, and let you into my heart, and you have no idea how scary that was for me. But I still don't really know you. You're all buttoned up and you don't like public displays of affection. I get that. But when you don't even like holding my hand when people are watching, it makes me feel shut out – as if you're slightly ashamed of me and waiting for someone better to come along.'

'Is that what you think?' Josh sounds exasperated and annoyed. 'Yes, I'm a private kind of bloke and I know I sometimes shut down when life gets complicated but that doesn't mean that I don't care about you.'

'I'm sure you do care about me, but you were quick to end our relationship after one disagreement.'

'A pretty big disagreement.'

'Granted, it was big. But I don't know where I truly stand with you. You never really tell me anything about your feelings. You never tell anyone. You broke my heart, Josh, and I don't think I can bear for you to do it again. I'm sorry. And anyway, you're here with Felicity.'

'I'm not here with her. She invited herself along and we're friends. That's all we are now, just friends.'

'But she wants more.'

'Maybe, maybe not. I know what Felicity's like and it's all a game to her. She always wants what she can't have, but I don't want more. Not with her.'

'Have you told her that? No, of course you haven't, because saying out loud what you really feel isn't your style, is it Josh?'

Without another word, Josh turns and strides back into the kitchen. A shaft of light falls across me until he closes the kitchen door and I'm plunged once more into star-strewn blackness.

The party is still in full swing when I slip back inside. It's deliciously warm in here and I gratefully accept the offer of a steaming coffee from Roger. Sitting in the corner, I sip it and warm my hands on the white china cup. I've just turned down Josh Pasco to protect my broken heart – the irony of it would be funny if it wasn't so painful.

'Where did you go?' Kayla's rust-red hair is almost sticking up on end. 'I've been dancing. That Gerald is quite a mover for an old bloke, with lots of jumping around and gyrating. I thought he was going to dislocate a hip at one point.'

Ah, that explains the hair style. Kayla is the kind of person who throws herself, body and soul, into whatever she's doing. And dancing is no exception. Her flailing arms and weird leaps cleared the dance floor when we visited a Penzance nightclub last month.

'Sit down and catch your breath.' I pat the chair next to me. 'I went outside for a bit of fresh air and to look at the stars.'

'Which are crap compared to—'

'—the Aussie outback. Yeah, I know. But they're still pretty damn awesome.'

Kayla nods grudgingly. 'I s'pose they're OK. Guess what I just did?'

'Made a spectacle of yourself on the dance floor?'

'Apart from that. I bought your sister a drink.'

'Not a Bacardi and Coke!'

'Of course not,' snorts Kayla. 'She's still underage. I just bought her the Coke bit which she well deserves 'cos her solo this afternoon took some guts. She's quite a lot like you, actually, once you get past the arsey attitude. Crikey, what's going on now? Has Gerald collapsed?'

The crowd in front of the bar and spilling across the pub is parting. People are moving towards the edge of the room in a wave and Roger has switched off the music. The sudden hush makes my ears ring.

'I think it's time for you to cut the cake,' whispers Kayla, clapping her hands together. 'About time. Maureen reckons there's half a ton of chocolate in that double-layer of delight and it's been calling out to me since the party started. Ooh, what's this?'

'This' is Josh, who's stepped forward with a half-drunk pint in his hand. Felicity appears to be pulling him back but she drops her hand and scowls when she realises it's not working.

Kayla groans. 'Ugh, is old grumpy pants going to wish you a happy birthday? He's got a cheek after dumping you, and it'll only delay the cake-cutting.'

'Shush, Kayla!'

Josh briefly catches my eye but looks away. The muscle in his jaw is working hard and I realise that he's nervous. Clearing his throat, he begins to speak.

'I'd like to raise a glass to Annie, who's thirty today.'

'She's just a baby,' yells Roger and everyone laughs, except for Josh, whose face remains deadly serious. He waits for everyone to raise their glasses and have a celebratory swig of their drink before he continues.

'As you all know, Salt Bay Choral Society pulled off a stunning victory this afternoon…'

'Stunning' is rather over-egging it, but everyone cheers.

'… a victory that would never have happened if it weren't for Annie's love of music and vision and general pigheadedness.'

Um, thanks, Josh, I think. Everyone is looking at me and I start to blush.

'You are so red,' giggles Kayla, which so doesn't help.

Josh hugs his pint tighter to his chest. 'Annie has become a part of Salt Bay and has been taken to your hearts. To all our hearts.' He lifts his head and his eyes lock on to mine. 'She thinks I'm a bit of a cold fish who doesn't wear his heart on his sleeve, and she might have a point, though I don't necessarily think that's a bad thing. I'm a man who doesn't find it easy to let his feelings show but, anyway—' he gulps '—now's as good a time as any to say that Annie is the most amazing woman and, in spite of also being hideously annoying at times—' he pauses and swallows '—I love her and can't imagine being with anyone else.' He looks at me and shrugs. 'And I don't care who knows it.'

You know when people say that time stands still and you think, what the hell do they mean? Well, now I know. And I want this moment and Josh's words – the most wonderful words ever – to exist for all eternity in a lovely Christmas bubble. So he mentioned that I was hideously annoying – that's fine! To be honest, Josh could have said I was a kitten-strangling psycho and I still wouldn't mind. Because he's just told a whole pub full of people that he loves me.

Out of the corner of my eye, I can see Marion and Serena in the crowd. Marion is beaming and, although Serena mimes putting two fingers down her throat and gagging, she smiles and gives me a thumbs up.

'Kiss, kiss!' the crowd start chanting. Cyril is banging his pint on the table in time to the words.

'Go for it!' hisses Kayla, pulling out my chair so I have to stand up. She gives me a hard shove in the back. 'Go and snog the life out of him, tongues, the lot. He deserves it after that.'

As I walk towards Josh, he gives the slow smile that makes my toes tingle. His face is flushed and we both resemble beetroots, which isn't the most romantic of looks. But he looks wonderful to me. When I reach him, he grasps my hand and his strong fingers interlace with mine. Then he leans so close, his lips brush my hair.

'So what did you think of my public declaration of undying love?' he murmurs.

'I can't believe that you just made a total tit of yourself in public.'

'Me neither.' He grins. 'It must be real love.'

Then he kisses me. Full-on. Passionately. In the middle of the pub. With everyone watching.

Chapter Thirty-Six

Christmas Day, growing up in London, was always a subdued affair. Usually it was just Mum and me, watching re-runs of Morecambe and Wise and eating Quality Street until we felt sick.

Since Mum died, I've spent the day at friends' houses, feeling my way around their various festive rituals which are a minefield for the uninitiated. Is opening presents OK first thing or do we wait until after lunch? Can I drink Buck's Fizz with breakfast or does that make me look like an alcoholic? Do you save the first family argument until after the Queen's Speech or launch right into a slanging match mid-morning?

Also, although it was lovely of my friends to have me round, it still felt like a pity invitation. Their good deed for the festive season was saving sad, lonely Annie from spending such a special day on her own. I had fun, and I appreciated their concern, but I always ended up a gooseberry at the feast and never stayed for too long.

So December the twenty-fifth at Tregavara House is my first ever 'proper' family Christmas and, to be honest, I've been a bit nervous about it. What if it's a let-down, or boring, or I still end up feeling out of place? But I needn't have worried. So far, Christmas Day in Salt Bay has been hectic and weird – and fabulous.

It began with us opening small gifts around the Christmas tree mid-morning and now, a few hours later, we're all stuffed to the gills with roast turkey. I lean back in my chair, pat my full stomach, and soak up the happy atmosphere.

There ended up being ten of us for lunch so Alice opened up the never-used dining room and we're sitting round the fancy table that she hastily ordered online as the guest list grew.

The brand new table now looks like someone has done that whipping-off-the-tablecloth trick, very badly. Wine has spilled across the red and green table runner which is strewn with discarded bits of pulled crackers, and the roast potatoes that fell out of the serving dish are scattered between them. Barry spears one with his fork and shoves it into his mouth before scraping his chair back and waddling slowly out of the room. I'm not surprised he's finding it difficult to move – I've never seen a man eat so much!

Alice watches him go and then knocks gently on the side of her wine glass with her spoon. The tinkling sound echoes round the room and halts the low buzz of conversation.

'That meal was absolutely magnificent. Thank you so much to the many cooks. Please do feel free to banish me from my kitchen again, any time you like.'

She giggles and almost pokes herself in the eye when she pushes her white hair back from her forehead. I do believe that my great-aunt might be a little tipsy. I'd better give Emily a hand getting her upstairs later. We don't want any accidents spoiling such a special day.

'It was a joint effort,' says Marion, who was supposed to be a guest but ended up taking off the sling on her left arm and helping a bit in the kitchen. She's looking so much better since her operation and is relishing having more energy. 'Can I just say thank you so much for letting me and my family join you today. It's very much appreciated.'

She grins and raises her glass to me and Alice.

Lucy's working today in a local hotel that's paying triple-time, but Serena has come along with Marion, and Freya too who arrived still wide-eyed with wonder at Santa's visit while she was sleeping. It's lovely having a child around at Christmas and she's really taken a shine to Alice. The two of them have been chatting for a while, their heads bent close together.

Storm and Serena appear to be fast friends these days and, to my relief, have made an effort to include Emily in their conversation over lunch. She's looking more like 'normal Emily' after the first heady days of her make-over though she's put on some make-up in honour of Christmas Day.

Her relationship with Jay is ongoing and still intense, though she let slip this morning, while we were cutting carrots together, that he's just a tad boring when you actually speak to him. I don't think there's much talking going on at the moment but the first sheen of her infatuation with shallow Jay has been tarnished and I don't suppose it will be too long before she realises that the sun doesn't shine out of his arrogant arse. Ah, young love! I remember it so well – and prefer mature love so much more.

I sneak a glance at Josh, who's sitting at the head of the table and looking particularly gorgeous. He's wearing the striped black and white top that I love, and his stubble is super sexy today. Maybe when he's older he'll grow a thick black beard so he looks even more like a Cornish pirate. And the two of us will still be together five years down the road, ten years, longer. A thought like that would have sent me running for the hills before I came to Salt Bay. Before I met Josh. But now it just makes me feel warm and fuzzy inside. Though that might be the wine.

Josh senses my eyes on him and raises a glass to me across the table-top detritus. And when I smile, he winks and purses his lips to blow me a kiss. He seems relaxed and at home, which isn't surprising seeing as he's spending most nights here now that Marion has recovered so well.

Next to Josh is our unexpected, last-minute guest. Toby declined his invitation (praise the Lord) to go to some swanky do in London so it was going to be just the nine of us until Storm stomped into the sitting room a couple of days ago.

'Do you know that Jennifer is spending Christmas Day on her own?' she demanded. 'What kind of village is this? I know she's a pain and even more annoying than Barry, but that's not right. She told me she likes spending the day on her own since her mum died. But that's what everyone without family says, even though they spend the whole day stuffing their faces with chocolate oranges, and crying.'

She folded her arms, crossly, and huffed at us.

'Would you like to invite her to join us for Christmas lunch?' asked Alice, which I thought was big of her seeing as Jennifer isn't the most relaxing of company.

Storm treated us to a faint smile. 'I might do, but she won't come.'

But Storm must have been extra persuasive because Jennifer turned up at midday in her best dress with a bottle of wine and the biggest box of chocolates I've ever seen. The conversation was stilted at first but it's got much easier as the meal's gone on.

Jennifer has had at least two glasses of wine and seems softer somehow. Or maybe that's just my vision getting blurry because – oops – I seem to have had even more wine than that. I'd better not have another glass or the Christmas pudding will end up on the floor before it reaches the table.

Leaning against the hard back of Alice's new chair, I survey our strange Christmas gathering. What a hotchpotch of people, all linked by family connections, affection and love. It's a complete mishmash but it seems to work. And I care about them all. They matter to me. And I matter to them. That fuzzy warm feeling starts working its way up from my toes as I take another sip of wine and make a silent toast in my head. *This is to you, Mum. I'm so sorry you never made it home but it's almost as though you're here through me.*

Storm, in particular, is having a lovely time and has even been laughing. But her smiley face disappears when Barry barges back into the dining room, carrying his guitar.

'Don't spoil it, Barry,' she mutters as he parks his backside on the edge of the table, sending cold roast potatoes flying in all directions.

'Spoil it? I'm going to add to the general ambience and convivial atmosphere of this festive gathering,' booms Barry, adjusting his paper hat that's slipped to the back of his head. He's definitely drunk.

'Are you going to sing, Barry?' asks Alice. 'That's nice. We can be your groupies.'

Eek, I don't think Alice fully understood Barry's explanation of the word. Josh catches my eye and bites his lip to suppress the grin that's playing around his eyes.

'You're going to be my audience, lovely Alice, while I sing a song to Annie. This is the special song I've composed for her as a combined birthday and Christmas present and it's to thank her for welcoming us into her home. Um, Alice's home.'

'You're such a cheapskate,' sighs Storm, settling back in her chair with a defeated expression. 'All right. Get it over with.'

'I will.' Barry tunes his strings for a minute while we all sit waiting but he suddenly stops and stares at me. 'Have I ever told you, Annie, how much you remind me of my grandmother Inga, God rest her soul? Especially when you've had a few. Same daft expression, and the eyes, of course.'

Inga? Surely not. Josh shrugs at me and gives a slow, sexy smile.

'Where was Inga from?' I ask, using my finger to chase a bead of wine that's rolling down the outside of my glass.

Barry thinks for a moment, swaying slightly. 'Watford. Though her parents came over here from Denmark before she was born. From Copenhagen, I think.'

And with those words, Barry unwittingly gives me the best Christmas present ever – bona fide Scandinavian heritage. Just as I imagined, when I was growing up fatherless and rootless in London. Maybe my father never made his way across Copenhagen with the wind in his hair but I bet some of my ancestors did.

I take a huge slug of wine to celebrate my confirmed Scandi roots as Barry strums a few chords and starts to sing.

To be honest, the song would probably be better if Barry wasn't drunk. And I could do without the loud burp between verses two and three that gives Serena a fit of the giggles. But, that aside, the words are lovely. Slurred but lovely. Barry sings about the joy of finding me and the pain of our lost years. And he sings of finding friendship in this small community that 'feels like home'.

Maybe it's the alcohol but I'm starting to feel quite choked. Barry might be an ageing rocker wideboy, but he's my ageing rocker wideboy and I've grown rather fond of him. Of Storm, too, who's mortified and appears to be draining Jennifer's wine glass.

We all clap loudly when Barry's song ends – even Jennifer – and he beams with delight.

'Did you like it, Annie? Did you?'

He sounds like a little boy desperate for approval.

'I did. It was a very unusual and unique present, and I loved the words. Thanks, Dad.'

Barry gulps and breathes alcohol fumes all over me when he leans forward and kisses me on the cheek. Then he whispers in my ear, just loud enough for me to hear, 'You're very welcome, Daughter.'

Chapter Thirty-Seven

Far below me, Salt Bay is stirring as first beams of pale sun strike the harbour wall and deep yellow sand. It's soothing up here on the cliffs and, even with the dull boom of waves hitting rock, and seagulls squawking and wheeling over my head, it's wonderfully peaceful.

I turn up the collar of my fleece and shuffle my backside on the Tesco carrier that's shielding me from the wet earth. Alice has a National Trust park-your-arse-on-the-grass-without-getting-soaked pad somewhere. I'll have to nab it sometime but she was still sleeping and I didn't want to wake her to ask where it was.

Alice is sleeping even more these days and hasn't been too well since Christmas, a fortnight ago. She seems older and more fragile and I'm terrified that I'm going to lose her. It's inevitable one day, I know that, but she's given me so much – stability, love, a home – and I can't imagine life without her.

But, then again, I couldn't imagine life without Mum and here I am, four years on since she died. And I'm happy, with a gorgeous boyfriend, a good job, and family around me. A new father and sister who are batshit crazy but OK.

The rising sun reaches my face and I turn towards the light, chin pointing to the sky. Sitting here, watching the day begin, wasn't planned but it seemed the natural thing to do when I awoke early. So I slipped out of bed, leaving Josh gently snoring with one arm thrown across the covers where my body had been, chucked on some clothes and headed for the cliffs before the house stirred.

And I'm glad I did. Pale pink trails are streaking the sky as the sun, a pale lemon ball, soars ever higher above the horizon, its light catching the fishing boats that are bobbing on a calm, almost translucent sea. It's going to be a lovely day in Salt Bay.

Sunlight has reached the walls of Tregavara House which are glowing honey-brown. And there's a dark shadow on the cliffs in the distance. As it moves closer, I realise that it's Josh. I'd know that tall frame and distinctive stride anywhere. I run my fingers across the heart-shaped gold locket around my neck that he gave me as a belated thirtieth birthday present – his heart always close to mine.

When I wave at Josh, he waves back and hurries towards me. He's pulled on his jeans and thick sweatshirt but looks sleepy with tousled bed-hair that's sexy as hell.

'Did I wake you? I'm sorry. I didn't mean to wreck your Saturday lie-in.'

'You're fine. It's a beautiful morning to be up and about,' says Josh, pulling a carrier bag from his back pocket and waving it at me. 'See, I've taken on board the Annabella Trebarwith method of avoiding a sopping arse.'

He spreads the bag on the ground next to me, drops onto it and leans towards me for a Colgate-y kiss in the sunlight. His face is chilly but his lips are warm, and mine soon warm up during a rather lovely early morning snog.

Eventually, Josh pulls away and smiles. 'I missed you when I woke up. I needed someone to snuggle up to. What have you been up here thinking about?'

'I've been thinking about how lucky I am that I found you and realised that you weren't a stone-cold swine after all.'

'That's a good thing to think about,' says Josh, deadpan, shuffling along on his crackly plastic bag until our arms are pushed up against each other. And we sit like that for ages without saying a word, as the sun rises higher over the sea and Salt Bay comes to life behind us.

'Who's that?' asks Josh when I'm beginning to think I'll have to move or my legs will start cramping. That's probably best avoided because leaping across a clifftop yelling 'buggering cramp' isn't terribly romantic.

Shielding my eyes, I peer towards where he's pointing. I think it might be…

'Blimey, it's Storm. And it's—' I check my watch '—well gone eight o'clock. She's supposed to be at work. Jennifer will blame me if she's late again. Is everything all right?' I call as she gets nearer. 'Shouldn't you be at the shop?'

'Nope. I'm going in at nine and staying late to do stocktaking, though Jennifer is taking the piss because she's only got about twelve things in the whole store. It's bright up here, isn't it?'

'The sun's shining,' says Josh with a grin.

'Yeah, I'm not used to it in what is, like, literally the wettest place in the whole world.'

Storm sits beside me, yanking the carrier bag along so I now have one dry buttock and one buttock that's already aware of seepage from damp grass to skin.

'Why are you up so early if you don't have to be at work until nine? You usually fall out of bed ten minutes before.'

'Which I would have done if Barry hadn't rung and woken me up so ridiculously early.'

'Is he OK?'

'Yep. Bit drunk but he usually is when he's on tour with a band. It's one long booze-fest interspersed with eating burgers. But he said it's going well and, in fact—' Storm pauses and chews her bottom lip '—they've been offered some more dates and he reckons some A&R bloke is interested in them, which is probably all in his head, but he won't be back for a while.'

She glances at me then stares steadfastly out to sea. 'Barry said I could go and stay with Jackie in Bethnal Green if I want.'

'And do you want?' asks Josh, sliding his hand under mine and linking our fingers.

'I don't know. I could go to Jackie's. She's got a yappy dog and her tower block smells of cabbage but Bethnal Green's on the Central Line so it doesn't take long to go shopping up west, and she's got Wi-Fi and more than four channels on her telly.'

'Sounds good. What's stopping you?' asks Josh, gently.

'Nothin' really. It's boring round here and everything but I think Jennifer would struggle if I wasn't giving her a hand. She's getting really old and senile.'

'She's in her late fifties,' I splutter.

'Yeah, like I said, really old and she's started relying on me, and she likes giving me singing lessons while I'm working.'

'Does she?'

'Yeah. It's a bit lame but it passes the time. And I thought you might need me around a bit to help you and Emily with Alice. But I could go to Jackie's.'

She starts picking blades of grass and bundling them up into a tight green ball.

Josh squeezes my hand and, when I turn my face towards him, he smiles and his beautiful gold-streaked eyes sparkle.

'Alice, Emily and I *could* do with some help for a while, Storm,' I tell her, 'if you could bear to spend a bit more time in Salt Bay and at Trecaldwith School.'

'Oh God, I forgot about the school. It's not as bad as it was to begin with, though most of the teachers are crap. Not you, sir,' she says hurriedly to Josh. 'You're not really one of the knobheads.'

'That's good to know.' Josh leans round me to grin at my sister. 'I hope you will stay for a little longer, Storm, because Annie needs you.'

Storm flushes and throws her ball of grass out and over the edge of the cliff. 'It'll be a sacrifice to give up the chance of going back to London but I suppose I could stay for a bit longer. Jeez, this carrier bag is rubbish!'

She jumps up, rubbing at her numb backside and takes a deep breath of salty air. 'It's quite pretty up here,' she says before sauntering back towards the village.

'What just happened?' I laugh and Josh shakes his head.

'I think you just invited Storm to stay for even longer and, to my great surprise, she's starting to appreciate the beauty of her surroundings.'

'It's a weird old life,' I say, snuggling up against Josh, who puts his arm around me and pulls me in close. 'And Tregavara House is full of weirdos and misfits.'

'Couldn't have put it better myself. Talking of which, I was thinking, now Mum is better, that I could perhaps move in, if that's OK with you. I don't want to pressure you if you're not ready but, when we're apart, all I can think about is you. So why be apart?'

'I can't think of anything I'd like more,' I say, kissing Josh's scratchy cheek and pulling myself into his lap. 'Will your mum mind?'

'No, she just wants me to be happy and she knows that I'm very happy with you.'

I rest my head against his chest and he puts his arms tightly around me. Over his shoulder, I can see the cemetery where my grandparents lie, and Alice's husband David.

One day Alice's name will be inscribed next to his and it will be an awful time, but I won't have to cope with it alone.

And one day maybe my name will be there too, in the tiny clifftop cemetery that overlooks the sea. Another Trebarwith who lived her life, surrounded by people who love her, in Salt Bay.

A Letter from Liz

Thank you so much for choosing to read *Annie's Christmas by the Sea* and spend time in Salt Bay. This is my first ever festive book and writing it has been a blast – a fabulous way of enjoying all the best bits of Christmas without the stress of panic-buying presents.

Annie's story isn't finished just yet so please sign up to my mailing list if you'd like to know when the next Salt Bay book is published. I promise your email address will never be shared and you can unsubscribe at any time, so there's no risk of spam swamping your inbox.

www.bookouture.com/liz-eeles/?title=annies-christmas-by-the-sea

I hope you had fun spending Christmas with Annie and Josh. If you did, I have a little request: I'd love it if you'd write a review. It doesn't need to be long – just a line or two is fine – but it's great to hear what you think. And reviews make such a difference, helping new readers to discover my books for the first time. Thank you so much.

Do get in touch if you'd like to say hello. Hearing from readers is one of my favourite things and I'm always happy to chat. You can contact me on my Facebook page, on Twitter or on Instagram.

And, if you're reading this around Christmas time, have a fabulous festive season!

Liz x

                lizeelesauthor

                @lizeelesauthor

                lizeelesauthor

Acknowledgements

Thank you to all at Team Bookouture for taking a chance on me. Being a 'proper author' at last, with two books under my belt, is wonderful and I feel lucky to have such a supportive and dynamic publisher.

My editor, the unflappable Abigail Fenton, deserves a special mention for her calm, spot-on advice that's so helpful – particularly on days when my confidence dips and I start hyperventilating. She and editor Emily Ruston, or as I know them 'The Dream Team', have made sure this book is the best it can be.

My fabulous friend Rachel Brown is a powerhouse when it comes to promoting my books and making people buy them. Thanks, Rach. And cheers, Sue Becker, for reading an early draft and coming up with great suggestions when my brain had seized up. Walking by the sea helps to clear my head and untangle plot problems, and it's so much more fun in the company of Carol Smith, Monique Kleinveld, Jo Osborne and Helen Dobbin.

Thanks to my family and in-laws for being so supportive – including Mum and Dad, Dave and Debbie, Jon and Megan, Sally, Andrew and Brenda, Iain, Adam and Cathy. I can't name you all or we'll be here all day but I'm very grateful.

And I truly appreciate the encouragement and support I've received from writing pals, readers, book bloggers and the marvellous choir I sing with, Shoreham Oratorio Choir.

This book would never have been written without my lovely husband, Tim, who doesn't moan when I shut myself away for hours and just lets me get on with it. He even brings me drinks and crisps. And finally, Sam and Ellie, you're awesome!

CPSIA information can be obtained
at www.ICGtesting.com
Printed in the USA
LVHW031049120519
617539LV00014B/648/P